MOSCOW AIRLIFT

by

Marc Liebman

PENMORE

Moscow Airlift by Marc Liebman
Copyright © 2018 Marc Liebman

This is a work of historical fiction. While based upon historical events, any similarity to any person, circumstance or event is purely coincidental and related to the efforts of the author to portray the characters in historically accurate representations.

ISBN-978-1-946409-44-7(Paperback)
ISBN 978-1-946409-45-4(e-book)

BISAC Subject Headings:
FIC014000FICTION / Historical
FIC032000FICTION / War and Military
FIC0012000FICTION / Action and Adventure

Cover by C. Horner
Editors: James Alan Gardner, Chris Wozney

Address all correspondence to:

Penmore Press,
920 N Javalina Pl,
Tucson, AZ 85737

or visit our website at:
www.penmorepress.com

Table of Contents

	Dedication	v
Chapter 1	Escape from Laos	1
Chapter 2	Terror Central	31
Chapter 3	Travelogue	42
Chapter 4	Cold Reckoning	46
Chapter 5	Leave No Man Behind	57
Chapter 6	Missile Matters	89
Chapter 7	What Are We Going to Do?	94
Chapter 8	Conversion	98
Chapter 9	Nukes for Dollars	115
Chapter 10	RatPack Assignment	151
Chapter 11	Old Flame	202
Chapter 12	Machetenum	220
Chapter 13	The Hits Keep Coming	224
Chapter 14	Disintegration	259
Chapter 15	Transfer Papers	290
Chapter 16	Field Work	316
Chapter 17	True Confessions	332
Chapter 18	Arriving	353
Chapter 19	Not for The People ...	405
Chapter 20	Joint Foreign Combined...	434
Chapter 21	Revenge is Sweet...	460

Dedication

This book is dedicated to three individuals who are have influenced my life and to a long persecuted minority. While I was writing this book, I couldn't help but think about my late father-in-law, Morris Yanowitz, and mother-in-law, Hanna Blum, both of whom had the good sense to leave the chaos, uncertainty and persecution they endured in Stalin's Soviet Union. Ultimately, they wound up in the United States and walked my lovely wife down the aisle at our wedding. *Moscow Airlift* is, in many ways, a tribute to their memory.

Both Morris and Hanna grew up in the part of the Soviet Union known as Bessarabia that is right on the border of Romania and the Ukraine. Depending on the day, it was a crapshoot as to whether my father-in-law hated the Russians or the Germans more.

When this book sees the light of day, I will have been married to Betty Kay Yanowitz for forty-eight plus years. I can't imagine life without her.

This book is also dedicated to Soviet Jewry. For centuries, they have suffered through pogroms, institutionalized anti-Semitism in the Tsarist, Soviet and Russian governments. In some ways, it created a warm, deep and unique culture, but mostly, it led to disease, poverty, exploitation and untimely death.

Most Russian Jews have left their homeland, and those who remain are discriminated against on a daily basis. When given the chance, they leave Russia. How and why the rest stay is beyond me.

Enjoy reading *Moscow Airlift*. If you have read *Big Mother 40, Cherubs 2, Render Harmless,* and *Inner Look,* you'll recognize some of the characters. If you haven't, don't worry. However, I hope you like *Moscow Airlift and* read the others!

Marc Liebman
March 2018

Other Books by Marc Liebman

Big Mother 40
Cherubs 2
Render Harmless
Forgotten
Inner Look
Moscow Airlift
The Simushir Island Incident (to be published in
November 2018)

Chapter 1
Escape from Laos

Wednesday, April 7th, 1971, 0717 Local Time, Laos

Danielle Debenard didn't know if her mother fell from the excruciating pain of burning to death or from the rain of bullets that met her as she ran from the house. Danielle didn't care; she ignored both the flames and the gunfire as she ran to where her mother had fallen. Three meters short of the charred smoking figure, Danielle was sent tumbling by a hammer blow to her left thigh followed by a searing, poker-hot pain. As she lay face down, she could smell her mother's burned flesh. Instinctively, Danielle closed her eyes as she reached to touch the bloody mass on her thigh sure she was about to die.

The sound of shooting faded into the distance, and Danielle opened her eyes as she felt hands gently roll her over on her back. Her father's face blocked out the sun. *"Ne tu inquiété pas, ça va aller."* Don't worry Danielle, it will be all right.

As her father, a retired French Foreign Legionnaire, bandaged the wound, Danielle watched Pathet Lao soldiers surround them, their AK-47s held ready to shoot. When he finished, she was carried on a stretcher by her father and her sixteen year-old sister Gabrielle.

The next thing Danielle remembered was waking in a large tent. Her father sat on a wooden crate next to her cot and held her hand. On her other arm, intravenous fluids fed through a tube into a vein on her wrist.

Danielle turned and looked at her father. Even through his grief, he smiled as he stroked her forehead. "Good evening. I'm glad you are awake."

"I guess this isn't heaven."

"No. It's a Pathet Lao field hospital. You were lucky—a French doctor operated on you. He's a prisoner too."

"How long will I be here?"

"I don't know. The doctor hopes two weeks at most, but it's up to the Pathet Lao."

The hospital commander had ordered the doctor to do only the minimal amount of surgery to save Danielle's life. He only had time to reset her femur, then stitch and bandage the wound. The motor nerves weren't reconnected and the severed thigh muscles weren't completely sewn back together. The doctor rationalized it was her karma to be crippled for the rest of her life.

The next day, Danielle stood up with the support of underarm crutches. A cast, bent at the knee, immobilized her leg from her hip to her ankle. Over the next few days, she began to move around. At the end of week one, the first cast was cut off, and after poking and pressing on the incisions, the doctor nodded and smiled. There was no sign of infection. In a few days, he said, it would be safe for Danielle to leave the hospital. In four weeks, the new cast he'd just put on could come off.

As a patient, Danielle was fed, but her father and sister had to scrounge for their own food on a daily basis. When dealing with Pathet Lao soldiers, Jacques Debenard allowed them to believe he was one of the foreigners impressed into service at the hospital. He guessed that the longer they stayed at the hospital, the better it was for all three of them.

Exactly two weeks after they arrived, the hospital commander said they were assigned to Re-Education Camp #3 and would leave as soon as the trucks arrived. On his afternoon rounds, the doctor handed Jacques Debenard a leg brace and two bottles of pills. One bottle held penicillin; the other contained painkillers. "Where you are going, there won't be much medicine. In four more weeks, soften the cast with water and peel it away. Give her the penicillin if the wound starts to be infected. Give her the hydrocodone for pain. The brace came from a man who had polio. She'll probably need one like it for the rest of her life. I'm sorry."

The Debenards left in a convoy of three trucks just before dark. Two held prisoners, the canvas tops raised so that the prisoners couldn't see where they were going. Each of the trucks had four soldiers riding as guards just in front of the tailgate. At a rest stop, Jacques counted twenty-four additional men riding in the third truck.

About an hour before dark, the trucks abruptly stopped and the guards ordered everyone to lie in a ditch beside the road. Jacques heard and then saw a pair of Laotian Air Force T-28s dive down to about five hundred feet as they buzzed the convoy. They were low enough that he could see the pilots' white helmets and their empty ordnance racks. Once the planes were gone, the convoy commander ordered everyone back into the trucks and the convoy raced down the pot-holed road. The Laotians wanted to find a place to hide before an Air America B-26 arrived.

After dark, the trucks resumed their journey into the mountains of Champasak Province in eastern Laos. The convoy stopped momentarily in Na Kai, a town not far from the Laotian/Vietnamese border.

Dawn was breaking when the trucks pulled into Re-Education Camp #3. The guards jumped down and opened the tailgates. As the prisoners got out, the men were separated from the women. Then the younger women were separated from the older ones. Danielle was leaning on her crutches when a Soviet officer, followed by the Laotian camp commandant, walked down the ragged line, looking at each young woman.

When he got to Danielle, he turned to the commandant, who ordered her to join the older women. She moved off slowly, awkward on the crutches; her sister Gabrielle stayed behind with the younger women: three Laotian and two Swedish aid workers. The six girls were taken to a small building next to the guards' barracks. Jacques's practiced eye estimated that the building was two hundred meters from the entrance to the prisoner compound.

As the youngest of the six women, Gabrielle was chosen first. She was given a bar of soap and told to go take a shower. When she finished, she was given a loose fitting garment and a pair of canvas shoes with soles made from tires.

Within minutes of coming out of the shower, two Russians grabbed her. One was a Soviet Spetznaz captain named Vladimir Koskov. He pushed her down on a bed. As Gabrielle fought back, the other Russian officer grabbed her hands and pulled them high over her head. Koskov shoved a pillow under Gabrielle's butt and shoved his erect penis into her. Koskov felt Gabrielle's hymen break and yelled, shouting that he'd taken the girl's virginity.

After Koskov emptied himself inside her, two other Soviet soldiers took their turns. When they were done, she was shoved back into the room with a shower and told to clean up—there were many more men who wanted sex with her.

Both Swedish women put up a fight and were beaten into submission. Like Gabrielle, they were handcuffed to their beds.

Anytime one of the camp guards wanted to fuck them, he just had to walk in and have at it.

Jacques lost count of the days, but guessed it was at least three months before another convoy with women prisoners arrived. The way the Soviet officers and the Laotians separated the women from the men reminded the World War II veteran of the *Auswahlprozess,* the selection process where SS guards at Nazi concentration camps sent the old men and women and children directly to the gas chambers. Young women became sexual toys for the guards, while young men were worked to death as slave laborers.

As the new line of women marched up to the guard barracks, Gabrielle and the five other women in their group were led to the prison. As soon as they were shoved past the wire surrounding the prisoner's living quarters, Jacques rushed to get his daughter.

Gabrielle was glassy-eyed and covered with bruises. She looked at her father and her sister and shook her head before collapsing in her father's arms. Jacques carried Gabrielle to their three-by-six meter room. It contained two bunk beds, a table and two chairs—one of sixteen similar rooms in the building. Interred families were allowed to live together; those who were alone when they were captured spent their time at Re-Education Camp #3 with strangers.

Jacques laid Gabrielle down on his bunk and held her close, hoping the sobs would stop. Each time Gabrielle tried to tell what she had been through, she started sobbing, unable to complete a sentence. Between sobs, she blurted out the name Vladimir Koskov. He was the Spetznaz captain who conducted the *auswahlprozess*; Gabrielle had been his favorite fuck.

Over the next few days, Jacques and Danielle pieced together what happened to the women. The prison was far

5

enough from the barracks that no one heard the screams of the women as they were raped. The young women who returned to the prison population either kept their experience to themselves or else they gave up and died.

Both Jacques and Danielle tried to comfort Gabrielle, but she grew more distant every day, staring absently at the wall. She ate little. Jacques forced himself to control his growing rage and anger towards the Soviet officers who'd repeatedly raped his youngest daughter. They were no better than the goddamned Nazis Jacques had fought for six long years.

Three weeks after she was returned, Gabrielle went to the camp doctor and found out she was pregnant. She could not contain her sobs of horror when she confided this to her father. The next morning, just before dawn, Gabrielle deliberately walked into one of the minefields near the fence. She kept walking, stomping her feet until she stepped on a mine.

The blast woke everyone. When Jacques reached her, one of her legs was blown off at the knee and the other at the hip. Her midsection had been ripped open by the blast. Her blood soaked through her father's clothes as Gabrielle died in his arms. The bloodstains never faded completely away.

For two days, Danielle cried. Then cold fury replaced her grief. She, no *they*, would get even; the question was, how? She and her father agreed that escape was the best option. Later on, at a time and place of their choosing, they would take their revenge. Somehow.

When Koskov came to conduct an indoctrination session after Gabrielle's suicide, Jacques forced his way past the guards around him and decked the man with one punch. Another Spetznaz officer stepped in, but Jacques jabbed him in the face with the back of his elbow, then spun and landed a blow to the man's sternum, followed by a second to his stomach. Jacques followed up with right and left cross to the cheeks. It took three

Laotian guards using their rifle butts to knock him to the ground.

After the guards pulled Jacques to his feet, Koskov beat him until he was unconscious. Two male prisoners dragged Jacques to his bed.

When her father's eyes opened, Danielle leaned over and kissed his forehead. "Papa, don't do that again. I need you alive. We'll get out of here, and when we do, we'll hunt Koskov down like the animal he is."

Jacques nodded. "Yes, we will. This is a matter of family honor."

Monday, December 16th, 1974, 2126 Local Time, Laos

Three years, seven months and three weeks from the day the Debenards arrived at the camp, Jacques leaned on the windowsill of their hut and looked at the night sky. The smell of decaying vegetation mixed with the ever-growing greenery wafted over the camp, but it couldn't conceal the putrid smell from the latrine. Its pungency overpowered everything else until the wind changed direction.

Jacques was thinking of one of his childhood heroes: Alfred Dreyfus, a fellow artillery officer, Alsatian, and like Jacques, Jewish. Dreyfus was wrongly accused of treason and sent to Devil's Island off the coast of French Guyana. Exonerated after five years of imprisonment, Dreyfus continued to serve his country and was made a member of the *Légion d'Honneur*, France's highest decoration for service and bravery.

Re-Education Camp #3 was Jacques' Devil's Island.

Tonight, a thin layer of clouds hid the normally bright stars. It was after the dry season; clouds might mean rain. Memories of his time in the camp flowed through Jacques' mind. Most were bad. Nevertheless, Danielle and he had survived. They were even reasonably healthy.

Yellow lights around the perimeter lit the fence well, but in the huts, each room only had one 75-watt bulb. No on/off switches—the Pathet Lao provided electricity at their whim as another way of saying *we control your lives.*

The prisoners of Re-Education Camp #3 worked small fields and rice paddies around the camp six days a week. Meals consisted of rice with a piece of fish. Any spare time was filled with mandatory lectures about the virtues of communism. The Pathet Lao political officers loved to point out the prisoners were in the camp to cleanse their minds of capitalist ideas about private property and individual ownership. Here, everything was shared: communism in in its purest form.

The sanitary facilities were communal—a row of holes cut into a sheet of plywood that was propped over a small ditch in a building at the end of the row of huts. Prisoners took turns dumping chemicals into the pit each day to speed decomposition. On Fridays, the prisoners shoveled the residue into wheelbarrows and dumped the stinking, slimy mass onto the compost pile, where it became fertilizer for the fields where they grew their food.

Cleanliness was also communal. They washed with water from a row of eight faucets attached to a long steel pipe on a wood frame. On the opposite side of the wall that held the sinks, eight shower nozzles were mounted at head height. A steel grating separated their feet from the mud below. Showers were permitted every other day.

Danielle never felt clean. She wasn't sure whether the feeling was psychological or physical, but it didn't matter: it never went away. Her once luxurious, shoulder-length hair was now crudely cut short so that it ended at the base of her head. The hair had thinned noticeably. She wondered if it would grow back once they got out of this hellhole.

MOSCOW AIRLIFT

Everyone wore the same style of clothes: dark, long-sleeve shirts and pants that soap and time had turned a dull, medium gray. Every inmate got the same size. Several prisoners handy with a needle and thread helped others resize the clothes to make them fit better. The pants were still baggy and tied with a string around the waist. Underwear of any type was non-existent.

Shoes were sandals made from tire rubber. If you were lucky, your pair came from the same tire. They only came in two sizes: ones that fit and ones that didn't.

One hut was a room with long benches and a kitchen, so it could double as a classroom and mess hall for their two meals a day. Another hut was a clinic where the sick went to die. Access to medicine and medical care was provided at the whim of the camp commander. The better your progress in your re-education, the more likely you would get medical care if you needed it.

Apart from the fence and minefield around the buildings, security was light. Each morning, the residents of the camp lined up for a formal muster. Sometimes, a muster was called when dinner was served.

The prisoners were a mix of former Laotian government officials and foreigners swept up in the Pathet Lao's conquest. The commander's orders instructed him to keep the foreigners alive because they were a potential source of hard currency: ransoms might be extorted from the inmate's employers or governments. On the other hand, what happened to the Laotians was of little concern. If they survived and the Pathet Lao thought they were re-habilitated, they would be released at some undetermined point in the future. If they died, it rid the country of potential political opponents.

On the first day of their arrival, the smiling Laotian commandant had announced that escape meant death from starving in the jungle or being shot immediately after being recaptured. Jacques saw himself as a prisoner of war; as such, it was his duty to escape. Neither he nor Danielle trusted any of their fellow prisoners enough to share their escape plans—the others might use information to curry favor with the guards.

Jacques turned away from the window and looked at his daughter. When he spoke, his voice was a whisper. "Are you sure you want to go through with this? You know what will happen if we are captured."

"Papa, if we don't try to get out, we'll die here. I'd rather be free and die starving in the jungle then spend another day in this place."

"We may have to live many days without food. Once we start, we'll be fugitives until we get to Thailand."

"Papa, I know, and I won't let my leg hold us back. I'll do whatever it takes to get out of this hellhole." She smiled. "This will be the escape of the old and infirm."

Jacques laughed softly. His daughter had been teasing him about his age ever since he'd turned fifty earlier in the year. As for Danielle, her leg was partially paralyzed from the damage to nerve and muscle. With the brace, she could walk by raising her left hip to get her foot off the ground and then swinging it forward. It was awkward, but she no longer needed crutches.

Danielle pushed herself upright and took her father's hands. Both she and he had rough skin from the years of manual labor. "Papa, we need to escape. We need to tell the world about this camp. It's what Gabrielle would have wanted. It's what *I* want."

"I agree. And we'll succeed because we know how to live and move through the jungle." It had taken Jacques months, but he'd hidden a machete, a spear, a bow and some arrows at the edge of the forest. Lately, he'd added some rope and other things they'd need. "We're ready. We're finally ready to get the hell out."

A former colonel in the French Foreign Legion, he had come to Indochina at the end of World War II. He'd fought the Vietminh and the Pathet Lao until the French pulled out of Indochina in 1954, then he'd stayed on as an attaché and worked for Michelin after retiring from the Legion in 1960. He knew the terrain they'd have to cover.

Curfew was in another forty-five minutes. Jacques hugged his daughter. "It's almost time for bed check. And, we have to get some sleep. Tomorrow, we'll be free. It's our Hanukah present."

Day 1—Tuesday, December 17th, 1974, 1702 Local Time, Laos

As they'd planned, Danielle joined her father where he was working near the edge of the forest, clearing the brush that always threatened to overwhelm the perimeter. This was hard work, so it fell to the few men still fit enough to do it. The guards allowed Danielle go twenty or thirty meters into the jungle to look for fruit because they were convinced she wasn't able to run away. For the past three days, she'd used this freedom to stock a pack with food.

Jacques was confident food and water would not be their problem. Avoiding capture was. Once they were away, his biggest worry was stumbling onto Laotians who might turn them over to the police. When they got to the more populated land near the Mekong, they'd have to stay away from locals— they would immediately report Caucasians.

When the whistle blew to tell the prisoners to return to their compound, Jacques simply stepped into the rain forest and disappeared from sight. A guard looked at Danielle, who waved and turned as if heading toward the huts. When he turned away, she too faded into the jungle. By then, Jacques already had two bamboo spears in hand, the bow was slung over his shoulder, and the feathers of the eight arrows stuck out of the makeshift pack on his back.

In the months leading up to their escape, Jacques had scouted the jungle for as long as two hours at a time, looking for trails and potential booby traps. The day before their escape, he'd disarmed four booby traps by disconnecting the trip wire from the grid of sharpened bamboo designed to impale its victim.

Now he took his daughter by the hand. "Let's go." He parted a bush with the machete he'd made and they started west.

By the time they'd moved five hundred meters from the camp, it was already dark under the trees. Jacques motioned for Danielle to sit on a rock. "We're going to rest a few minutes and let our eyes become accustomed to the dark. Then we want to put several more hours' distance between the camp and us. We'll find a place to sleep off the trail."

Danielle nodded and stood up. Gently, she pushed the brace's locks back down on both sides of the knee so it was rigid from her hip to ankle. "Let's go."

For the next three hours, they picked their way through the jungle. It was very slow going. Every so often, Jacques would hold up his hand and both would freeze. Jacques would listen until the normal night noises of animals, bugs and birds reassured him there was no danger, from either a human or other large predator.

After crossing a small stream, Jacques led her parallel to the water until he found a bowl-shaped group of rocks. With a few slashes of the machete, he cut leaves off plants and laid them down. "We'll sleep here tonight. Tomorrow we have to start at first light. If they don't come tonight, they'll send patrols as soon as they figure out we've gone. We have about a kilometer head start. By ten tomorrow, I want it to be two or three."

MOSCOW AIRLIFT

Day 2—Wednesday, December 18th, 1974, 1639 Local Time, Laos

Light was just beginning to filter through the trees, making it easier to see the trail they were following. Suddenly, Jacques held up a fist, then pointed into the trees. Within a minute, he and Danielle were lying on the ground behind a thick stand of bamboo, ten meters off the trail.

Three minutes after they were on their stomachs, a patrol of eight Pathet Lao soldiers came down the trail. They stopped within three meters of where Danielle and Jacques lay. From their hiding place, the two could hear the soldiers talking. After drinking from their canteens, the Laotians headed back in the direction of the camp.

Danielle and her father waited thirty minutes, counting their breaths to measure the passing of time. When no one appeared on the trail from either direction, they headed southwest.

Coming over a rise just before their midday break, the pair stopped at the edge of a clearing and spotted a small farm. From inside the tree line, they watched another Pathet Lao patrol buy food and depart.

They skirted the clearing, avoiding the farm. Not long after, Jacques held up his fist, and they hid off the trail again. Two young men passed within five meters of where they lay. The men were looking up at the trees, talking about finding more fruit. Jacques and Danielle waited until they were sure the men were gone.

Three hours later, after climbing to the top of a ridge, Jacques found a group of rocks in a crescent. Jacques pointed to the middle. "Here we spend the night."

Danielle froze. In a hushed voice, trying to control her fear, she said, "Papa, there's a large snake in there."

Jacques poked at the snake with his spear and the meter and a half reptile started to uncoil. The machete flashed. Smiling, Jacques held up the headless snake, its black diamond pattern on its light brown skin clearly visible. "Tonight we have fresh meat."

"We don't have matches. How will you build a fire?"

"Leave it to me. Can you clean and skin this?"

"I've never done it before."

Jacques spent three minutes explaining the process. When he was finished, he said, "Don't worry if it's not perfect. There's a small pool of water a few meters down the hill. When you're finished, wash the snake and your hands. Meanwhile, I'll make us a fire—a small one."

When she came back, Jacques was crouching, blowing on glowing embers that were struggling to become a fire. When flames began to flicker, he gently added shreds of dry bark. The embers flared into a fire. "*Voilà.*"

He sliced the cleaned snake into three-centimeter long chunks and wrapped each in a Malay Gooseberry leaf before shoving a bamboo sliver through the assembly. "Hold this over the fire for about five minutes."

Danielle cooked the first one. Jacques made five more and tossed several leaves on the fire to make a sweet-smelling smoke. They were both ravenous; the meat had a texture someplace between fish and chicken. The smoke from the leaves made it palatable, even tasty.

Day 3—Thursday, December 19th, 1974, 0626 Local Time, Laos

When Danielle awoke, she couldn't believe how tired she was. Before they'd left the camp, she'd worked in the fields, thinking it would be excellent preparation for what she referred to as "their walk to the Mekong." It was not. She was exhausted, but still she pushed her fatigue and the pain from her aching joints out of her mind. Freedom was more important than pain.

When she asked her father if following trails was too dangerous, Jacques explained that breaking trail through the jungle was not realistic. First, it would be grueling, and neither of them had the stamina to do it for days on end. Second, it would be noisy and time-consuming. Time was not on their side —the longer they were on the road, the greater the chance they would be captured or starve to death. They had to stick to trails and move carefully.

The trail they followed led southwest. Every so often, Jacques stopped and looked for booby trap trip wires—local farmers set them to capture small animals for food.

Cresting a ridge, the pair stopped to survey a wide valley stretching off to the horizon. Jacques took his daughter's hand and pointed. "Out there is freedom!

With no compass, Jacques kept the sun on the back of his right shoulder in the morning and on the front in the afternoon. Despite knowing they were going west, his greatest fear was not going far enough south. He wanted to intercept the Mekong River before it turned west.

They started down the hill and came across a large hole in the middle of the trail. Going around, they stumbled on a clothed skeleton that they could tell had once been a soldier. The man's harness held seven full thirty-round magazines. Danielle spotted a rusted AK-47 a meter away and partially buried.

It was time for a break anyway, so they moved off into the trees. Jacques made some cleaning rags from the dead soldier's clothes, then fieldstripped the rifle. He shoved a small wad of cloth down the bore with a bamboo shoot, then held the barrel up to make sure that light shone clean through. Reassembling the weapon, Jacques pulled the trigger and smiled when he heard a loud click as the firing pin moved forward. Next, he emptied each magazine and wiped each bullet clean.

To Danielle it seemed to take hours, but it was less than 40 minutes. As Jacques slung the weapon over his shoulder, he told Danielle they were no longer defenseless. In addition to the rifle, the dead man provided them a canteen, a mess tin, a pack, ammunition, a bayonet and another machete.

A kilometer later, the ground dropped sharply. Jacques told his daughter to move off the trail and wait while he scouted. Danielle shook her head and asked her father not to leave her behind. She was scared of being alone in the jungle; if something happened to him, she didn't know how to survive. The retired Legionnaire hugged his daughter and promised her he would not be long.

When he returned, Jacques led her by the hand to a waterfall dropping into a pool almost thirty meters across. He pointed to the other side. "I'll cover our tracks. You find a place three or four meters from the bank. Get a fire ready to start while I catch some fish. We'll eat well tonight, clean up, and then get some rest. Tomorrow is another long day."

Day 4—Friday, December 20th, 1974, 1248 Local Time, Laos

As she was waking up, Danielle felt a weight on her stomach. She raised her head slightly and saw the black slitted eyes of a snake looking back at her. Its forked tongue flicked the air several times. It was her worst nightmare. What if it was poisonous? Laos was famous (or infamous) for its deadly snakes. One bite and you were dead.

Danielle held her breath and whispered, "Papa."

Her father, already up and heating water in the canteen, turned around. Seeing the snake, he told Danielle not to move. He slowly positioned a bamboo spear under the front third of the snake. With a flick of the wrist, he launched the snake across the clearing. It landed on a fallen tree trunk and slithered off.

"What kind of snake was that?"

"I don't know." Jacques lied. It was a Malayan Pit Viper. Sometimes they were aggressive and sometimes they were passive. Their venom, while not deadly, could make you very, very sick.

Before they left, Jacques fieldstripped the AK-47 again. This time he used water from the stream to rinse off the dirt he'd missed in the first cleaning.

Each previous day before they started out, Jacques had used the machete to cut small branches that he stuffed into the webbing of their makeshift pack. Now with two backpacks, both of them got the branch treatment: it broke up their silhouettes and made them harder to see when they moved off the trail.

Most of the time, trees prevented them from seeing the sun. Danielle was beginning to wonder if they would ever make it to the Mekong and Thailand. The jungle seemed endless. She forced away the thought that it may have been better to stay in the camp.

After walking for two hours and taking a twenty-minute break, they got back on the trail. They hadn't gone far when Jacques held up his fist, and then knelt to examine some tracks in the dirt. Once he was satisfied men and dogs had not made them, Jacques stood back up and nodded. The trail wove back and forth, but led downward and to the west. To Danielle, both those traits were important. The thought of Mekong and, beyond it, Thailand kept her going.

Around a bend the trees suddenly ended, leaving them standing in the late morning sun, surrounded by grass and small bushes. Their end of the clearing was higher than the far side. The earth was heavily dimpled in every direction.

Jacques held up his fist and patted the air as he slowly dropped to one knee. Danielle stuck her braced leg out diagonally so she could kneel next to her father. He cupped his hand over the rifle as he slid the safety off. Even so, the loudness of the click surprised Danielle.

Her father whispered, "American B-52s caused this years ago. Be careful. Look for things we can use as we move across, but don't pick anything up until I examine it."

They'd gone fifty meters when Jacques pointed to a clump of bushes to his right. He mouthed, "Voices." He and Danielle lay on the ground. Jacques rubbed dirt on their faces and arms so they wouldn't reflect light. Carefully, the two of them slid into a crater. Only the top of their heads edged above the rim so they could see.

Danielle felt bugs crawling over her legs and thighs. She willed herself not to react. *After four days of this, I should be used to it, but I'm not. When we get home, I'll never lie in dirt again.*

From where they lay, she could see four soldiers approach and stop, not fifteen meters from the crater. Two of them pointed their weapons at a tree near the edge of the bombed-out area. They held the triggers down and emptied their AK-47s. Bullets zinged over the far edge of the crater.

When the first two shooters cradled their rifles in their arms, another soldier put his rifle to his shoulder. He sprayed a row of bullets that stitched the far side of the crater, nowhere near the tree. Danielle thought that if the soldier's aim was so bad, he would never hit anything in an actual firefight, except by accident. The final man actually turned towards the crater and laughed as he emptied a magazine into the far side of the big hole. Danielle ducked, thinking the soldier was shooting at her.

If the soldiers came over to check their shooting, Jacques was afraid of being spotted and recaptured. He felt he had no choice but to take the initiative. He made sure the selector switch on the AK-47 was in the semi-automatic mode. Raising his head just enough to see over the edge, he took aim, praying that the weapon would work.

Jacques squeezed the trigger and thanked Mikhail Kalashnikov for the rifle that bears his name. It fired. Jacques sent two bullets into each of the two closest shooters. Before the other two realized what was happening, Jacques fired double taps into their chests too.

Once the soldiers were down, Jacques leaped from his hiding place and beheaded each one with the machete. Only then, did he kneel and search the bodies.

Danielle was horrified by the brutality of her father's actions. The wounded men had been defenseless. As soon as she joined him, Jacques explained, "We can't afford to leave witnesses. They had to die."

He handed Danielle an AK-47, then a harness with its pack and magazine pouches. He put his partially used magazine into his pack and added fresh ones taken from the dead soldiers.

Danielle rummaged through the soldiers' packs. All the rice balls, tins of fish, and matches were dumped into one pack. Into the other, she put the mess tins and a small pocketknife, plus four pairs of socks.

Jacques examined the dead soldiers' boots and gave Danielle the smallest pair. The boots were too large, but with an extra pair of socks, they were much better than the crude sandals she currently wore. It took her several minutes get the baseplate of her brace into the bottom of the boot and to adjust the laces so they wrapped around the brace's ankle joint. If the boots hurt their feet, she could always shift back to the sandals. Maybe she'd have to—after almost four years not wearing shoes, the boots felt very strange.

Jacques found a pair of boots that fit. Before they started walking again, he adjusted the load-bearing harness and straps on the pack Danielle carried. They now had two much newer

AK-47s with ten full magazines, two bayonets, eight rice balls, six tins of fish, five cans of fruit, four canteens, two metal mess tins, a pocketknife, two machetes, and a watch for each of them.

After walking in silence for half an hour, Jacques pointed to the side of the trail. Time to take a break. After taking a drink of water, Danielle looked into her father's face. "Papa," she said tremulously, "what you just did was murder."

Jacques gave Danielle a cold stare she had never seen before. "No, it wasn't. We're at war with the Pathet Lao. They put us into that re-education camp when there was no reason to do so. In war, you kill as many of your enemies as you can to convince them to either quit or surrender. While you're doing it, you hope to survive. We killed and we survived. It was either kill them or risk being captured." He took a deep breath. "Now we go on to the next battle.

"Papa, I didn't like it."

Jacques hugged his daughter. "If you did, I'd be worried about you."

Day 5—Saturday, December 21st, 1974, 1629 Local Time, Laos
The land was getting flatter. It soon divided into fields and rice patties separated by stands of trees. They kept inside the tree lines, only exposing themselves when they had no alternative. For lunch, they ate from the tins of fish and fruit, along with a rice ball each. Not long after they set out again, their noses detected the faint smell of rotting vegetation and sewage. It could come only from one source: a large river.

As they headed west, the smell got stronger and the odor gave them the strength of hope. By midday, they could hear chugging of single-cylinder diesels, the puttering of small outboard motors, and the roar of V-8 engines hooked to a single screw. Even so, they couldn't yet see the river.

MOSCOW AIRLIFT

From the top of an irrigation canal, Jacques spotted a major obstacle between them and the Mekong: a busy road. They stopped a hundred meters short, hunkering down in a small stand of trees. They were two hurdles away from Thailand. First was the road, but they could cross that after dark, when the traffic died down. The second was the river. Swimming was out of the question, due to the current and the distance. Building a raft would take too long; it would attract attention; and be hard to control in the water. Stealing a boat was the only answer.

Getting across the road was much easier than they'd thought. They didn't even have to wait until nightfall. A gap came in the traffic; when they couldn't see trucks in either direction, they crossed. The brush along the riverbank was fifty meters thick and went all the way down to the water. As they reached the river, a gray patrol boat flying the Pathet Lao flag passed within a hundred meters of the bank. The crew was more interested in the fishing boats than a man and a woman in dirty gray clothes sitting on shore.

Danielle gazed across the river separating them from Thailand and freedom. "Papa, I wonder if our fellow prisoners are being tortured because we escaped."

He was silent for a moment, and then said, "More than likely, the commandant decided to frighten the prisoners, by telling them we died horribly in the jungle. At the same time, he probably sent out a bulletin to tell all the police in the area to look for us. Fortunately for us, most policemen probably just shrugged when they got the news; they think we're starving in the jungle, if we haven't already been killed by snakes." Jacques put his arm around his daughter's shoulder. "We're very close to Thailand. We just have to stay careful and we'll make it. Tomorrow or the next day we'll be safe."

After dark, they climbed back onto the road and started walking south, away from a small village to their north. Nearby, the Mekong looked like a menacing black ribbon beckoning and waiting to strangle them. The trees on the Thai side looked like a solid black wall, ready to repel them.

Both were exhausted. Jacques found a place above the river where the road headed inland. It was dry, and hopefully not home to any snakes.

Danielle was about to cut a branch when she heard voices. As she undid the knee lock on the brace, it made a loud metallic click. She froze. Hoping the sound hadn't given them away, Jacques took one of the machetes and slunk away into the darkness.

When he returned an hour later, she could see, even in the darkness, that her father was smiling. He led her down to the riverbank and pointed. Fifty meters from where they stood, six boats with outboard motors were tied to a rope between bamboo pilings. A plank walkway connected the shore to the boats, and another led to a cluster of huts on pilings.

Jacques put his hand around her shoulder and whispered, "When I overheard the men talking about their boats, I followed them here and saw these. And look!" He pointed to lights on the opposite side of the river. "That's a Thai village. That's where we're going."

Day 6—Sunday, December 22nd, 1974, 0736 Local Time, Laos

When Danielle woke up in the twilight before sunrise, her father was nowhere to be seen. She panicked, until she saw his pack and AK-47 lying where he'd left them. Only his machete was gone.

She refilled their four canteens and resisted the temptation to drink the untreated water. Instead, she collected dried sticks and bark. Then she gathered a few dead branches to make a small stack. As her father had taught her, she pulled the lint from her belly button and readied the small bow-and-stick arrangement they used to start the fire.

Within two minutes of pulling the bow back and forth, the lint began to glow. Danielle gently blew on it until it flared with a flame. She added a piece of dried bark, which started to burn. Carefully, she put the burning sliver of bark under the pile of dried sticks and gently began to puff on it. Soon she had a small fire.

"Fantastique, bien fait." Fantastic, well done. The whispered words in French came from her smiling father, who held up two fish.

"How did you get them?"

Jacques tossed a small fishing rod onto the ground. "I took this from one of the boats. I'll clean them while you boil the water in our canteens. We can filter it through the clean rag in my pack."

The sky was dark gray with building storm clouds. After eating, Danielle and Jacques cut branches and limbs to make a small lean-to. They hoped the ever more frequent thunder and the noise from the road masked any noise that they made. To keep the shelter together, Jacques showed her how to strip bark from small branches and soak the strips to make them flexible. The strips of bark were then used to lash the frames together. After putting six alternating layers of leaves and branches on top of they lean-to, they laid branches on the ground to keep themselves above the rainwater that was soon to come. It still wouldn't keep them completely dry, but it was better than nothing.

With the lean-to done, Danielle gathered dry wood to build a small cooking fire for dinner, in case her father caught more fish. The dried wood was stacked on top of a pile of branches to keep it off the ground.

While Jacques sat on the river's edge waiting for a fish to bite, he studied the water and the stand of huts and boats to their south. He was particularly interested in how the villagers started the outboard motors. By the end of the day, Jacques was sure he'd memorized the steps: uncover and connect the battery, open the fuel valve, pull out the choke, and press the starter button.

In mid-afternoon, the rain began. It was light at first, but got much heavier by the time darkness fell. A little water dripped down through the leaves, but the dirt on the floor didn't turn muddy.

Just before dark, they heard outboard motors through the patter of the heavy rain. Two boats appeared out of nowhere and nosed up against the riverbank.

Danielle and Jacques watched two men carry red fuel cans down the bank and along the rain-slickened planks. The cans were put into two boats and hooked up to the engines. Before they left, the men started each engine and let them run in neutral for a few minutes before shutting them down.

The Laotians easily lifted the empty fuel cans and brought them back to the beached boats and departing. The Debenards smiled at each other; they now knew which boats were primed. Danielle could see the joy in her father's face, despite the streaks of rain and mud.

Back in their lean-to, Jacques broke open two bullets and dumped most of the contents on the pile of sticks. A couple of grains went into the small hole where he began to use the bow to twirl the stick. Seconds later, the strip of bark began to burn and the fire started with a whoosh.

After eating, Jacques described the plan he'd been formulating all day.

Day 7—Monday, December 23rd, 1974, 0016 Local Time, Laos
Jacques shook his daughter's shoulder. Danielle wasn't asleep—she was too excited for that. The sound of rain on the lean-to's leaves and branches was loud in the darkness. The

cheap watch she'd taken from one of the Laotian soldiers told Danielle it was a few minutes past midnight. She patted the watch affectionately. It was the first timepiece she and her father had had since the Pathet Lao confiscated Jacques' Rolex.

Her father checked her pack and her AK-47, and then inspected his own equipment before looking into Danielle's eyes. "Are you ready to kill anyone who tries to stop us?"

Danielle nodded. "Yes, Papa, I am." Danielle released the bolt and watched the rifle chamber a round.

I am ready to die and to kill, rather than stay in Laos. Laos, I love you and I hate you. I love your beauty, culture, and gentle, peace-loving people. I hate the Pathet Lao for what they did to my family, my country and me. The Laos of my childhood no longer exists. It's time to leave, probably forever.

Moments after crawling from the shelter of the lean-to, both Danielle and Jacques were soaked. They slipped and slid in the mud as they moved toward the boats. Sporadic bolts of lightning helped them see the way, and thunder masked whatever noise they made.

They were within fifteen meters from the plank pier when Jacques held up his hand and patted the air. With the palm of his hand, he pointed to the pyramidal shape of a man wearing a poncho sitting on a small box. An AK-47 was propped between his legs. The sentry's drooped head indicated he was asleep.

Jacques pulled his machete out of its scabbard. With his AK-47 in one hand, he moved from tree to tree and covered the ten meters separating them from the sentry. Danielle didn't want to watch; her eyes were riveted to the scene unfolding in front of her.

As her father raised the machete, the man sensed danger and turned around as he woke. The last thing he saw in the blue light from a bolt of lightning was the flash of steel. Jacques' downward slashing blow severed the man's head from his body. The head splashed in the mud before rolling to the river's edge.

Danielle didn't wait for her father's signal. She was on her way, AK at the ready, just as her father had showed her. As she passed the sentry, blood still oozed from the dead man's neck. It made her sick but she kept going. *Freedom waited!*

Jacques took her hand and led her across the two twenty-five-centimeter-wide planks lashed to a row of pilings, which shifted under their weight. The boards were slick from the heavy rain.

As they were approaching the last boat in the string, a bolt of lightning lit the sky, immediately followed by thunder. Startled, Danielle lost her balance and slipped into the choppy, muddy water. Jacques dropped to his stomach, held onto a piling, and pulled his gasping daughter back onto the plank. He was proud of her; she had not once cried out.

The boat at the end of the pier bobbed wildly, driven by the wind and the rain. Jacques got in first, taking the two packs and the rifles. Danielle's gear went just behind the forward thwart, which was widened slightly to make a seat. Jacques placed his own equipment forward of the gas can. Steadying himself, he held out a hand to help his daughter step into the boat.

At a nod from her father, Danielle cut the mooring line with a machete and Jacques pushed the boat away from the piling. As soon as it was free, both father and daughter started paddling, angling out and letting the boat drift silently past the huts.

Once they were far enough from the bank, Jacques spoke in a normal tone of voice. "Stop paddling and save your energy. I'm going to try to start the motor."

He went through the drill he'd memorized; when he pushed the starter button, the motor spun but did not start. He made sure it was primed and tried again. Nothing.

Jacques pulled off the fuel hose, sucked on it for a few seconds and spit gasoline out into the river. He tried again. Nothing. He turned off the choke and tried again. Nothing! The boat was ten meters from the Laotian shore, but the waves were pushing it closer. Jacques tried again, and this time the engine coughed, sputtered for a few seconds, before it roared into life.

The noise of the engine running was a harsh contrast to the rain pounding the river. Despite its noise, it was the best sound that Danielle had ever heard.

Jacques steered the boat west, straight across the river to get to the Thai side as fast as they could. Theoretically, the border ran down the middle of the river. Once they were on the western side, they could go downriver to the village they'd spotted earlier.

The wind in Danielle's face had a cool pleasant feeling that added to her excitement. After walking for a week and living in the camp for three years, they were about to reach freedom. The rain stopped, even though lightning continued to flash and thunder rumbled in the distance; Danielle wondered if God was sending a signal that he wanted them to be safe. Then a searchlight started sweeping the water at the same time that she heard the low rumble of a diesel engine.

Jacques throttled the engine down so as not to leave a wake and steered the boat to where the searchlight beam had been. He spoke loud enough for Danielle could hear but not so loud that it carried over the water. "Get down."

In the glow from the searchlight, they could see the shape of a heavy machine-gun on the patrol boat's bow. A two-man crew swept it back and forth, trying to stay synchronized with the searchlight.

"Danielle, get your rifle ready. If they find us with the searchlight, aim at it. After you shoot it out, spray the rest of the magazine and another one along the deck of the boat."

She nodded numbly. The Pathet Lao patrol boat was between them and the Thai side, but it was *not* going to stop them. Jacques had slowed the boat to minimize engine noise, but the next flash of lightning would make them visible.

Automatically Danielle went through the drill her father made her practice before they went to sleep each night and when they got up each morning. Make sure the magazine is seated; pull the bolt back to make sure a round is in the chamber. If there wasn't a round in place, use the bolt to chamber one. She was about to take the last step—select semi-automatic or full automatic and flick off the safety—when she heard shouts from the deck of the patrol boat.

The beam swept across their boat, then stopped and started to come back. Danielle pulled the AK-47 back into her shoulder and put the sight in the middle of the light, forcing herself not to close her eyes as she squeezed the trigger. The rifle banged against her shoulder and the sharp pain reminded her to pull in tighter.

From the bow, the crew of the heavy machine-gun started firing. Tracers zipped over their heads. Then bullets started raising short rows of geysers in the water around them as the gunner adjusted his aim. Danielle forgot to select fully automatic and aimed at the bow. When the gun only fired once, she kept pulling the trigger until the searchlight shattered with a flash and a loud bang.

With the light out, Jacques gunned the engine and shouted, "Keep firing!"

Danielle dumped out the empty magazine and fed in a new one. This time she remembered to change to fully automatic and aimed at the accelerating patrol boat as it turned toward them. She aimed at the source of tracers and pulled the trigger. Sparks from rounds hitting the boat told her where to aim.

She followed her first burst with a second and a third. When the machine-gun shopped firing, she replaced the magazine and aimed the next burst at the bridge.

Jacques turned the boat sharply and Danielle almost dropped a magazine over the side. It fell into the boat and, rather than search for it, she grabbed the last one from her pack. Their six-meter-long boat was passing the patrol boat, headed west. Green tracers from the machine-gun on the stern flew over their heads. Confident the gunners on the patrol boat couldn't see them; Danielle held the trigger down and sprayed the back of the open bridge. Sparks flew wildly, and several men went down before the AK-47 had fired all thirty rounds.

Danielle turned to her father. As he erratically swerved the boat, he leaned forward and handed her his pack. In it were their last four magazines. Danielle loaded one into her rifle. Another flash of lightning showed the patrol boat chasing off in the wrong direction; they'd lost Danielle and her father in the dark.

* * *

On the Laos shore, the village had little electricity and practically no lights. Not so the village on the Thai side. It was well lit, almost cheery. Jacques looked for someplace they could tie up.

Danielle shivered in the wind, despite the twenty-five degree Celsius temperature. She was wet and cold. Goose bumps covered her body.

They came to a number of short docks, then a larger one sticking thirty meters into the river. Jacques eased the boat alongside a ladder. Danielle grabbed a hanging piece of rope and tied it to a cleat in the front of their little skiff.

"Leave everything in the boat."

Danielle pulled herself up the ladder one rung at a time. By the time Jacques joined her on the dock, a man in uniform was running out of a small building, waving and shouting. A rumble of thunder drowned out his voice. In the arc lights, his steel gray Thai police uniform shirt and blue trousers were easy to identify.

His pistol drawn, the police sergeant came toward Danielle and Jacques. Two more policemen armed with M-16s emerged from the shack and aimed their guns at the escapees. Father and daughter raised their hands in surrender.

Danielle spoke in Thai. "We are French citizens who just escaped from Laos. He is Jacques Debenard, and I am his daughter, Danielle. We were held at the Pathet Lao Re-Education Camp #3 near Na Kai since April 1971. We would like to speak to the French ambassador in Bangkok who can verify our identity."

The closest Thai police officer advanced cautiously. His shoulder tabs indicated he was a *cha sip tri,* or master sergeant. Without saying a word, he patted both the Debenards down. Then he peered into the boat. "We heard a Laotian patrol boat report it was shot at. Four of their sailors were killed and six more were wounded. Was that you?"

"Yes. We didn't want to get captured and executed."

"Who are you?"

Danielle replied, "Before we were captured, my father managed one of Michelin's largest rubber plantations in Laos. I worked for the French diplomatic corps."

The *cha sip tri* studied the two of them for a few seconds before he spoke. "Come with me. We have to keep you in our jail until we make sure you are not criminals. We will put you a separate cell, allow you to clean up, and give you clean clothes."

Danielle forced herself to stand as straight as the brace allowed, even though she felt like sagging with relief. Soon she would be clean, warm dry. The nightmare of the last three years was over.

Chapter 2
Terror Central

Sunday, October 23rd, 1983, 0630 Local Time, Beirut

Two trucks were parked in the warehouse. One was a yellow nineteen-ton capacity rated Mercedes stake truck; lying in its load area was an eight-centimeter thick sheet of marble, on top of which sat an equally thick slab of concrete with hoops of rebar sticking up. Workers had just finished lashing barrels of butane to the wood frame around the bed.

The second truck was a pick-up. On its bed, propane bottles were lashed together vertically. Due to weight restrictions, there was no concrete or marble on the floor to create the base for a shaped charge.

Mohammed Safdar was the man who'd come up with the idea of using readily available materials—concrete poured into a form on the floor of the garage—to create a plate that would direct the blast upward rather than letting its force expend wastefully in all directions. After the concrete was poured, U-shaped rebar hoops, with the bottoms bent out at ninety degrees to ensure they would not pull free, had been pressed into the wet concrete.

For Safdar there was only one thing left to do. He climbed on the Mercedes truck and checked the plastic explosive packed around each gas bottle, the bricks all linked together with det cord. Over the past four days, assistants had helped him arrange a total of 9,525 kilograms of explosive. As for the pick-up trick, it had only taken Safdar a day to place five hundred kilograms of explosive PETN around the butane bottles there.

Now, with the wiring and circuitry tested, it was time to put the detonators in place. This was the first moment-of-truth. If there were any stray voltages, either vehicle could explode and set off the other in a sympathetic detonation. Safdar and the garage would disappear, leaving a large hole in the ground.

The second moment-of-truth occurred when the vehicles were started. Safdar used the safety procedures he'd learned while blasting rock in the Hassai Chromium mine in Sudan. Although confident of his design and his work, there was always a chance he had made a mistake. If he had, six months of work would have been lost in a flash, not to mention his life and the lives of all those around him.

The two trucks started without incident. They sat idling, waiting for the signal to go.

Unknown to the drivers, each vehicle had two radio control detonators hidden amongst the explosives: a primary and a backup. Safdar had been instructed by his employers to install the extra detonators in case one or both drivers got cold feet, or were killed before they could set off the bombs.

With the vehicles ready, Safdar handed the transmitter for the van to a chosen assistant and kept the one for the truck himself. He got into a battered Volkswagen Beetle and headed for the apartment building on the edge of Beirut International Airport to watch the fruits of his labor. From a seventh floor apartment rented by a front company, Safdar saw the four-story building that was his target.

He'd been in position for at least ten minutes when he saw the Mercedes truck approach the gate for the barracks and headquarters of the First Battalion, Eighth U.S. Marine Regiment. A short distance away from the gate, the truck turned off from the approach. Concerned that the Iranian-born driver, Ismail Ascari, was getting cold feet, Safdar flipped open the cover on the remote detonators. Both green lights came on, indicating that his transmitter was connected to both receivers on the truck and the remote detonators were armed.

The truck turned back toward the gate. Perhaps Ascari had decided he needed a longer run at the target. Safdar could see the vehicle gathering speed, and U.S. Marines scurrying in response. From Hezbollah, Islamic Jihad had found out that while the Marines carried loaded magazines in their weapons, their rules of engagement didn't allow them to have rounds in the chamber. They couldn't shoot unless they saw clear evidence of a threat.

Islamic Jihad's leaders were confident the Americans would be reluctant to shoot at what appeared to be a lost truck. This was essentially the same tactic the organization had used to destroy the U.S. embassy in Beirut back in April. When Safdar had been designing and building the bomb, his contact had estimated it would take the Americans ten to twenty seconds to realize they were in danger and react. By then, the truck should have crashed through the gate and be on its way to the main building.

Safdar placed the transmitter down on the windowsill. He watched the truck plow through the concertina wire that crossed the road. Green-uniformed Marines dove for cover. Others frantically cocked their weapons. He couldn't tell if they had fired when Ascari drove the truck into the building's lobby, just as planned. Safdar could no longer see the vehicle; he was about to pick up the transmitter when he heard a rumble. Seconds later, the building shook from the concussion.

The blast lifted all four floors off the foundation and the building collapsed in a smoking pile of rubble. Safdar hurried downstairs. He would later find out from the local news that his bomb had killed the most Marines on a single day since the World War II battle for Iwo Jima: 220 Marines, 18 sailors and three soldiers. All told, the U.S. suffered the most casualties in a single day since the Tet Offensive during the Vietnam War.

Across town ten minutes later, the pick-up truck stopped in front of a building housing men from two French Parachute regiments. Suspicious, the soldiers started shooting and killed the driver. From a nearby building, a member of Islamic Jihad flipped the switch to send a coded pulse to the remote detonator. Fifty-eight French paratroopers—fifty-five from the 1st Chasseur and three from the 9th Chasseur Regiment—died in the explosion.

Friday, September 28th, 1984, 0830 Local Time, Teheran

The first man through the door was the head of Iran's Ministry of Intelligence. The second man was a general who led the intelligence arm of the Army of the Guardians of the Islamic Revolution, a.k.a. the IRGC, a.k.a. the Pasdaran. Both were members of Iran's National Supreme Defense Council, but they rarely met or even communicated directly. Their presence in the same place at the same time automatically made this an event of the highest importance.

Each man had arrived thirty minutes before the scheduled start of the meeting to allow plenty of time to go through the security protocols. They arrived in separate armored limousines in a three-vehicle convoy. Once inside the Supreme Leader's residence, their bodyguards waited in a special area while the principals were escorted to the conference room. Once they were seated, a small leather folder was placed in front of each on the polished wooden table.

The men stood when a man was in his early fifties entered and sat in a chair at the head of the table. The chair stood on a raised platform so the man's head and shoulders were always well above those seated before him. He had a long and well-trimmed white beard, streaked with black. He wore the traditional black headdress of a mullah, and his white shirt contrasted sharply with his black robe.

The Supreme Leader pursed his lips. "It is Muharran. Before we go over our plans for this New Year, let us review what we have accomplished. We provide men, weapons, intelligence, money and logistics support to Islamic Jihad and Hezbollah. Last year, they blew up the American Embassy on August 18 and the Marine Barracks on October 23. On September 20—just a few days ago—they destroyed the U.S. Embassy Annex in Beirut. I would call these attacks a good start, yet we need to strike much harder at the Great Satan. I want an organization created to carry out a series of devastating attacks in America itself as soon as possible. We also need to continue to arm and support Hezbollah and Islamic Jihad in their efforts to destroy Israel. Use whatever weapons you consider necessary. Work together and report directly to me on the success of your endeavors."

The Minister of Intelligence nodded. "My people have always been interested in conducting operations in America. We have outlined possible approaches. With your permission, let us call this new group the Sword of Allah. There will be no shortage of volunteers who want to help chop off the head of the Great Satan."

The Supreme Leader nodded. "Make it so. We will meet in thirty days to review your plan."

Monday, November 30th, 1987, 1846 Local Time, Tel Aviv
Tacked to a bulletin board on the wall in Avram's office were three photos from three different bomb attacks. One was from March 27th, 1987, when a bomb in a bus station injured

fifteen Israeli soldiers. The second came from a camera outside a police station just before a bomb went off on November 11th, 1987. Luckily, only one person had been hurt. The third was taken from a camera outside a bus stop on November 26th before a bomb injured fifteen soldiers.

One of Avram Gutman's favorite sayings was, 'Sometimes you are good, and sometimes you are lucky.' This time it was a little of both.

All three photos were on the wall because they had one thing in common: the same man. Gutman was sure it was not coincidence that this particular man was at all three locations just before bombs were set off. In the last photo, it was clear he had a small box in his right hand that could have been the detonator.

As Avram drummed his fingers on the table, his mind raced. *Who are you? Where did you come from? Where are you hiding?* The grainy blow-ups weren't much help. The mystery man could have been any resident of the West Bank, or even an Israeli citizen.

What Gutman didn't know was his man was named Mohammed Safdar—born in Tyre, Lebanon, and Islamic Jihad's primary bomb designer. His factory was in Nablus on the West Bank. He used Israel as a venue for his experiments. On Safdar's drawing board were far more sophisticated and deadly designs.

Thursday, August 11th, 1988, 1145 Local Time, San Diego

The windows were down, so Josh Haman could hear gravel crunching under the tires of his 1965 Porsche 356SC coupe as he drove slowly forward. At the end of the road, Josh parked and got out, standing still for a moment to take in the quiet. The only noise was the soft rustle of wind through the trees.

He picked up three rocks from the gravel parking lot of Home of Peace Cemetery and headed down the path he'd followed more times than he could remember. This was a visit his wife Rebekah didn't object to his making. Josh had taken the murder of his first wife and her parents hard, and the memory still hurt.

So every year, if he wasn't at sea, Josh made this pilgrimage on the anniversary date of Natalie's death.

When he got to the three light gray granite gravestones, Josh gently put a rock on top of each one, signifying that a family member had visited the site. He stood there for a few seconds and then, as he did each time, he gave Natalie an update on his life, his children and his wife. On some visits, tears flowed down his face and made his grief feel lighter. Three headstones, but it should have been four. On that fateful night, Natalie had gone to tell her parents she was pregnant and was planning to surprise him when he returned from deployment.

Josh remembered reading the calling card the assassin had left with the bodies, the card from a KGB agent that stated Natalie's father, Artur Vishinski, had been targeted for execution because he'd deserted the Red Army in July 1945. When the war ended, Artur hadn't wanted to go back to the Soviet Union to live under Stalin; apparently, the Soviet Union's deterrence policy against defections had turned retroactive.

Josh finished by saying, "Natalie, I still haven't found the KGB son-of-a-bitch who killed you and your parents, but if I don't find him while I'm in the Navy, I will when I retire. Someone has to bring the bastard to justice."

Wednesday, March 2nd, 1989, 0846 Local Time, Beirut
It was hard for Mohammed Safdar to imagine Beirut as it was in the 1950s and 1960s, when it was s a glamorous city. The

rich and famous from all over the Middle East and Europe came to play on its beaches and stay in its hotels. For some, it had been a city where enemies could sit in its cafés and make deals, free from the scrutiny of official politics.

Now Beirut was a city of ruins. There were streets lined with nothing but heaps of rubble. Buildings that still stood were pockmarked with shell holes, or showed walls of nothing but burned concrete. Somehow, families turned these into residences. Along the beachfront, the once luxurious hotels were a shadow of their former glory. All of them needed updating, and to afford that, they needed customers. Apart from a few locals or visitors from Syria, tourists were staying away.

Despite thirteen years of civil war, Safdar could feel Beirut's pulse. The city was not dead or even dying; it just needed to find its way out. The traditional balance between Maronite Christians and Muslim rule was gone, and no unifying replacement had materialized. Safdar's native Lebanon needed to heal itself and end the war that killed over a hundred thousand of its citizens.

Then there were the Israelis. In Safdar's mind, they'd made it worse with their 1980 invasion and support for the Southern Lebanese Army. The Jewish state shouldn't have been allowed to be created, much less still exist. The Arabs should have pushed the Jews into the sea in 1948 when they'd had the chance.

Lebanon was the home of his birth, but he'd grown up in New York City, where his father worked for the Palestine Liberation Organization in the U.N. After graduating with a degree in mechanical engineering from Cornell University, Safdar had taken a job working in the Haddai Mines in the Sudan. It had been a two-year contract, and he'd been assigned the work of figuring out where to place dynamite for blasting rock in search of chromium ore.

In the end, the government who owned the mine couldn't afford to keep it open. The money the mine generated went to corrupt politicians and black market weapons. What little stayed with the mine wasn't enough to pay operating expenses. Safdar's contract was not renewed. When he got to the airport, the ticket he was given as part of his severance pay had not been paid for; he had to pay his own way back to Lebanon.

There had been no jobs for a mechanical engineer with expertise in explosives and blasting until one afternoon when a stranger had sat down at Safdar's table at an outdoor café. The man introduced himself as Rami Dagher and said he had a simple proposition: Help Hezbollah and its "affiliates." The rewards would be handsome.

Safdar asked, "When do I start?"

At first, he had been kept secluded from others within Hezbollah, but as his bombs proved to be more deadly than those built by others, his value increased. When it came to designing and building specialized car bombs, he was "the man"; he had created the one used to kill the former president of Lebanon, Rashid Karami.

Some said that the small bomb placed on the Puma helicopter was planted by a member of the never before heard of Secret Lebanese Army. Ten men went to jail, but not one of them knew how the bomb was made or how it was gotten on board the Puma.

* * *

The day before, Safdar had driven just east of Louaizeh where the road climbs into the mountains. He'd stopped the car to look back, wondering if he'd ever see Beirut again. He'd been warned not to go near either the Iranian embassy or Hezbollah's office in Damascus. Instead, he'd been given the address of a small hotel on the edge of the wealthy Malki suburb. A message waiting for him at the front desk instructed him to take a seat in Tishreen Park where he would meet his contact.

On his way to the meeting, Safdar checked for surveillance, but no one seemed to be shadowing him, no one cared who he was. His worry was he was sent here to be eliminated.

According to his watch, he'd been sitting on the bench for ten minutes when a stranger sat down next to him. The man gave no sign of making contact. Safdar resisted the urge to move and decided to wait five more minutes before leaving.

Out of the corner of his eye, he studied the man. He was casually dressed, with blond hair going gray hair and a neatly cropped beard.

"Safdar." The stranger spoke in a barely audible voice.

"Yes."

"We have a very important mission for you to undertake in America. We understand you have lived there."

The man's accent was odd. *I wonder where he learned Arabic.* "My father worked for the PLO at the U.N."

"Then I presume you will take this mission in the U.S."

If I don't take it, what then? Will they kill me? Probably, because it will show I am not committed to their cause. "What am I supposed to do?"

"Build an organization and strike at the Americans. We have assets already in place, but they need someone with your skills. Tehran thinks you are the perfect man for the job." The man turned his head to scrutinize Safdar; his eyes were hard, and the coldest blue Safdar had ever seen.

Leadership? I just build and teach others how to build bombs. I am not a leader.

"I am honored I am thought of so highly."

"So you will go?"

Safdar hesitated for only the sliver of a second. "Yes."

"Gut." The man unbuttoned his jacket, took out a thick envelope, and placed it on the bench. "In there, you will find new passports, credit cards to use for expenses, and plane tickets to get you to England. From there, you will go to Canada. There is also a list of phone numbers for you to use, and one to call when you get to New York. A driver will be waiting to take you to your apartment."

Former SS-Brigatenführer and war criminal Hans Graebner, who had advised the Syrians and now Hezbollah, looked at the young man. "You are to depart as soon as possible. This afternoon, I will have a courier drop off detailed instructions you must memorize, and then flush down the toilet. Here is my business card. Call from a public phone if you have any questions."

With that, the man put his hands on his thighs and stood up. Looking down at Safdar, he said, in his oddly accented Arabic, "May Allah be with you and guide you."

Chapter 3
Travelogue

Sunday, March 7th, 1989, 1147 Local Time, New York City

Mohammed Safdar walked into the apartment on East 56th Street between First and Second Avenue, dropped his bags in the short hallway and went into the small living/dining area. At one end, there was a couch, coffee table and TV set on a stand. At the other, a small table with four chairs; on the table, laid out in a neat row, was his renewed New York State driver's license, a box of checks, a Master Card issued by Barclay's Bank, and a three-by-five card with the apartment's phone number.

The cabinets had a set of Mikasa dishes and the drawers enough silverware to serve eight, or at least eight single person meals before he'd have to wash dishes. There were pots and pans, a toaster, and a wooden knife block on the counter holding a nice set of recently sharpened knives.

Safdar carried his bags into the bedroom and quickly unpacked. Still full of energy, he decided to walk down to the small market at the end of the block and pick up enough food for a late lunch and dinner. Tomorrow he would walk around and learn the ins and outs of the neighborhood. Pleased with this prospect and his setting, Mohammed lay back on the bed and reviewed his actions of the past few days on his way to the United States.

He'd left Damascus on Thursday, March 3rd, on a Syrian Air flight to Doha in Qatar.

From the airport, he'd called a hotel in downtown Doha and booked a room. The next day, he'd used the second ticket from the packet to fly to Gatwick Airport in England, using a year-old Lebanese passport and a valid U.K tourist visa in the name of Hussein Yehia.

After checking into a hotel just off Bayswater, he'd strolled around, had dinner and noted several travel agencies. The next morning, he selected a small one and bought a one-way ticket to Toronto on Air Canada leaving March 5th. When the young agent asked him for his passport, he handed her a Qatari one issued six months earlier to Farooq Khan. It had a valid tourist visa for Canada. Satisfied, the agent wrote out the ticket after charging his American Express card.

Upon landing in Toronto, Mohammed had taken a cab into the central business district and booked a room at the Chelsea Hotel on Gerrard Street. From prior visits to Toronto he knew there were many travel agents on Yonge Street, a few blocks to the east of the hotel. At 0930 on Saturday morning, he bought a ticket to LaGuardia leaving on a nine a.m. American Airlines flight on Sunday. This time, he presented his Lebanese passport and green U.S. Immigration and Naturalization Agency card that indicated he was a legal resident of the United States. When the travel agent asked why he'd stopped in Toronto, Safdar had replied he was on vacation and it was cheaper to fly through Toronto and spend the night than taking a direct flight from London. The polite agent handed him the ticket and wished him a pleasant trip.

That evening, he'd called the New York number from a pay phone in the hotel, giving the person at the other end his flight number and time of arrival on March 7th. He'd slept well, then departed early for his flight, which had been uneventful. In La Guardia Airport's baggage claim, an elderly man wearing a black suit had been holding a sign with his name. Without saying a word, he'd led Safdar to a parked Lincoln Town Car and driven him to this address. On the seat had been an envelope with two sets of keys to the apartment.

After reviewing the events and his diligence in ensuring he'd not being tailed, Mohammed relaxed and closed his eyes for a nap. Shopping could wait.

* * *

When he'd gotten off the plane in Doha, Safdar hadn't spotted the man taking pictures of every male passenger arriving on flights from Damascus. A copy of the manifest was surreptitiously acquired and couriered to the Israeli embassy in Athens. There, the embassy looked at the photos, ran the passport numbers against the photos, and matched the surveillance pictures against those on their "persons of interest" list.

Hussein Yehia's photo was close enough to those on the wall with no name. The Mossad agent called an apartment in Doha and told the officer he was to watch the airport tomorrow the next few days to find out where Yehia was going. If he spotted Hussein, he was to use his law enforcement credentials to find out what flight he boarded.

Before Safdar got on the plane in London, an investigator in the Israeli Ministry of Justice had called his counterpart in Ottawa and asked for information on Hussein Yehia. Because it was a weekend and the Israelis didn't have a warrant for Yehia, all the Canadians would offer was the information on his passport and visa application to be delivered Monday. It was then they learned Yehia was not on board any flight to the U.S. or Canada.

Hiding his frustration, the Israeli representative asked to review the surveillance tapes for Sunday for those boarding flights to the United States from Toronto. It took three hours of looking at photos of passengers entering and leaving Canada in the past forty-eight hours and comparing them to the photo of Yehia before a familiar face popped up on the screen.

A copy of the image was made, and the Israelis now knew Hussein Yehia entered the United States on a Lebanese passport as Mohammed Safdar. The address on the passport was faxed to the Mossad office in the U.N. mission in New York. By Tuesday afternoon, the address on the green card was determined to not be valid. It existed, but the Safdars no longer lived in the apartment, and there was no forwarding address. The Mossad database listed an Ahmed Safdar, deceased, who had been a member of the PLO U.N. Mission. The Mossad had a name to go with a face. Now they had to find out where he was in the U.S., and why?

Chapter 4
Cold Reckoning

Monday, December 10th, 1990, 0859 Local Time, Moscow

Monday, December 10th, 1990, 0859 Local Time, Moscow

By Moscow standards, it was a balmy late fall morning. The sun was out, the sky was clear, and the temperature was -5° Celsius. Supposedly, it would get to +1° for a few minutes in the afternoon, which was good. The bad news was that the damp, gusty twenty-kilometer an hour wind from the northwest made it feel much colder.

Inside the Kremlin walls and in the main administration building, the General Secretary of the Communist Party of the Union of Soviet Socialist Republics sat at the polished antique desk used by Tsars as well as Communist leaders. For a man in his position, it was remarkably free of clutter. He was reading a four-page briefing document.

Three phones—two private lines to connect him to anyone in the world and a red phone with a direct line to the defense minister's desk—were within arm's reach on the right side of the desk. On the credenza behind him were photographs of the General Secretary with other foreign leaders. To his left, a ten-centimeter tall stack of bright red folders awaited his attention.

MOSCOW AIRLIFT

Kremlin is the Russian word for fortress or citadel. It was an apt description for the Soviet Union's seat of power. The twenty-seven hectare complex started out as a wooden fort in the 11th century. In the middle of the 13th century, the oak walls were replaced by white limestone. In the 1500s, Grand Duke Ivan the Third, a.k.a. Ivan the Great, hired two Renaissance Italian architects to make improvements: Petrus Antonius Solarius to redesign the walls and towers, and Marcus Ruffus to design three churches plus a new palace for the Grand Duke.

The fortress had its ups and downs. From September 21, 1610 to October 26, 1612, the Poles occupied it. Peter the Great barely escaped an assassination attempt in 1682 and moved the seat of government to his beloved St. Petersburg. For almost a hundred years thereafter, the Kremlin was only used for ceremonial purposes until 1773, when Katherine the Great decided to have a new residence built inside its walls. Since then, the only non-Russian leader to live in the Kremlin was Napoleon, who moved in for a brief time in 1812. The last leader to put his imprint on the Kremlin was Stalin, who ordered two of the three churches on the grounds destroyed.

A soft tap on the door caused the man to look up. His expected guest was ushered in.

The two men shook hands and sat in chairs used by Catherine the Great. A tray of tea and mineral water was placed on a side table made from Siberian white birch sometime in the late 19th century and covered, like many of the tables in the Kremlin, with a wide strip of red cloth. The General Secretary often wondered if the Tsars, particularly the last one, Nicholas II, ever considered that red would be the color of the revolution that ended their "divine rule".

Neither man smiled, nor did they speak until the servant left the room and the door closed with a soft click. The wood floor and the ceilings, seven meters above the floor, absorbed sound like dry sand absorbs water.

The General Secretary spoke first. "Eduard, are you confident your analysis is accurate?"

The Minister of Finance, Eduard Schvardze, spoke softly, but with authority and confidence. "Yes, Comrade General Secretary. In fact, I think it is understated. No matter how we look at the data, the conclusion is the same. The Soviet Union is almost out of money."

The General Secretary slid a report across the table. "Have you seen this?"

Schvardze picked up the document. "No, what is it?"

"The latest estimates on our food supply. It says food production throughout the Soviet Union was down at least five percent from last year, and six percent less than the year before. Meanwhile, our population is growing at about three percent a year. Eduard, you do the math. We're somewhere around fourteen per cent short on what we need, and winter is upon us. We have to buy food from the West with money we don't have. And we have to get it here quickly, so we don't have riots in the street."

The General Secretary sat back in his chair and took a long sip from a glass that Schvardze suspected held vodka, not water. "Eduard, what do we do?"

Wednesday, December 12th, 1990, 1936 Local Time, San Diego
It was supposedly a happy night, the first night of the Festival of Lights, more commonly known as Hanukah. In the Haman household, there were eight presents for each of the three children: sixteen-year-old Sasha, fourteen-year-old Sara and ten-year-old Sean. After the candles were lit, each family member got to choose one present. There was no shaking or examination of boxes; each child simply went to the fireplace and chose one. The rest would be opened in turn, one each the

next seven nights. It was a gentle lesson in patience ands the power of anticipation.

The six-hundred-pound gorilla in the living room was the absence of their father, Captain Joshua Haman, who was on board the *U.S.S. Blue Ridge* in the Persian Gulf. He and a small team of recently recalled Reservists designated Zulu Lima were responsible for operational command and control of over a hundred and forty helicopters from fourteen different countries. They were part of Operation Desert Shield, planning for their part in a war.

Central Command's naval component commander had handpicked Josh for Zulu Lima. In the U.S. Navy's battle force command structure, Zulu Lima was the designator for the individual or group responsible for tasking and operational control of all the helicopters assigned to Battle Force Zulu. Everyday, his team had to juggle the number of helicopters available to fly, the missions Zulu Lima was tasked to complete versus the actual capabilities of the helos, and the restrictive rules of engagement imposed by their national governments as one of the conditions for their participation in the coalition.

Josh had spent most of August and September commuting between San Diego and Riyadh, and when the Seventh Fleet Flagship, the *U.S.S. Blue Ridge*, had arrived, he'd moved on board. When the *U.S.S. Ranger* reached the gulf in late December, he and his staff would move on board the carrier and work for Commander, Carrier Group Seven, the Anti-Surface Warfare Commander designated Zulu Sierra.

After the blessing over the candles was completed, Sara turned to her mother. "Mom, the best present would be if Daddy was here."

"I'd like him here, too." Rebekah was worried about the safety of her husband. The question Sean had asked the last time Josh was home was running through her head like a litany, almost like a dirge. She forced that comparison from her mind.

"Daddy, how many aircraft carriers were sunk during the Vietnam War?"

Josh's quick answer had been, "None." Then he'd turned to his son. "Why did you ask?"

"Because you're going to be on an aircraft carrier and everyone thinks Saddam Hussein is not going to leave Kuwait, so there will be a war."

"Hopefully, he'll get smart and leave."

Sasha had added, "Or you're going to kick him out."

"Not me personally, but all the coalition soldiers in Saudi Arabia can."

Sasha was ready with a follow-up question. "Dad, are you going to fly combat missions?"

Josh didn't want to lie to his children, but he also didn't want them to worry unnecessarily. "I'm not planning to."

Rebekah's immediate thought had been, "Good answer." She was afraid her husband would find a way to put himself in harm's way. He usually did. They'd been married almost sixteen years and her greatest fear was that the odds would finally catch up to him.

Friday, December 14th, 1990, 0936 Local Time, Moscow

Until 1946, the nondescript building on 9 Ilinka Street had been the headquarters for the People's Commissariat for Finance, or *Narodnyi Komissariat Finansov*—Narkofin for short. In the post-Stalin era, it was renamed the Ministry of Finance, but to those who worked with and within the bureaucracy, the agency was still referred to as Narkofin.

Through its Department of Revisory Control, the Ministry of Finance's stated mission was to impose financial discipline throughout the U.S.S.R. by enforcing laws, and by auditing and controlling each ministry's adherence to their budgets. It was also responsible for examining the activities of the Soviet

Union's equivalent to the U.S. Federal Reserve Bank. The ability to look at any business or government agency's finances, print money, impose taxes and control the purse strings made the Minister of Finance one of the most powerful members of the Central Committee and of the Soviet Union's vast bureaucracy.

In her fourth floor office overlooking Ilinka Street, Olga Gregorenko frowned like a schoolteacher in the midst of grading a set of papers in which it was obvious the students didn't understand the material. She was the head of the Department of Revisory Control; in a western business, Gregorenko would be considered the firm's chief financial officer. Her boss, the Minister of Finance, depended on Gregorenko to develop accurate reports on the Soviet Union's finances. She was the source of the financial reports that had given the General Secretary a migraine headache.

Sitting in front of her desk was an older man with a full, but neatly trimmed, gray beard. His beard and triangular head made him resemble Lenin.

Olga templed her fingers and spoke in a hushed tone. "Eduard, a U.S. dollar on the black market will get you thirty to forty rubles, even though the official exchange rate is one point seven rubles to the dollar. Printing more rubles only delays the inevitable. Even the Cubans want to be paid in U.S. dollars... or British pounds or Swiss Francs. In the international currency markets, the ruble is almost worthless. Yet you say we must buy food from the West. With what money?" Olga clasped her hands on the desk.

Eduard Schvardze knew the country's options were as cold as its winter weather. "If we were a Western company, we would file for bankruptcy. At my advanced age, the last thing I need to do is preside over a bankrupt country."

Schvardze was looking forward to retirement. He had just turned sixty-five and could feel his body breaking down. Six years in the Gulag for publishing a paper suggesting the Soviet Union adopt a Western European style banking system hadn't helped the aging process. Five years after he'd been released, Andropov, the man who'd put him there, was dead, and the current General Secretary had installed him as the Minister of Finance with a mission to reform the country's finances.

"We have, as the capitalists say, no leverage. So, how do we avoid paying a premium?" The minister turned to the third person in the office. "Seraphim, my good friend, what would you do?"

Seraphim Olshansky was the creative force behind the July 1990 trade agreement requiring the Soviet Union to buy at least four million tons of wheat and four million tons of feed grains annually. The young trade minister's KGB file had a note stating he was a "practicing Jew." Under prior administrations, that notation would have kept him from senior positions in the government. It was still a stigma, but ability and expertise had a way of overcoming centuries of prejudice.

"We have a way to get more food, and we do have some leverage. The latest grain deal makes the Soviet Union the largest customer for American wheat. I think I can get the Americans to take crude oil, natural gas and raw materials at below market prices as payment. The potential for larger profits and dividends will make it easy for the Americans and other Western governments to accept. So I think we should talk to the Americans as soon as possible. They will bring their allies along. What I need to know is, how much more we need, and how soon. Do you know?"

"Yes." Schvardze handed Olshansky the report he'd been given by the General Secretary. "It will not be popular with the hardliners. They are already unhappy with Gorbachev's loosening the government's hold on the people; it scares them. You need to think carefully how to propose this, because you will make enemies."

"No more than I already have, Eduard." Seraphim knew this government, like the ones before it, often blamed its failures on its Jews; it wouldn't be the first time and probably wouldn't be the last. "I can use my strong relationships with the American Secretary of Commerce and the European Common Market trade ministers to get their support. Believe me, the last thing they want is for our government to collapse. The prospect of millions of Russian refugees heading west gives them all heart attacks."

The finance minister shook his head slowly. "Getting the members of the Presidium to agree will be a problem—they will see it as another public admission that our socialist system has failed to meet the needs of the Russian people. They're more worried about negative publicity than taking care of their fellow citizens. They will take a lot convincing. Many ministers still resent the budget cuts the General Secretary imposed. They want to return to the spending levels of the 1970s and 80s."

Olga Gregorenko broke the uncomfortable silence. "The Politburo has three choices. One, wait until our fellow citizens are dying of starvation and then act to put down the riots. That will be bloody, but maybe the hardliners think it is a way of re-establishing control. Two, buy food from the West, as Seraphim is suggesting. Three, come up with their own plan. But they won't step forward with a plan because if it fails they are dead politically, and it ends their dreams of becoming the next General Secretary."

Olshansky leaned forward with a smile on his face. "Let's use their caution against them. We present our plan and, if given the authority to carry it out, offer to take responsibility. If it works, we're heroes. If it doesn't, they think they've won and it doesn't matter, because Russia will disintegrate into civil war and none of us will survive the chaos."

The forty-year-old technocrat reached into his briefcase for a pad and a Mont Blanc fountain pen he'd bought on one of his many trips to Geneva. "Let's look at the votes in the Politburo. That is where the real power lies."

After discussing each of the eighteen members of the Politburo, Olshansky had two short lists. Those who would oppose an expanded barter deal were:

- Viktor Babenko—Minister of Justice
- Piotr Talyzin—deputy head of the Committee of State Security

Those who might be on the fence:

- Vasily Beriev—Minister of Defense
- Dimitri Ulyanov—head of the Red Army's General Staff

The consensus was the remaining members would go with whichever way they thought the wind was blowing. None of them would upset the apple cart unless their own position and power were threatened. Olshansky grinned and quoted the Russian proverb: "Teeth are all friends among each other."

Olshansky and Schvardze agreed that the old warrior Ulyanov was the key. The armed forces would follow his lead.

Boris Yeltsin, the candidate member to the Politburo and the popular vocal mayor of Moscow, was the wild card. The chubby, red-faced alcoholic Yeltsin knew all the players, but the degree of his influence was unknown.

"General Ulyanov is non-political and will support what is right for the country," Schvardze said. "I've heard rumors about his health, however. If he has a heart attack, who takes command of the general staff?"

The finance minister used the traditional Russian term *stavka* for the Main Command of the Armed Forces of the U.S.S.R., also known as the general staff. It had been created by Tsar Nicolas II at the beginning of World War I and re-established by Stalin when Germany invaded in 1941.

Eduard had been around the government a long time, and he knew this was the pivotal question. It was a very delicate subject, but it had to be asked. Until he'd been released from the Gulag, he'd kept his thoughts to himself. *Now*, he told people, *I will do what is right. What can the government do, send me back to the Gulag? I've already been to that hell.* When no one replied, he sighed and asked an easier question. "Seraphim, how long do you think it will take to come up with a plan?"

"It depends on whether I get arrested by the KGB or not." Neither Gregorenko nor Schvardze laughed at his attempt at humor. "I will start putting feelers out today. By the end of the week, I'll know if the Americans and their allies are willing to help. There is one potential problem. Iraq's invasion of Kuwait has distracted everyone's attention. The Americans and the others may be slow to deal with anything else."

Wednesday, December 19th, 1990, 1546 Local Time,
New York City

Safdar's fourth stop of the day was at the large post office at 909 Third Avenue between East 54th and 55th Streets. Riding up the escalator let him scan the people around him for a possible tail. He was pretty sure there wasn't one, but that was no excuse to be careless.

On the second floor, he stopped at one of the long tables in front of the rows of boxes, ostensibly looking at the forms for certified and registered mail. It was his last stop to check for surveillance before he opened his post office box.

Besides junk mail, telephone and utility bills for the shop he leased in Queens, there was one letter with a hand-written address. Safdar deposited the promotional material in the trash, kept the bills and the letter, and rode the escalator down to the main floor.

Back at his apartment, he tossed the envelopes on the dining room table and got his copy of T.E. Lawrence's *Seven Pillars of Wisdom* from the bookcase in the living room. He slit open the hand-addressed envelope and opened the folded note. The date, 12/15/90, directed him to the fifteenth page of chapter twelve. The formula to decipher the six-digit code groups was simple. The first two were the line number. The second two were the number of the word on the line. If the last two digits in the code group ended in 66, the word was Allah. If it ended in 99, it was infidel.

The decoding process took ten minutes. *Continue building network and capability but take no action to antagonize the Infidels until after the current situation in the Persian Gulf resolves itself.*

Chapter 5
Leave No Man Behind

Sunday, February 17ᵗʰ, 1991, 2146 Local Time, Persian Gulf
It was the thirty-first night of Operation Desert Storm. By now, the planes of the Iraqi Air Force were either hiding in Iran or piles of rubble and twisted metal. Air strikes now focused on hunting mobile Iraqi Scud missile launchers, destroying Iraqi armor and artillery, and isolating the Iraqi Army in Kuwait.

The weather was terrible. Clouds and rain obscured the stars. Gritty, sulphurous smoke from the burning oil wells coated everything with an oily slime.

As a helicopter pilot, Josh Haman was most concerned with forecasts of dense fog and visibilities close to zero. Such conditions would make landings interesting.

On board the carrier *U.S.S. Ranger,* interior spaces were cold wherever they were open to the raw damp outside; cool where spaces were kept at sixty-eight degrees Fahrenheit that made a long-sleeved shirt comfortable; or hot where heat made areas downright sweaty.

Whether he was wearing his khaki uniform or his flight suit, Josh Haman wore one of his flight jackets wherever he went on the *Ranger* since his duties usually kept him in the colder spaces. Tonight, he decided to wear the insulated olive green nylon jacket with the orange liner—much warmer than the beloved brown leather one issued to him when he was a student Naval Aviator back in the sixties. That well-worn jacket with its fur collar was a much-prized possession.

Above his head, he could hear the banging and clanging made by chocks hitting the steel flight deck as the flight deck crew moved airplanes for the next launch.

After dark, passageways or spaces opening to the flight deck or to the catwalks running around its perimeter were lit by a dull red light to protect the night vision of anyone who had to go "on the roof", as the flight deck was known. The red lights made everyone's skin look ghostly pale; the green floor tile looked light gray, and the blue a noticeable shade darker. The blue tile denoted the spaces allotted to the Commander, Carrier Group Seven and the staff of Zulu Lima. Only members of Zulu Lima's and the admiral's staff were permitted to go through the area with blue tile. All other members of the ship's crew and the air wing used the port fore-and-aft passageway around the flag spaces, as they were known. A few frames aft of the staff's offices in the port passageway, the blue floor tile changed back to green.

The helicopters that Zulu Lima tasked were part of the Arabian Gulf Battle Force known as Battle Force Zulu. Under the warfare commander designation system the first letter was the one assigned to the entire task force. The second letter, in this case L, was given to the officer responsible for coordinating the operations of all the helicopters in the battle force.

Back in late August, on his first trip to Riyadh, Josh had learned that the body of water separating Iran and the states on its southern coast was known by different names. If one lived in Tehran, one used its traditional name, the Persian Gulf. However, if one was in Riyadh, it was called the Arabian Gulf.

MOSCOW AIRLIFT

The *Ranger* had been commissioned in 1957, the first U.S. carrier built from the keel up to have an angled deck. Josh had picked the *Ranger* because its carrier group staff got tasked with the less glamorous Zulu Sierra—anti-surface warfare—mission and had to keep track of the ships in the Arabian Gulf, of which on average, there were just over 6,000. Zulu Lima had a logical supporting mission. If there was going to be a war, the Iraqi Navy was not much of a threat; however, it would still be important to perform combat search and rescue; assault some of the oil platforms; and know what every ship in the Arabian Gulf was doing.

Every day, the Zulu Sierra staff had to task ships, airplanes and helicopters to classify every ship in the Arabian Gulf as either blue for friendly, green for neutral, white for unknown and red as a possible threat. The helicopters were often used to confirm ship identities.

At just under six feet, with longish hair starting to turn gray, newly promoted Captain Josh Haman looked like a slightly older version of everyone else on the *Forrestal* class carrier. He turned the polished brass knob to open the door to Helicopter Anti-Submarine Warfare Squadron Fourteen's ready room. Starting roughly in the middle of the ship, HS-14's was the sixth in a row of nine. The last two were under the arresting gear.

"Attention on deck!" The squadron's petty officer of the watch recognized Josh, even though the light was too dim for reading the gold letters under the gold wings on his name tag.

Everyone in the red-lit room stopped what they were doing and came to attention. While Josh understood the gesture was a courtesy and tradition due to his rank, he disliked interrupting any tasks being performed.

Josh's quick "As you were" sent everyone back to work. A young lieutenant named Chris Cranston walked up. "Good evening, sir. The Air Tasking Order assigned us the call sign of Comfy Five Five. My co-pilot, Lieutenant Junior Grade David

Wellington, is up on the flight deck checking on the spot of the helicopter. He should be right back. We're supposed to launch from the forward part of the angle."

During a January briefing, Josh had looked at the young officer and asked him if he was old enough to drive. When the young pilot turned red, Josh kept the heat on and asked him if he bought his wings at an Army Navy store. Everyone in the room had laughed. Cranston had responded to the light-hearted barb with, "Sir, I ordered my wings from Sears & Roebuck! I do have a learner's permit and plan to get a real license when we get home."

Josh had laughed. "Excellent. So we know you are at least fifteen."

"Yes, sir. My ID card says I am old enough to buy a drink."

Now Cranston showed Josh to a seat in the front row, sat down next to him, and leaned over to say, "Captain Haman, if you want to fly in the right seat, let me know. I'll fly as the co-pilot, and Wellington can ride in the back or, if he wants, stay here and get a good night's sleep."

"Thank you, but that won't be necessary. I'll fly co-pilot for some of the mission, then Wellington and I can switch."

"Sir, one more thing. The skipper told everyone to pick your brain whenever they get a chance. I hope Wellington and I don't get annoying."

"Lieutenant, I'll let you know if you do."

* * *

When the H-3 lifted off, the *Ranger* was north of the "thumb," as the Qatari peninsula was known, and east of the Saudi city Al Jubayl. It took the SH-3H an hour to reach its assigned orbit about five miles southeast of Kuwait City. On the way up, they could see, smell, and taste the oily, gritty, sulfur-filled smoke from the burning oil wells in Kuwait.

Josh shined his flashlight on the chart marked with all the oil rigs in the northern Arabian Gulf. Those occupied by the Iraqis were circled and avoided, because they had Iraqi Army detachments manning thirty-seven and fifty-seven millimeter anti-aircraft guns.

"Chris, what's the plan if we hear a beeper?"

"We head toward the beeper and if the pilot is inland, we ask for clearance to go get him?"

"What happens if you don't get an answer?"

"We have to make a judgment call?"

Josh stuffed the chart between the instrument panel and the side window. It was time for some coaching. "Let me suggest an alternative way of making the—"

The ear piercing, warbling sound of a beeper filled their headsets. Josh looked down at the instrument panel as he flipped a switch on the UHF radio to get a bearing on the beeper. "Chris, turn right to heading of zero-two-zero to get us headed toward Bubiyan Island, and speed up to one hundred and ten knots."

"Head zero-two-zero. Sir, you do know to conserve blade life, we are not supposed to fly above ninety knots."

"Humor me, Lieutenant. This is wartime and peacetime policies go by the wayside, particularly when time is of the essence."

He was about to key the mike when the radio came alive. "Comfy Five Five, this is Sun King Seven Zero Zero. Are you up?"

Josh pointed to his chest as if to say, I'll talk. As the senior officer and helicopter qualified Naval Aviator, he was by Navy regulations the officer in tactical command, even though he wasn't designated as the helicopter aircraft commander. "Sun King, Comfy Five Five is with you."

"Comfy Five Five, this is Sun King Seven Zero Zero, Diamondback Two Zero Four is down. We have comms with him on two-eighty-two point zero. He thinks he is on the east side of Bubiyan Island. Can you make the rescue?"

This is the early days of Vietnam all over again, when HS squadrons were pressed into service for combat search and rescue. Back then, the helicopters had no armor plate, no self-sealing tanks, and equipped with just two M-60 machine guns to defend themselves. And guess what? We're in the same situation tonight. They made rescues then, and we're going to make one now. Some things never change.

"Chris, here's the plan. We're going to go as fast as this fucker will go and as low as we can safely fly, which is about one hundred feet. If we start taking enemy fire, we maneuver out of range. If it gets too hot, we abort."

"Sir, the rules of engagement say we are not supposed to attempt rescues over land because the Air Force is supposed to make them."

"True, but if you were Diamondback Two Zero Four, would you want to wait for the Air Force to confirm your identity before it figures out how and when it is going to come get you?"

"No, sir."

"Good. Now you know why we're going to attempt to make the rescue." Josh felt the helicopter shudder a bit at a hundred and fifteen knots and then smooth out as Chris slowed it to one-ten; he keyed the mike. "Sun King Seven Zero Zero, Comfy Five Five is buster and on its way." By using the word "buster," Josh told the crew on the E-2 his own H-3 was going as fast as it could.

Josh turned around to see Lieutenant David Wellington standing between the seats, peering out into the night and searching the sky. In the distance, they could see the tracers from fifty-seven millimeter guns searching for targets before they slowly arced downward and disappeared from view as the chemicals burned out.

"Comfy Five Five, fly zero-zero-five. Heartless Five Oh Four and Five Oh Seven are available for support. Have more help on the way."

Josh clicked the mike twice to acknowledge the radio transmission. "Chris, two things. One: if we start taking fire, when you jink, cross-control with the rudders going one way and the stick the other. Slow by at least twenty knots and then speed up erratically as you jink back and forth. Two: fuel. We have thirty-one hundred pounds, enough to get there, make the rescue and get the hell out, but it may not be enough to get us back to the *Ranger*. As soon as we make the pick-up, we'll ask Sun King for vectors to the nearest ship in the northern gulf with a helicopter deck to get fuel. We'll 'high-fer' if needed." Josh pronounced the acronym for the Navy's helicopter inflight refueling, or HIFR procedure, in which a helicopter picks up a fuel hose with its hoist and then takes on fuel by hovering alongside the ship.

"Got it."

"Comfy Five Five, Sun King Seven Zero Zero."

"Comfy Five Five, go." Josh wanted to keep his transmission brief so they would not give their position away. The Iraqis were known for their ability to home in on radio transmissions.

"Diamondback Two Zero Four is immobile. Believes he broke his back and leg on landing. We show you about twenty miles out. Copy."

"Comfy Five Five copies." Josh rotated the mike switch to the intercom. "The survivor can't move so we're going to have to go get him. Everybody locked and loaded?"

"Yes sir. This is Petty Officer Grassly, we're ready to go in the back."

"Grassly, what do you recommend?" Out of the corner of his eye, he saw Cranston's surprised look. *Lieutenant, the air crewmen know more about what to do with an injured survivor than either one of us.*

"Sir, I won't know for sure until I get to him. My guess is we're going to have to carry him out strapped to a backboard on a litter. If we don't, we may really fuck him up."

"Knowing what you know now, Chris, what's the plan?"

"We're going to have to land and wait while Grassly goes and gets him."

"You've got the answer partly right. Assuming he's not in one of the marshes at the north end of the island, we land as close as we can, Grassly goes out with the backboard and gives him a once-over, then calls us on the radio. Meanwhile, we find a place to circle and keep from being shot down. Staying on the ground makes us a sitting duck and tells the Iraqis where the survivor is. Plus, we risk sucking enough sand into the engines to cause one to fail. When Grassly is ready, we go back in, land, and another crewmember runs out with the Stokes litter; they load the pilot and come back to the helicopter. We'll have to provide covering fire with the M-60s and M-16s if needed."

"Yes, sir. Got it."

"There's the island. Everyone call fire if you see any. Dave, you've got the left front from twelve o'clock until about nine, so Chris can keep his head down and focus on the instruments."

"Yes, sir." The lieutenant junior grade was connected to the intercom with a long mike cord plugged into to a receptacle where the sonar consoles used to be. In this and two of the squadron's other eight helicopters, the anti-submarine warfare equipment had been removed to enable them to carry more passengers and cargo.

"Comfy Five Five, Diamondback Two Zero Four knows you are on the way. Fly zero-two-zero. You are five to six mikes out."

Josh clicked the mike twice and watched the instruments as Chris rolled the helicopter into a coordinated turn to change headings. Once they were level, he reached for the map. "Diamondback Two Zero Four is about ten miles from the gulf, which puts him on the sand on the eastern side of the island. Everything to the west of a narrow spit of sand is marshy."

"Comfy Five Five, Sun King Seven Zero Zero, contact Diamondback Two Zero Four on two-eight-zero point two. Authentication complete."

"Sun King Zero Zero, Comfy Five Five switching." According to his kneeboard card, the search and rescue frequency was pre-selected as channel sixteen. Josh twirled the knob until the numbers one and six were in the window, and then counted to five to allow the radio to re-tune. When he had a side tone, Josh keyed the mike. "Diamondback Two Zero Four, Comfy Five Five, you copy."

"Diamondback copies."

"Diamondback, mark us on top. No flares. Copy."

"Diamondback, roger."

"Sir, this is Grassly. I am pretty sure I saw four or five big trucks on the sand running without their lights as we crossed onto the island."

"Thanks. Hopefully, we'll be in and out before they get here."

"Tracers, eight o'clock." Grassly's voice was higher pitched than usual.

Josh craned his neck around just in time to see the next burst. "Break hard left, NOW!"

The helicopter rolled into a twenty-degree bank.

"Chris, twenty degrees is not steep enough. You need to roll into forty-five or sixty degree bank and change speeds as soon as the call comes in. Don't worry about being smooth or in balanced flight. In fact, a skid or a slip will help toss off their aim."

The young lieutenant nodded his head in acknowledgement.

"Comfy Five Five, you just passed me in front of me by about two hundred yards."

"I've got the helicopter." Josh didn't wait for Chris's hands to come off the controls; he pulled back on the cyclic as he pushed it to the left and fed in a boot full of left rudder. The collective went down as the helicopter slowed. "Show us a quick light."

Three flashes from a strobe light lit the sky. "Turn it off, we see you." Josh rotated the mike switch to the intercom. "Chris, do the landing check list."

"Gear down and locked. Landing check list complete."

"You've got the helo. Do a fast air taxi at about forty feet to minimize the amount of sand we blow around and find a flat place to land as near him as possible. Grassly, you ready?"

"Yes sir."

"There he is. One o'clock." David Wellington pointed his finger at a form in what looked like a deep ditch. The white nylon of the parachute lying on top of the sand dune reflected a little light.

"Got him."

"Land here on this side and turn so Mitchell can cover him with the M-60."

Josh felt a bump as the helicopters main mounts touched down. "Grassly's out."

"Go and turn hard left. Let's get out over the marshes about a mile north of here and orbit at one hundred feet."

Josh felt the helicopter lift off and the nose pitch down as the H-3 accelerated. In peacetime, there was nothing wrong with Cranston's technique. In wartime, it was too smooth, too slow and too coordinated. *If we were off North Vietnam, he'd get us killed!*

"David, ever fire an M-60?"

"No sir."

Shit! Josh looked over his shoulder at Wellington. *We're going to need another pair of hands to bring Diamondback Two Zero Four back. This is why I recommended each SAR helo carry three air crewmen, but I was overruled. They didn't believe they would ever need to make a rescue over the beach. Once more, the Navy is penny-wise and a pound-foolish when it came to combat SAR.*

"David, let's swap seats." Josh flipped off the straps and started to get out of the seat. By the time he got in the cabin, Grassly came on the air.

"Comfy Five Five, this is Grasshopper." Grasshopper was Grassly's nickname. "Pilot is bleeding with two broken legs and I think a vertebrae is out of place. I heard trucks, and when I peeked over the top of the ravine I could see Iraqi soldiers about four hundred meters out. The trucks turned on their lights for a few seconds and I got a good look. Hurry."

"Grasshopper, we'll be there in less than two mikes." By the time Josh finished speaking, Chris had the H-3 headed back toward the two men on the ground.

Good, at least Cranston doesn't look lost. "Okay gents, here's the plan. We land where we did before. Petty officer Mitchell and I get out and help Grassly load him on the Stokes litter and bring him back to the helicopter. Give me all the bandoleers of M-16 ammo because I smell a firefight. Chris and David, what follows is a direct order. If you start taking fire and the helo is being hit, get the fuck out of here and circle north of

Diamondback Two Zero Four. If you lose a hydraulic system or an engine, head home. Once we get on the ground, have Sun King get the A-6s on the SAR frequency so I can give them a brief of where to drop. On the ground, I am Skierman Actual. Got it?"

"Yes, sir."

"One more thing. As soon as you depart south, call Sun King for vectors to the nearest aviation capable ship. If you've got Diamondback on board, tell the ship about the pilot's injuries."

"Sir, it sounds like you're planning on not coming back with us."

"That's the last thing on my mind, but remember, we're all expendable. This is combat and you must have plan A, B and C in order survive and win."

"Sir, what's plan B?"

"Plan B starts with doing the unexpected, and at the moment I don't know what that is, but as the HAC you'd better start thinking of something based on the concept we don't leave people behind unless there is no other option. Got it?

The young lieutenant nodded his head vigorously. Seeing the acknowledgement, Josh pulled off his helmet and pulled on a black wool hat after he stuffed the PRC-80's earpiece into his right ear.

Josh didn't wait for the main mounts to touch down before he jumped. Loaded down with his survival vest, an M-16 and two bandoleers, each with six 30-round magazines, his run to where Grassly lay was more of a fast jog than a sprint; Mitchell followed, carrying the wire-framed Stokes litter.

"Sir, what the hell are you doing here?"

"Same thing as you are, Grassly. Getting this guy home."

Grassly unlatched his night vision goggles from his helmet and handed them to Josh, who peered over the top of the ravine. "Sun King Zero Zero, this is Skierman Actual. We have bad guys about three hundred and fifty yards south-east of our position moving towards us. Have Heartless look for the trucks to find the Iraqis."

Josh looked down at the two air crewmen. "How long is going to take you to get this guy on the stretcher?"

"Less than three minutes, sir. We have to splint his other leg, slide him onto the backboard, strap him down and then get him into the litter before we move."

Josh heard the metallic pop of the first two cluster bombs open and put his head down, hoping the A-6s were on target. A second or so later, he could feel the heat and the concussion of thirteen hundred bomblets exploding. When he stuck his head above the edge of the ravine, he saw four of the six trucks burning, and many men, silhouetted against the flames, headed towards him.

"Grassly, bad guys, three hundred yards." Josh keyed the mike. "Sun King Seven Zero Zero, Skierman Actual. Tell Heartless good work, but we have a hundred-plus bad guys moving towards us between the burning trucks and our position. We will mark our location with a flare when they're inbound. The bad guys are danger close. Copy."

"Skierman Actual, this is Heartless Five Oh Four. We copy, rolling in now. Give us the flare."

Josh rolled on his side and fumbled for a second as he pulled the combination flare and smoke out of the front pocket of his survival vest; he felt for the ring of bumps around the flare end and pulled the toggle. A bright red light ignited, and he shoved the non-burning end into the sand at the bottom of the ravine. "Heartless, flare's lit."

"Skierman Actual, Heartless Five Zero Four, we've got it and the helo, keep your heads down."

Pieces of shrapnel zinged over their heads from the next round of exploding bomblets. When they stopped, Josh popped his head over the edge and was greeted by a burst of fire from an AK-47. The bullets chewed up the earth about four feet to his left and Josh blinked a couple of times to get the sand out of his eyes. The silhouettes were now less than two hundred meters. With the M-16A2 set in the three-round burst mode, Josh squeezed the trigger at the first shape. It went down. He targeted another. After dropping five, he dropped back down and moved about ten feet and again peered over the rim. He counted five and fired at the closest one, then one after another. All started emptying magazines in his direction so that the sand erupted near and around him as he dropped down.

"Ready?"

"Yes sir."

"O.K. When I start shooting, you two move out and keep going until you get to the helicopter. I'll call everyone on the radio and let them know you're on the way."

Grassly nodded and the two air crewmen picked up the Stokes litter. Seeing their movement, Josh squeezed the mike button on the survival radio. "Comfy Five Five, Skierman Actual, Grasshopper is on his way with Diamondback."

Josh moved off to the side and raised his head over the edge. He fired two bursts and the weapon clicked empty. *Shit, piss and corruption!!!* He dumped out the empty magazine, slammed another into the weapon, and fired. This time the men were really close, i.e. about seventy-five yards. He looked over his shoulder and saw Grassly and Mitchell loading the Stokes litter on the helo. *Too late for you, idiot!* He fired, shifted to another target, and fired again.

"Skierman Actual, this is Comfy Five Five, are you coming?"

Josh ran down the bottom of the ravine to another position where it turned just before it emptied into the mouth of the Tigris/Euphrates River. "Negative. Repeat Negative. Get out of here and I'll contact you later. Skierman Actual out."

Fuck, now what I do? Survive, that's what!

With the helicopter's noise fading fast in the distance, it got quiet, really quiet. In the distance, Josh could hear the groans of wounded men and the occasional popping of ordnance exploding in the burning trucks. In the faint moonlight, he saw Iraqi soldiers creeping toward his old position. His strategy now was not to fight, but to get away, unnoticed if at all possible. He had plenty of ammo if he had to get into a firefight.

Josh pulled out his .45 and made sure a round was in the chamber and flicked off the safety. He then checked the magazine in the M-16 and replaced the half-empty one with a full one. From his position, he watched an Iraqi soldier pick up the night vision goggles he'd forgotten and examine it before handing them to an officer. It was clear neither knew what they were. If they did, they'd be using them now instead of putting them in an empty ammo pouch.

Slowly, Josh raised his head above the edge, grateful his view was partially blocked by some dead grass. *They live if they don't come towards me. I count six men. They die if they do, and maybe I do as well. Officer, you die first, and I want those goggles back.*

After finding nothing at the far end, the Iraqis started down the ravine towards Josh. He looked around. *Shit, there is more concealment and cover on the other side and I should have moved. Too late now!*

The bottom of the ravine forced the Iraqis to walk in single file and made them easy targets because from his position he could fire at an angle. *When they are about thirty yards, I open up. First with the M-16, and when they get close, the .45. What did Marty say? At this range, it is like a knife fight and every one can be cut. Do what you can to avoid getting cut!* Josh hugged the sand as he slid the muzzle of the M-16 through the grass.

Fifty feet. He pulled the trigger and the first man staggered into the man behind him, who dropped his weapon to help his wounded comrade only to catch Josh's second three round burst in the chest. The officer was the third to be hit. The last man in the group started running, and for a second Josh felt guilty, but he pulled the trigger, putting the man down with three in his back.

I got four. Where are the other two?

A stream of bullets sent geysers of sand flying and Josh flattened himself on the sand. He crawled back to where he'd started and a longer stream of tracers zipped overhead. Josh moved farther down the small ravine and found himself at the end. There was no way to go except up and over or back where he came from.

He heard a noise and took a quick glance over the edge. Nothing. He hard two rounds being fired and then a loud click. Josh popped up and saw two Iraqi soldiers. One was kneeling while he loaded a magazine into his AK-47. The other was watching for him, his weapon on the ready.

Josh aimed the M-16 and fired a three round burst at the soldier with the loaded weapon. The last soldier released the bolt and was putting the rifle to his shoulder when three .223 rounds from Josh's M-16 stitched him across the chest.

With the Iraqis all down, Josh ran back to the officer with the night vision binoculars. He was still alive and tried to aim his pistol. Josh kicked him in the chin with his boot and yanked open the pouch. With pistol and goggles in his right hand and M-16 in his left, Josh turned west into the high grass and the marsh. He walked quickly in ankle-deep water for about thirty minutes, hoping the flow through the reeds would wash away his footprints.

An hour later, Josh found a dry spot large enough for him to lie down. He took a long look around in every direction with the night vision goggles before he settled himself. With his breath and pounding heart under control, he keyed the PRC-90's mike.

"Sun King Seven Zero Zero, this is Skierman Actual. Do you copy?"

"Skierman Actual, Sun King Seven Zero Zero. Good to hear from you. Say status?"

"Skierman Actual is a full up round."

"Skierman Actual, this is Sun King Seven Zero Zero. Continue to evade. We'll let everyone on Gray Eagle know and we'll work on an extraction plan. Contact our relief at your pre-briefed time. Copy?"

"Skierman Actual copies." Josh turned off the radio and looked at his watch. Gray Eagle was the call sign for the *Ranger*. It was 0207. *I have an hour and eight minutes to wait.*

Monday, February 18th, 1991, 1206 Local Time, Baku, Azerbaijan
The narrow streets of the Old City gave the two men what they wanted most—privacy and protection from the incessant, icy, thirty-kilometer winds blowing from the north. The winds were the norm, not the exception; they gave Baku its nickname of "City of the Winds." February was the coldest month, but compared to Moscow, the normal highs of four degrees Celsius made it balmy. In summer, the wind provided a form of air conditioning and made living bearable in the capital of the Soviet Socialist Republic of Azerbaijan. In winter, the wind simply made the city cold... but the cold ensured the sort of privacy that could never be found inside a building. Out here, it was impossible for police or intelligence agencies to record conversations. Passersby gave the two men a wide berth, and the narrow streets made it easy to spot a tail.

Private enough.

The taller of the two men, a colonel in the KGB, sniffed the air and savored the aroma of coriander and basil from cooking kebabs before it was snatched away by a gust of wind. Elchin Rajabov's mustache, build, and dark skin made him look like the second coming of Josef Stalin, but the resemblance did not do him any favors. The forty-two-year-old had been born after Stalin died, and by the time the KGB recruited him, Stalinism and everything it represented was out of favor in the Soviet Union.

Born and raised in Shirvan, a town eighty kilometers southwest of Baku, Rajabov had proven himself in firefights with the Chinese People's Liberation Army along the Amur River and then again in Afghanistan. His performance had earned him the trust of his superiors and an assignment in his native land, where corruption was the norm.

Colonel Rajabov turned to the other man, also dark-skinned but a few centimeters shorter. "Tarana, you look good in the uniform of a KGB captain. I hope you have the documents to go with it."

"I'm here with the head of the KGB's border troops in Azerbaijan. Why would anyone question my papers?" The documents were, of course, false, prepared by a fellow Muslim in the KGB's Baku offices—a man responsible for preparing the papers for troops assigned to posts in Azerbaijan. Tarana Aliyev had purchased his uniform from a KGB officer who needed some extra cash. It was one of many uniforms he kept in a house in Parasabad, Iran, just south of the Azerbaijani/Iranian border. Once the walk was over, Tarana planned to hurry back to his truck and return to Iran, resuming his role as the head of a small transportation company.

Rajabov waited until they finished the loop in the oldest part of the city known as Boyuk Qala. "Things are changing in Moscow. There is much uncertainty about the future of the Soviet Union. In some ways, I have more control, and in others, I have less. I do not want to bore you with the details, but I need

74

more money for the documents I provide to you. Ten percent more."

Tarana didn't respond for a few steps. His shipments of drugs and consumer goods never had any trouble getting through the border crossing checkpoints. Once they were inside Azerbaijan, however, the trucks needed travel permits—provided by Rajabov—to reach their destinations. Another ten percent was nothing, considering he was making almost five hundred percent on the opium and four hundred on the toasters and TV sets. He had been expecting Rajabov to ask for fifteen percent... but then, the KGB colonel didn't know about the opium, or the extent of his profits. To maintain Rajabov's ignorance, Tarana couldn't give in too easily. "How about five?" he said.

"No, it has to be more. Ten percent."

"I can give you eight."

Rajabov walked a few more steps. "O.K. Eight, but it starts with the last shipment."

Tarana spoke grudgingly, as though reluctant to concede. "Done."

The Same Day, 1415 Local Time, Persian Gulf

The shrill calls from the gulls and the warmth of the sun woke Josh at sunrise. The air smelled and tasted salty. To the south, he could see the black cloud of smoke from Kuwait's oil wells.

Josh rolled on his back and stretched. His watch told him he'd managed four hours of fitful sleep, despite his fear and the distant crump of bombs and guns firing in the background. Before he'd drifted off, he'd watched tracers heading skyward. A few seconds later, he'd heard a rapid series of four cracks, signifying the gunner had fired all four rounds in the clip.

Getting to one knee, Josh studied the area around him. He was convinced the Iraqis had not given up searching for him. He was sure they'd found his footprints by now and wondered what was taking them so long.

Josh took inventory of the most critical items. He had an M-16 with one partial and ten full magazines, his .45 with three clips, a PRC-90 survival radio with a spare battery, a day/night flare, two ChemLights and one quart of water, plus a pair of night vision goggles with an unknown amount of battery life.

Water was his most pressing problem; the quart wouldn't last the day. He ripped open the two candy bars he'd stuffed into the pocket of his flight jacket. As he surveyed the mostly flat sandy land around him, he enjoyed the sweetness of the chocolate and the coconut filling. After two swallows of water, Josh stood up, looked at his compass and headed west, thinking the marshy section of Bubiyan Island was a better place to hide.

As he trudged across the sand, Josh felt horribly exposed and it kept him alert. He was out in the open and there was no place to hide.

A chugging diesel engine and the clashing of gear teeth sent him retreating behind a nearby dune. From a hundred yards away, he watched three trucks drive slowly by. Each was packed with Iraqis soldiers. However, they were all scanning the sky for airplanes rather than looking for a lone American on the ground.

After ten minutes, Josh estimated they'd reached the north end of the island. He scrambled to his feet. Carrying the rifle in his right hand and using his left to keep his survival vest from bouncing around, he jogged a hundred yards. Out of breath, he sank back down between dunes and listened for the trucks while he took a drink. Satisfied they weren't coming back, he headed west and almost immediately found a trail with many fresh footprints. He added his own prints to the trail for five hundred yards before checking his compass and heading directly northwest. That would take him closer to the Iraqi mainland.

Four hours and two radio check-ins later, he found the bay in the north central part of the island where there were a group of smaller islands. According to his chart, the southern end had two sandy areas big enough to land an H-3.

By one in the afternoon, he'd waded through the chest-high water and located a hiding place at the northern end of one of two small side-by-side islands. After verifying that no one was around, he pulled out the survival radio and keyed the mike. "Any station, this is Skierman Actual, repeat, any station, this is Skierman Actual, over."

"Afternoon Skierman Actual, this is Sun King Seven Oh One, are you ready for pick-up?"

"Affirmative, Sun King Seven Zero One."

"Skierman Actual, any bad guys around?"

"Negative, none I can see."

"Check in on schedule and we'll provide an update."

Why the fuck can't they come get me now? There's not a soul on the ground near me and they can easily get a helicopter in here. I don't understand. Deflated, Josh keyed the mike twice and turned off the radio.

* * *

A hundred and twenty miles to the south of where Josh Haman was hiding, Commander Jack D'Onofiro stood in the flag command center on the *U.S.S. Ranger* with a radio handset in each hand. Each was attached to a radio control box in the overhead. The one in his right hand was tuned to a UHF frequency so he could talk to the E-2 orbiting about sixty miles north of the *Ranger*. If he spoke into the other, his voice would travel via a communications satellite to the Air Force rescue unit's command center at King Khalid Military City in northeast Saudi Arabia.

Everyone in the command center knew getting Josh back alive was more than just another rescue. For Jack, it was intensely personal, because he and Josh had flown together in Vietnam. They were very, very close friends.

Secure satellite radio was both a boon and a curse. The signal went at the speed of light, i.e. one hundred and eighty-six thousand miles a second from the ship to a satellite in a geo-stationary orbit twenty-six thousand miles above the earth, where it was received, processed by its on-board computer and radiated back to earth. If you were within the satellite's broadcast footprint, you heard what the other person was saying a few seconds after he spoke. In most cases, the words, even though encrypted, were clear. That was the good news. The bad news was a lack of privacy—anyone using the channel with the same code key could listen to your conversation.

D'Onofrio impatiently tapped the satellite handset on his left thigh as he studied the three large screens at the front of the command center. The middle screen portrayed all the ships and aircraft on a simplified map of Kuwait and Southern Iraq. If they wanted to change the scale, a couple of keystrokes would show the entire theater of operations or just a few square miles.

Jack put the red phone-like handset to his ear. He was using the call sign plus the words "zero one actual" to indictate he was the second in command. Josh had given the team their call sign. "Jolly Green Central, this is Rotorgod Zero One Actual, over."

"Roger Rotorgod Zero One Actual. Pass on to your survivor the delay is caused by a lack of assets. Estimate we will have the assets in seventy-two to ninety-six hours. Also, uncertainty over the survivor's location is leading to a reluctance to risk assets, over."

D'Onofrio bit his lip. *Bullshit. By lack of assets, you mean helicopters, and picking up survivors is supposedly your mission.*

Out of the corner of his eyes, he could see the men in the command center turn towards him, hearing the words broadcast over the speaker so they could be recorded for review and for the official log. *This was unmitigated Air Force bullshit. If it were their own guy, they'd be all over the rescue.* He counted to three and took a deep breath before he squeezed the mike button "Jolly Green Central, be advised your information about Skierman's location and availability for rescue is incorrect. Repeat, incorrect. Sun King Seven Zero Zero, Seven Zero Four and Seven Zero Three all have had radio contact with Skierman Actual and have authenticated. We have enough cross-bearings to locate him on the northwestern side of Bubiyan Island."

"Rotorgod Zero One Actual, Jolly Green Central Actual says best estimate is ninety-six hours and still needs more accurate location information before they launch... Out."

Well, fuck you. Nothing has changed since the Vietnam War. God help us. We will never win a war with an independent Air Force. They're very good at paper work, publicity, building officer's clubs and runways, but not much else. Jack bent over the intercom box, flipped a row of switches. Satisfied he had them the way he wanted, he keyed the mike. "Admiral, this is Commander D'Onofrio. May I have a word? All I need is five minutes."

The Same Day, 1946 Local Time, Moscow

Boris Vavilov picked the bar off Nevesky Prospekt for its crowded, noisy atmosphere. Spoken words couldn't be heard two meters away. The background music could be heard if one listened, but mostly it just added to the noise level.

At the entrance, he handed over his heavy brown overcoat with the gold shoulder boards and the three red stars of a Lieutenant General. The green color tabs indicated that the wearer, General Vavilov, was a member of the Soviet Union's Rocket and Artillery Forces. A separate badge on his breast pocket told the knowledgeable observer he was a member of the Red Army's General Staff.

"Welcome back to Vadim's." The coat check girl with East Asian features bowed her head as she took his coat and handed him a numbered token he would use to retrieve his overcoat. The combined restaurant and bar was named for the owner, who Vavilov assumed was well connected, for the bar was always well stocked with the best Western liquor. It never ran out of anything.

The second reason Vavilov had picked this bar was that the food was good. They made their own pickled herring and the best beef borscht in all of Moscow. It was served with a spring of dill and a large dollop of sour cream. Vadim had access to smoked meat, which gave the soup a pleasing aroma and taste.

A bottle of sparkling water was waiting at his table and his nostrils identified the smell of freshly baked peasant bread rising from a cloth-covered bowl in the center of the table. After sitting, Vavilov ordered a bottle of red Georgian wine, thinking it a better choice than vodka. The decision of what to eat could wait until the second person arrived.

Born and raised in Leningrad, Vavilov's Red Army personnel dossier noted he was politically reliable enough to be sent to postings in Egypt and India, where he'd taught Soviet artillery doctrine. Papers in the four-centimeter thick file noted he'd commanded a Soviet artillery battalion in Poland and had been the senior artillery officer at the 57th Guards Armored Corps stationed in East Germany.

MOSCOW AIRLIFT

Before returning to Moscow, Vavilov had been an artillery division commander whose unit drew a partial allotment of 203mm ZBV2 nuclear rounds with one-kiloton warheads. The crews spent two days practicing handling and loading them into the magazine racks of their 2S7 Pion self-propelled guns. Afterwards, the units returned the shells to their underground magazine.

The exercises taught Vavilov the ins and outs of the process needed to requisition nuclear and chemical shells, how to account for them when they were loaded into a truck or self-propelled gun, and how to count and inspect them as they were returned to their storage sites.

"Good evening, General." The words interrupted Vavilov in the process of eyeing ladies of the evening as they leaned over a nearby table and displayed their cleavages. The man who had captured the women's attention was wearing a suit sold only in the stores where a select few Soviet citizens could buy Western products. The women knew perfectly well the suit meant that the man had a great deal of cash.

Vavilov stood up. "Good evening, Yuri. It is good to see you again." They shook hands.

"I hope I'm not interrupting anything," Yuri said.

Vavilov laughed. "No. I was just wondering what those two women over there would cost tonight, and how that man would go about deciding whether he slept with one or both."

Vavilov's guest turned to scrutinize the women: one was blonde and one dark haired. He curled his lip as he looked at the women and then turned away. He took the glass of sparkling water proffered by his host and held it up. "Your health, General."

The man called himself Yuri Panichev; Vavilov doubted it was his real name, but for now the fiction didn't matter. The papers Yuri presented the first time they met almost a year ago said he was Georgian. A cursory check had indicated they were genuine; asking an official to conduct a more thorough check would involve the GRU or the KGB. Vavilov did not wish to attract the attention of either.

Vavilov knew he was playing a dangerous double game, but if things got too hot, he could always turn Panichev in. What would be harder to explain were the millions in his bank account at Credit Suisse.

Vavilov waited until they ordered and his wine arrived before getting down to business. "So, Yuri, what brings you to Moscow?"

"I am on a shopping trip."

"The GUM department store is just down the street. And of course, with your connections, I am sure you can get access to the stores selling goods from the West." The suit Yuri was wearing did not have a "Made in the Soviet Union" label.

"No, my friend. *You* are the one who controls what I want."

"Like what?"

Yuri leaned forward to speak, but stopped and pulled back as the waiter arrived with their food. When he was sure the waiter was gone, he bent forward again. "ZBV2s."

"Impossible." Vavilov took a fortifying swig. "We'll sell you those when pigs fly. They require very special paperwork."

"Perhaps. Our research says you can provide the paperwork to authorize their movement. That is all we need. My men will do the rest."

Vavilov was surprised Panichev knew he could issue orders to move the nuclear artillery shells around. "People will ask questions. These shells are very closely controlled."

"You can move them as part of an exercise. The Red Army does it all the time."

"If I agree to this, how many do you want?"

"Twelve would be ideal."

"Not possible." The words shot out of Vavilov's mouth.

"How many did you take out of the storage centers in Poland and East Germany?"

"Four." Vavilov lied. The real number was twenty-four.

"We will make it worth your effort. I can offer you 10 million U.S. dollars deposited in your Swiss bank account."

Vavilov cut him off. "Not nearly enough."

"You didn't let me finish, my offer is ten million American dollars *per warhead*. Half when we get the paper work and half when we take delivery."

There was a long silence.

"If I decide to facilitate this, this ..." the Russian struggled to find the right word, "...transfer, I would need *all* the money up front before the transfer of the weapons. And the price is twelve million each."

"This means I have to trust you completely not to turn me over to the authorities."

"True, but I am taking all the risks. The very fact that we are having this discussion could get me a bullet in the back of my head in the Lubyanka."

"We can get you out of the country if necessary."

"How soon do you need the paperwork?"

"Within a month would be ideal."

"Do you know where the ones you want are stored?"

"Yes." Panichev rattled off the name of several weapon storage facilities in Uzbekistan and Turkmenistan.

"I will let you know if it is possible."

"Then you will do it?"

"I will think about it."

"When will you decide?"

"I need at least a week to figure out if it is possible and evaluate the risks. We'll meet here at the same time and I will give you my answer then." Vavilov drained his wine glass.

Tuesday, February 19th, 1991, 0113 Local Time, Persian Gulf
The two blacked out H-3s were in loose formation, with the second helicopter a half-mile behind the first. The leader was at one hundred feet above the choppy waters of the Arabian Gulf, while the second was stepped up fifty feet higher. Above them at eighteen thousand feet and ten miles from the southern tip of Bubiyan Island, four A-6Es, each loaded with twelve CBU-57s and two external tanks to maximize their on-station time, orbited at their most economical airspeed. Four more were slowly climbing to join them in an orbit at twenty thousand feet.

"Charger flight, this is Sun King Seven Zero Two, we see you're about to go feet dry. We'll see if Skierman is awake. Stand-by."

Jack hadn't flown an H-3 in years, so he stood between the two pilots with his helmet hooked to the helicopter's intercom and radio. He clicked the mike twice.

"Skierman Actual, this is Sun King Seven Zero Two, you awake?"

"Sun King, this is Skierman Actual, that's a roger."

"Skierman, lay low. Cavalry is on the way with new authentication questions in less than five mikes. Over."

"Skierman Actual, standing by." Josh could feel his heart begin to race. He turned on the NVGs so he could see better and farther in the dark. He saw nothing. He dropped the batteries out, wiped off the contacts and re-inserted them. Still nothing. The batteries must be dead. Josh slowly pulled down the cover on the right front pouch of his survival vest so the Velcro wouldn't make its distinctive ripping sound; he made sure his two green chemical lights and remaining night flare were handy. Confident he could get to them in a hurry, Josh crawled to the top of the berm on the island, hoping no one on Bubiyan spotted him on this trapezoid-shaped pile of sand.

"Skierman Actual, this is Charger Eight Oh One, say brand of favorite ski?"

"Dynastar."

"Name of favorite ski area?"

"East or west?"

Up in the H-3, Jack keyed the intercom. "That's Captain Haman, no doubt. But I'll continue to go through the drill." Jack rotated the mike to the radio transmit position. "Give me both."

"Mad River Glen and Snowbird."

"One last question. Make and model of your first car?"

"Sunbeam Alpine Series Three." Josh released the mike. He almost added a sarcastic "Satisfied?" but knew the drill. During the Vietnam War, he'd been asking the authentication questions. The pickup crew had to be sure—during the few seconds the helicopter was hovering with a cable out to hoist a survivor, it was a sitting duck.

In the distance, Josh heard the sound of an approaching H-3 but also saw fire from fifty-seven millimeter guns. Tracers just above the horizon showed the Iraqis were shooting at something flying low. He heard the screech of a jet and saw the tadpole shape of a blacked out A-6 streaking by at what he guessed was about a thousand feet. In the distance, he heard a ripple of small bangs and then silence.

"Skierman Actual, Charger Eight Zero One, do you have any ChemLights?"

"That's affirmative."

"Light them off and toss them out on the sand."

Josh picked up the first of the two eight-inch long sticks, bent it and waited until it glowed a dull, slime green before he tossed it out onto the sand dune. It was followed by the second about six feet from the first; they gave the dune an eerie, pale color.

"Skierman Actual, gotcha. We're coming around."

The blacked out H-3 loomed out of the darkness off to the side. He could see the dull red glow from the dimmed lights in the cockpit as it banked in a steep right turn. As the nose came up in a flare, Josh saw tracers and heard the rat-tat-tat of a machine gun aimed at the helo.

"Charger Eight Oh One, you're taking fire. Abort, abort."

"Keep your head down. We can see about forty bad guys on the island to the south of you."

Josh watched the nose pitch down as the helicopter accelerated away, jinking to the right. Three lines of green tracers followed it, all falling behind, and answered by a single line headed toward the source of the ground fire.

Josh heard two distinct pops and put his face in the sand. After about five seconds of silence, the island to the south of him exploded. As the flashes started to subside, the ear-piercing whine of a tail rotor and engines announced the presence of an H-3. Josh was up and running as fast as he could toward the passenger door even before the helicopter touched down. He tossed the M-16 into the helicopter and bounded onto the bottom step. He felt someone grab his survival vest and arm to pull him further into the helicopter as the nose of the helicopter pitched down.

Josh landed in an uncoordinated heap against the broom closet and at the feet of Jack D'Onofrio. He had rearranged himself so he was sitting on the floor when Petty Officer Grassly knelt down beside him.

Grassly held out a bottle of water. "How are you doing, sir?"

"I'm fine, I think. Thanks for the water."

"As soon as we get south of the island, I need to check you out."

MOSCOW AIRLIFT

Two hours later, Josh was sitting on a bed in the *Ranger's* infirmary in a blue and white striped robe with the Navy's Medical Corps insignia on the left breast pocket. After an exam by a flight surgeon, a corpsman drew blood and let him take a shower before handing him two small vials of brandy. He'd just opened the first when Jack D'Onofrio walked in.

"The docs say you're just fine. How do you feel?"

"Tired and hungry, but O.K." Josh emptied the bottle. "What the hell took so long?"

"You want the short or the long version?"

"Right now, I'll settle for the short one."

"It took a day to convince the Air Force that Grassly's story was true. Then they didn't believe the person on the radio was you. They also didn't believe we knew where you were. We tried explaining we weren't dumb enough to ask you for a description on an open circuit because we were sure the Iraqis were listening. The Air Force AWACs copied enough transmissions to know where you were, and so did we. When the Air Force told me it would need another ninety-six hours before they could launch, assuming we could prove it was you, I lost it and went to the admiral with a plan. He said go, and when he told the battle force commander what was going on, the three-star came unglued. He went right to Schwarzkopf, and by the time we were halfway up to Bubiyan Island, the Air Force called the guys on the *Ranger* saying they would get you tomorrow!"

"Jack, thanks." Josh downed the second bottle. "Does Rebekah know?"

"No, I asked the admiral to hold off."

"Good. I'll tell her when I talk to her."

"Be advised, my good friend, you may get your ass chewed twice: first by an admiral, and then by your lovely wife. Then you're probably going to get another medal. Grassly and

87

Mitchell have been telling everyone within earshot you are a pretty cool customer when shit hits the fan and they ought to give you the blue ribbon with five white stars."

"I don't want the Congressional Medal of Honor. What I did was pretty stupid."

"Yes and no. Josh, you did what you thought was needed to get the injured pilot out. Oh, by the way, the pilot is on a hospital ship and will be fine in a few months. The doc said he can fly again."

"Good."

"You, my good friend, have two problems. First, you're not twenty-five anymore. Second, you believe everyone thinks like you do, and trust me, they don't. Cranston and Wellington were as green as they come, even more so than we were in Vietnam. Back then, we had some training in combat search and rescue, and they've had none. My point is, it never crossed your mind that you would be on the ground for more than a few hours."

Josh sat back on the mattress, gripped the sides and dropped his head. "Yeah, you're probably right."

"You know goddam well I'm right, and we're both getting too old to do this kind of shit."

"You maybe, but I'm not ready to hang it up!"

Jack shook his head. "I give up!"

Chapter 6
Missile Matters

Thursday, February 21st, 1991, 1023 Local Time, Shiraz, Iran

If one studied a satellite photo, the road ending at the side of a mountain was not the only indication of a cave. Guard stations and a double fence suggested whatever was inside was important. Anyone lucky enough to be allowed to enter would quickly realize no expense had been spared to equip the Pasdaran Weapons Test and Evaluation Facility lab.

The complex was in the Zagros Mountains fifteen kilometers west of Shiraz. The mountain range begins along the northern border Iran shares with Turkey, Armenia and Azerbaijan and runs southeast paralleling the Persian Gulf, ending at the Straits of Hormuz.

Located in a valley at 5,200 feet between seven-thousand-foot peaks, Shiraz is known as a city of poets, literature, wine and flowers. It is one of the oldest known cities in human history; references to its existence begin as early as 2,000 BC.

Every day, Dr. Stefan Zimmerman and two other foreigners working with him were driven from their guarded quarters in Shiraz to the cave. Zimmerman had designed the lab, the workstations, and specified the test equipment so he could create circuit boards to withstand the shock and vibration

89

created by a missile in flight. His workstation, desk, and chair were built to accommodate a man two hundred and twenty centimeters tall.

First time visitors, particularly shorter ones, were invited to sit in this swivel chair while Stefan talked. He found it amusing how uncomfortable they looked with their shoes nearly a third of a meter off the ground.

Now the German watched with satisfaction as the Hewlett Packard Apollo 9000 computer went through his data test routine. Disk drive noises followed by "test complete, no failures" message on the NEC MuliSync monitor told him the new arming circuitry for the Soviet 203mm nuclear artillery shell worked.

What remained was to test a dummy warhead on a missile to make sure it survived the flight and would detonate the weapon. Then his job would be done, and the Iranians could have as many nuclear missiles as they had ZBV2 warheads.

He had assembled the prototype boards and had trained Iranian engineers and programmers so they could reproduce his designs without him. As he tapped away on the keyboard, ensuring his precious test data was saved, Stefan's mind wandered.

Ten months ago, the Iranians had contacted him. To an out-of-work electrical engineer from East Germany, it was the offer of a lifetime. Now it was almost over: in a few weeks, he'd buy a villa on the Spanish Riviera and retire. The millions of Deutschemarks in his Bank of Zurich account, plus the money due to him at the end of his contract, meant he'd never have to work again.

Zimmerman never asked what the Iranians would do with the shells. It didn't bother him that the most likely target was Israel. Killing Jews, as his father, a former SS officer who'd helped liquidate the Warsaw Ghetto had often told him, was always a good thing to do.

At the other end of the laboratory, Helmut Schulz, a fellow East German, and Igor Rylin, a Russian, inspected newly machined parts on a soft foam mat. From Zimmerman's perspective, they looked like two peas from the same pod. Both were short and stocky, but not pudgy. Both wore thick black-rimmed glasses—their poor vision kept them from being drafted. Both had black hair and eyes and liked to drink Czech pilsners.

"Very good," Schulz said, measuring the tolerances of the artillery shell's circuit board mount. "These should hold the boards in place during the rocket's acceleration and free fall."

"Who would have ever thought to connect a Soviet artillery shell with a North Korean rocket?" Rylin said, recording a micrometer's measurement. "Particularly one designed in Russia, modified and redesigned by the North Koreans, and sold to the Iranians. Who, in turn, with Russian and East German help, modified the rocket again to hold a nuclear artillery shell designed and built in the Soviet Union. It could be the basis of a plot for a good novel, no?"

They often talked about what they were going to do "after the project." They all were planning new, richer lives free from the suffocating control of the Iranian secret police and the poverty of their respective homelands. Once they left Iran in few weeks, they only had to keep their mouths shut and enjoy life.

In another hollowed out area in the cave, Esmail Zadeh, Iran's deputy minister for weapons research and development, was listening to a briefing on the progress of the program and the upcoming missile test. Each speaker began with the answers to Zadeh's standard four questions:

1. What progress have we made since the last meeting?

2. What other materials, if any, do we need?
3. What new problems have come up, and what are their solutions?
4. How will those problems affect the timetable?

Zadeh never discussed money. The men and women working in this lab were asked to produce based on their technical skills. How much it cost was the worry of others.

Today, however, Deputy Minister Zadeh had a new question. "Abas, how far is it from the launch site to the target area?"

Zadeh knew warhead and guidance package weight affected how far the missile could go. Range was critical, because the missiles had to reach Tel Aviv from the pre-surveyed launch sites near Hamadan. He didn't want the test missiles making impact near any of Iran's cities on the coast or outside the target area.

Abas Ali Banki, the missile warhead program manager, put down the part he was holding gently on the foam pad in front of him. "The target area in the Hamun marshes is approximately 1,100 kilometers southeast from the pre-surveyed launch sites and our test site. Riyadh, Tel Aviv, or Ankara are all well within this range from the sites we will use when the missiles become operational."

Zadeh nodded. "Excellent."

How the missiles were deployed was not Ali Banki's worry. His job and life depended on making sure the warheads worked. "The test warheads will have a complete firing system but no nuclear material, and will be set to simulate initiating a nuclear explosion at one thousand meters above the ground. There will be just enough explosive inside the shell to tell us if the detonator worked. Should the shell survive the impact into the marshes—and we believe it will—we've installed a low powered homing device to help us find it."

Zadeh nodded. He had this job because the head of the Army of the Guardians of the Islamic Revolution knew he had a mechanical engineering degree. His other qualification was demonstrated ruthlessness to get jobs done. For his bravery and leadership in the Iranian/Iraqi war and for helping clean house of army units that did not perform well against the Iraqis, Zadeh had been promoted to brigadier general. His job was to make sure the Iranians had a deliverable nuclear capability. Al Banki and everyone in the cave worked for him. If he wanted, he could have them all imprisoned or executed if the warheads failed to work.

"Deputy Minister Zadeh, I understand you will be with us at the target site. We've timed the launch so it occurs between passes of the American photographic satellites. By the time the Americans react, the missile launchers will be hidden and we'll be gone from the target area."

Zadeh rubbed his thin black mustache and smiled as he imagined the devastation the one-kiloton warhead could do to an enemy.

"Sir, the foreigners know we are planning the test in a few days. They are also sensing their part in the project is over and are anxious to finish their work."

"Excellent. Make sure they are happy and keep working." Zadeh glanced in the general direction of the foreigners as he walked out of the room. He planned to keep them alive as long as they were needed, but they'd never live to spend the money he'd been putting in their Swiss bank accounts... on which he was also a secret signee.

Chapter 7
What Are We Going to Do?

Sunday, May 12th, 1991, 2011 Local Time, North of San Diego

The setting sun was still a red half-circle above the horizon, yet the water of Pacific Ocean, as far as one could see, was already gray-black. Even with the shadows on the redwood deck lengthening and darkness coming, it was warm in the hills east of La Jolla and the coast called Muirland Mesa. The houses along the edge of the ridge stood high enough to give the homeowners on the bluff a clear view of the ocean a mile or so away.

Rebekah Haman held out her glass for a refill. Josh poured the remaining Merlot; she sniffed the wine to enjoy the bouquet before taking a sip. "O.K. Josh, you've been home almost a month and life is more or less back to normal, so what's next? Your assignment on the Commander, Air Forces, Pacific Fleet staff is only for a year."

"I don't know."

"When will you find out?"

"Not a clue. I'll start bugging the detailer in a month or so."

"Have you thought about retiring? We're comfortable financially."

"I'm not ready to retire yet." That much he was sure of.

"Josh, I know you love the Navy and what you do, but there comes a time when you can't keep going off to save the world. You've been lucky, but some day your luck may run out. I'm not ready to be a widow, and our kids would like to have their dad for many more years."

"What would I do if I retired?"

"Go back to grad school. Become an airline pilot, become a professor, write your memoirs, be a consultant. Who knows? Find something you like that doesn't involve being shot at. After Jack got home in April, he filled me in what you did during the rescue. Good God, Josh! What were you thinking?"

"No one else on the crew was trained for combat rescues. I didn't think I would be on the ground for a couple of days. They were supposed to circle around and come back and get me."

"But they didn't. Most pilots aren't ready to take the same chances you do."

"Point taken." Josh looked at his wife over the rim of his wine glass. "Are you asking or telling me to retire?"

"Neither. What you do and when you do it is your decision. Every time you leave, I wonder if the next time I see you it will be in a box. I married you because I love you and wanted a life with some adventure, but I think it is time you start thinking of what you want to do when you're no longer a naval officer."

Josh pulled Rebekah into his arms. "Being a naval officer is what I am. I know my career may be coming to an end. The Navy may tell me to go away if I don't get another command or am not selected for admiral. Right now, I'm not ready to walk away."

"Oh Josh," Rebekah put her head on his shoulder. "This country has others who are ready to take your place. "

Josh smiled as he spoke to show he was kidding. "But none are as good as me."

Rebekah playfully slapped him on the cheek. "I knew you would say that."

Monday, May 13th, 1991, 1646 Local Time, New York City

The words were seared into his mind: *Plan and make ready for the first devastating attack. Advise when plan is ready.*

Safdar sat back in his chair looking at the pieces of torn paper on which the message was written. He already had a plan and willing volunteers.

After flushing the bits of paper down the toilet, letting the tank refill and flushing again, Safdar prepared his response.

Thursday, May 16th, 1991, 1849 Local Time, Moscow

Piotr Talyzin, first deputy chief of the Committee of State Security a.k.a. the KGB, busied himself by putting the loose papers lying on his desk in the proper folders, then placing them in a drawer of the open safe behind him. Task completed, he poured a fresh glass of tea and dropped in two lumps of Cuban sugar. As he stirred, Piotr tried not to let the clinking of the spoon on the glass disturb the man sitting across from him at the conference table.

When Vladimir Koskov, commander of the Soviet Union's special operations forces known as Spetznaz, looked up from reading the report, he had a pained look on his already dour face. "How sure are you of this information?"

Talyzin pushed his wire-rimmed glasses back up his large nose. "Very. In the West, they would call this market research. I call it frightening. It documents real changes in the people's attitudes and tells me we're losing our grip."

Koskov knew what Talyzin was referring to when he used the word "grip." For decades, Soviet Union citizens feared its government's secret police. First it had been the Cheka, then the OGPU, which became the NKVD. Now it was the KGB. The names changed, the mission didn't—*use whatever means necessary to find and punish subversive elements. Stamp out any opposition to the government.* Together with the vast Soviet bureaucracy, the KGB controlled every aspect of citizens' lives.

Under Stalin, the NKVD had created a network of slave labor camps known as the *Gulag.* Most were in remote, cold and desolate Siberia. Once a person entered the *Gulag,* the chances of coming out alive were slim. Gorbachev had decreed the *Gulag* should be emptied. Sentencing records were being reviewed and prisoners released, leaving in place only those convicted of the most heinous crimes.

The loosening of the reins was noticeable throughout the country. Gorbachev was trying to improve the economy and curtail the country's thriving black market by forcing the bureaucracy to focus on creating consumer goods. In the minds of Talyzin and Koskov, Gorbachev's worst sin was his plan to dissolve the Union of Soviet Socialist Republics and create the Federation of Soviet Republics by the end of 1991. In the newly elected Soviet parliament, there was wide support for the plan. In the proposed FSR, the individual Republics would have much more autonomy and could, if they wanted, refuse to join.

Koskov put the document down. "Yeltsin and Gorbachev must be neutralized. Either they go to their dachas and keep quiet, or we silence them forever. Once they're gone, we can make the people forget them."

"I agree."

"Then I am ready," Koskov said. "My men are ready. We will not allow the Soviet Union to fail. We have sacrificed too much for our country."

Talyzin nodded, although he wondered what sacrifices Koskov had made, other than losing men in combat. Koskov never got anything less than exactly what he wanted.

Chapter 8
Conversion

Friday, May 24ʰ, 1991, 0715 Local Time, New York City
The sun was starting to stream into the tenth floor apartment on the upper east side of New York City. Large windows in the master bedroom and the living room gave a panoramic view of Roosevelt Island in the East River, already showing the rich, dark greens of early summer. Long Island City lay beyond, on the other side of the river.

James Broughton loved the view. He often sat on the apartment's small balcony, high above most of the noise from 74th Street. The building was a short three-block walk from the 77th Street subway station, where Broughton could pick up the local Number Four, Five or Six trains. In one stop, he could be at the 59th Street station. From there, he'd wait a few minutes to board one of the express trains, and fifteen minutes later, he'd be at the City Hall/Brooklyn Bridge station and had two options to get to the Jacob Javits Federal Office Building. He could take Chambers Street to Broadway, or Lafayette past Foley Square to Worth Street and head west. His destination: the New York Field office of the Federal Bureau of Investigation, where he was the Special Agent in Charge of surveillance for diplomats and potential terrorists.

If they knew what it was, his morning ritual would have startled his associates. Before Broughton ate breakfast, he laid out his prayer mat so its length faced east-west. To make the alignment easy, he'd put a small plant on the windowsill of his living room, and on the opposite wall, he'd hung a photograph of Istanbul's Sultan Ahmed Mosque he'd taken while on vacation five years ago. The trip had marked the tenth anniversary of his conversion to Islam.

On his first full day in Istanbul, Broughton had been sitting alone at a table in a café in the Grand Bazaar sipping coffee when a man asked if he could sit in the unused chair. Later, he'd learned the meeting had not been an accident. The man worked for Iran's Ministry of Intelligence; he'd been tipped off by someone at the Islamic Center in Long Island City, to whom Broughton had mentioned his upcoming trip to Turkey. By the time Broughton landed in Istanbul, the Iranians knew where he was staying and had followed him to the bazaar.

Monday, May 27ᵗʰ, 1991 1809 Local Time, Moscow

One of the things Danielle enjoyed, even during the winter when the cold made her leg brace freezing to the touch, was walking back and forth to the embassy from her flat on Bolshoya Yakimanka. It gave her time to enjoy the sights, even though the smoke and vehicle exhaust fumes made the air smell awful. Today was different. Danielle wanted to shop at GUM, the *Gosudarstvennyi Universalnyi Magazin* or State Department Store, and her fiancé Avram Gutman had offered to drive her there.

Catherine the Great had commissioned the building near the end of her reign. For a while, it had served as a trading center. Destroyed when Moscow was burned as part of Tsar Alexander I's plan to keep the city from being occupied by Napoleon, it had been rebuilt in the original neoclassical architectural style and expanded by the Italian-Russian architect Joseph Ivanovich Bové who was retained by Alexander I to supervise the rebuilding of Moscow. By the 1917 Bolshevik Revolution, it was home to about twelve hundred shops. After the revolution, the facility was nationalized under Lenin's New Economic Plan. Stalin turned it into office space in 1928 for bureaucrats creating the first Five Year Plan. In 1953, it had been re-opened as a department store; the Communist Party thought it would be the ideal retail operation where every citizen could shop. GUM was one of the only places that managed to maintain an inventory of items made in the Soviet Union.

Shopping at GUM was an adventure because the lines to get in were long, often wrapping around Red Square, unless you were a Westerner—noticeable by the clothes one wore—and willing to pay in dollars, Euros, pounds or Swiss Francs. Those suspected of being Westerners were asked for their passports and quickly ushered inside, attended by sales people wanting to liberate cash from their wallets. High-ranking members of the party had to show their identity cards and were let inside. They got the second tier help when Westerners were around.

Danielle wanted to buy Russian made toys for her nephews, and GUM always had the best selection. As she walked towards their agreed upon meeting place, Danielle wondered what the future with Avram would bring. When she'd started dating the Israeli, she'd reported the relationship to her supervisor and received permission to continue. Now that they were to be married, it presented a thorny security problem for them and their employers. She might have to leave France's Directorate of External Security and was prepared to do so. Danielle had worked for the agency for twenty years—they had generously given her credit for the years she'd spent in the re-education camp in Laos—so she qualified for a pension. The money would be modest, but enough to live on. She'd invested the lump sum for back pay she'd received for the time she was a prisoner, and the investments had done well and was, as *les Americans* say, financially secure. Nonetheless, Danielle kept putting off setting a retirement date, and she didn't know why. It was as if she were waiting for something.

During the last few weeks, Danielle often felt she was being watched. Avram had assured her that it was not the Mossad. That left her wondering if it was either her employer or the KGB.

Danielle didn't give the white UAZ-451 van a second glance as it pulled to the curb. Such vans were common all over Moscow.

The panel door opened and a man grabbed her. He was strong enough to lift her off the ground. He took two steps and dumped Danielle on the floor of the van.

* * *

Avram's Volga was poking along in a line of slow moving cars on Zhitnaya Street. He looked at his watch. He was going to be at least five minutes late. Looking beyond the traffic, he could see Danielle standing a few feet from the curb. He thought of honking his horn and waving out the window, but it did n to do to attract too much attention. He could wait. He smiled thinking good things were worth the wait

He saw everything that happened. A white van, one of the ubiquitous vans of Moscow, stopped beside Danielle and a man's arms reached out and pulled her in, the panel door slammed to, and the driver aggressively inserted the van into the flow of traffic. Avram felt his face drain of blood.

The car in front of him didn't move. Furious and frustrated, he wrenched the steering wheel and drove up on the curb. He got to Bolshoya Yakimanka just in time to get a glimpse of the van. As he pulled in line a few cars behind it, he grabbed his satellite phone and dialed the number for his counterpart at the French embassy.

* * *

The van's interior reeked of body odor, vomit and who knew what else. Danielle's assailant grabbed her flailing wrists and held them together as he tried to get a rope around them. She managed to get her left foot wedged in one of the panel van's frames and her brace kept her rigidly in place. While her attacker stood hunched over and was focused on wrapping the rope, Danielle slammed her right foot into his crotch. The man grunted in pain and fell to his knees. The position gave Danielle another clear shot, so with all the strength she could muster, she drove her right heel into his groin.

Her shoe had a square, sturdy two-inch heel, the highest she could wear with the brace.

The man's face contorted with pain as he rocked back against the rear door of the van. Danielle rolled forward and jabbed her index and forefingers into his eyes, just as her father had taught her. She felt the muscles holding his eyeballs give way and the man howled in pain.

Danielle yanked the Makarov from his belt and turned around just in time to see the man in the passenger seat aim his own Makarov at her. Just then the van lurched around a corner, throwing his aim off. His three bullets punched holes in the rear door. Danielle, now wedged in the corner, fired twice. The first one went into the seat back. The second one splattered the man's brains all over the front windshield.

The driver started weaving erratically. She yelled for him to stop and pull over. He ignored her, and the van's violent movement tossed her around, preventing her from setting up a shot.

She glanced at her attacker. He was screaming, clutching his face with his hands, and blood was dripping down through is fingers. For a second Danielle thought about putting him out of his misery, but getting the van stopped was more important. She didn't know how many bullets she had left. If she had only one, she wanted to make sure she hit the driver in the head. Each time she pointed the gun at the driver, he turned the wheel sharply and threw off her aim. She was about to fire anyway when there was a jerk, the crunching of metal, and the van screeched to a stop. Before the driver could get the van headed back down the street, she shoved the barrel of the Makarov against the back of his head. "Freeze!" she snarled.

A heartbeat later, the driver's door opened and Avram yanked the man out of the van. The man fell to the ground and desperately tried to roll away. *Militsiya* officers were running toward the van, drawing their pistols. The man pulled a Makarov out of a shoulder holster and pulled the trigger as soon as he got the barrel under his chin. The top of his head exploded in a red mist of blood and brains.

Danielle sat down on the back bumper of the van, shaking. She hadn't felt such cold rage and determination to survive since the escape from the re-education camp. As the adrenalin flowing through her body began to dissipate, Danielle steeled herself for the interrogation ahead. The *militsya* would want to know why the *mafiya* would kidnap a commercial attaché. The answer that wouldn't blow her cover was simple. They wanted to extort a ransom from the French government. She hoped it would fly.

Tuesday, May 28th, 1991, 1120 Local Time, New York City
Three days after he'd pulled the letter addressed to Nasir Ghannan from his P.O. box, Jim Broughton walked into a restaurant selected by the man he was to meet. The special agent wasn't worried that the man might be tailed; any surveillance request would have to go to Broughton himself for approval.

Broughton had chosen the use-name Nasir Ghannan. Nasir loosely translated in Arabic to "protector" or "helper," and the last name "to shepherd." Broughton had given a great deal of thought to the meanings; when he retired from the FBI, he would legally take on the name. Until he left the FBI, making the change was career suicide.

Mohammed Safdar had picked this Mediterranean restaurant on the east side of the financial district, not for its cuisine or its quality, but because it was a place where no one would give a second look to an Arab having lunch with an Anglo-Saxon. Unlike most restaurants in Manhattan, the tables were set far enough apart so that he and Broughton could have a conversation without anyone nearby overhearing. Furthermore, two members of the wait staff were Palestinians belonging to Safdar's network. Still, neither Safdar nor Broughton would speak of anything important. It was simply a place to meet and eat before they moved to someplace more private.

Safdar stood to greet his guest. Broughton towered over the Palestinian, who was barely five-foot-six. The first time most people met Jim Broughton, they either wondered or asked why he wasn't in the NBA. At six-foot-eleven and two hundred and fifty pounds, he looked like a basketball player, but he was uncoordinated as hell. Just surviving the physical training courses at the FBI academy had been a challenge. To stay in shape, he worked out several times a week with weights and the NordicTrak ski machine in his second bedroom.

"It is good to see you, Nasir," Safdar said. "I presume you are healthy."

"I am."

Safdar smiled; he truly cared about Broughton's health. Safdar got rid of men he didn't trust by giving Broughton tips. An excellent arrangement: Safdar eliminated problems, while

Broughton got credit and commendations for making important arrests.

The food was served within minutes of their order and they ate in easy silence. Safdar finished the last bite of his falafel, drawing out his simple meal so that it ended simultaneously with Broughton's attack on his more substantial platter. Safdar said, "Come, my friend, let's take a walk."

Broughton dropped three five-dollar bills on the table and picked up the receipt.

Once outside, Safdar asked what sounded like a perfectly innocuous question. "How is your new boss?"

Broughton had previously mentioned that the new Special Agent in Charge of the New York office was Jewish. "Occasionally he asks me questions, but I never see him except in staff meetings. He's focused on the Italian Mafia and white-collar crime. To him, Islamic terrorism is not a major threat."

Safdar nodded his head. "Do you know there over two million Jews in the New York Metro area?"

"No."

"We're going to kill a lot of Jews in America. They will pay for their support of Israel and the Zionists, pay with their blood. With Allah's help, when I am done they will think Hitler was a nice man."

"You'll also kill a lot of innocent Americans."

"Americans are not innocent," Safdar insisted. "They are co-conspirators. My mission is to make America end its support for Israel. I will kill as many American Christians and Jews as Allah lets me. To me, they are no different."

"You know I could arrest you for what you just said."

"You could, but you won't."

"Mohammed, you can't be sure I won't."

"Yes, I am. You are a Muslim, and in your heart, you want me to succeed."

Safdar spoke easily, persuasively, but privately he thought, if you had me arrested, I would trade telling them about you for deportation back to Lebanon. I'd get away, and you'd go to jail. He was in control, and he liked it that way.

Wednesday, May 28th, 1991, 1436 Local Time, Moscow

While the French ambassador was in the offices of the Soviet Foreign Ministry, filing a vigorous protest that one of its employees covered by diplomatic immunity was almost kidnapped, the *Direction générale de la sécurité extérieure* (General Directorate for External Security—DGSE) station chief and his assistant along with the legal attaché were grilling Danielle in a sound proofed room. It started at 0900 after the official *militsiya* report of the attempted kidnapping arrived at the embassy.

She felt it was more of an interrogation than an interview. They started with the event and went backwards in time asking her to remember every detail of her life outside the embassy. On a pad, Danielle listed all her non-French embassy employee contacts over the past six months. At the top of the list was Avram Gutman, then she started listing the Soviet army and air force officers she'd met at embassy, Soviet foreign and trade ministry functions. When she was done, they asked if that was all, her answer was probably not, but if the DSGE reviewed the reports she filed, it would have a complete list.

The question and answers got testy early in the interview because Danielle felt as if she was being treated as a possible traitor or spy. After assurances and apologies that her loyalty to France was not in doubt, the session continued.

Now, five hours and a half hours later, none of the people in the room could answer the question as to why the *mafiya* would want to kidnap her. Their hypothesis, based more on experience than fact, was that someone in the KGB, GRU or the *mafiya* thought she was either a threat or knew something that would expose one of the leaders. It could be any one of hundreds of men and trying to determine who was beyond the capabilities of the office.

After an admonition to be careful, Danielle walked out of the room. She accepted the interview as needed, but felt the way it was conducted made her feel uncomfortable as if she was the cause of the attempted abduction.

Thursday, May 30th*, 1991, 1336 Local Time, the Pentagon*

Jeff Gainesville walked down the corridor of the E ring, the innermost of the five rings of offices in the Pentagon. He kept glancing at his shoulder boards as if they weren't real and as if the promotion ceremony three weeks ago had been a practical joke. Instead of being black with a gold star and four gold stripes, they were solid gold with a single white star. That star meant he was a rear admiral, lower half. If he had been an Air Force, Army or Marine officer, the single star would have meant brigadier general.

Gainesville had been "frocked", a Navy tradition in which a promoted officer is given a new ID card and allowed to wear the insignia of the new rank, but doesn't get the increase in pay until he or she receives their date of rank. At the ceremony, Jeff had been presented with a new hat with the extra row of lightning bolts—otherwise known as scrambled eggs—to go along with his new shoulder boards. He still couldn't believe it; he kept looking at the shoulder boards to make sure he wasn't dreaming.

"Good morning, Admiral Gainesville." The speaker was a middle-aged woman who'd probably worked in this office for twenty years; she must have seen many newly promoted admirals come and go. "The Chief of Staff for Operations will be here in a minute. Please have a seat in his conference room. May I get you anything?"

"No, thank you." He still hadn't gotten used to being addressed by his new rank, but as Josh Haman had told him, his first name was no longer Jeff, it was "Admiral." Jeff seated himself at the highly polished table and started to read the stack of messages in the blue folder he'd brought with him.

The room had flags from all the services, standing on either side of a red flag with three gold stars—signifying that this was a conference room of a three-star, or lieutenant general. Marine generals, because of their experience in ground, naval and air operations, were often selected for operational billets requiring coordination of all four services.

"Good afternoon, Jeff. I hope we didn't keep you long. At ease." At the sound of the man's voice, Jeff had stood and come to attention. A Marine three-star general wearing a khaki shirt and blue trousers with red stripes followed the Chief of Naval Operations. Jeff, like the Chief of Naval Operations, was wearing his summer whites, the uniform which some wags inside the Navy called "the Good Humor Man outfit."

"Thank you, sir, I just got here."

The four-star admiral inclined his head. "Good. You're going to be yanked out of your current billet and assigned to work for General Feltzer and me. Your relief should be in your office by the time you get back today, tomorrow morning at the latest. Turn over your duties properly, but as fast as you can. I'd like to see you here at 0730 a week from this coming Monday. You're going to be my special projects slash action officer, and your first hot potato is looking at food shortages in the Soviet Union for implications from a military perspective. Your second concern is harder to specify. Intelligence thinks the Iranians are up to something, and we smell a rat. We just don't know what kind of rat. When you get here, I'll give you more details. I'll take care of the necessary clearances."

"Yes, sir. I'll report back as soon as I finish my turnover." There was nothing more to say.

"Great."

Friday, May 31st, 1991, 1925 Local Time, New York City

For Jim Broughton, working on Friday, the Muslim Sabbath, was a travesty, but if he wanted to stay in the FBI he had no choice. Now he was on his own time, and he went to prayers at a mosque on Manhattan's lower east side on the way home. After preparing dinner, he read the Koran for an hour and made notes where he had questions to ask the Imam on Saturday.

In the evening, he studied books and listened to tapes to learn how to speak Arabic. Broughton struggled with the Arabic script's intricate swirls and dots read from right to left. He persisted and the proof was that he could have conversations with members of the congregation in his accented Arabic.

He studied the two books on the coffee table. The blurb on one trumpeted that the Holocaust was a hoax. The other claimed the author had uncovered a Zionist plot to take over the world and that the creation of Israel was the first step. Broughton agreed with the author's premise. The British should never have agreed to create a Jewish state. The United Nations should not have taken land away from Muslims and given it to Jews. He deliberated for a few seconds before deciding to read the book about the Holocaust first.

Saturday, June 1st, 1991, 2136 Local Time, Moscow

The sun had set, leaving the sky a bright red for a few moments before everything turned to darkness. "Red sky at night, sailor's delight"—if the old saying held, the weather the next day would be fair. Its counterpart, "Red sky in the morning, sailor take warning" was a good indication of storms. The sayings weren't always accurate, but most mariners used them as a check on the forecast.

Piotr Talyzin wasn't a mariner nor did he know the sayings. He walked into Vadim's, ignoring the band of red sky on the horizon and not giving a damn about the weather. It was hot, muggy and he was sweating. Vadim's was one of the few places in Moscow where the air conditioning really worked. It would be twenty degrees Celsius or colder inside no matter how crowded the club was. He smiled as he thought how the cool temperature made the waitresses' nipples stand out under their skimpy bras.

Solving how and where the club's owner got the equipment would get a commendation from an enterprising *militsiya* officer. It would also get him killed before he finished the investigation.

Loud as the music was, Talyzin's customary booth was far enough away from the band that, if he wanted to talk to someone, he could use normal tones. The booth was a small cubicle separated from four similar ones along the same soundproofed wall. Each had a comfortable U-shaped couch and a small, polished wood table. The semi-privacy was one of four reasons Vadim's was a favorite of high-level Soviet officials. The other three were attractive women willing to do anything, good food, and Western liquor.

Piotr slid onto the couch and made himself comfortable. Soon he had help. A bottle of Famous Grouse was deposited on the table, along with four glasses. A young blonde in a mini-skirt leaned over him. Her breasts were barely contained by her blouse and her nipples were as erect as a tree. She filled Talyzin's glass while a well-endowed redhead began to nibble his ear.

As the blonde poured two fingers of the amber liquid with her right hand, she kept her left on his back, making sure her breast rubbed against his bicep. When she finished pouring, she slid next to him and her right hand found Talyzin's thigh.

Valentina was a natural blonde. Katerina's reddish-brown hair was made redder by dye smuggled into the Soviet Union by Vadim's friends in the *mafiya*. Both women were college graduates who'd given up working as teachers for more lucrative jobs at Vadim's.

Occasionally they performed sexual favors, for which they got a generous bonus. Their real work, however, was enticing customers to spend lavishly and drop tidbits of information that their employer could use. The more valuable the information, the bigger the reward. When they'd arrived earlier this evening, they'd been told to make Talyzin comfortable and provide whatever he needed, even if that meant fucking his brains out. Out of the corner of her eye, Valentina eyeballed a man sitting at the bar nursing a bottle of mineral water. The man had followed the First Deputy of the Committee for State Security into the nightclub; he'd spend the evening trying to pretend he was not Talyzin's bodyguard.

Valentina excused herself. Rather than going to the ladies' room, she went to the manager's office and dialed the house phone. The head bartender listened and then spoke a few words to one of the unoccupied girls. By the time Valentina sauntered back onto the dance floor, the other girl was perched on a stool beside the bodyguard.

Meanwhile, Katerina had unzipped Talyzin's fly. She had a firm but gentle grip on his fully erect penis. Katerina's sparkling eyes told Valentina what her partner was doing, so before she sat down Valentina drew the curtain across the front of the booth. Without saying a word, she pulled the table back so Katerina could get on her knees and use her mouth to finish the job she'd started.

Fifteen minutes later, when Katerina finished bringing the First Deputy Chairman of the KGB to his second orgasm, Valentina opened the curtain. She saw that Talyzin's bodyguard and the girl who'd sat beside him were no longer at the bar. Vadim and a tall man with shoulder-length, shaggy blond hair had taken their spot. Both men nodded; together, they approached Talyzin's table.

"Piotr, I hope you have been well taken care of." The blond haired man was Evgeny Karlov, head of the *mafiya* in Moscow. If he wanted, he could make you disappear, never to be heard from again.

Piotr was still glowing from his orgasm. "I'm very well, thank you. The scotch and the ladies are wonderful. I really like the redhead; she can service me anytime."

"Excellent." A slight nod of Karlov's head told the ladies their work was done. On the way out, Valentina let her hand brush her lover's behind as they headed to clean up in the private washroom next to the office.

Karlov didn't have to check to know the booths on either side were empty; that was prearranged. He sipped from the glass of German wine he'd brought with him to the booth. "So, Piotr, are you ready to talk about the future?"

Talyzin nodded.

"Good. You and I know changes are coming. My associates and I think there will be opportunities for us to acquire government-owned businesses at a good price. I'm sure that government leaders like you are looking to the future. If you find yourself out of work, you need enough money to survive. The... skills required to succeed in the Soviet bureaucracy will not serve so well in a capitalist economy much less a democracy."

His statement got another nod from Talyzin. Piotr felt too at ease to bother speaking.

"Then we can help each other. My friends and I know things even the all-seeing and all-knowing KGB misses. Important things. Who really needs money? Who has bank accounts in the West? Who has already contacted western businesses to sell certain government factories and businesses when the time comes? You're in a position to help us buy the businesses we want. In return, you'll be handsomely compensated."

Talyzin cocked an eyebrow. "You know I could have you arrested for what you just said."

"You could, but you won't. You know I am right."

This was true. The remark served to remind the arrogant prick KGB officer who was really in charge. The *mafiya* was just as powerful as the KGB—in some ways, more so. It had its own rules and, unlike the KGB, didn't have to maintain the appearance that it was following the law when it wanted a specific result. That done, it was time to move on to the heart of the matter. "How would I be paid?"

"U.S. dollars deposited in the bank of your choice. I would suggest a Swiss one with offices here in Moscow. They are properly tight-lipped about their clients." Karlov was neither impressed not distressed by Talyzin's chest-thumping. He could have Talyzin killed or so compromised that he would be removed from power, and no one would ever figure out who was behind it.

"How much?"

"Millions. The exact amount depends on what we manage to buy and how much you help. Think in terms of five percent of the purchase price. You are the number two man in the Committee for State Security. You'll know what others are doing. In a pinch, you can even arrest our competitors, on whatever charges the KGB wishes to invent. If a competitor becomes a *real* problem, both of us have ways to deal with them..." Karlov paused and shrugged his shoulders to make sure Talyzin understood the *mafiya* was different from the government. "... but the end result is the same." He judged that the implied message—that Talyzin could also be dealt with if he made himself a problem—had penetrated the Deputy Chairman's alcohol and sex-induced complacency. Effective communication was all about nuance, he reflected.

Monday, June 3rd, 1991, 1421 Local Time, New York City

The sun was fully behind Safdar's back, brightening the waters of the East River and lighting the buildings of Brooklyn on the other side. Beside him on the slats of the green painted bench rested a bird recognition manual, its title easily read by anyone passing. On Safdar's lap was a steno notepad and around his neck was a Nikon F with a 105–300 millimeter zoom lens. Fully extended, the lens magnified anything Safdar looked at by roughly six times.

Every so often, he adjusted the focal length, snapped a picture, and made a note on the pad. An intent observer might have noticed that Safdar never looked at the book. Nor was he taking pictures of birds. The objects of his scrutiny were the trusses and steelwork under the lower roadways and the towers that held up the cables of the Brooklyn and Williamsburg Bridges.

Chapter 9
Nukes for Dollars

Wednesday, June 5ᵗʰ, 1991, 1626 Local Time, The Pentagon

"Turds" is Navy slang for assigned tasks whose scope and political fallout have a distinct odor to them. Depending on how they're handled, they can be completed successfully and the officer moves on to the next job. Or, they can become FUBAR (Fucked Up Beyond All Recognition) and affect one's career.

When Jeff Gainesville started going through the data, he thought he was stuck with a turd: figuring out why the Soviets wanted to buy more food. CNO wanted it done very quickly. His hypothesis was the Red Army needed food to fight, but it made no sense to be feeding them! *Isn't this why we have a DIA, CIA, and State Department? What am I missing?*

Suspicious, Jeff began reading all the reports and kept coming to the same conclusion. It wasn't news that the Soviet agricultural system was painfully inefficient. Jeff couldn't find any report where an analyst pulled together all the information in a simple chart that a dumb Naval officer could understand. Gradually, by digging through the data and highlighting the numbers he could verify, the information began to make sense.

Soon he had a spreadsheet in Lotus 1-2-3 on the computer screen. Most of the raw data came from the annexes in a CIA document called *Soviet Food Shortages, Making of the History of 1989*. From that data, he created a chart keyed to the same symbols used by the CIA analyst. His next step was to type in the numbers associated with the symbols. Those went on the second sheet.

After saving the first document, Jeff created a "dash one" version and used the spreadsheet to calculate the Soviet decline in food production every year over the past five years. With mounting excitement at the prospect of having an answer, he used the data to create a chart on graph paper, with food production on the vertical and the year on the horizontal axis.

The answer was clear as a bell. Soviet food production, for the past five years, had been declining on average by three to four percent per year. Last year's decline had been five percent. Over five years, the total drop was almost eighteen percent.

To get the other side of the issue, he took data from a joint report produced by the U.S. Commerce Department and the Soviet State Committee on Statistics for the U.S.S.R. It indicated that the Soviet population was growing at about three-and-a-half percent per year.

Jeff copied the food chart and then drew a line showing population growth versus time. The gap caused by lower food production versus population growth was getting wider. He now had the data to confirm why the Soviet Union needed to buy food in the short term. They simply didn't have enough to feed their people. In the long term, it was obvious that the Soviets would have to make major changes in their agricultural system; otherwise, they'd face famine and/or a huge increase in the money they spent buying food from other countries. Two more reports from the Department of Agriculture and CIA documented the specific issues. They became notes to support Jeff's assessment.

Quickly, he tidied up his charts and asked General Feltzer's admin if there was a graphics person who could produce high-grade versions suitable for a presentation. She arranged it, and said the charts would be ready when Jeff came in the next morning and scheduled a meeting with General Feltzer.

Thursday, June 6th, 1991, 1246 Local Time, Moscow

Moscow in summer can be a magic place. Along the snaking course of the Moskva River, the Tsars had built parks for the nobility, wealthy landowners, and merchants to enjoy. Despite the harsh climate, Catherine the Great ordered trees planted throughout the parks. They'd flourished, only to be cut down in 1812 to make barricades in a failed attempt to keep Napoleon out of the city. Tsar Alexander I had planted new trees the following summer; they had grown until 1941 when they were sacrificed to make defensive positions to keep out the Nazis.

The winding paths served another purpose: they were wonderful places for Soviet citizens to have private conversations out of range of the KGB's microphones.

It was along one such path in Fallen Monument Park that Arkady Kishniev, a Lieutenant Colonel of the *militsiya*—the city's uniformed police—waited while his sister Valentina bought ice cream from a vendor. Arkady was a member of the Ministry of Internal Affairs police force, known as the MVD. He led one of the special teams assigned to investigate high profile murder cases. The more spectacular, the more bizarre and bloody, the more likely Arkady's unit would be called in to investigate. Arkady was proud of that; he considered himself a *real* policeman, not a thug from the armed forces or the KGB.

He told his sister, "You realize too much ice cream will make you fat?"

Blonde, fair-skinned Valentina was a full ten centimeters taller than her darker, black-haired older brother. Despite such differences, however, their similar facial features made it easy to tell they were brother and sister.

Valentina's mid-thigh-length skirt showed off her long, well muscled legs. They also showed off her authentic Nike running shoes, a present from Vadim. Real Nikes were status symbols and hard to get in the Soviet Union. She replied, "I'm not worried about my weight. I got the skinny gene from our parents."

Arkady chuckled. "I had dinner with mother and father last night. They asked about you. They'd like to see you."

Valentina licked the melting vanilla ice cream. "How are they?" She hadn't seen them in quite some time. They had kicked her out because they disapproved of her job and lesbian life style.

"They're doing as well as may be expected for people their age." Arkady didn't want to add, "They don't have much time left." He walked a few steps beside his sister before broaching the subject he'd been dwelling on for months. "*Mama* and *nana* will welcome you back with open arms. They're old school and it's hard for them to admit they made a mistake, much less make the first move."

Valentina stopped. "What brought this on? My last memory of our mother and father is them pushing me out the door and throwing my clothes at me while screaming insults." Valentina slurped the soft ice cream. "Are they willing to accept me for what I am? Are they going to apologize?"

"There'll be hugging, crying and a lot of 'I'm sorry's. Then there will be joy. I don't know if a formal apology will be forthcoming, but they want to see their beautiful daughter."

Valentina finished her ice cream and took a large bite out of the cone as they started walking again. "O.K. I'll come home with you. When?"

"They'd prefer a Friday night."

"I can't, I work Fridays and Saturdays."

"It's Shabbat..."

"I know, but I still can't make it. How about this Sunday night?"

"Deal. I'll tell them to set an extra place for dinner. It will be my surprise. I'll pick you up at five-thirty."

"Afraid I'll chicken out if you don't come and get me?"

"You better not. I do have to warn you: they desperately want grandchildren. And... I'm getting too old to start another family."

"Well, *I'm* not having children ever! Arkady, you need to stop grieving for Rachel and the baby. May she rest in peace, but she's gone and you need to find someone else. Do I have to play yenta for you?"

"No."

"Then get your ass in gear. Find another wife!"

Arkady didn't answer. After a few paces, he changed the subject.

"Anything interesting happening at Vadim's?" Arkady knew his sister helped Vadim separate men from their rubles. Valentina was Vadim Durov's number two—she kept his books and made sure their suppliers, both legal and illegal, delivered what was ordered. Valentina also personally greeted important guests and oversaw the services provided. She knew what was going on... and she had no qualms about telling her brother.

She started with the meetings between Evgeny Karlov and Piotr Talyzin. While she hadn't heard the actual conversations, Valentina had overheard Vadim and Karlov talk about upcoming investments in hotels that might soon be for sale.

Arkady listened intently to his sister. Planning investments wasn't a crime, but Arkady still found it interesting. "Do, you think they're preparing for a capitalist economy?"

Valentina laughed. "Nooooo!!!! I think they're preparing for chaos."

Friday, June 7th, 1991, 0812 Local Time, the Pentagon

As an admiral, Jeff Gainesville had to get used to more than fancy shoulder boards with stars. He had to get used to the notion of having an aide.

On his desk were officer summary records for six lieutenants—three men, three women—along with the Navy instructions that described the role of an aide. On top of the pile of records, a Post-it note said, "Pick one." The Chief of Naval Personnel had initialed the note.

Jeff knew what an aide was supposed to do—he'd learned all about it at the two-week class known as "knife and fork school" where he'd been taught the do's and don'ts of being a flag officer in the U.S. Navy. Jeff just never thought he'd have to make the pick. *Au contraire, mon admiral!*

Since he was a surface warfare officer, custom dictated he select an aviator. Rather than interview the young officers during the workday, he invited each one to the Pentagon's flag mess so they could have lunch with Jeff and his wife, Beth Anne.

Joining Jeff and Beth Anne at the table today was the fourth candidate from the list of prospects: a slim, very attractive, dark-haired Naval Aviator by the name of Phyllis Johnson. The three of them had finally got through the usual small talk about the weather and why Phyllis wanted to be an admiral's aide. Jeff decided to ask about her choice of schools. "Lieutenant, I understand you went to Norwich University outside Montpelier, Vermont. Why Norwich?"

"I'm from Boston, sir. I wanted to go someplace where I could ski that had a Navy ROTC program." Johnson pronounced the acronym for the Navy Reserve Officer Training Corps as "rot-see."

"Not the Naval Academy?"

"I know that's the prestigious school, but it's not near a ski slope. At Norwich, I could be at the base of a lift forty-five minutes after I left my dorm... provided the road wasn't blocked with snow."

"How often did you go skiing?"

She laughed. "Sir, I skied sixty to seventy days a year and managed to graduate with honors and a degree in mechanical engineering."

"I've heard the same story from another Norwich grad... except he admitted that while he earned a degree in mechanical engineering, he really majored in skiing, girls and race cars." Jeff looked at Beth Anne, who smiled. Her face told him she liked this woman. That was important, considering that he'd spend as much time with the aide as he did at home. From the beginning, Jeff had made it clear Beth Anne had a vote in the decision. More importantly, he trusted her judgment in evaluating people.

"Sir, may I ask who this Norwich grad was?"

"One of your fellow rotorheads by the name of Josh Haman. He's a captain out at COMNAVAIRPAC." Jeff spoke the acronym as "com-nav-air-pack."

Phyllis' eyes opened wide with surprise. "*The* Josh Haman? The one who provided covering fire to help an injured pilot get helicoptered out during Desert Storm? And then evaded the enemy for several days before he was picked up?"

"Yes, that Josh Haman. We lived together on the *U.S.S. Sterett.* My second tour in Vietnam, his first. We became good friends."

"Oh wow! Admiral, sir..." " Phyllis Johnson caught herself. *Don't be an idiot and ask the admiral if he could introduce you to Josh Haman.* "Captain Haman spoke at alumni weekend while I was at Norwich. He's the reason I picked helicopters."

"Good. Just don't treat him like a movie star if you get to meet him. Definitely no autographs. He wouldn't know what to do if you asked him, and it would just piss him off."

"Yes, sir. I'll be on my best behavior if he comes calling."

"Lieutenant, just out of curiosity, you were in one of the first squadrons with both SH-60Fs and HH-60s. Am I correct?"

"Yes, sir. I was one of the first female pilots to get qualified. Almost all of my time is in the HH-60H."

"What's your call sign?"

Phyllis said proudly, "Sir, my squadron name tag says Phyllis 'Kno' spelled K N O Johnson. I love it." She spelled out the letters with a straight face. Beth Anne giggled but didn't blush at the call sign. "No Johnson" was a double entendre for "no penis."

A week later, Lieutenant Phyllis "Kno" Johnson reported to Jeff's office as his new aide. As more than one O-7 (rear admiral) had found out when assigned an O-3 (lieutenant), Phyllis Johnson took less than three days to take over Jeff's professional life. She even coordinated Jeff's schedule with Beth Anne to make sure he was never late for meetings or commitments to his wife. All his routine messages were answered, and other tasks attended to. She did everything she could to free up 'her' admiral for the things only he could do: make decisions.

"Sir...."

Jeff recognized Lieutenant Johnson's soft voice and looked up in time to see the Chief of Staff for Operations walk through the door. Jeff came to attention, as did his aide.

"At ease." The three-star held out his hand toward Jeff's new aide. "I'm General Feltzer."

"Lieutenant Phyllis Johnson, sir."

"Welcome aboard." After they shook hands, General Feltzer turned to the brand new admiral. The normally easy-going

Chief of the Joint Staff for Operations' face looked grim. "The fun and games have started."

Sunday, June 9th, 1991, 1021 Local Time, San Diego

The sun was already high and bright at the start of what would become another day with temperatures in the high seventies. Josh set the table for a family brunch on the deck, which boasted an unobstructed view of the Pacific Ocean. Rebekah was making buttermilk pancakes that would soon be swimming in the genuine and expensive Grade B Vermont Maple syrup Josh insisted on buying. He'd just put a pitcher of fresh squeezed orange juice, thick with pulp, on the table when the phone rang.

"Hello, Josh Haman speaking." He wondered who was calling on a Sunday morning.

"Josh, it's Lev Mogen. How are you?"

"Lev! Long time, no speak. How are you doing? It's been a couple of years."

"Yes, it has. Too long, as a matter of fact."

"Where are you?"

"I just got off a plane in Los Angeles. I'd like to come talk with you in person. It's important." Lev Mogen was one of the top two or three members of the Mossad. The first time they'd met, Josh had been an exchange pilot with the Royal Navy in Yeovil, and Lev had wanted to share information with the U.S. government outside normal channels. Josh was beginning to figure out this was not just a social call. The word "important" caught his attention and caused his gut to tense in anticipation.

Josh said, "How long will it take you to get here?"

"An hour. Our consulate is providing a driver and a car."

"Wonderful. Rebekah is making pancakes. We'll wait for you."

Rebekah put the batter in the refrigerator and spent fifteen minutes directing the kids to help Josh clean up the living and family rooms, as well as their bedrooms. Josh protested that Lev knew they had three children and no matter what they did, the house would look lived in. His statement got "the laser look" from Rebekah, which told him without her uttering a sound to *shut up, don't argue and do what you are told.*

Fifty-five minutes after Josh hung up the phone, Lev Mogen was at the front door. After tight hugs all around, Josh invited the driver to come in. Josh was sure he was an armed bodyguard for Lev.

Each of Josh's kids greeted Lev as a long lost uncle. Holding Sean, his youngest, Josh asked, "Where were you when you called? You made great time."

"We were passing Newport Beach. The car has one of those new mobile phones."

"That's convenient. We'll eat and then talk out here on the deck."

"Great. Knowing Rebekah, the food will be five star!"

Over brunch, they learned the young driver/bodyguard, whose name was Asher, was a former paratrooper assigned to embassy security, and that Lev was now a grandfather to six kids. They all talked comfortably, but it was clear that Lev was impatient to get down to business. The moment they'd finished dessert, Rebekah ushered the kids away. The paratrooper cleared the table, leaving Josh and Lev to talk.

"So what brings you to San Diego?" Josh asked quietly.

"We've got some very sensitive intelligence on Iranian activities, and I don't want it to get buried."

Josh contained his grimace, but just barely. He knew, too well, and at a terrible cost in human lives, how ignoring information could backfire. During Viet Nam, higher ups had repeatedly dismissed the warning signs that a double agent was leaking intel to the Russians, and many pilots had died or been captured as a result.

"I need your advice of whom we should contact," Lev continued. "The San Diego number I have for Marty doesn't work."

"Marty is assigned to Central Command at Tampa in some super-secret counterterrorism role. Do you have something he'd be interested in?"

"We're ninety percent sure the Iranians think they can buy nuclear artillery shells from the Soviets. We don't know if the Russian government sanctions the sale or if it's a rogue operation. What we have is a trail of money starting with the Iranian Revolutionary Guards and ending in a numbered Swiss bank account owned by a Russian. We're trying to get the name on the account, but as you know, that's tough."

"How many warheads?"

"It could be as many as a dozen."

Josh's head snapped back and his eyes went wide with shock before he spoke. "So the Iranians are using this as a shortcut to becoming a nuclear power, and the Russians are ignoring the non-proliferation treaty they signed. Maybe they're doing an end-run around it."

"Exactly. The Iranians don't have guns big enough to fire the shells, so they either want to turn them into bombs, or..." he said grimly, "mount them on rockets."

Josh was silent for a moment. "And you want a contact person who'll realize the significance of this and have the clout to take action." *Please do not let this be Viet Nam all over again.*

"Yes. Do you think Marty would know who?"

"I don't know, but a good friend of mine just made admiral. He works right in the Pentagon. We'll call both of them before you leave."

Tuesday, June 11th, 1991, 2016 Local Time, Moscow
Arkady was almost home when the radio in the car blared. It was the dispatcher, directing him to a wealthy suburb called Rublyovka. It was west of Moscow and had been the city's wealthiest neighborhood back in the days of the Tsars. Unfortunately, Arkady was not sent there to admire the houses or the well-kept landscaping. He had been sent by the head of the Moscow *militsiya* to investigate two murders. One victim was the head of the Soviet Air Force's Military Transport Aviation. The other was a foreign ministry official who'd worked on the rain agreement recently signed between the U.S.S.R. and the United States.

After inspecting each crime scene, Arkady suspected the same murderer had killed both victims, using the same gun. He'd have to wait, however, for the forensic team to confirm that the shell casings came from the same pistol.

Arkady and his driver and deputy, Captain Anton Dorotkin, were leaving the second crime scene when Arkady spotted a man who'd been at the first scene. The man didn't back away when Arkady approached and asked for his identity papers, which identified him as one Vitaly Migunov. Arkady doubted that Migunov was the killer—the murders were too professional to be committed by someone foolish enough to be caught standing around. On the other hand, Migunov didn't have a convincing story for how he happened to be at both locations, so Arkady handcuffed him and escorted Migunov to his car.

Once Migunov was stashed in the back seat of the Lada, he opened up. He gave Arkady a detailed description of a man he saw enter the Air Force general's apartment building. When the man came back out, Migunov had followed him to the diplomat's building. Then, Migunov said, he saw the same man go to a third building from which he never left.

How convenient to have such a useful witness! Was Migunov telling the truth, or baiting a trap?

Arkady had no choice but to follow-up. He went to the third apartment building and spoke to the concierge, giving the description provided by Migunov. The concierge identified Comrade Igor Gabashivili as the man in question. Gabashivili lived on the fifth floor in apartment four. The concierge confirmed that Gabashivili had returned to the building when Migunov said he did.

One of Arkady's men remained with the concierge to make sure he did not contact Gabashivili. Back in the car, Arkady again questioned Migunov. How did he happen to be in the right place twice? Migunov explained he'd been paid to watch the apartments and not who came and went. When he handed his notes to his contact, he was given twenty thousand rubles.

Arkady called in three other members of the *militsiya* for a raid on Gabashivili's apartment. Between them, they had two AK-47s, a flash bang and an anti-personnel grenade. Officially, only members of OMON, the *militsiya* special weapons and tactics unit, were supposed to have such grenades, but the head of OMON's unit at his station slipped him the grenades "just in case." Arkady didn't want to wait to run through the procedures to get an OMON unit out here in the middle of the night. It could take hours; and who knows? They might know Gabashivili and alert him. Allegiances in the *militsiya* were sometimes murky.

In pairs, the four stood on either side of the doorframe, against the concrete walls. Arkady reached out and rapped sharply before shouting. "*Militsiya!*"

"Its open. Please come in."

Cautiously, his point man twisted the knob and nudged the door open. A burst of bullets from a suppressed weapon spun the *militsiya* officer and sent him bleeding to the floor. A second burst tattooed the concrete on the far side of the hall.

This is bullshit! Arkady had the anti-personnel grenade ready and pulled the pin, released the spoon and rolled it into the room. He put the palms of his hands over his ears. An instant later, the grenade exploded, spewing hot metal fragments everywhere and creating enough smoke to provide cover for Arkady and the two remaining *militsiya* to dash into the room.

They found Gabashivili bleeding from shrapnel wounds behind a teak table he'd laid on its side for cover and concealment. The table was shredded by the blast; metal and wood fragments had found their way into Gabashivili's body. Arkady called for an ambulance, then he and his men searched the rooms, collecting bundles of rubles, American dollars, British pounds, foreign passports and several weapons. They also found Gabashivili's documents that said he worked in the Tbilisi KGB office.

A member of the KGB could obtain weapons and forged passports easily enough with the right authorizations. The first question in Arkady's mind was, why did Gabashivili have an apartment in Moscow when he was supposed to be in Georgia? The second question was, just how much shit was going to roll over him for taking down a KGB agent?

Four possibilities ran through his mind. One, they would kidnap, torture and probably kill him as a lesson to the *militsiya* to not fuck with the KGB. Two, they would pressure the *militsiya* leadership to discipline him. Three, was this a set up to have the *militsiya* do the KGB's dirty work? Or four, was this a personal vendetta by someone high in another organization?

* * *

Arkady continued his thorough search after Gabashivili was carted away in an ambulance that would take him to a prison hospital. It didn't take Arkady long to find two loose floorboards hiding a secret compartment, which contained more dollars and pounds, plus more ammunition for the fully automatic Stechin pistol they'd taken from Gabashivili. Arkady knew many of his fellow *militsiya* would be satisfied with finding so much illegal contraband, but Arkady had a feeling there was much more in the apartment.

After moving all the furniture away from the walls and looking behind all the hung pictures, Arkady's started on the apartment's three closets. A hollow sound on the wall of the bedroom closet told him there was a cavity behind the wall. He removed all the clothing and searched for a latch. Finding none, he pushed on several places, but nothing happened. He was about to try to kick the wall in when he spotted a small wire loop on the floor. Pulling it op caused a loud click, and the back wall pivoted ninety degrees, providing entry into a small room filled with weapons, ammunition, and a radio transmitter and receiver.

So, was Gabashivili a spy or an assassin or both? Arkady went back to Migunov and was convince he knew little more than what he was told. He was tempted to hold the man for a few days to sweat him for more information. For Migunov, that would be a death sentence—Migunov's employer would assume he talked and would kill him as soon as they could.

It was close to 2330 when the forensic team left Gabashivili's apartment. The weapons and ammunition were photographed and catalogued before being carted off. The money was counted, and along with the identity documents, photographed and inventoried. Arkady kept the money and passports, afraid that much of the cash would disappear on the way to the evidence locker. Instead, he signed the custody log saying he had the valuables and would turn them into the station in the morning.

* * *

Militsiya procedures required Arkady to return to the police station before going off duty to turn in his Makarov pistol and ammunition, depositing them into a locker with his name on it. Usually he complied. Tonight, however, he directed Anton to drive him directly to his flat. It was damned late, and driving to the station would add an hour to his trip home. Arkady rationalized that getting home early would make it that much faster to finish his report of the night's activities.

Once he got to his flat, Arkady put his holster on the nightstand. He began planning the next day's activities in his mind, starting with a visit to the prison hospital where Gabashivili was being held under *militsiya* guard. Within a minute, Arkady fell asleep, exhausted.

The clunk of the door-lock awoke him. Only one other person—his sister Valentina—had a key. Arkady pulled the Makarov from it holster and quickly left the bedroom. There weren't many places to hide in the one bedroom flat. Whoever had picked the lock was waiting a few seconds to see if they got a reaction before they cracked open the door. The delay gave Arkady time to crouch down in a corner behind his couch in the combination living/dining room.

Light from the hallway silhouetted two men moving stealthily into the apartment. In the dim light, he could see that their pistols had long barrels—suppressors. He waited until the first man went into his bedroom. He though he heard four shots, presumably into his rumpled bed that the shooter, in the total darkness, couldn't tell was empty. The living/dining room had more light from the glow of the streetlights five stories below.

Swiftly Arkady stood up and fired twice at the man remaining in the living room. Both bullets hit the man in the chest, and the sound of the Makarov thundered off the concrete walls. The muzzle flash temporarily blinded him. He eyes watered as he squeezed his eyelids closed. Instinctively, he crouched and turned towards the bedroom door.

The man who had been in the bedroom came out firing. Four bullets slammed into the concrete walls behind him. The shooter was firing blindly in the darkened room, and after the fourth shot, Arkady heard the slide on the man's pistol lock open. It was the Makarov's way of saying, *reload me!*

Before the man could finish reloading, Arkady stood. "Drop your weapon or I'll shoot."

The attacker slammed a spare magazine into his pistol and pulled the slide back to release it. For a split second, Arkady hoped the man would reconsider and surrender, but the slide slammed forward. The man started to extend his arm to bring his pistol into a firing position.

Arkady fired first. The ninety-five grain bullet hit the man someplace in the chest; the man grunted and tried again to point his pistol at Arkady. Each attempt got him another bullet in his upper body. After the sixth bullet, the man's arm dropped and he collapsed to the floor.

Arkady looked down at his pistol. The slide was open, telling him he was out of bullets. In his haste to get out of the bedroom, Arkady hadn't brought the spare magazines.

Realizing he'd been very lucky, he sat down heavily on the couch. Before he dialed a number for a forensic team, three thoughts ran through his brain.

I am not going to get any more sleep tonight.

Who wants me dead?

In the morning, I'm going to have a long talk with Gabashivili and find out what he knows.

Wednesday, June 12ᵗʰ, 1991, 0846 Local Time, Moscow

Built in 1870, Butyrka was Moscow's largest prison. It was run by the *militsiya*, which was why Arkady had directed the ambulance to take Gabashivili there. It would be hard—though not impossible—for the KGB to kill him there, unless one of the doctors or medical attendants who worked on Gabashivili was a KGB operative. In which case, it would probably be a *fait accompli* by daylight.

When Arkady and Anton arrived at the Butyrka, Gabashivili was in the morgue. They were told the man had died of a heart attack in the middle of the night. After a moment of standing there, trying to contain his anger, Arkady decided there was no point in trying to find out if Gabashivili had been murdered or had died of his wounds, but he would go on the assumption the man was killed until it proven otherwise. He would try to have a medical examiner he trusted get involved in the autopsy, but that was a long shot.

The Same Day, 0929 Local Time, Denver, Colorado

From several hundred miles up, an infrared sensor on a Defense System Program satellite detected the flash of a rocket motor igniting. Within three milliseconds, the plume's chemical composition was spectrographically analyzed and transmitted to an Air Force Space Command operations center deep underground at Buckley Air Force Base, outside Denver, Colorado.

The launch triggered both visual and aural warnings to the watch officers in the command center. Less than a second later, the rating of "probable missile launches" changed to "two confirmed missile launches." The watch officer on duty pushed a button to connect to both the command duty officer in the Pentagon and the command duty officer at the North American

Aerospace Defense Command (NORAD) buried in Cheyenne Mountain less than a hundred miles to the south.

A projected trajectory was calculated and refined every few milliseconds. The computers further analyzed the trajectory data and fed it into the Joint Tactical Ground System (JTAGS), making it available to the appropriate theater commander. Since the missile had been launched in Iran, Central Command was also alerted. The conversation only took thirty seconds; everyone concluded the missile launch was not a threat to the U.S. or its allies or any country in the region.

JTAGS had been created to provide target quality locating data on missile launch sites and impact areas. In a matter of seconds, the system gathered data from national air, ground and space sensors. Classified artificial intelligence software analyzed sensor input before displaying it on a computer screen to give the user a coherent picture of the missile type, its launch site, and its target.

The launch puzzled Air Force Lieutenant Colonel Cheryl Hancock. Telemetry normally associated with a missile test had not been detected by any U.S. sensor platform, nor had the Iranians followed the usual protocols for a planned missile test by sending out Notices to Airmen and Mariners. There were no other indicators at all—no explosion, no radio beepers from a test capsule. Only those clear indications of two missiles fired within seconds of each other, both aimed at Eastern Iran.

Hancock, who'd been in the missile shoot monitoring business since the early 1980s after getting her degree from Stanford University in astrophysics, couldn't believe the Iranians were shooting missiles at their own people. The trajectory was not a "normal" test flight path. Their prior shoots had sent rockets into the North Arabian Sea or the desolate areas in Northwestern Iran near the Afghani border.

Hancock dialed the satellite operations control center at the National Reconnaissance Office. As the command's watch officer, she had the authority to authorize a photo pass over the impact area. The unannounced missile firings made the impact area a high priority photo target of interest, and she was sure the National Reconnaissance Office would support her request. Unfortunately, she was told the next KH-11 satellite orbit allowed only a long oblique photo of the Hamun Marshes. Detailed photos would take another 24 hours.

At her workstation, Cheryl scrolled through the reconnaissance asset status boards. She found the locations and mission tasking of all the Navy's EP-3Es electronic surveillance, as well as the Air Force's U-2R high altitude reconnaissance aircraft. EP-3Es were modified P-3B airframes for the ELINT mission, while the U-2Rs were descendants of the original U-2 and had large sensor pods on each wing.

An EP-3E had just taken off from Masirah, a fifty-mile long island in the Arabian Sea off the east coast of Oman. The "Remarks" section of the mission tasking order noted it was under the operational control of Central Command, along with several U-2Rs based at Taif Air Base in Saudi Arabia. One was currently on a reconnaissance mission over the Arabian Gulf.

Hancock pushed the speed dial on the STU-III. A voice sounded over the speaker.

"CENTCOM Ops. Colonel Jones. This is not a secure line." The officer was speaking from headquarters in Tampa, Florida.

"Colonel, this is Lieutenant Colonel Cheryl Hancock, Air Force Aerospace Command Operations Watch Officer. Let's go secure." The green light came on, the liquid crystal display indicating Colonel Jones was in a Top Secret facility. Impatiently, Hancock used her thumb to push down on the silver top of her government ballpoint pen, making the pen's point click in and out, in and out.

When the phones finished synchronizing so that the conversation would be encrypted, Hancock leaned forward to get closer to the monitor on her desk. "You see the JTAGS data?"

"You bet," Jones said. "It got everybody around here pretty excited. The J-2 is in with the boss right now. Do you have anything to add?"

She looked at the screen in front of her, one of five with the status of all the U.S. national reconnaissance assets. The data was updated every hour. "We can't get any decent satellite imagery for at least another day, so no, we don't. But I have a suggestion for you."

"Go ahead."

"A Navy EP-3E took off from Masirah about thirty minutes ago and an airborne U-2R is flying down the Iranian coast as we speak. The U-2 has high-resolution video cameras and electronic sensors on board; we can get a pretty good look at the impact area if it's within range. Suggest you redirect both the EP-3 and the U-2R to see what they can pick up electronically. From its cruising altitude, the U-2R should be able to get excellent pictures of the Hamun Marsh area. I don't believe the Iranians can touch the U-2R with missiles, so they may scream a lot but the plane should be safe."

"Good idea. I'll get on it and get back to you. We'll send you copies of whatever we get."

Hancock pumped her fist after she hung up. *Yes!!!*

The Same Day, 0947 Local Time, On Board Nestor 06

From eighty thousand feet, far above any clouds, dirt, or anything else in the Earth's atmosphere, the pilot of the matte-black U-2R could see the curvature of the earth. Unlike the straight-line horizon seen by airlines, general aviation, and non-U-2 military pilots, the view from eighteen miles above the earth was different. If the pilot, Major Garrett Richmond, looked straight up, he stared into the blackness of space. Ahead to the right and left, the horizon was a black line tinged with a little light blue above and either brown or darker blue below.

The U-2R looked like the original U-2, but was slightly larger, had a more powerful engine, and two long sensor pods on each wing. It cruised in the dangerous part of the flight envelope known as the "coffin corner." Flying a few knots faster than the designed speed of the airplane could lead to overstressing the airplane and large pieces flying off. Fly a few knots slower and the airplane stalled. While the U-2R stall was relatively benign, it was not something one wished to do at high altitudes. A stall recovery, no matter how well executed, could overstress the airframe, as well as screw up the images that were being recorded. Flying a little too high put the airplane above its designed service ceiling, which stressed the pressurization systems to the point where they might fail. Any of the three could ruin your day. Even so, flight planning was the easy part. Prepping for flight was the real ordeal. This was Richmond's fifth year flying the U-2R, so by now he was familiar with the process. Like all of the others who flew the airplane known as the Dragon Lady, he had volunteered for the dangerous assignment.

Several mission equipment specialists had to help Richmond don the pressure suit, hook up the pee bottle, zip the suit, and then put on his gloves and helmet. Once zipped up, the suit was connected to a portable air-conditioner. The next step was an hour breathing one hundred percent oxygen to purge as much nitrogen out of the blood as possible. This was designed to prevent the bends. After that, the pilot waddled from the truck and up the ladder. Technicians hooked up the U-2R's ventilation and pressurization hoses, then hooked up the harness to the ejection seat.

Once ensconced, the pilot would go through the checklist and start the engine. Like everything else about the U-2R, taxiing was different from most airplanes. The forward pair of the two tandem sets of wheels pivoted, allowing the pilot to steer the plane. The pilot's helmet and bulky pressure suit, however, made it difficult for him to turn his head, so he followed a truck which went just fast enough so the U-2R's wing tips were flying (so they wouldn't drag on the ground) but slow enough so the plane's long, thin, high-lift wing didn't generate enough lift to get airborne.

One of the best things Richmond liked about the airplane was the takeoff from the runway. When he released the brakes and pushed the throttle to takeoff power, the U-2R was airborne in an amazingly short distance, despite being one-third bigger and heavier than the original U-2. Once it left the ground, the U-2R was a jet-powered glider, and he loved the way it climbed like a homesick angel.

Nestor Zero Six's route plan called for flying east along the Iraqi/Saudi border and then down the Arabian Gulf parallel to the Iranian coast. At eighty thousand feet there was no wind, so the airplane tracked steadily along its heading.

The Bahraini peninsula had disappeared behind him thirty minutes ago. Using the big yoke the designer had thoughtfully installed to accommodate a pressure suit, Richmond banked Nestor 06 gently northeast. His track would take him past the Iranian port of Bandar Abbas, then east into the Gulf of Oman before heading back to King Fahad Air Base outside Taif, on the west side of the Arabian peninsula.

Since half the plane's fuel had been burned, the autopilot kept re-trimming the airplane to compensate for its lighter weight. The Straits of Hormuz were passing under Nestor 06's nose at a steady three hundred and seventy-five knots. Richmond was admiring the panoramic view when the radio crackled. Other than reporting turn points, he rarely talked to his controllers via the satellite radio system.

"Nestor Zero Six, Ratchet Control, over."

All the levers and switches the pilot of U-2R could be expected to reach were oversize to make it easier to operate with the pressure suit's thick gloves. "Nestor Zero Six, go."

"Nestor Zero Six, we have new tasking. You ready to copy?"

Richmond picked up the pencil attached to his kneeboard with a length of kite string added so if he dropped it he could, theoretically, pull it back up. Bending over in the U-2R cockpit to get something off the floor was not an option. "Ratchet Control, go."

He wrote down the new headings and times along with what sensors had to be on and then he read them back to Ratchet Control. The new headings had the U-2R cruising along the Iran's coastline less than five miles offshore until it reached its border with Pakistan. Then he would make a right turn to head back to King Fahad.

"Ratchet Control, Nestor Zero Six estimates the extra leg will extend the mission by two-plus hours. Fuel may be a problem."

"Nestor Zero Six, Ratchet Control, understand. Once you turn back toward home plate, we'll determine whether or not you will land on Masirah or fly all the way home."

Once the U-2R was on its new heading, Richmond grabbed the chart he kept stashed between the instrument panel and the forward section of the canopy. As part of the preflight planning, he plotted the courses to familiarize himself with the terrain over which he'd be flying. It was also a backup in case he had electrical problems and the autopilot or the inertial navigation system failed.

No one could see Richmond's raised eyebrow or hear his murmured *hmmmmm* when he finished drawing the new courses on the map.

Beep. Beep. Beep. The tone in his headset meant a Soviet-made radar was targeting his plane. Richmond made note of the time on his kneeboard.

If the tone changes and gets more rapid, then I'll know they are shifting from surveillance to targeting. If it gets higher pitched, I know the missile is aimed at me! When it starts screeching steadily, it is locked on to my plane.

Richmond glanced at the three-inch display on the upper left part of the instrument panel. Sure enough, it showed that radar was on and tracking him.

Do I abort? Before I launched, I was cautioned not to fly over or into Iranian airspace. What changed? What are they not telling me?

"Ratchet Control, Nestor Zero Six is being tracked by a Square Pair radar normally associated with the SA-5 Gammon missile. Tracking began at 1549 local, over."

Square Pair was the radar normally associated with the SA-5 missile. The intelligence he'd seen on the Iranian air defense system said they had SA-5s, but no one knew whether or not they were operational. Intelligence photos showed the SA-5 to be a very big multi-stage rocket. Theoretically, it could get up to one hundred and thirty thousand feet.

"Nestor Zero Six, roger. Continue mission as planned. Intel says the missile can't get up to you."

Easy for you to say that—you're not the target. The goddam missile is designed to bring down airplanes two hundred miles from the launch site. The beeping continued and got stronger as he neared the target area. He flipped the switch to put the U-2R's jammer into the stand-by position, figuring he would have enough warning to use it once any missile was in flight. Turning a jammer on now would technically be an act of war, more so than just violating their airspace, which could be explained as a simple navigational error. An activated jammer would also make it easier for a missile to home in on his plane.

To make himself feel better, Richmond eased the throttle up one percent. He was now just five knots shy of the not-to-exceed airspeed, but it changed the Iranian's firing solution. He turned the temperature controller on his pressure suit to make it colder; his hands were clammy and he could feel sweat dripping down his back and face.

The beeping increased in rapidity, and then changed to a solid tone. He keyed the mike.

"Ratchet Control, Nestor Six is targeted. The radar warning system confirms SA-5 missile launch at my ten o'clock."

No answer. *What could they do? I'll bet they're looking up the procedure for what to do if the Iranians shoot down a U-2R. Assholes!*

Even for a missile flying at twice the speed of sound, it takes time to cover the ground from the launch site to a targeted airplane, and climbing vertically takes a lot of rocket fuel. Richmond searched the sky beneath him, looking for a plume, and sure enough, it was at ten o'clock low. Jammer on!

He watched the SA-5 missile climb. Its exhaust plume left a long snaking trail as it hunted for its target. The tone in Richmond's headset became shrill as the terminal seeker lit up the U-2. He couldn't believe the size of the second stage of the SA-5 as it struggled to lock on to his airplane. Confused by his jammer, the SA-5 passed three hundred yards from his wingtip, and Richmond started talking aloud to the missile. "So what are you going to do? Run out of fuel? Or, are you going to come back at me and detonate in the hopes a piece of your shrapnel brings me down? Or are the jammers going to work and make you go stupid until you run out of fuel?"

The plume was now out of sight. Richmond unlocked his shoulder harness and pulled himself forward to see the missile's trajectory. When he couldn't see it at all, he settled back down in the ejection seat and re-locked his shoulder harness. *Are you going to come down on my ass? SA-5, what are you going to do? Am I going to die?*

The thought had just passed through his mind when he heard a muffled *whump* and the U-2R shook as if it were flying through turbulence. Richmond figured the SA-5's four hundred and seventy-eight-pound blast fragmentation warhead had detonated. *I hope none of the fragments damaged my fragile airplane.* The pitching and rolling eased as the autopilot struggled to keep the plane level. Richmond scanned the instruments. *No caution lights. All temps and pressures are normal.* The pilot patted the top of the instrument panel and again spoke out loud. "Baby, we're going to finish the mission and get home today. All I have to do is get you back on the runway in one piece and it's Miller time!"

* * *

Below Richmond's U-2R, Iranians huddled around the warheads. Even though the transmitters radiated less than a watt and a half, Zadeh's recovery teams had had no trouble homing in on the 203mm shells. Both were well within the two-kilometer target circle.

Unknown to Zadeh, the U-2R's sensitive receivers had detected low power VHF transmissions coming from the area its cameras photographed. The receivers recorded the signals. Later, Air Force technicians would plot the location of both warheads within a couple hundred yards.

Esmail Zadeh was delighted by what a smiling Zimmerman and his cohorts showed him. The electrical circuits had performed as designed, setting off the few grams of explosive at three thousand feet. He could now report the North Korean-made missiles met their requirements for accuracy. In fact, both warheads had landed within a kilometer of the center of the target. Under Zadeh's supervision, the heat-scarred warheads were loaded onto trucks and moved out of the area—before U.S. satellites photographed the area.

In a private office at the Iranian Air Force base in Jask an hour and a half later, an excited Zadeh called Defense Minister Bagdhani and told him Iran was now only a few steps away from having deliverable nuclear capability.

Tuesday, June 13th, 1991, 0536 Local Time, the Pentagon

One would think that, this early in the morning, there wouldn't be much northbound traffic on I-95 between the Marine Corps Base at Quantico and the Pentagon. One would be wrong. As General Feltzer rode in the back seat of the staff car, he wondered, *who are these crazy people going to work at 0530 in the morning?*

The ride gave him an hour of private time to sort through messages, read reports, and prepare for meetings. It was, however, hard on his aide, who got up an hour earlier than Feltzer did to pick up his message traffic and meet his driver before they headed to the general's quarters.

At 0106 in the morning, Feltzer's phone had rung, the duty officer for Joint Chiefs of Staff Command Center calling to tell him the Iranians had fired a missile at a U-2R. After listening to the few facts the Pentagon had, Feltzer gave the man a list of people to call and have them in his office at 0730.

Feltzer's conference room was on the E ring. It had thick blast-and-bullet-proof windows overlooking the courtyard three stories below. When he arrived, there was a stack of photos from the U-2R showing the missile in flight ready for his review. Next to the pictures was a Defense Intelligence Agency assessment of the SA-5's capabilities. As a Marine fighter pilot with thousands of hours in the F-4, Feltzer was familiar with the missile's capabilities. The SA-5 was designed to take out bombers at long range, but wasn't much of a threat to a highly maneuverable fighter. A U-2 flying at seventy thousand feet, however, wasn't very maneuverable and would fall into the category of a "sitting duck" for an SA-5. If one got bagged by an Iranian missile, there would be hell to pay and he didn't want that on his watch. The big picture worry was that the Soviets could equip the SA-5C with a nuclear warhead to take out formations of American bombers. That was scary because, no amount of maneuvering would save you from the blast and radiation. He wondered were the Soviets dumb enough to send nuclear armed SA-5s to Iran.

In Feltzer's conference room, a Navy captain assigned to the Defense Intelligence Agency sat opposite an Air Force Colonel from the Aerospace Defense Command. Rear Admiral Jeff Gainesville came in and took a seat, three chairs down from the intelligence analysts.

The fighter pilot in General Feltzer pushed him not to waste time once everyone was seated. "What happened?" he demanded.

The Air Force colonel turned down the lights in the conference room and moved to an overhead projector. His first slide was a map of Iran. "Sir, my name is Colonel Grant and I specialize in analyzing missile capabilities and performance."

His presentation included the data Cheryl Hancock had provided. Next, Navy Captain Brooks went to the front of the room and opened his presentation with a genealogy chart of the Scud missile and how it evolved into the Shahab 4. He only had an artist's conception of the North Korean versions to show.

"Here's what we know about the Shahab 4. It is the longest-range version of the North Korean NaDong series they fired over Japan a few years ago. Like the Scud, it can be fired from a mobile launcher and has a range of about fifteen hundred nautical miles. The missile is trucked to the launch pad, then fueled while the launch point and target location data are loaded into the guidance system. We estimate this sequence takes about thirty minutes. After the missile is fired, the truck can be reloaded with another missile in another thirty minutes and the process starts all over. All this means..." The captain paused while he waited for another slide to show with a range circle on a map. "...from the launch site, the Iranians can hit Tel Aviv and most of South Eastern Europe. Moscow is only just out of range."

Brooks turned off the projector and looked at General Feltzer, then to Admiral Gainesville, to see if there were any questions.

"General, we believe the Shahab 4 can be fitted with almost any type of warhead. We know the North Korean fired unitary warheads with approximately twenty-five hundred pounds of high explosive as well as simulated chemical rounds. It is probably safe to assume the missile can easily carry a nuclear warhead in the ten to twenty kiloton range."

Feltzer listened intently. After Brooks finished, the general summarized the findings and thanked them for the briefing. He turned to Jeff Gainesville. "Jeff, go wake up our State Department liaison officer. Find out what they know. Find out what the CIA knows. See if there's an arms control angle to this. My guess is they're as much in the dark as we are."

"Yes, sir."

"And Jeff, the intel guys liked your analysis on the Russian food situation. Good job. So dig deep, there may be more to this story. I'm one of those who think the Soviet Union is about to unravel. Food shortages may cause riots the government will have to put down, but then what? They still don't have enough food. The question I'm asking is, what do hungry, greedy officers who control tactical nukes do when they can't afford food and their families are faced with starvation?"

"Thank you, sir." The new admiral paused. "I'd like some help."

General Feltzer smiled. He'd been wondering how long it would take for Jeff to figure out he needed a staff. "Do you have anyone in mind?"

"Yes, sir. A Navy captain who's a helo driver by the name of Josh Haman. I've worked with him before, and he speaks Russian like a native. I'll keep the missile issue myself and toss the Russian angle into Josh's lap. He'll sort it out pretty fast. We may not like the answer, but I'd bet he gets it right."

"Where is he now?" Feltzer asked.

"Out at AIRPAC," Gainesville said. "I can get him here TAD easily." TAD: Temporary Additional Duty. AIRPAC: short for being on the staff of Commander, Naval Air Forces Pacific.

"Fantastic," Feltzer said. "I've heard what he did during Desert Storm. I know people who call him first when the shit hits the fan. Between crises, they'd like to keep him stuffed in a box marked 'Open only in time of war.'" General Feltzer laughed. "Having a warrior like Captain Haman around the Pentagon will give the shoe clerk flag officers nightmares. Get him here as fast as you can, and before he talks, meets, or sees *anyone* in D.C., have him in my office for a brief."

The Same Day, 1248 Local Time, Moscow

Rank allowed General Boris Vavilov the perk of having a driver take him back and forth to Ekaterininskiy Park. It was a great place to take a walk and one of his favorites. It had three man-made lakes, broad paths lined with trees, and benches every few hundred meters. After the ten-minute drive from his office in Znamenka Street, Vavilov told the driver to be back in an hour.

The general took a walk every day. It gave him a chance to be alone and enjoy being outside, rather than cooped up in a stuffy office. Indoors, cigarette smoke always drifted down the hall from the other offices, making his eyes water and his nose run. Whenever Vavilov commanded a unit, smoking was not allowed in his presence.

At the end of the paddle-shaped pond and as far away from the Central Armed Forces Museum as he could get, Vavilov found an empty bench. Before sitting, he deliberately fumbled with his net bag to let a wrapped piece of food fall out. Retrieving it let him look underneath the seat for a hidden microphone.

Satisfied there was not one, he gazed at the cumulus clouds darkening the sky. Later this afternoon it would become noisy and rainy. Vavilov appreciated thunderstorms. Humans could make more noise and lights with their machines, but there was a grandeur to thunderstorms that was primal and exhilarating.

The sight of a Soviet Lieutenant General in uniform was usually enough to deter others from sitting on the same bench, unless they knew him. He gently placed his net bag on the seat, took out a bottle of mineral water and an embroidered napkin, and then removed a paper bag holding a large chunk of homemade dark black bread and pieces of sausage and cheese.

As was his custom, Vavilov laid the bread and cheese on the napkin that his wife of thirty-plus years provided, and used a pocketknife to cut chunks of sausage to fold into pieces of torn bread. As he chewed, the general watched the birds. Pigeons flapped and scurried over, knowing crumbs would soon be on the ground.

The general was halfway through his meal when another man, wearing the uniform of a Soviet Army colonel, sat at the other end of the bench and opened a book. It was Panichev.

Vavilov had cause to thank his mother for the dark olive skin he'd inherited. At a height of 2.2 meters, Vavilov was tall for a Moldavian. His height had kept him out of the tank corps;

there was no way he could fit inside one. Panichev had similar skin color and a bushy Stalinesque mustache, as well as broad-shoulders, but he would be at least a head shorter. Vavilov wondered if Panichev had ever been assigned to a tank unit.

Panichev read for a minute or so before he spoke quietly. "General, we are ready to place our order."

Vavilov looked up at the sky as if to say, *God, here we go.* "And it is?"

"Twenty-four ZBV2s and a dozen RA-115s. Five million U.S. dollars for the ZBV2s and a million for each RA-115."

"What's an RA-115?"

"A small man-portable nuclear device. The GRU has supposedly smuggled them into Western Europe and the U.S.— for use by the Spetznaz, if the Soviet Union ever went to war against the United States and NATO."

"I know nothing about RA-115s, nor do I control any." *I need to find out who does.*

Panichev nodded. "O.K., then twenty-four ZBV2s."

Vavilov pursed his lips and shook his head. "My good colonel, twenty-four is not possible. ZBV2s aren't the same as the 203mm high-explosive artillery shells I sold you before. We never release more than six ZBV2s at any one time. I can get you six, at fifteen million each."

"We think twenty-four is possible. We can get them other ways. I came to you first as a courtesy."

"Any release order has to be signed by me. Attacking storage facilities can be very messy. You might get the weapons, but you'll never get them out of the Soviet Union."

"A dozen at eight million."

"Six is all you're going to get. And the price is fifteen per warhead."

The colonel didn't say anything. Not hearing a response, Vavilov finished his mineral water and neatly folded the three sheets of off-white butcher paper that had held his lunch.

"Six at ten," the colonel said finally.

"Comrade, your Russian is rusty, and your hearing is faulty. I said fifteen. You're not the one who will be in the basement of the Lubyanka, looking at a wall and expecting a bullet in your brain at any second." Vavilov put the bottle in the net bag and made it appear he was ready to leave. "However, for you, I will come down to twelve."

The man wearing the colonel's uniform gritted his teeth. "Six at twelve. Half when we get the paperwork and half when we take delivery."

"No, half *before* I start on the paperwork and half when you get the documents."

"We won't agree to payment before delivery!"

Vavilov stood up. "Then you won't get any ZBV2s." He was ready to walk away. Without the money, he was ready to report the man as a spy. *Does this make me a capitalist?*

"We agree to your terms," Panichev ground out.

"Excellent. When the money is in my account, I'll start on the paperwork. I'll get in touch the usual way when I have the documents ready. If the money isn't there by this coming Monday morning, the deal is off."

Vavilov let a slip of paper fall to the ground in front of the colonel. On it was the name of the Swiss bank and an account number set up by a relative in Finland. *Once I have the money, my retirement is secure and I can leave this god-forsaken country and all its troubles.*

The Same Day, 1546 Local Time, the Pentagon

Jeff waited until everyone had left the conference room. A quick glance at his watch told him he had fourteen minutes before his next meeting, according to the sheet generated by the efficient Lieutenant Johnson. A single black rotary phone occupied the corner of the room. It couldn't connect to the outside world unless you dialed the operator and she switched the user to an outside line. Technically, it wasn't a secure phone, but the chances of someone tapping it were slim.

He picked it up the receiver, listened for a tone, and then spun the dial seven times, entering his aide's phone number. Her clear voice sounded before the first ring had time to complete. "Lieutenant Johnson. This is not a secure line." If the other extension had rung, she would have answered, "CNO Special Projects Office."

"Hi, it's Jeff." Mentally, he cursed. He still wasn't used to introducing himself as Admiral Gainesville. He'd have to work on that. Even with an aide, it wasn't O.K. although an occasional slip might be excused. With others, it wasn't. Once he put on the gold shoulder boards, his first name was Admiral, even to his friends... unless they were one-on-one in private, and not discussing Navy business. It was a change the informal Jeff Gainesville had a hard time getting used to. I'm calling from an internal phone," he went on. "I've got a hot one you need to jump on right away. It will be a labor of love and shouldn't take you long."

"Yes, Admiral, what do I have to do?"

"Write a message to Captain Haman ordering him to report to General Feltzer and me for at least thirty days of temporary duty: initially working here at the Pentagon, but possibly going to the Soviet Union. Get the accounting codes from General Feltzer's administrative assistant and put it all in a message for me to release. Then call Haman and tell him I need his ass here, as in tomorrow or the next day. I know he's going to ask, so tell him the work involves Soviet nukes going to Iran illegally, and he may get to work with Lev Mogen's friends again. Also ask him to call you when he has his ticket in hand, so we'll know when he'll arrive."

"Yes, sir, I'll get right on it."

He could practically hear the grin competing with alarm behind her words. "Lieutenant, one more thing. When you talk to him, try not to gush too much."

Jeff smiled as he hung up.

The Same Day, 1622 Local Time, San Diego

On the way back to his home, Josh stopped at the cemetery where Natalie was buried. Standing in front of her grave, he told her he was going to the Soviet Union. He knew he had to try to find out who'd ordered her father's murder.

He'd made the stop despite promising Rebekah he would only visit on the anniversary date of Natalie's death. Josh rationalized that this visit was special. He wasn't sure if he had the courage to tell Rebekah; she'd be afraid he'd be killed avenging his first wife's death. It was bad enough he had to tell her he was going to the Soviet Union.

Chapter 10
RatPack Assignment

Friday, June 14th, 1991, 0700 Local Time, the Pentagon

Josh had been directed to an anteroom to wait. He was the only person in the small room, which was furnished in typical military bleak: three desks, two steel four-drawer safes, a credenza, and four simple metal chairs lined up along one wall. The central desk with a polished wood top belonged to the administrative assistants assigned to General Feltzer, a.k.a. the Chairman's Chief of the Joint Staff for Operations, informally known as the J3. The other two desks, noticeably smaller, had seen better days and many occupants. Currently those desks were assigned to the aides of the flag officers, whose offices were also accessed through the anteroom. All the metal chairs were well used, with deep indentations where the cheeks of one's ass rested, assuming of course, it hadn't been chewed off by a general or flag officer for some real or imagined mistake.

Josh picked one of the chairs along the wall, put his briefcase on the floor, and pulled out John Grisham's bestseller, *The Firm*. He'd started it yesterday on the plane ride from San Diego. At 0702, an aide, a Marine major, offered Josh coffee.

When Jeff Gainesville strode in at 0710, Josh came to attention. Jeff quickly waved him to "At ease" and they exchanged greetings. An Admiral has many demands on his time, so Jeff got right to the point.

"Welcome to a CNO rat pack assignment. Normally, they're for post-command COs waiting their next billet, but I wanted you, so you can blame me. We'll talk on the way to General Feltzer's office." Jeff turned to the smiling Lieutenant Johnson a pace to the right and a step behind him. "And this is Lieutenant "Kno" Johnson. She's a fellow rotor head. I believe the two of you have met."

The two helicopter pilots shook hands. "A pleasure to meet you, Captain." Johnson tried not to stare at Josh's ribbons; they showed he'd been awarded two Navy Crosses, three Silver Stars, four Distinguished Flying Crosses—and that was just the top row! The third Silver Star was for his actions during the rescue of Diamond Back Two Zero Four.

"Josh, let's not keep General Feltzer waiting. Lieutenant, I'll be back in time for my 0800 meeting. Make sure no one stole the office down the hall; Captain Haman can work there."

On the way to the general's office, Jeff summed up recent events, explaining that he was working on the food shipments and Iranian missiles; Josh got to deal with loose nukes in the Soviet Union. Outside the general's door, Jeff turned to face his friend. "There are people in this building with very long memories. Some of them would like your head on a platter."

Josh didn't say anything. He was in receive mode.

"As I'm learning," Jeff went on, "defying conventional wisdom in the five-sided puzzle palace is not popular. We've been lucky because we worked for flag officers who understood the warrior mentality. With Desert Storm over, the shoe clerks are large and in-charge, trying to collect the Peace Dividend. In this building, doing your paperwork, shining your shoes, and keeping your hair short is more important than strategy and how well you can lead men in a firefight. It's all about your service's share of the defense budget."

Josh shrugged. "I see the same thing every day at AIRPAC. The war fighters want more free play in exercises, while the people farther up the chain of command want the exercises toned down to little more than paperwork drills. Less cost, more safety. Accidents of any kind in training are career threatening. When you push back with 'Train as you plan to fight,' the paper-pushers shake their heads and say. 'You don't understand.' My answer is that I understand all too well. Those guys are all about not doing anything that might jeopardize their next promotion."

"You got that right. Well, welcome to the lions' den."

In General Feltzer's office, there were introductions and handshakes. Under the general's gold wings, Josh saw the ribbons for the Silver Star and Distinguished Flying Cross, followed by his Air Medals. Feltzer had seen his fair share of action in Vietnam. Josh and Jeff sat on opposite ends of the couch. Josh's sense of history had him wondering who else had sat on its well-worn leather.

Feltzer spent ten minutes putting his spin on what he wanted Josh to do, then summed up his instructions. "Read the material and come up with your own analysis on what weapons are changing hands, whose involved, and why. The Chairman of the Joint Chiefs wants an operator's opinion, not just one from a spook who sits in a cubicle."

The Marine tossed an envelope on the table. "This is what came from Lev Mogen on rumors that the Iranians were trying to buy tactical nukes from the Soviets. It got a lot of people's attention. His trust in you is one of the reasons you're here now, and why you're going to Moscow as soon as we get the paperwork done."

Josh listened to the general as intently as he could. It was like drinking out of a fire hose. He wondered what he would simply not take in because he was still thinking about what had just been said. Feltzer went on: "The President is sending food to the Soviets. To make that possible, the Soviets have agreed to allow a limited number of our cargo planes to land at selected Aeroflot-served airports—just as a stopgap until ships arrive with the bulk of the food. It's called *Operation Deny Famine.*"

The general knew that many on the Joint Staff thought the Soviet Union was on the verge of unraveling. Josh was to be Feltzer's boots on the ground in Moscow: the J3 wanted raw intel on the nukes, not filtered stuff that had gone through layers of analysts who'd either left things out or spun the data in a direction reflecting the analyst's perspective. Feltzer wanted as much real, raw data as Josh could dig up... and he wanted it sooner rather than later.

The general leaned forward. "The senior military attaché will only provide administrative support. He's not cleared for your mission and you do not, repeat do *not* report to him. You report to me, through Jeff. I have the ear of the Chairman who talks to the President and the National Security Advisor on a daily basis. Am I clear?"

"Yes, sir, absolutely." Josh knew a clear chain of command when he heard one. "Sir, how long do you think I'll be in Moscow?"

General Feltzer frowned. "Captain, the honest answer is I don't have a fucking clue! All I can say is that you'll come home when you've got it figured out or I decide to call you back."

Feltzer stood up. "One last thing, Captain Haman. Please keep in mind, at the moment we're not at war with the Soviet Union. Please don't start one. I've got enough on my plate as it is, and by the time I finished the paperwork documenting the start of a war, the Soviets will have landed on Virginia Beach and artillery shells will be falling on the Pentagon."

All three officers were smiling when Josh said, "Aye, aye, sir."

Five minutes later, Josh was walking down the hall with Lieutenant Johnson toward the secure room he'd use as a temporary office. "Sir," she said, "the material Admiral Gainesville wants you to read is on the desk. He wanted me to tell you he'd like to have lunch with you. I'll come get you at 1115 and take you to the flag mess."

"Sounds like a plan." More stuff from the fire hose!

"Yes, sir. If you need any additional material, call me. Admiral Gainesville gave me a number to call to help motivate people to get you what you need."

"Lieutenant, does the office have secure phone?"

"Yes, sir." She reached into her pocket. "Sir, here's the key for the STU-III. Dial eight to get an outside line and you're good to go. The number for the office is on the phone; but sir, I would recommend you have them call me if you're going to be out of the office. I'll know where to find you."

"How will you know where I am?"

"Captain, Admiral Gainesville said one day soon you'll be a flag officer and you'll need to work with an aide, so you might as well start with me! And part of my job is to manage your schedule."

"Jeff said that?"

"Yes, sir. I'm quoting him verbatim."

"That's both amusing and alarming. Many flag officers have made a point of telling me they're going to end my career and I'll never make the next rank, much less admiral. So far, I've been promoted beyond my wildest dreams. I wonder if the powers that be will demand I get a lobotomy before I get selected for promotion to rear admiral so I can become a shoe clerk. If and when that happens, I'll retire."

Lieutenant Johnson tried to hide her smile as she busied herself with entering the six numbers on the cipher lock to open the door.

* * *

On the desk were three piles of documents. One had intelligence reports on Soviet nuclear weapons, including the information Lev Mogen had given Gainesville. The second contained a series of messages containing reports and analysis of the political situation in the Soviet Union. The third was a pile of recent satellite photos.

"Captain, here's the combination to the door and my direct dial number. The head is down the hall to your right. There's a coffee bar and vending machines near there too. Commander Cabot's direct dial number for his STU-III is on the paper, in case you didn't have it. He's expecting your call sometime this morning."

"Am I that predictable?"

"No, sir, Admiral Gainesville suggested I give the commander a heads up. He has the Navy current ops billet at Special Operations Command. If we have to do anything in the Soviet Union, Marty will be the starting point. I read everything that comes to Admiral Gainesville, and I sort it out so he knows what to look at first. From what I've heard, Captain, if anyone can figure out what is going on in the Soviet Union, you can."

"Lieutenant, thanks for your confidence, but I must warn you, being around me may be bad for your career."

"Sir, with all due respect, that's bullshit and you know it. I'm not worried, and neither is Admiral Gainesville. If he'd let me, I'd go to Moscow with you."

The Same Day, 1503 Local Time, New York City

Shadows from the buildings along the Manhattan side of the East River made the water look dark gray. Flow and swirls around the bridge abutments showed the tide going up river toward Long Island Sound, as opposed to the Atlantic Ocean.

Mohammed Safdar had picked this location to get a good look at the Williamsburg Bridge, as well as to give himself another angle of the Brooklyn and Manhattan Bridges. He alternated looking at the bridges with his binoculars and taking pictures with his 75–300mm f.4.5 to f.5.6 zoom lens on his Nikon camera. He was studying how the bridge was built and looking for security measures.

What Safdar didn't know was that two of the joggers running past him were confirming his identity. A hundred yards to his left, a passing photographer took his picture so it could be compared with others in an archive in Tel Aviv.

This was the third time today Safdar had been photographed. The first had been while he was taking pictures of the 59th Street Bridge, the second when he had lunch with a remarkably tall American. The observers made a note to see if the American could be identified.

Friday, June 14th, 1991, 1422 Local Time, Moscow
The conference room several levels below Znamenka Street was neither as big nor as luxurious as one would expect, considering that it was for the private use of the Chief of the General Staff of the Soviet Armed Forces. It was used it when he was briefed on war plans or top-secret operations. The table and chairs, inherited from the Tsars, were dilapidated shades of their former grandeur, because the Red Army had used them since the 1930s. Maintenance had not been high on the list of priorities; in fact, contempt for relics of the oppressive past had encouraged neglect.

Cigarette and cigar smoke had permeated the worn leather. The reek overwhelmed the aroma of the freshly brewed coffee that non-smoker Major General Vladimir Koskov preferred when he scheduled the room. For this meeting, he sat at the head of the table. Konstantin Rybalov, the commander of the Moscow Military District, closed the door as he came in and sat in the chair next to him.

Koskov always wondered what was discussed by the men whose asses had occupied these seats during Stalin's rule. One day you could be here, and the next standing in front of a firing squad. In reality, little had changed in the thirty-eight years since Stalin's death, other than the frequent purges of hundreds or thousands of party members. Show trials based on trumped up charges, forced confessions, and made-up evidence still went on to give the perception that Justice was being served.

As a captain, Koskov had served as an advisor to the North Vietnamese Army and the Pathet Lao in the 60s and 70s. Then he'd fought the Afghan rebels for four years in the 80s. Unlike many of the staff officers with whom he served, most of his decorations were for bravery and leadership in combat. He was known for his brutal treatment of Fedayeen captured by his men in Afghanistan. In Koskov's mind, torturing prisoners to get usable intelligence was simply efficient. Generous too: once he'd tortured the prisoners to death, they'd supposedly go meet Allah and receive however many virgins they were promised. What could be kinder than that?

A fragment from a grenade tossed by a burka-clad woman killed Koskov's best friend and peppered Koskov's own body with fragments, leaving a long scar where one piece of shrapnel laid his cheek open. Despite the wound, Koskov had been back in the field two days later. That experience spelled the end of his trust of anything Afghan or Muslim.

Two years ago, he'd been made the head of the Operations Directorate of the Soviet General Staff, responsible for control of all the Red Army and Navy's Spetznaz units. As such, he could task as many specialized KGB and MVD units as he needed.

"General, are you sure this room is safe?" Rybylov was a Lieutenant General whose command included the elite 4th Guards Armored Kantemirovskaya Division, the 2nd Guards Motor Rifle Tamanskaya Division, and the three Spetznaz companies assigned to guard the Kremlin and its occupants. Rybalov had served as an infantry officer with Koskov in Afghanistan.

Koskov laughed. "The room is perfectly safe. The KGB and the GRU sweep it for bugs every couple of days. The only people who have not searched it for bugs are the CIA."

"You never can be too safe," Rybalov replied. "The old people say, *Usluzhlivyy durak opasnee vraga.* A complacent fool harms more than the enemy."

"Agreed." Koskov poured a glass of vodka and pushed the glass to Rybalov. The gesture allowed a pause so he could get to the point of the meeting. "We can't keep trading oil and gas for food from the Americans and the Europeans. It makes us ever more dependent on the West. This can't be allowed to continue."

Rybalov agreed with a sneer.

"Is the air force with us?" Koskov asked. This was the question of highest concern. "We need their planes to move the troops loyal to us around the country."

"General Zhilin assured me the air force would do what is needed. Those who don't support us have been neutralized. Admiral Dolgikh has let it be known that the Navy will not go along, but we don't need them to control the country."

"Good." Koskov wrote five names down on a piece of paper and slid it across the table. "Many people oppose us, but these are the most troublesome. If we eliminate them, no one can stop us."

Rybalov looked at the paper and his bushy eyebrows went up.

Koskov was now in command mode. "Memorize the names, destroy the paper. Have Piotr place his men so they're ready, but take no action. We'll make our move the next time Gorbachev leaves Moscow."

"Vladimir, once I talk to Piotr, we're committed. There is no turning back."

Koskov leaned across the table and put his hand on the infantry officer's shoulder. "Konstantin, remember when we took our oath of office? We agreed to die for the Soviet Union. In Afghanistan, we didn't know when death might overtake us. Now we are home, in *our* land and if we risk death, we pick the time and place of our own choosing. I do not anticipate it is we who shall die. And I will not sell our birthright and our motherland for American bread."

Sunday, June 16th, 1991, 1047 Local Time, Tehran

From both the air and the ground, the square building, halfway between the Saadi metro station on Tehran's Red Line and the Baharastan station on the Blue Line, didn't spark any interest. It looked nondescript, until a photo interpreter at the Navy Intelligence Center Pacific spotted one unusual detail while looking for potential Tomahawk missile targets in Tehran.

First, the array of satellite antennas on its roof caught his eye. Then he saw the parking lot full of sport utility trucks used by leaders of the regime. After each KH-11 photo satellite pass, he checked the building, and each time the parking lot had one or more of the same type vehicles.

The petty officer recommended the building become an "item of interest." Two days later, the National Security Agency added it to its list of targets and started recording transmissions.

Three facts piqued NSA's interest. First, ninety percent of the communications to and from the building were encrypted with codes not used by the Iranian military. Second, the keys for the codes changed in random patterns. Third, the vehicles observed in the parking lot indicated that many important people were coming and going. Put together, these facts pointed to an operation the Iranian government wanted to keep secret.

The Iranian codes, based on a modified 64-bit DES type algorithm, became a priority target. Brute force attacks on the encryption deciphered enough data to confirm that the building housed offices of a Pasdaran unit conducting special operations in Syria, Egypt, Lebanon, Kenya, the Sudan, Eritrea and the Gaza strip. Decoded segments of transmissions indicated that a special procurement organization was buying material for an operation called *Shamshi Shekaraar*. The Persian words translated to "hunter's sword." that was further interpreted by the NSA analysts as a probable code for an attack.

Out in front of the six-story concrete and cinderblock structure, a rectangular piece of marble listed the names of six innocuous companies, all of them fronts. In the lobby, a concierge sat behind a large wood-faced desk next to a turnstile. The wood facade concealed a twelve-centimeter thick concrete wall backed by an inch of high strength steel.

The "concierge" was a member of the Quds special operations unit. His orders were that random visitors were not permitted. If someone entered without the proper papers, he would politely escort them to the door. If any visitor refused to leave immediately, the concierge was authorized to make an arrest. If they resisted, the concierge was authorized to shoot to kill.

To get to the elevators, a visitor first had to show a proper badge to the concierge. He examined it, recorded its number, and then pointed to a slot on the turnstile. Before employees pushed any elevator buttons, each had to insert his or her badge into the slot. The employee would only be granted access to the floor where he or she worked.

After the elevator opened on a floor, workers were met by another Quds Force checkpoint. Again, the guard examined the employee's badge and entered a code of the day. If they matched, the office door popped open with a loud metallic click.

In his office on the top floor, Esmail Zadeh slit open a double-sealed envelope. It came in the diplomatic pouch from Moscow and had been couriered straight to this building. Inside the pouch was a single coded note with familiar penmanship. When deciphered, using the one-time pad Panichev and he were using, it read:

Esmail,

General Vavilov agreed to provide paperwork to allow us to take delivery of six (6) ZBV2s. Location of the weapons is still unknown, but I suspect they are stored either in Uzbekistan or Kazakhstan, where we have many operatives.

We plan to transport them to Iran using Tarana Aliyev and his men, supplemented by a platoon from the Quds Forces. They will have documents showing that they are part of a transportation regiment. Tarana is an old friend we have used before. He has the contacts and can get the trucks and documents. No one besides me will know what the cargo is.

Vavilov insisted on US$12 million for each weapon. Terms are half now and half when the documents are ready for us. Documents will contain details on where *the weapons are located and provide authorization to transfer them to our men.*

Let me know when US$36 million has been transferred to the following Bank of Zurich account— CH96 1176 2062 6118 5395 08. Once the money is in Vavilov's account, I will inform him.

No money, no documents, he insists. But we can deal with the general once we have the weapons.

Allah be praised and He will deliver.

Ali

Zadeh pulled out the small, black, Franklin Covey phone book he always carried. It was one of those products from the hated Americans that he really liked. He ran his finger down the letter tabs and flipped to the page he wanted. With his left forefinger on the number, he dialed the phone with his right.

In six seconds, the satellite telephone connection went from the roof of the building to a tower in the outskirts of Tehran, then via a satellite to a number in Geneva. Up in space, the hundred-meter diameter antenna of a U.S. Jumpsat 'heard' the call and its onboard computer recognized it as a 'number of interest.' The Jumpsat started recording. Twelve seconds later —two for processing and compressing the file, and ten for transmission from the satellite in a geosynchronous orbit more than twenty-two thousand miles above the earth to a ground station—the entire conversation was being sent to a computer at Fort Meade, Maryland.

At the NSA facility, two copies were made automatically. One was sent to the archives. The second went to a computer center where an attempt was made to decode the conversation. Seventy-six minutes from the conversation's arrival at Fort Meade, a computer-generated message went to the NSA action officer, reporting that the conversation had been partially decoded.

The action officer looked at the decrypted transcript on his screen. Other than the date of the desired transfer, the bank name, account and routing information, the numbers six, twelve and thirty-six, the message was gibberish. Six times twelve was seventy-two and half was thirty-six. The officer sent a report to the NSA's Iranian desk, with copies to the Defense Intelligence Agency and the Central Intelligence Agency. The report said the Iranians were buying six of something at twelve million each, making two payments to a Swiss bank account.

The Defense Intelligence Agency analyst looked up the routing numbers and determined it was an account at the small and very private Bordier et Cie Bank, located in Geneva. A second series of digits gave an account number in a Finnish branch of Bank Nordea. The analyst also noted he had not yet decoded the message so he couldn't definitively say what was going on. He added more addressees to his note: Rear Admiral Jeffrey Gainesville, and analysts at the CIA and NSA. He asked them to please notify him if any more deposits or withdrawals were made to this account, and to invest some computer time trying to further decode this conversation and the transfer.

The Same Day, 0846 Local Time, San Diego

Rebekah shook her head as she watched her daughter Sara walk toward the car. Rebekah thought, *her father will have a hard time when she starts dating.* Despite not being a Southern California blonde, Sara had the look that attracted men. Budding breasts and a long, lithe figure toned by playing sports caught the attention of passers-by; long hours in the dojo with her mother gave Sara an air of confidence. She also had the brains to do anything she wanted. Yet, as Sara walked, even wearing a comfortable pair of denim mini-shorts and a halter-top, there was a child-like innocence about her.

Sara opened the door to the red 1965 Porsche SC coupe and tossed her backpack in the back. "Morning, Mom. Why the Porsche?"

"I like driving it and you're the only passenger."

Sara said, "Cool. Much better than the Suburban. I'm glad we don't have a minivan... They're soooooo ugly. Let's bone out...." Sara caught herself, knowing her parents didn't like their children using current slang. "I mean, let's get going. I need to get back to our crib so I can take a shower."

Rebekah slipped the Porsche into reverse and backed out of the driveway. "You mean house."

"Whatever."

"So how was the party?"

"Great, until Renate started bitching about everything, like always. I don't know why Faith likes her." Sara rolled down the window. "Are we going straight home?"

Rebekah gunned the engine. The Stinger exhaust made a ripping sound as the Porsche accelerated. "No, I'm stopping for bagels and to get a few things for dinner."

"Are your parents coming over?"

"You mean your grandparents?"

"Yeah. Your dad's such a downer. All he does is rant about Dad and the Navy. It's brutal."

Rebekah was between a rock and a hard place. Her stepfather Stan had gone to Canada to avoid the draft and hated the U.S. military. He had been after her to dump Josh almost from the day they started dating. As Stan got older, his message became more strident. Now he claimed that what had happened in the Persian Gulf was just another example of Josh's death wish. Pained, Rebekah said, "Brutal or not, he's your grandfather."

"Duh!!!!"

"And you have to respect his opinions, even if you don't agree."

Rebekah loved the responsiveness of the Porsche as she downshifted. The blat from the tailpipe added a punctuation mark to her comment, like a signal to change the subject.

Josh kept updating the Porsche as it aged. He'd replaced the original seats with a pair of Recaros with bolsters for hip and thigh, as well as for the side of the torso. The last mod had been an electronic ignition system to give it more power and better gas mileage. Best of all, Josh no longer had to change the points and condenser every three thousand miles.

Sitting at a stoplight, Rebekah watched Sara admire a Lotus Esprit Turbo passing through the intersection.

"Mom," Sara asked, "is dad going to give the GTI to Sasha?"

The 1990 Volkswagen GTI 16V was Josh's daily driver. The bright red car had a five-speed gearbox, European cams to give it 137 horsepower, Recaro seats, BBS alloy wheels, and a factory-approved free-flow exhaust he'd installed right after taking delivery. Normally, for a teenager, it was uncool to accompany parents on shopping trips, but Sasha went with his dad on every trip to the VW dealer. After his son completed driver's education in school, Josh had taught Sasha how to drive a stick shift car, and it was no secret the GTI 16V was the car the sixteen-year-old wanted.

The Hamans had, so far, resisted buying a car for Sasha. Sasha's friends drove everything from beat up Volkswagen Beetles to relatively new Porsches and BMWs as "their" cars, and peer pressure was excruciating.

"We haven't decided and won't until your father gets back from Russia," Rebekah said. "Why?"

"I want an Audi Quattro Coupe."

Rebekah had no idea what the car was, but Audi meant German and German meant expensive. "Why an Audi Quattro Coupe?"

"They're dank, I mean, really nice. At least it's not a Ferrari, a Maserati or a Corvette. And no one at school has one."

"But expensive." It was the best Rebekah could say as she focused on driving.

Sara said, "Mom, do you remember what I told Grammy, when she asked me what I wanted to be when I grew up?"

Rebekah glanced at her daughter. The scene was a part of family lore. Sara had been eight, and was baking cookies with Leah, Rebekah's mother. Leah asked Sara what she wanted to be when she grew up. Sara's forehead had wrinkled as her brain processed an answer. The eight year old put her hands on her hips, thrust one out to the side and told her grandmother, "I want to be expensive!"

The Same Day, 1458 Local Time, New York City

The Islamic Center in Long Island City was a short subway ride from Broughton's apartment. To get there, his preferred route was taking either the #5 or the #6 train one stop to 59th, then getting on the M train. Two stops later, Broughton got off and walked three blocks to the center, which looked like it had been a warehouse or a factory before the Imam blessed it.

The people who came to the center were Muslims who'd immigrated from Pakistan, India, and Central Asia. When Broughton was not working Sundays, he came for two discussion groups. The first was on the weekly passage in the Koran, the second on world politics.

An easel in the lobby noted that today's political topic was "The Fiction of the Holocaust." Broughton took a seat on the outside aisle so he could stretch his legs and put his cup of mint tea on the floor. It was impossible to turn off his instincts as an

FBI agent. Without thinking, he'd picked a seat that allowed him to scan the audience with a slight turn of his head. Many, but not all of the men in the room had dark hair, dark skin, and a mustache or full beard. Broughton was glad he wasn't the only Caucasian in the room. There were Yugoslavs and Albanians who ranged from blond and blue-eyed to a more traditional Mediterranean look. To Broughton, the men from the Balkans looked like stereotypes for the Italian Mafia.

The FBI agent turned his attention to the speaker, the author of a book called *The Holocaust, Fact or Fiction?* The man's research had received favorable reviews. His biography neglected to mention he was from Bosnia and had joined the 13th Waffen-SS Mountain Division, also known as the SS Handschar or 1st Croatian division. It also left out how, after the war, thirty-eight men from that division had been tried for war crimes and ten had been executed. He was one of the many suspected of war crimes, but, due to a lack of sufficient evidence, not indicted.

While Broughton didn't take part in the discussion, there was nothing in it he disagreed with. He disliked Jews and everything they stood for. His father, a moderately successful commodity trader, had hated Jews because they were always at the top of the pile when bonuses were handed out. Broughton senior had cheered the day President Roosevelt died. "Now," he'd said, "all the goddamn Jews advising Roosevelt will be replaced."

When Julius and Ethel Rosenberg were arrested in 1950, Peter Broughton studied every article he could find on the trials of the Rosenbergs and other members of the spy ring—David Greenglass, Klaus Fuchs, Martin Sobell. Their convictions were a cause to celebrate. When the Rosenbergs were executed, Broughton senior told his son over a glass of his favorite bourbon, "Two more Goddamn Jews got what they deserved.

Too bad for the rest of us, the Germans didn't kill them all. The world would be a better place."

At first, Broughton had dismissed his father's prejudices as bitterness over his lack of success in his chosen profession. He had changed his opinion when, as an FBI agent, he found himself on a witness stand being questioned by a defense lawyer named Albert Ginsberg. Broughton's testimony collapsed in the face of the defense attorney's pointed questions that flustered Broughton. By the end of his time on the stand, Broughton was exhausted, defeated and discredited.

It seemed as if each time he went into the court room, no matter how well he was prepared by the government's lawyers, he would get hammered by a Jewish defense attorney who created enough doubt in the minds of the jurors to lead to a "not guilty" verdict.

Broughton was sure his failures in the witness chair were the reason he had been pulled from criminal investigations and assigned to intelligence. His boss at the time, a Jew by the name of Gary Blumfeld, had said it happened a lot and wouldn't affect his career... but between the Jewish lawyers and what he felt was a demotion by a Jew, Broughton had come around to his father's way of thinking.

At work, Broughton held his anti-Semitic opinions to himself. If the Bureau found out he attended meetings the Islamic Center, at best they would question his judgment. At worst, he'd lose his clearance, and without clearance, he'd lose his job.

Broughton headed for the subway, thinking about what he'd heard. He didn't notice the man a few steps behind him. Across the street, a man in a panel van with glass windows made to look like steel squeezed the trigger on a motorized Nikon F with a five hundred millimeter lens. The camera sat on a tri-pod with sandbags around its feet to keep it steady.

The man following Broughton soon turned away down a side street, while a new man, loitering at the corner, picked up the tail and stayed fifty feet behind Broughton. Two different men got on the subway and sat opposite the FBI agent. Broughton simply stared into space, not aware he was being followed.

Monday, June 17ᵗʰ, 1991, 1538 Local Time, Moscow

Josh couldn't help thinking he was walking into a den full of hungry, angry bears as he approached the immigration booth at Moscow's Sheremetyevo Airport. Trying not to be obvious, he eyed the electronic and human surveillance, suspecting there was more than he could see. The overt security and the sense he was being covertly watched made the hair on the back of his neck stand up.

Throughout the terminal, uniformed KGB Border Guards studied the stream of passengers. Josh's paranoia suggested there had been also KGB officers in civilian clothes on his flight.

When he'd called Rebekah from the hotel Sunday night, just before leaving for Dulles to catch a British Airways flight to London, he could tell she was putting on a brave voice. Both suspected the KGB had a file on Josh. Rebekah accepted but didn't believe his reassurances that a diplomatic passport protected him. "Even the Soviets don't kill other country's diplomats." The words had sounded hollow then and sounded even hollower now as he tried to reassure himself.

When Lieutenant Johnson had handed Josh his tickets, the diplomatic passport, and a visa to enter the Soviet Union, she'd smiled and said, "Good flights, good seats, good hunting and good luck, Captain."

Hunting? Hell! Here I'm probably the target.

Josh spotted the immigration booth for aircrew members and those with diplomatic passports. Unlike the other lines with hundreds waiting, there were only a few members from an Air France crew ahead of him.

By the time he got to the baggage area, suitcases were being unloaded from the baggage carts and placed on a stainless steel ramp. Fifteen minutes later, he exited customs with a hanging bag over his left shoulder, a briefcase in his left hand, and a B-4 bag full of clothes in his right. Before he could leave the secure area, his passport, visa, and paperwork were examined again and his customs form stamped. The KGB Border Guard put the form in a stack with others from his flight.

A young man strode toward him. Although he wore civilian clothes, Josh immediately thought, *Marine.*

"Captain Haman, sir, I'm Gunnery Sergeant Jesus Velasquez. Let me help you with your bags. The car is just outside the door."

Josh followed as Velasquez marched to the door carrying Josh's luggage. A black Chevrolet Suburban with a driver, an American flag on the right bumper, and diplomatic plates waited at the curb.

Once the car pulled out, Gunnery Sergeant Velasquez, riding shotgun in the front passenger seat, turned to address Josh. "Captain, sir, there's been a slight change in plans. The flat you were scheduled to use has a bad water leak and we don't know when it'll be repaired. The embassy has reserved a small suite for you at the Hotel Rossiya for the next two weeks. I'll be your assistant, and your driver here is Sergeant Lester Brown."

"Assistant as in body guard?"

"Sir, I didn't think it was obvious."

"You're carrying a .45 in a shoulder holster with at least two magazines that I can see."

"Sir, I carry two more magazines in each sport coat pocket and the head of the Marine detachment told me he would have my ass if anything bad happened to you. Apparently, he got a call from a Marine three star in the Pentagon who passed the word."

"Good. I want a .45 as well. Can you get me one?"

"Sir, we're not supposed to be armed outside the embassy... except in very special circumstances."

"I understand, but you didn't answer my question."

"I'll see what I can do."

"Good. What time do you come on duty in the morning?"

"Do you need us tonight, sir?"

"No, I'm going to order room service, have a drink and go to bed. It's been a long day."

"Sir, we'll be at the hotel in the morning any time you want."

"How long from the hotel to the embassy?"

"Sir, normal traffic, fifteen minutes."

"Gunny, please pick me up at oh seven fifteen. That should get us to the embassy by oh seven thirty, right? I've got a long list of people I'm supposed to meet."

"Oh seven fifteen it is, sir."

Josh spent the rest of the thirty-minute trip from the airport looking at the drab apartment buildings lining the streets. By western standards, the roads were empty of traffic. When the Suburban entered the city center, Josh recognized some buildings, but most were a blur to his tired eyes. For years, he had studied Russian and Soviet history, spending long hours looking at pictures, trying to get insight into the soul of his country's primary Cold War enemy. Now the Cold War was over and he was here, in the belly of the bear known as the Soviet Union.

Josh was headed toward the elevators when a voice called, "Captain Haman, *ein Wort, bitte?*" The speaker wore the uniform of a Major General in the KGB. *How did he know I speak German?* Before responding, Josh pocketed the key and pulled his briefcase off the luggage cart. He gave the bellman a twenty-ruble note to deliver his bags, then he popped open the briefcase's latches and dropped in the sealed envelope he'd received from the hotel clerk. Only then did he look at the man from the KGB.

"And you are?" Josh said in Russian.

"Allow me to introduce myself. I am KGB General Oleg Krasnovsky. I would be pleased to have an informal chat with you over a drink." Krasnovsky was thinking, *Haman's dossier didn't mention he spoke Russian. His accent is very good.* The dossier also didn't describe Haman's blue eyes and their intensity. They just bored into you and told you not to try any bullshit. Had the general known that more than one of Josh's commanding officers and peers had been made uncomfortable by that gaze, he would have experienced a flash of sympathy. As it was, he felt moment of pure apprehension. Krasnovsky was taking a risk meeting the American out in the open.

"An informal chat about what? Things the KGB will do to me if I try anything undiplomatic?"

"Oh no, Captain. I'd like to talk about Red Hand."

Josh tried not to react, but he blinked. "Look, I just got here. This is my first night in Moscow. I just want to eat and go to bed."

"I understand. I am in the Seventh Chief Directorate and responsible for investigating individuals who want to enter the Soviet Union. Your visa application came across my desk and I approved it personally. You and I have a lot to talk about. If not today, later."

"General, what do we have to talk about?"

Krasnovsky was thinking, *he reacted to my mention of the German terrorist organization.* The KGB general's brow creased slightly, but he smiled. "Other than how you managed to capture Dieter Stiglitz, I would like to talk to you about

173

several topics you should find both professionally and personally interesting."

Stiglitz? Josh thought. *Now you have my attention.* "General Krasnovsky, with all due respect, sir, please pardon my skepticism. I've been on Soviet soil for less than three hours, and out-of-the-blue, a KGB general wants to talk to me. Don't you think this is a little strange?"

The Soviet officer looked down at the carpet, then right into Josh's eyes. "Captain, my timing may be awkward, but it's important we talk. We can help each other."

Josh could tell from the ribbons on Krasnovsky's tunic that he was a World War II veteran, old enough to be Josh's father. He also knew that Russian generals tended to retire much later in life than those in the U.S. "All right, General, as long as it doesn't require me to betray my country, I'll give you thirty minutes to convince me that further discussions are warranted."

"I'm not stupid enough to even try to turn you into a traitor. Agreeing to at least one more conversation is all I ask."

"I'll busy for the next few days. How do I contact you?"

Krasnovsky handed Josh a card. "Call this number during the day. It's not monitored and I am the only one who answers it."

Josh watched Krasnovsky walk out of the door, not knowing what to think. *What's this about Red Hand? Was the KGB involved up to its red eyeballs, or had Krasnovsky heard about it through a leak? The operation to capture Stiglitz had been in 1976; those who authorized the operation are retired or out of public life. How did he know I was involved? That isn't public knowledge.*

Mind racing, Josh headed toward the elevator.

* * *

The lever doorknob to Josh's room opened with a Germanic thunk. The window in the living room gave him a panoramic view of Red Square and the Kremlin.

Josh expected to see his B-4 and hanging bag in the middle of the room. Not seeing either, he opened the closet, where he found his suits and uniforms neatly hung and his shoes aligned in a precise row. In the dresser, his rolls of t-shirts and shorts were placed next to his socks. On the counter in the bathroom, his toilet kit was carefully unpacked, with his toothbrush and razor resting on a porcelain plate on the glass shelf above the sink, his shaving cream and toothpaste alongside.

For a few seconds, he wondered if the porter had done this because of Josh's generous tip, or if he'd been told to inspect his belongings. Well, if the man had been looking for something, there was nothing to be gleaned from his clothes, other than where he went shopping.

Josh picked up the phone and ordered a plate of fruit and cheese, peasant bread and a bottle of locally brewed Zhigulevskoye beer. Next, he sat down at the ornate desk; it was made from Siberian birch, and Josh guessed it had been made especially for the hotel when the place was built in the 1930s. Josh opened his briefcase and started making notes on a yellow pad. He began with a recap of the conversation with Krasnovsky, a description of the general, and then a list of questions. As a postscript, he wrote the names of all the individuals who were either members of the 66th Joint Observation Group, whether they were alive or dead, and where their careers had taken them. At the bottom of the list was the name Lev Mogen. Josh wondered if and how he was involved?

His meal arrived. He ate as he continued making notes. The hearty flavor of chunks of the aromatic cheeses on crusty dark bread brought back memories of his first father-in-law—Artur Vishinski. He would have said, "This is *real* bread."

Josh was about to turn out the light when he remembered the envelope in his briefcase. Holding it up to the light, he saw it contained a large card. After slitting it open, he dumped the card and saw a neatly handwritten note.

Lev Mogen suggested we meet sooner than later. Dinner on Wednesday? If that suits you, be in the lobby at 1830. If not, please leave a note in a sealed envelope at the concierge desk with a more convenient time.
Avram Gutman

The note from the Israelis didn't surprise him. Someone in the Pentagon or their own sources had probably alerted them he was headed for Moscow. He concluded that Feltzer had let Mogen know.

Tuesday, June 18ᵗʰ, 1991, 0800 Local Time, Moscow

At this hour in the morning, Josh was surprised at how few people were in the embassy. In most shore-based Navy units, the workday started at 0730 and COs, XOs and department heads were usually at their desks well before.

Given the choice of taking the elevator or the stairs, Josh turned to Velasquez and said, "Stairs. It'll help us live longer." It also gave him the opportunity to assess alternate routes.

Just before they entered the conference room on the third floor, Gunnery Sergeant Velasquez handed Josh a sheet of paper. "Sir, here's your schedule for the rest of the day. You meet the ambassador at 0900. It's not optional." Velasquez realized he might have crossed the line with his tone and his words, but chain of command did not take much regard for niceties.

Josh took both in stride. "O.K., the ambassador at 0900. Then we meet the other attachés. I'll get questions I can't answer, so let's keep it as short as possible. My brief said you and Brown now work for me, which means you work for General Feltzer. I need eyes, ears, and people with good heads on their shoulders. According to what I was told before I got here, you fit the bill."

Gunnery Sergeant Velasquez nodded. He thought, *I am going to like working for this dude.* His "Yes, sir" was heartfelt.

"Good," Josh said. "I need a secure phone, a safe with a combination no one knows but Brown, you, and me, and a secure room I can use as an office. No CIA and no other attachés can have access. I'll tell you what this is about later." In Russian he added, "How's your Russian?"

Velasquez smiled and responded in kind. "Excellent, Captain. When I went into recon, I was a linguist. I speak Spanish, Russian and French, sir."

"Good. My Spanish is so-so, but it's good enough for informal talk. We'll have four languages we can converse in."

"Yes, sir."

"You married?"

"No, sir." Velasquez's answer was emphatic.

"Divorced?"

Another emphatic no.

"Girlfriend here in Moscow?

The gunny didn't hesitate. "No, sir!"

"Confirmed bachelor?"

"Absolutely, sir. I got close to getting married once, but a month before the wedding, she walked away when she realized my first wife was the Marine Corps."

Josh thought, *I'm living through the same problem, being here.* "For the record, Gunny, I'm married with three kids."

"Yes, sir. Your wife is Rebekah and you have two boys— Sasha 15, Sean 10—and a daughter, Sarah, 13."

Damn, he was well briefed. "What about Brown?"

"Sir, he's single too, with no attachments. He's learning Russian but struggling. However, he was the top man in his class at Marine sniper school. If the target is under fifteen hundred meters, one round and it's dead."

"I like him already."

"Sir, may I speak candidly?"

"Gunny, when there's work involved, there's no other way. Go!"

"Well sir, we have a mutual friend in retired Master Chief Jenkins. I called him to get the dirt on you as soon as I found out about this assignment. He said many good things about you and ended by saying he'd cut my balls off with a dull serrated knife if I let anything happen to you. He was the second person who said it. General Feltzer was the first."

Josh laughed. "Next time you talk to the Master Chief, tell him I said hello."

Velasquez stopped by a closed door. "Sir, all the attachés are in this conference room. They're a good group. Some have held operational assignments, but they spend most of their time writing reports on conversations they've had at cocktail parties. Your fruit salad may scare them. Most of these people never met the elephant. In fifteen minutes, I'll knock on the door to say you have an important phone call, and then I'll escort you to the communication center with direct lines. I need you off the phone at oh eight fifty, because it takes five minutes to get to the ambassador's office and he doesn't like his appointments to be late. And sir, if you piss him off, he calls the President, whom he counts as a friend."

Josh knew Velasquez use of the word 'elephant' was a reference to the attachés not being combat veterans, i.e. they never were shot at. "Got it."

Eighteen minutes later, Josh was dialing a number from memory in a tiny communications chamber. With the door closed, it felt like a coffin standing on its end. The soundproofed cubicle had a shelf for a desk, a single chair, and a secure phone.

The phone rang six times before a well-remembered sleepy voice answered, "Cabot...."

Josh looked at his watch—it was 0028 in the morning in Tampa, Florida. "Good morning Marty, its Josh. I'll initiate secure while you wake up. What I'm about to tell you will clear all the cobwebs from your brain."

The light on Josh's phone flashed to show that the security level had gone all the way up to Top Secret. It was highly unusual for an apartment to have that kind of security, but this was Marty Cabot, a Navy SEAL who held a special operations billet at Special Operations Command. All Josh knew that Marty's billet had him approving and often being the action officer for covert operations around the world.

"When did you get to Moscow?"

"Yesterday. I need you to dig up everything you can find in the DIA/CIA archives about a KGB Major General by the name of Oleg Krasnovsky. He stopped me in the lobby of the Rossiya Hotel not two hours after I cleared customs. Among other things, he wants to chat about Dieter Stiglitz."

The last two words acted like a combined shot of adrenalin and caffeine. Marty was now fully awake. "Oh, fuck!"

"I figured that name would wake you up." Josh recounted the conversation with Krasnovsky.

When he was done, Marty said, "I'll wake some people up, and hopefully they'll have something by the time I go in to work. Do you have an office number I can call?"

Shit, Josh thought, *I was in too much of a hurry to get a number.* "Not yet. I'll call you by the end of the day today, your time."

Josh hung up the phone and stared at the light gray soundproofing that surrounded him. He felt a sense of foreboding. *How far in over my head am I?* Krasnovsky was the first curveball. *How many more were coming?* This was not flying a helicopter in combat; there he had a degree of control. Here in Moscow, his options were far more constrained, and there was no radar to indicate incoming missiles... unless you counted your intuition. Josh did. That sixth sense had saved his life before, and he had a horrible suspicion it would have to do so again. Soon.

The Same Day, 0944 Local Time, Moscow

On the way back from the ambassador's office, Velasquez took Josh on a tour of the embassy. It took the better part of half and hour, after which they stopped at the cafeteria so Velasquez could fix a cup of coffee, black, while Josh emptied packets of creamer into a cup. Josh added hot chocolate powder before pouring in hot water and stirring it with a wooden stick.

"Maybe I should mention," Josh remarked, "that I'm completely lost."

"No worries, Captain," Velasquez replied. "You'll find your way around here after a day or two. Just remember, your office is behind locked doors waaaaay in the back with the other attachés and the spooks. Sometimes, you'd think the State Department regards this as a leper colony."

"We do make their life difficult at times."

"That's an understatement. Working for you is going to be much more interesting than standing guard."

"It may also be career-threatening."

Velasquez smiled. "I like the pointy edge of the sword, so I'll take that chance!" He looked at Josh. "Sir, are you ready to head back?"

They were about twenty feet down the hall of the secured corridor when Josh heard a voice behind him. "Captain Haman, a word, please?"

Josh turned around to see a brigadier general wearing a green Class A army uniform. "Yes, sir."

Velasquez gave Josh a wry smile as if to say, *have fun.* "I'll be in your office, sir." He hurried off, leaving Josh to follow in the wake of the general. The man had pivoted away before Josh could read his nametag.

The brigadier general strode ahead to his office. By the time Josh entered, the man was standing behind his desk. "Close the door."

No please, no hi. Just a command. With a sense of déjà vu, Josh approached the desk as if he were a midshipman reporting to a senior officer. He stopped three feet from the front edge of the massive wooden desk. Several piles of paper and stacked wire baskets formed a barrier, indicating how busy the embassy kept the general.

"I'm Brigadier General James Grant, senior attaché. Your assignment here was a complete surprise. There's been much head scratching in DIA about why the Navy decided to send another senior officer. We have a full staff. So tell me, why you are here? Your orders were rather vague on the duties you're to perform."

So basically, why the fuck are you here on my turf with no warning? "General, sir," Josh said, "I'm here on a special project. The J3 on the Joint Staff wanted me to work out of the embassy." *See, I can be polite and obtuse too.*

"Captain, every day I get a summary from each branch on their activities. I review all reports before they are forwarded to D.C. No exceptions. Are my requirements clear?"

Josh thought, *I'm not going to answer that question. I'm not a defense attaché and my chain of command goes from me, to Jeff, to General Feltzer to the Chairman of the Joint Chiefs, not up through the DIA like the rest of the attachés.*

"Captain, I didn't hear you answer. Did I make myself clear?"

"General, you did. There is, however, a problem."

"Which is?"

"Sir, I wasn't sent here to work as an attaché. I'm on what can best be described as a special assignment from the chairman of the JCS." *In other words, I don't work for you.*

Grant tapped his desktop with his index finger. "Captain, I am the *senior officer* of the United State military in this country! As a Naval officer, you are a member of the U.S. military, and therefore work for me."

This was familiar territory, unfortunately. "General, sir. When I left the States, Admiral Gainesville made my reporting relationship very clear. I report to him, and he works for the Joint Chief's J3, Lieutenant General Feltzer, who works for the Chairman of the Joint Chiefs."

Grant came around his desk strode with the bearing of a senior commander about to chew out a junior officer. Josh did a proper left face to face Grant.

"*Captain*, why are you in Moscow?" The emphasis was an unsubtle reminder of who outranked whom.

"General, I'm on a special assignment for General Feltzer, sir."

The Army general made a face. "I expect, let me clarify, *require* daily reports by 1700 on your activities of your 'special assignment'. *Nothing* goes back to the Pentagon without my approval. Understood?"

"Yes, sir, I understand." *I just can't comply with your requirements. Shit, I've been here less than twenty-four hours and already I have two problems. A shoe clerk brigadier general is giving me orders I can't obey, and a KGB major general wants to 'talk'. I don't know which is going to give me more headaches.*

"One last thing," the general said. "I run a tight ship in order to prevent any incidents. I don't want any attachés sent home *persona non grata* for stepping over the line or arrested for committing a crime. I understand you spent a lot of time in the special operations community. I view them as a bunch of loose cannons who like to operate on their own. Word from the Pentagon is there are many flag officers who would like to see you out of the Navy, or in a cell at Leavenworth. So if I have to send you home, it will be the end of your career, and you may end up sitting in front of a judge at a court martial."

General, what leadership! Threats in the first meeting, and you don't know my mission or me. You're a typical rear echelon motherfucker.

"Sir, thank you for your guidance."

"You didn't hear a word I said, did you?"

"General, I heard and understood every word."

"But you are going to do what you want?"

General, you don't really expect me to answer that question. "General, I'm sure you are busy. Is there anything else?"

Grant shook his head. "Get out of here. Just remember, I'm watching. The first time you screw up, you'll be on a plane back to the States."

"Understood, sir." Josh executed an about-face that would have many any Marine drill instructor smile with pride and marched out of the office.

Wednesday, June 19th, 1991, 0916 Local Time, Tel Aviv
Lev Mogen stood in front of a whiteboard that held two rows of surveillance photos. He picked up a black marker and wrote under one row:

183

James Broughton, FBI—undercover or traitor?

The second row showed Safdar taking pictures of bridges. Under it, he wrote:

Mohammed Safdar, Hezbollah

Why are you in the U.S.?

Are those bridges your targets?

Are they linked to the sale of ZBV2s?

Lev stared at the board and wondered how his questions fit with three facts.

Fact one: A source in a firm that processed SWIFT transfers for banks had informed the Mossad that thirty-six million U.S. dollars had been transferred to a bank in Switzerland from a bank in the Arabian Gulf. The remarks section of the transfer required notification to be sent to a customer in Finland. Finland was close to Leningrad. Some Soviets are allowed to travel to the Finnish capital. Lev wrote on a pad:

Find out who?

Fact two: Another source in the bowels of the Soviet Army's Rocket Artillery forces said papers were being prepared to allow the transfer of six ZBV2s from a depot in Uzbekistan to a destruction facility. The source reported the destruction facility did not exist. Next questions:

Where are they going?

Why only six and not a larger number?

Six factors neatly into thirty-six.

Fact three: The Iranian nuclear program needed help to build an electrical power plant. It was far from being able to build a bomb, even with imported Russian talent. More questions:

Do the Iranians want to take a shortcut and mount ZBV2s on a missile?

Do they have, or can they hire, the skills?

MOSCOW AIRLIFT

The Same Day, 1956 Local Time, Moscow

The admiral was unconscious when he went out the eleventh floor window. The rush of air past his face and the sense of his impending demise brought him back to consciousness as he cartwheeled through the air. He realized he only had a second to live. He hoped he would die quickly without much pain.

In the still evening air, passersby heard his bones snap on impact. Blood from his shattered head turned the concrete dark red.

Police were stationed at guard posts around the complex near Patriarch Ponds. They came running when they heard witnesses screaming. The police surrounded the body in an attempt to keep the crowd away from the scene.

Lieutenant Colonel Arkady Kishniev arrived ten frantic minutes later, his ears still ringing from the wail of the siren atop the police car. He knelt beside the mess that had been a body. Looking up, he could see an open window on the top floor.

Kishniev glanced at the other *militsiya* nearby. "Who is he?"

The sergeant held out a folder containing the dead man's identification. "Admiral Sergei Dolgikh, commander of the Soviet Navy, sir."

Arkady pointed at two *militsiya* standing behind the sergeant. "You and you. Go upstairs, but don't go into, nor let anyone in or out of the apartment. Don't touch anything. I'll be up in a few minutes." Seeing their hesitation, he commanded, "Go, *go, GO!*"

Still on his knees, Arkady gestured and asked the crowd to move back. When they did the opposite, two *militsiya* drew their pistols. The onlookers still didn't retreat. Arkady wasn't sure if he saw defiance or hatred in their eyes.

Hostility toward the police was not something new. In the Soviet Union, the police forces are part of the Ministry of Internal Affairs. To many Soviet citizens, the *militsiya* and their brethren in the KGB were not to be trusted because of their roles in Stalin's purges and the show trials of the 1930s. Both agencies were known for torture and fabricating evidence to frame innocent citizens.

Arkady stood up and placed himself between the crowd and the nervous *militsiya*. The last thing he wanted was to have a scared police officer fire into the crowd because he felt threatened. In a soft voice, he told the guards to holster their weapons. They hesitated, then saw their sergeant nod approval.

Turning to the throng, Arkady addressed them directly. "Okay everyone, go home. An admiral jumped out of a window and died. He just reduced the potential number of pensioners by one. Go home and we'll clean up the mess."

By the time the coroner arrived, only a few hardcore citizens remained. Arkady gave the head of the forensic team phone numbers where he could be reached after the autopsy was finished. He checked that they had no questions, then he went into the building.

The two *militsiya* stationed themselves by the door to the three-bedroom flat. They reported that no one had come out or gone in after they'd arrived. Arkady studied the doorframe and handle: no sign of forced entry. Inside, papers were scattered all over the floor, and a desk chair was overturned on its back.

Arkady squatted to read some of the papers, but didn't touch them. *Nothing immediately noteworthy.* He stood again and examined the pictures and memorabilia in the room, trying to get a feel for the dead man.

The files on the floor and desk dealt with personnel and military matters. One was a file of reports on the readiness of Navy ships. Another contained reports of shortages of ammunition, fuel, parts and uniforms. Arkady had spent two years as a draftee in the Army, but he couldn't tell how bad the shortages really were. *Were they bad enough to drive the commander of the Soviet Navy to suicide?*

Whom should he ask? If Arkady followed official channels, the military would declare the papers state secrets and not tell him anything after they were confiscated. He had to find a way to learn their significance while protecting them from compromise. Carefully, he gathered the papers, put them into folders from Dolgikh's desk, then stuffed them into a soft-sided briefcase he found on the floor.

The room at large was the neat, not the messy jumble of a place that had been ransacked. Arkady's initial opinion was that any assailants had been after Dolgikh the man, not what was in his office. If they'd wanted something specific, they would have beaten him until he gave it to them. There was no splattered blood. The overturned desk chair and scattered papers might have been the result of a struggle, or the frustration of a man about to jump out the window. Perhaps the object of a search was small enough to be carried away without anyone noticing. If it were a small diary or one of those new computer diskettes, it was gone and Arkady might never know that it existed or what it contained.

* * *

A few minutes later, Captain Dorotkin came into the apartment and reported that the *militsiya* had gathered potential witnesses: neighbors who were home in their apartments, and people who'd been passing in front of the building. Each would be interviewed by one of Arkady's investigators; some might be brought to police headquarters for a more thorough interrogation. So far, though, no one had said they'd seen strangers enter the building. Furthermore, the concierge swore he had logged everyone who came in.

Conceivably, the killers were arrogant enough to log in, perhaps using false names, so as not to raise alarm. At the very least, it was a place to start his investigation.

Arkady thanked the man and went back to trying to visualize the admiral's last moments. He was still thinking when a *militsiya* officer arrived, escorting Dolgikh's wife, Vera. Speaking sincere words of comfort, Arkady quickly moved her out into the hall, away from the office. Vera broke down and sobbed. She was, Arkady noted, in her early sixties, a hundred and eighty centimeters in height and fifty kilograms in weight, still slim and attractive. She was far too small to have shoved the tall, heavy admiral out the window without help.

When the woman could finally speak, it was with a mix of anger and sorrow. "Why did this happen? He was such a good man. Sergei would never just leap out a window. He had so much to live for! Our sixth grandchild was just born."

"I don't believe he jumped," Arkady said. "But if I am to catch the criminals, Mrs. Dolgikh, I have to ask you some questions."

She took a deep breath and wiped the tears off her cheeks. "Go ahead. I have nothing to hide."

"How long have you been married?"

"Forty-seven years. It would have been forty-eight this September."

"Do you know anyone who'd want to kill your husband?"

"No!" she said fiercely. "He was straightforward, honest. He didn't play politics. He joked he got this assignment so the KGB leaders would not have to travel to Severomorsk or Vladivostok to watch over him. The sailors loved my Sergei. He got calls all the time from those who he'd helped to promote. Deep inside, I think he was happy the Soviet Union was trying to become more democratic and open. He'd seen so many abuses by the government."

"Do you know what he was working on?"

"No. But, he was very concerned about some of the readiness reports from units around the country. I heard him talking to one of his friends. He said the country is dying from a cancer and no one seems to care."

"Do you know what he meant by a cancer?"

"He was afraid some of those in power want to return to the old days, as it was under Stalin. He also worried about corruption. He said our shipyards turn out crap and Soviet sailors die unnecessarily because of it. Sergei believed some of our leaders spent more time stealing from the people than running the country."

Arkady tried not to react. In the Soviet Union, such statements could lead to jail time. Or worse. Suicide was looking less and less likely. "Vera, did Sergei have friends outside the Navy?"

"General Dmitri Ulyanov and he were friends. The general came to our flat many times. He and Sergei would talk for hours at the kitchen table. When they did, I always went into the bedroom to read, so I didn't hear their conversations. Oh, and Vasily Beriev, the defense minister, occasionally came for dinner. President Gorbachev used to call my Sergei all the time! Apart from those three, most of Sergei's friends were in the Navy. Am I being helpful?"

"Definitely." Arkady closed his notebook. "I'd like you to make me a list of all his friends and how often they met with your husband or talked outside work. It doesn't have to be anything formal. I'll come back to pick it up tomorrow afternoon around three."

"Will it get them or me in trouble?"

Arkady shook his head. "I'm not KGB, and I'm not looking to blame someone for Russia's troubles. I believe your husband was murdered; my job is to find out who."

189

As Arkady slowly returned to his car, the question that bothered him was, why? Was this something to do with payoffs... drugs... weapons... political favors? Or, had Sergei Dolgikh been as straight and honest as his wife believed?

Perhaps *too* straight and honest.

The Same Day, 2107 Local Time, Moscow

Josh had been eager to meet Avram Gutman, once he'd checked with Lev to verify that Avram was real, not Memorex. The agent met him promptly in the lobby. After dinner and small talk, they departed to walk around Red Square, away from any microphones and eavesdroppers in the hotel.

Avram had just summarized what the Mossad knew about Iranian efforts to buy nuclear warheads, and about a terrorist organization called Sword of Allah. Josh had agreed to forward the information to Gainesville via the diplomatic pouch. Then Gutman dropped his first real bombshell: the Israelis wanted help in stopping the transfer of nukes, and Lev wanted him involved. That suddenly took Josh's mission from gathering and reporting information to a possible special operation.

Josh was still digesting how to answer this question when Avram put his arm on his Josh's shoulder. Bombshell two: Avram was Rebekah's cousin. His father was her natural father's brother!

No matter how he tried, he couldn't be sure knowing his wife was related to Gutman wouldn't color his judgment. Would telling her compromise his mission? Did Rebekah know Gutman was in the Mossad *and* in Moscow? If she did, why hadn't she told him?

Thursday, June 20th, 1991, 1915 Local Time, Moscow

The summer sun was about a third of the way down the horizon. According to the calendar on the wall in Josh's temporary office, sunset was not until 2120. Twilight wouldn't start for another couple of hours. It was a subtle reminder how far north the Soviet capital was located. The twenty-four degree difference between San Diego's thirty-two degrees north and Moscow's fifty-six meant that the Southern California city was about fourteen hundred miles south of Moscow. After the sun went down, Moscow's temperature would drop from the low seventies into the mid-fifties. It was why Josh had a light windbreaker draped over his shoulders.

He was on his way to meet with Krasnovsky. Josh wondered if this encounter could possibly be as surprising as yesterday's meeting with Avram; he hoped not. *What does Krasnovsky really know about Stiglitz and Red Hand? Maybe he was just fishing for information.*

As he walked, Josh reviewed what little the CIA and DIA had on Krasnovsky. Undoubtedly, a KGB major general wanting to have a private dinner with Josh had started conversations in Langley and the Pentagon about why. The local CIA station chief had been dead set against the dinner, believing it would compromise Josh. He'd gone so far as to announce that the meeting could be grounds for declaring Josh *persona non grata* and pulling him back stateside, under investigation.

General Feltzer had let Josh decide. So here Josh was, alone on a Moscow street, headed to a dinner with a stranger who worked for the enemy's version of the CIA. As Josh left the embassy, Velasquez had reminded him that Master Chief Jenkins was holding him responsible for Josh's safety. Velazquez also pointed out that he didn't command the assets to raid the Lubyanka to get Josh's ass out.

Velazquez and Brown followed Josh at a discrete distance. They wore clothes made in the Soviet Union, giving them a grubby appearance that let them blend in with the locals. The two Marines planned to hang out in the park across the street from the restaurant. When Josh came out, they would watch for a tail on the way back to the Rossiya. They were not worried about being accosted. In the Soviet Union, people rarely spoke to strangers; you never knew if they were from the KGB or some other government agency spying on its citizens.

The small neighborhood restaurant was on the corner, with a couple of tables set out on the sidewalk. Despite Josh's attempt to look like a local, several patrons gave him the once over as he paused on the threshold. Pungent blue cigarette smoke assaulted his nostrils. Peering through the haze, he looked for Krasnovsky.

"Ahhhhhh, Captain Haman, I'm so glad you came." Josh turned to see a man wearing a light blue shirt and faded gray slacks. Major General Krasnovsky was definitely here incognito. The general held out his hand and spoke in Russian. "I'm happy you didn't recognize me without my uniform. My camouflage is good, no?"

"*Da.* I hope I don't look too much like a Westerner."

"I'm afraid, Captain, you do. People in Russia would kill you for your jeans alone, if they could figure out how to make sure your blood wouldn't stain them."

Josh smiled at the Soviet general's attempt at humor. He'd been briefed on the thriving black market in Moscow for genuine western made goods. Much of what was sold in stores was cheap fakes made in countries where adherence to intellectual property rights and laws were largely ignored.

Krasnovsky led Josh to a table in the back of the room. When they sat, Josh suppressed a smile of genuine amusement as both of them automatically positioned their chairs to place their backs against the wall to give them a view of the entire room. Krasnovsky opened a bottle of sparkling water and filled two glasses before he emptied it. *He's showing me the water is safe to drink.*

"What language do you prefer?" Krasnovsky asked. "English, German, Russian?"

Josh replied in Russian. "You choose, General."

Krasnovsky spoke in his native tongue, rationalizing that if they spoke another language and someone overheard them, it could be reported.

"Relax, Captain. I'm not going to drug you or have you arrested. I have information to share, and you have something I want. We can trade, no?"

"Maybe." Josh struggled to keep his body language and tone neutral.

"*Doroga lozhka k obyedu.* That is an old Russian proverb: 'A spoon is valuable only at dinner.' In other words, timing is everything."

Josh couldn't help smiling at the Russian's hint.

Encouraged, Krasnovsky continued. "Before the Ministry of Foreign Affairs issued your diplomatic visa, they asked if the KGB had a dossier on you. We wouldn't want to let a known spy into the country." Krasnovsky chuckled. "I got to read your entire dossier so I could assure the foreign ministry that you aren't a spy. I must say, however, your dossier is very interesting reading. The Vietnamese called you 'the ghost' because they could never shoot you down. You flew a helicopter with the call sign Big Mother 40. I love that name! I believe you captured a Russian officer by the name of Alexei Koniev during an attack on a missile base in North Vietnam. No?"

"Go on." Josh wasn't going to give Krasnovsky anything to work with. He was trying to decide if he would even engage in conversation. Right now, he was trying to be deadpan and non-committal.

"During a raid in 1976, you captured the German terrorist Dieter Stiglitz. Stealing a Mi-2 helicopter and flying it to Denmark was brilliant. The East Germans, even with our help, never learned how you got commandos into their country. They did figure out that the men who came on the ferry from Sweden weren't the ones who drove out. The Stasi were...not amused."

Josh gritted his teeth and forced himself not to move. He was sure he blinked. *What else do these KGB bastards know? I can't deny this, but I don't have to confirm it either.*

"Maybe you will tell me some day. Maybe you won't. A colonel by the name of Grünewald was in charge of Stasi's covert operations in West Germany back then, and I was one of the KGB officers assigned work with him. Over time, we became good friends. Grünewald retired in 1988 at the rank of major general. I would be pleased to be able to tell him how it all happened before he dies." Krasnovsky sighed. "But alas, he was a chain smoker. He has lung cancer now and only a few months to live."

Josh tried to remain stone-faced, but the words just popped out of his mouth. "Why are you telling me this? You still haven't told me why I am here."

Krasnovsky waved his hand philosophically. "*Svoya rubashka blizhe k telu.* That's another Russian proverb: one's shirt is closer to the body. It means I have to be careful to look out for my own interests... but please be patient with a man who, like you, considers himself a warrior. In the Great Patriotic War, I joined an armored unit in early 1942 and helped push the Germans out my country. I first saw Berlin through the commander's periscope of a T-34 tank."

Krasnovsky took a sip of his mineral water before he changed subjects. "Captain Haman, if we can, as you Americans like to say, make a deal, then I can share information which I am sure will help you."

"Like what?"

"I am well connected within the KGB and the Foreign Ministry. It is no secret my country is in trouble. Many forces are at work: some good, most bad." Krasnovsky pursed his lips and waved his hand. "I can help your country understand what is really happening in the Soviet Union. Your government would like to know this, yes?"

Oh, shit!!! Has the KGB been listening in on the conversations I had with Jeff and General Feltzer? "It depends what you tell me."

"Understood." Krasnovsky leaned forward and spoke softly. "When I saw you were coming to the Soviet Union, I read your file, which led me to other related ones. This is called connecting the dots, yes? The more dots you connect, the more you learn. I know who ordered the killing and who killed your in-laws and your first wife. Both live here in Moscow."

Josh flinched as if someone had just stabbed him with a knife. Natalie's killer had left a card identifying the assassin him as KGB. He'd often dreamed about becoming Natalie's avenging angel. The possibilities of what he would do to the killer raced through his mind. He hoped Krasnovsky didn't see him flush with thoughts of revenge. "So what do you want from my country?"

"Ahhh, you don't waste time, do you?"

"No, General. There's no need to dance."

"I want money to fund my retirement. I think the Soviet Union may collapse. The cost of living will go up, so I'll need lots of money. Defecting to another country is possible, but I'm Russian to my core. I'd be unhappy living someplace else." Krasnovsky cocked his head slightly. "I prefer to stay."

"And the KGB would be unhappy if you left?" Josh didn't want to use the word defect.

"If the country is falling apart, those running the KGB may be too busy trying to stay alive, and my departure would be one of many. Of course, I would rather live someplace else than be stood against a wall and shot for imagined crimes."

"Even assuming my country or I have any interest in this, you know I can't commit to anything." *Why did I add the 'or I?' Because he dangled a very powerful piece of bait on what could be a rusty hook. The question is, will I take it and get tetanus?*

"Captain, I connected three dots that tell me otherwise. I found dot one while reading your file. It tells me you're a resourceful officer; if anyone can arrange this money, you can. Dot two is the urgency with which the United States wanted you accredited. It suggests your mission is sponsored by someone very high in your command structure. Dot three is personal." His already deep voice lowered even further. "If I were you, I would want to know who killed my wife and in-laws."

This is one very smart officer who knows what buttons to push.

"General, you have to give me something to get the attention of my government. Saying that you have information to trade is all very nice, but how do I know it's true?"

Krasnovsky sat back and rubbed his chin. "Before we get to that, I have one condition. My name must not be shared with either the CIA or the FBI. They both have leaks who get people like me killed."

That did it. Josh was hooked. He could almost feel the rusty iron enter his mouth. Double agents, traitors, and moles were a threat to his mission. Josh knew his country had benefited from the information Colonel Alexei Koniev had shared after his defection, and that marked him as a traitor in the eyes of the KGB. Walker's treason and giving cryptographic codes to the Russians allowed them to give some information to the Soviets. There was no doubt in his mind that the Soviets gave details of U.S. air strikes in North Vietnam and had caused many American pilots to be shot down. Some were captured, and many died. Searing memories flashed through Josh's mind:

watching pilots shot down because the North Vietnamese had known *exactly* when and where they'd be. Josh forced himself to relax and unclench his jaw and fists. "Can you give me examples?"

"Certainly. The KGB executed four of its officers for spying on behalf of the USA—Dimitri Polyakov, Leonid Poleshchuk, Vladimir Pigasov, and Boris Yutzin. All were identified by a Soviet agent in your CIA or FBI. Start with these and check them out. I can get more names if you really need them."

Josh mentally repeated the names several times to get them memorized. "All right, we'll give you a code name. I'll keep the number of people who know your real name to a minimum. I'm guessing less than six or seven."

"Excellent... Let me tell you more. There are very senior officers in both the Army and the KGB who are very unhappy with Gorbachev and his policies. I'm not sure which they resent more—his policies and attempt to grant our people more freedom, or his dissolving the Soviet Union and creating the Russian Federation."

"This isn't news."

Krasnovsky nodded slowly, then took a sip of tea. "But your analysts don't know the names of men who may be plotting a coup. I do."

* * *

It was still twilight when Josh and the two Marines emerged from the tube station on the Number 3 line near Moscow's Red Square. Across from the entrance, the twenty-one stories of the thirty-two-hundred-room Rossiya Hotel loomed large. As Josh trod the cobblestones, he again felt the strange sensation he was being followed. He told the other two he was going to check. He headed toward St. Basil's Cathedral and after a few hundred feet, he stopped abruptly and swung around. No one looked surprised or as if they were following him. Nevertheless, the feeling remained.

Josh wondered if he'd even know what a tail looked like in the Soviet Union. Things were different here, and had been for a very long time.

Josh paused at the entrance of the Rossiya to let four couples come out; it gave him another chance to look around. Again, there was no obvious tail. He put his hands on his hips as a signal to Brown and Velasquez that he was in for the night. As he entered the hotel, his mind kept telling him paranoia was fine, so long as it didn't take control of the mission.

Friday, June 21st, 1991, 1909 Local Time, Moscow

Admiral Dolgikh had been murdered. No other explanation fit and Arkady Kishniev still had no suspects. In two days of interviews, all the men on Vera Dolgikh's list expressed shock and surprise, but no one had offered any helpful observation or recollection.

When Arkady had called to make an appointment with Beriev, the Minister's secretary had taken his number and made no commitment. Arkady had been surprised to get a return call thirty minutes later, telling him a member of the Minister's staff would be waiting to escort him to the office at 1000. Nothing of note had happened at the meeting —the defense minister's body language indicated he was being open and truthful, but he'd had nothing to offer other than that Dolgikh would be missed.

Perhaps Beriev had made a phone call. After lunch, Dimitri Ulyanov called Arkady, asking him to meet for a drink on his way home. As he approached the bar Ulyanov had specified, Arkady wondered if this meeting would make a difference in the investigation.

The watering hole was dark and smoky. A dozen men sat at the bar drinking in a steady, desultory manner. Rachmaninoff played in the background. The general waved at Arkady from a table in the back corner. A bottle of vodka and two glasses were already in place. Ulyanov stood as Arkady approached; they shook hands and exchanged polite greetings. As soon as they were both seated, Ulyanov filled the glasses.

"To Sergei Dolgikh: a very good man, a friend, and a first rate Naval officer."

Arkady touched the rim of his glass to the general's. "Sergei Dolgikh." Both men emptied their glasses.

Over a second round of drinks, Ulyanov asserted that Dolgikh had not been suicidal. The general refilled and emptied his third glass of vodka, then grimaced as he put the glass down with the air of a man who had to force himself not to pour a fourth. Ulyanov said, "Some of those in power don't like the direction our country is heading. I fear they may try to take power by a coup. Sergei's death may be their first move."

"Do you know who?"

"I have my suspicions, but no proof." The general poured a fourth glass of vodka and drained it. As he put the glass down, he stood. "I can't trust anyone on the general staff to lead the investigation. You, however, are an experienced investigator with an excellent reputation. Find me proof, and I will take care of those responsible. Then perhaps Sergei Dolgikh's soul will rest in peace." He sighed heavily. "But I doubt it. There is no one who will look out for the Navy as he did. Some men are hard to replace."

The Same Day, 1217 Local Time, New York City

The sea breeze was just enough to cause the tassels on the umbrellas to flutter. The smell of the Atlantic Ocean hung lightly around the table. From where Broughton sat, he could see Governor's Island where the Coast Guard had its base. Closer, Lady Liberty's green coat contrasted with the blue sky. To the right of the island where the statue stood, Broughton could see Ellis Island; two of Broughton's grandparents had entered the United States through the Ellis Island facility, as part of the flood of Irish immigrants in the late 1800s. The facility had closed in 1954 and had been turned into a museum only last year.

Broughton loved the view. He could sit for hours, watching the ferries ply their trade and sailboats heel as their sails filled with wind.

"I'm sorry I'm late."

Broughton turned to see Mohammed Safdar starting to pull out a chair. The chair legs screeched as they scraped along the cement. "Not a problem," Broughton said. "I enjoy the view." He reached for the pitcher of lemonade and poured the Palestinian a glass.

"Thank you." Safdar took a long sip.

Neither man said anything for several minutes after the waiter took their order. Broughton let the other man initiate the conversation. Finally, Safdar murmured, "So what do you have for me?"

"Copies of the reports from FBI investigations into terrorist organizations. They're wrapped in the newspaper." Broughton tapped the folded newspaper held down by a glass ashtray. "You have nothing to worry about. No awareness of your activities."

"Excellent. We have to end the influence the Jews in this country and return our land to its rightful owners. We will ensure that as long as Zionists guide American leaders, American citizens will die. Eventually, the people will get the message."

"Be careful, Mohammed," Broughton warned. "Killing hundreds or thousands may cause a reaction you may not like."

"We'll take that chance. No one has listened to us since 1948. Palestinians are living in squalor in camps in Syria, Lebanon and Jordan. It's time they went home."

Neither man paid attention to a nearby young couple with a baby carriage. However, the hood of the carriage was a parabolic antenna for a very sensitive microphone. A tape recorder was hidden under the doll used instead of a real baby. Leaning on the railing, the father aimed his camera at his wife. In reality, he was using the full magnification of his 110 to 300 millimeter lens to take pictures of Jim Broughton and Mohammed Safdar.

A third man in the café rested his video camera on a bench so that it was aimed at the two men and recorded their faces. Later, a trilingual lip reader at the Israeli embassy would translate their words into a transcript.

Chapter 11
Old Flame

Saturday, June 22nd, 1991, 1945 Local Time, Moscow

In a formal letter, General Grant ordered all of the attachés to attend the embassy's reception honoring the fiftieth anniversary of the day the Soviet Union entered World War II on the side of the allies. The reception was held at Spaso House, the historic building that has been the U.S. Ambassador's residence since 1933. Originally built in 1913 by the industrial magnate Nikolay Vtorov, the structure got its name from Spasopeskovskaya Square across the street. In 1917, Vtorov joined the Bolshevik Revolution and was assassinated by an unknown attacker in 1918. Spaso House and all of Vtorov's factories were seized by the Bolsheviks, and some are still operated by the Soviet government.

General Grant's order had specified wearing mess dress. Josh had known he'd be expected to have a full suite of dress uniforms for formal events, so before flying out from Washington, he'd called Rebekah. With his guidance, she'd found all the miniature medals, wings, studs, cummerbund, cuff links, blouse and pants for all his uniforms and had shipped them by Federal Express to Moscow. The gear had arrived the next day at the Marriott Hotel in Crystal City.

Now, as Josh approached Gunnery Sergeant Velasquez in the Hotel Rossiya's lobby, the Marine came to attention. Since Josh was wearing his dress blues and white hat, Velasquez rendered a proper crisp salute, with his tucked thumb aligned with his fingers and touching his eyebrow, his elbow parallel to the ground. Velasquez was a Marine, and saluting was a sign of respect to a fellow warrior. "Good evening, Captain."

Josh's return salute would have made a drill instructor proud. "Good evening, Gunny. Are you ready to do battle with the buffet table, wine, and vodka martinis?"

Velasquez smiled. "Sir, I prefer a good shot of José Cuervo Silver tequila myself. Sergeant Brown is waiting in the car."

"Excellent."

On the back seat was a notebook with pictures and biographies of the Soviet and allied officers Josh was supposed to meet and greet. He'd already spent an hour with the book earlier in the afternoon; after a few pages, the faces began to look alike. Putting it on the seat was Velasquez's hint to study more.

At the entrance, Josh paused as he handed his bridge cover to a woman from the embassy staff. She gave him a plastic card with a number so he could retrieve it later. He tucked the card into a pocket, then proceeded into the reception.

He surveyed it as he would a battlefield. Josh was surprised by how many Soviet officers were in attendance, as well as officers from U.S. allies in Europe and Asia. Nearly everyone he'd met at the embassy was present. In all likelihood, General Grant had assigned the junior most attaché to take attendance, and anyone who didn't show would be chastised. The general himself had not yet made his entrance, nor had the ambassador. No doubt, Grant had arranged to meet the ambassador in private first—face time with the ambassador and making a grand entrance together were more important than greeting each guest when they arrived.

Most of the Soviets were clustered around the two buffet tables in the center of the room. Josh deemed that the tables held enough food to feed the residents of a Russian apartment complex for a week. One table bore a majestic prime rib, along with fish, poultry, pork, and vegetable sides. The other had a selection of cold cuts, cheeses, and fruit. Against each end wall, bartenders served European and American beers, wines, and whiskeys along with the best gins and vodkas. Velasquez said the toasts would begin once the dessert tables were rolled out and the ambassador was sure everyone had a drink in his or her hand.

Between the buffet tables and the walls, the embassy staff had set up rows of small bar tables along with larger tables with chairs. Each was covered with starched white tablecloths bearing the seal of the United States.

Josh said, "Care to join me for a drink on Uncle Sam's nickel, Gunny?"

"My pleasure, sir." Only Marine guards who could speak Russian were invited. The others were assigned guard duty.

Drink in hand, Josh turned to the sergeant. "I guess I need to follow my orders and mingle with our Soviet guests. Learn what I can."

"Yes, sir. You're learning the new attaché drill. The Soviet officers know you just arrived in Moscow, so they'll try to get you to tell why you're here. Think of yourself as a new toy just given to a roomful of five-year-olds."

"Sounds like fun."

"Expect to be approached by sharks smelling fresh blood in the water. Your best move is to initiate conversation with a Soviet officer of your rank or higher. That tells the rest you're 'taken,' so to speak. The Russian will invite others to come and join you as he sees fit. If you need help, just give me a nod. By the time I get to you, I'll have come up with a reason to pull you away."

"Deal. Wish me luck."

"You won't need any, sir."

Two hours later, Josh looked at his watch. He'd survived conversations with a Russian admiral and two captains and he was ready to leave. He spotted Velasquez and waved him over. "Gunny, let's have another drink before I head to the hotel."

"Yes, sir."

They were halfway to the bar when Josh stopped abruptly. He stared as if he'd seen a ghost.

"Something wrong, sir?"

"Velasquez," he said, and cleared his throat, which had gone suddenly dry. "I'm either about to make a fool of myself or to reintroduce myself to a woman I haven't seen since 1970. Can you find us a private table for two?"

Josh didn't wait for acknowledgement. He headed in the direction of a Eurasian woman wearing an emerald green cocktail dress. She was at the buffet table, putting a piece of chicken on a bed of rice.

A single word came out of Josh's mouth as his heart pounded. "Danielle?"

Danielle Debenard looked at the six-foot tall American who'd addressed her. He looked familiar. *Could it be...?* She'd never seen him in mess dress, or with hair graying along the temples.

For a moment, Josh's heart sank, afraid he was wrong, or worse, that she didn't remember him.

"*Mon dieu.* Josh Haman." There was no questioning in her voice, just the well-controlled recognition of a fact.

Josh nodded. "*C'est moi...*"

"It's been a very long time." Hand trembling, Danielle put her plate down between trays on the buffet.

"Yes, it has," Josh said. "It must be twenty years since I saw you last."

Josh stepped forward and they hugged tightly. When they separated, Danielle stepped back awkwardly. "The years have been kind to you."

"And you as well. You're just as beautiful as I remember. How's your father?"

"Older and as difficult as ever, but he's well. Papa lives in the south of France near Toulon. He says he needs the warmth to keep his old bones from getting cold. Really, it's because he's living near his girlfriend." Her black eyes still sparkled, just as Josh remembered.

He'd been captivated by Danielle from his very first sight of her. They'd met in 1970 at a cocktail party in Singapore. The dress she'd wore then was almost the same color as the one she wore now: an elegant contrast with her brown skin, exotic eyes, and Eurasian features.

"Danielle, do you have time to talk?"

"Of course. I'm here with the French attachés, but if they need me they'll find me."

Josh searched the room and spotted Velasquez. "Gunnery Sergeant Velasquez has a private table for us over in the corner."

Josh's head was swimming, so he didn't notice Danielle's awkward pivot. As they walked to the table, however, he saw her pronounced limp. He held his tongue as a smiling Velasquez pulled out Danielle's chair for her, then disappeared toward the bar. As soon as they were seated, Josh picked up Danielle's hand. "I heard you were captured by the Pathet Lao. Then nothing. I tried to find out what happened to you but never had any luck."

In fact, Josh had barely been restrained from barging into Laos and committing an act of war with a rescue mission.

Danielle struggled to find middle ground between emotion and sounding too cold or clinical. "When the Pathet Lao attacked our plantation, I was shot when I went to help my mother. After two weeks in a field hospital, we were taken to Re-Education camp #3 near what was then North Vietnam. My father and I were kept there three years." She let her voice trail off rather than reciting the exact number of days. "But we escaped. Eventually. When I returned to France, I sent letters your fleet post office box, but they all came back stamped 'Addressee not at this address.'"

"Sorry. By then, I was back in the States. How are your brothers and little sister?"

Danielle's jaw tightened noticeably before she spoke. "My brothers are fine. One lives in Paris and the other is in Singapore. How long will you be in Moscow?"

Josh knew better than to point out what she'd omitted. "I'm here a month or two. Are you still a translator?"

"I'm an assistant commercial attaché. At least that's what I am officially." She casually glanced around, making sure no one was close enough to overhear, and raised her hand to her face as if patting her hair, half covering her mouth in the process, so that no one would be able to read her lips. "When we got back to France, the *Corps Diplomatique* suggested I go into intelligence. I'm now an analyst for France's General Directorate for External Security. At events like this, I'm both an interpreter and an analyst." Lowering her hand, she resumed a normal voice. "My tour in Moscow ends in December. Now tell me about *you*. Did you ever marry?"

"I did. I have three children: Sasha is sixteen, Sara is fourteen, and Sean is ten."

"And your wife, is she here?"

"No, Rebekah is back in San Diego."

A French officer came up to the table. After a short conversation, Danielle turned to Josh and fished through the small purse. "I must go, but here's my card. Call during the day and I'll give you my apartment phone number. We have much to talk about."

Josh watched Danielle limp off. He sat at the table for a few minutes, studying and twirling the half-empty wine glass in front of him. *Knowing Danielle, she wants to tell me something, but couldn't or wouldn't do it here. So, what is it?*

Velasquez approached the table. "Captain, who was that?"

"A very old..." Josh started to use the word flame but stopped. "...friend."

Life in Moscow had just got even more complicated.

Sunday, June 23rd, 1991, 1346 Local Time, Moscow

The mild, warm front from the northwest brought a band of booming thundershowers and a rain-filled morning. In the humid air, the large puddles on the uneven sidewalks evaporated slowly. The sunshine was a cause for Muscovites to come out of their flats and enjoy the summer. Winter was only a few months away.

Talyzin wanted to give his driver the day off, but his bodyguard protested it was much too dangerous for the first deputy of the KGB to walk around Moscow alone. As a compromise, the bodyguard agreed to stay a hundred meters away from Piotr as he headed toward the pistol-shaped park south of Moldavskaya.

Two hundred meters into the park, the main path turned ninety degrees. Three picnic tables stood there, topped with wide, weathered planks whose gray color almost matched the cement. Sitting on one side, Vladimir Koskov read his book and sipped from an open bottle of mineral water. Occasionally he glanced at the birds clustered around him, eager for a snack.

Talyzin approached. "Is this seat taken?"

Koskov pushed the Prussian blue bottle of mineral water across the plank. "Have a seat, Piotr. I saved a bottle for you."

"*Spasibo.*"

"Any loose ends?"

Talyzin leaned over the table and spoke in a hushed tone. Even a man in his position couldn't be too careful—he had no idea if there were microphones nearby, and if their conversation was recorded, it would put them both in a cell in the basement of his own headquarters. "I've collected information from my people with access to the investigation. The *militsiya* are convinced the admiral was murdered, but they don't have any leads."

Koskov smiled grimly. "Then I think Maksimov should be next. We'll wait to remove Uylanov."

If Koskov is being this candid, he must have checked for microphones. "Comrade general, I think Schvardze or Grachkov should be next. We can use their deaths as an excuse to implement martial law."

"No, Maksimov should be next. Without him, Ulyanov doesn't trust anyone high up in the GRU. We can do the politicians later. They have no troops; they can't arrest us."

Talyzin scowled. "Maksimov is well protected."

"Just another challenge for your friends."

"Murder or an accident?"

Koskov thought a few seconds. "Murder. It will set off a witch-hunt, and we can spread rumors it was the *mafiya*. If that gets a few of your *mafiya* friends jailed or killed, so be it."

"They'll ask for more money."

Koskov leaned back. "Give them what they want, if it's reasonable. Once we're in power, we can deal with the *mafiya*.

They're leeches sucking the blood out of our country with their drugs. We just need a plan to eliminate them once they cease to be useful."

"I have one."

"Then eliminate Maksimov." Koskov stood and walked leisurely away.

Monday, June 24th, 1991, 0730 Local Time, Moscow

When Josh walked into his office in the embassy, two sets of folded utility uniforms lay on the desk. On their collars, eagles—insignia of rank for a Navy captain—were pinned in the proper position with the beaks pointed in. The gold wings of a Naval Aviator were pinned over the left breast pocket above the embroidered "U.S. Navy." Over the right pocket was embroidered "Haman." Neatly placed between the two sets of utilities was a camouflaged field cap with the Naval officer's crest. A pair of highly polished boots with several pairs of athletic socks spread neatly atop sat on the floor.

"Gunny Velasquez, what's going on here?"

"Field trip, sir. I took the liberty of getting you two sets of BDUs and boots in the proper sizes. Better than walking around in khakis or summer whites."

Josh thought, *I'm not going to ask how he got my size. I'd prefer not to know.* He said, "I thought we were supposed wear the low visibility insignia on BDUs."

"Sir, in the Marine Corps, we only wear the low visibility insignia when we're going into combat. The rest of the time officers proudly wear their rank."

In other words, *Captain, don't be a pussy swabbie!* "Got it," Josh said. "Where are we going?"

"Domodedovo Airport," Velasquez replied. "That's where the food flights coming to Moscow land. The Russians shifted everything away from Sheremetyevo to Domodedovo so the rest of the world won't see the number of planes coming in. Also, Domodedevo has far more ramp space. We'll observe the offloading of several U.S. C-141s and C-5s. I'd like to leave at 0830, sir."

"I'll change after I make a phone call."

"Yes, sir. Rear Admiral Gainesville and Commander Cabot requested callbacks when we return. I've got a secure room arranged later this afternoon."

"Good work. I'll change and meet you outside."

The sergeant took his cue and left. As the door closed, Josh dialed the number on the card Danielle had given him.

* * *

As they pulled away from the embassy, Velasquez turned around in the front passenger seat. "Sir, we're going to take a detour on our official trip to Domodedevo. The KGB and the foreign ministry may get pissed, but since you're supposedly here for a look at the *Deny Famine* operation, we'll be doing our job."

"And what, pray tell, Gunny, do you have in mind?"

"We're going to stop at food distribution sites on the way."

Twenty minutes later, Brown pulled the black Suburban into a space along the curb. "We're a block away from the site, sir. I'll stay with the car while you and the Gunny go have a look."

As soon as they turned the corner, Josh spotted four food lines, each with hundreds, maybe thousands of people. Pairs of armed KGB troops patrolled up and down the lines with their AK-47s held at the ready. At the entry checkpoint, two U.S. Marines waved Josh and Velasquez over. After a smart salute, which Josh returned just as crisply, a sergeant whose name tag read "Bellamy" checked Josh's and Velasquez's ID cards and embassy badges. He handed the badges to his corporal, who logged them in. "Would the captain like a guided tour?"

"Absolutely."

"Sir, please stand by." The sergeant went inside and picked up a radio handset. When he came out, he handed back their documents. "Captain Garcia will be here in a minute."

Josh looked at the lines snaking around the block. Movement was slow but steady. At the makeshift gates where the Russian citizens entered, KGB officers inspected each person's internal passport and their *propiska* or residency permit. *Propiskas* had been implemented under Stalin as an additional means of controlling the movement of Russian citizens. The data in one's *propiska* had to match what was in your internal passport; if it didn't, it was a crime.

Those whose documents didn't match were sent to a holding pen. If the discrepancies were sorted to the satisfaction of the KGB major working in a small shed, the document holder was re-inserted in line. If not, they were carted off for further questioning.

After introductions, Garcia explained the rationing system. Just before the exit, a KGB officer glued a ration card to the back of the internal passport, then noted the amount of food received both on the card and in a ledger. Garcia explained that some people tried to get more food by removing the added card. If they were found out, the lucky ones are admonished and turned away (after standing in line for four hours); the unlucky ones were arrested.

The Marines' barracks and workplace was an old factory turned into a warehouse. The only weapons Josh saw were Beretta M9s on the hips of officers and NCOs; Garcia said their M-16s, ammo and M-60s were locked and guarded in the building.

Inside the warehouse, crates of food were neatly stacked and catalogued. Working parties made up of local citizens arrived at 0800 every day to offload the trucks that started arriving around 0900. Payment was a bag of food, not entered on the worker's internal passport. Who was selected for work duty was up to the Russians, not the Marines.

The Marines guarded the storage facility twenty-four hours a day, but there was still some "leakage" in the food supply. Not one of the shipping manifests matched what arrived from Domodedovo, Garcia said disgustedly. He had no proof, but he estimated the Red Army was siphoning off about twenty-five percent of each delivery. He duly noted the discrepancy on his daily reports.

After thanking Captain Garcia, they went back to the car. Josh rode along in silence as Brown drove down the Don AutoRoute leading south out of Moscow. Traffic was light. Soon they passed the ring road known by its initials MKAD: the outer administrative boundary for the City of Moscow.

Josh kept brooding over the long lines of people waiting for food. It reminded him of the photos he'd seen of bread lines in the U.S. during the Depression, and the ones of concentration camp prisoners and PoWs queued up for whatever morsels of food might be given to them by their Nazi keepers.

At least there were no riots, and the KGB was not firing into the crowds indiscriminately. What worried Josh was the Red Army stealing food from its citizens. Why? He said, "Gunny, can you check with the other distribution points run by the U.S. military? See if their manifests don't match. If we spot a pattern, that's something I need to tell Admiral Gainesville."

The Same Day, 1826 Local Time, Moscow

A SCIF was a Specially Compartmented Intelligence Facility. The SCIFs at the U.S. embassy in Moscow were built to prevent eavesdropping from either inside or outside the building. The defense attachés area had a large conference room SCIF, as well as the smaller ones Josh referred to as "phone booth coffins."

A pause in his conversation with Admiral Gainesville gave Josh time to review the notes he'd taken:

1. Krasnovsky
   a. CIA thinks he's a plant. Beware!
   b. Pay what you think is reasonable. JG and J3 will back
   c. Cut K if JH thinks we're being played
2. Gorbachev
   a. No one in DIA or CIA really knows what's happening
   b. Lots of conflicting opinions in DC, few facts
   c. Get Gen. K's insight?
3. Israelis
   a. Good connections in USSR
   b. Suspect Iranians are buying suitcase nukes and nuke artillery shells; source is generals wanting money, not Soviet gov't
   c. Want help in stopping the transfer. JG says stand-by on offer
   d. JG to get CIA data on nukes
   e. CIA doesn't believe the ZBV2s can be mounted on missiles. JG got ass kicked in meeting with CIA and DIA on topic.

With the official report concluded, Josh had one more item. "Sir, I met someone out of my deep dark past. This'll take you back to our days on the *Sterett*. On our first trip to Singapore, do you remember who I met?"

"Yeah, the hot chick who was half-French, half-Laotian. I don't remember her name, but the two of you were getting serious when I headed home. What about her?"

"Her name is Danielle Debenard, and... she was at a cocktail party in the U.S. embassy this past weekend. She works for the French version of the CIA."

"Didn't you tell me she was captured by the Pathet Lao?"

"She says she and her father escaped after three-plus years. Apparently, she wants to tell me something important outside the walls of her embassy. I don't think it's, 'Do you want to sleep with me?'"

"You better hope not." Jeff Gainesville paused before asking the obvious question. "Are you going to tell Rebekah?"

"Absolutely... once I figure out what Danielle wants. You'll recall that my wife has several black belts in various forms of martial arts. It's unwise for me to keep certain kinds of secrets." Josh took a long drink of water to wash away images of what his wife might do if she thought he was fucking around. "Jeff, I need you to do me a favor." By using his boss's first name, he was making it personal.

"What is it, Sport?"

"Can you run the traps through Langley or DIA and see what they have on her? Discreetly."

"I'll take it as an action item. Think she was flipped?"

"Anything's possible."

"How's Gunny Velasquez working out?"

"Overprotective, but topnotch. He gets stuff done. Why?"

"He's got friends in the snake-eater community. Feltzer said Velasquez is on the new E-8 list, and you know as well as I do that making E-8 in the Marine Corps is a big deal. He'll get the word in about two weeks."

Good news. Too bad I have to keep it a secret.

He had one more secure call to make. Josh turned to make sure the door to the mini skiff was still latched. The chrome door handle looked like something from a commercial freezer. Then he dialed.

"Cabot." Marty's voice was terse and business like.

"It's Josh."

"How's Moscow?"

"Drab but not dull. Let's go secure." A sign on the wall in big bold letters reminded users that the booths were only for official conversations and secure calls. Using satellites was expensive, so users should minimize the chitchat.

"Secure," Marty said. "What do you have?"

Josh summarized his conversations with Krasnovsky and Gainesville. "I'm going to ask the Russian for a copy of my KGB file. Do you want a copy of yours?"

Marty didn't hesitate. "Yes."

"I got more."

"Go."

"A former flame. Remember Danielle Debenard from our first tour in Vietnam?"

"The good-looking linguist who got captured. You almost did something dumb, like go into Laos to try to rescue her from the Pathet Lao, even though you had no idea where she was."

"I met her here in Moscow at an embassy reception. She's working for the French intelligence community. She wants to talk."

"The plot thickens."

"Marty, this is a distraction I don't need."

"Challenges, challenges, challenges! That's why they pay us the big bucks."

"Here's the third reason I called. I need to know how you'd smuggle a nuclear weapon out of the Soviet Union. Assume the destination is Iran and the cargo is six nuclear artillery shells in their original crates. How would you do it?"

"Where do they pick up the weapons?"

"Uzbekistan or Turkmenistan."

"The smuggling route shouldn't be hard to figure out. Give me a day or two."

"Before you go, I need to ask you one more question...."

"Josh, I know you. This is where you ask for help because you think you're in over your head."

"True. Can you get your scrawny ass over here?"

"Let's work on creating a reason."

"I will try to make that happen."

The Same Day, 1633 Local Time, New York City

The mental itch wouldn't go away and made Safdar nervous. After a trip in a cab followed by a ride on the A train to Columbus Circle, he walked along the paths on the south side of Central Park to Fifth Avenue. From there, he went down the steps to the platform for the R train and went one stop to Lexington Ave. He spotted no tail, but the sense he was being watched didn't go away. Trying not to be obvious, he checked again for a tail as he got into a cab outside the station to take him to Catherine Park on 72nd Street and Second Avenue.

In the park, Safdar found a bench and scanned the world around him. Nothing even hinted surveillance. With no links between the identities he'd used to get to New York, he didn't think anyone could trace him. Besides, if the Israelis knew he was in the U.S., they would have screamed to the U.S. Government to have him arrested. Broughton would have caught wind of that and warned him.

If not the Israelis, then who? The Jordanians? The Saudis? Either would sell him out to curry favor with Washington. Or, was Broughton a double agent? Were they both under surveillance?

Safdar felt wetness in his armpits. He wasn't sure if it was the humidity or nervousness. For the first time since he'd arrived in the U.S., Safdar felt a sense of impending doom. Could he finish his mission? Or, was Allah calling him?

Safdar closed his eyes. In 1948, a year after he was born in Acre north of Haifa, his family had fled to Tyre in Lebanon. Like many Palestinians, the Safdars left the newly formed State of Israel voluntarily, drawn by the promise from neighboring Arab states that they would destroy Israel and let the refugees return home.

It didn't turn out that way, but Safdar's mother Aribar often reminded both her husband and Mohammed that they had not been forced out. All they would have had to do to stay was become Israeli citizens and pledge their allegiance to the new state. Safdar's father had refused to do so, and they'd taken the train to Tyre where a cousin lived.

In 1950, Yasser Arafat asked the Oxford educated Dr. Hakem Safdar to join the Palestinian delegation to the United Nations. The Safdar family had moved to New York. Mohammed went to an international school in Manhattan with the children of diplomats from other Arab countries. By the time he applied to colleges, he spoke American English without an accent, as well as French and Arabic.

He was welcomed as an engineering student at Cornell because he had the grades to get in and his parents paid full tuition. By the time he graduated with a degree in mechanical engineering, his mother wanted him to find a job in the U.S. because she believed there was no future for him in Palestine. Mohammed had wanted to go his own way and found the job with Hassai.

When his father died suddenly in 1983, the Israelis allowed Dr. Safdar to be buried in an Arab cemetery outside Acre as long as the ceremony was quiet and peaceful. Safdar's mother arrived the day before and left two days after the funeral. A practicing pediatrician, Aribar had applied for U.S. citizenship.

She said there was nothing left in Palestine for her. She wanted to make a new life in America, not one dedicated to creating a Palestinian state on the West Bank. She didn't approve of terrorism, or her son's hatred for the Israelis. After the funeral, mother and son had a long discussion. Some would call it a fight. Either way, communication between them stopped and Safdar returned to Acre.

At the cemetery, Mohammed made sure the three balls of dirt were in place on the simple white shroud, and that his father's body was placed in the grave with his head facing east toward Mecca. By the time the gravediggers finished covering his father's body, Mohammed Safdar had stopped crying. All that was left in his body was rage.

Now here he was, back in the U.S. He'd entered legally as Mohammed Safdar, but Bashar al Bishi was the identity he used on a daily basis. For bomb-making projects, Safdar had other identities.

Sword of Allah's backers in Iran wanted a major bombing event every year, which meant that, surveillance or no surveillance, Safdar had to get on with his mission. Whether or not he survived was God's will.

Chapter 12
Machetunum

Tuesday, June 25th, 1991, 1552 Local Time, Moscow

Danielle opened the windows to her bedroom and the combination living/dining room. The breeze was strong enough to push out the bottom of the curtains and create a pleasant freshness through the apartment.

Satisfied with the 'air-conditioning,' Danielle took a sip of red wine and placed the glass on the windowsill. She looked down at Bolshaya Yakinamanka, six floors below. A moment later, she squeezed her eyes shut as suppressed memories of Pathet Re-Education Camp #3 flooded back.

What do I tell Josh?

Dinner in her flat for just the two of them was probably not appropriate, but it was the only place she'd feel safe. The rooms were swept for bugs every few days; so far, none had ever been found. The French had even gone to the extreme of setting up scanners across the street and having her speak as she walked around the apartment to make sure nothing was transmitted.

A black Suburban stopped below, and Josh got out. The bundle of flowers of flowers he was carrying made her smile; they didn't surprise her.

Two minutes later, the flowers were on a small table and Josh was hugging his former girlfriend. He put his hand on the back of her head and gently pulled it to his shoulder. After they separated, Josh followed Danielle into the kitchen and watched as she trimmed the stems of the white roses and put them in a vase.

Twenty years had matured but not dimmed her beauty. "You look great!" he said.

Danielle smiled, knowing she had aged. "I was down to forty kilos when Papa and I escaped the re-education camp. It took a year for my hair to grow back. From a legal standpoint, we'd come back from the dead—all kinds of records had to be changed, and the paperwork never seemed to end."

"I thought you had died," Josh said somberly, remembering his anguished trip to Laos. He'd wanted to try to find where the camp was and attempt a rescue.

"We *would* have died if we hadn't escaped."

"How did you?"

"Do you really want to hear the whole story? Isn't it enough to know that Papa and I escaped, and that it took us a week to get to Thailand?"

"If you're willing, I'd like to hear it all. It's good to talk about these things, no?"

Danielle shrugged. "I've told it to French intelligence and to a psychiatrist. Why not you too?"

Danielle poured Josh a glass of 1988 Puilly Fuisse and the two of them settled on the couch, wine glasses in hand. When she got to the part about Gabrielle, she had to stop several times to compose herself. Anger, rage and grief surfaced, as raw as they'd been at the time. Josh held both her hands and didn't interrupt. At times, his own eyes welled up—it hurt to hear what she'd endured, not only in Laos, but what she and her father had to go through to restart their lives in France.

When she finished, Josh held her tightly. Neither spoke for several minutes. Finally, he asked, "Do you have nightmares?"

Danielle raised her eyebrows. "No. My father and I waged a private war to get to Thailand. We did what we had to do. I can live with a clear conscience."

"Thank you for telling me. So where are your brothers now?"

"Andrei is an investment banker with N.M. Rothschild & Son. Henri lives in Singapore and works for *Banque du National Paris.*"

"When you got back to France, couldn't doctors do anything for your leg?"

"No. It was too late." Danielle made a typically Gallic face as if to say, *c'est la vie.*

"The story gets better, or maybe worse." She rose and refilled her glass, standing for a moment with her back to him.

"How?"

"In May, I was at a reception commemorating the end of World War II in Europe. I was directed to talk with a Soviet general named Vladimir Koskov. Supposedly, he spoke fluent Laotian and Vietnamese. When I saw him, I recognized the bastard who raped my sister. He doesn't remember me, but I remember him. He's one of the most vocal hardliners opposed to bartering oil and natural gas for food. I think he's up to no good. You need to meet him. I'll set up a lunch with the three of us."

"Why?"

Danielle smiled and cocked her head to one side. "It is part of your job, no?"

"I suppose so. I'll meet him." Josh knew it would give General Grant and the CIA fits, but Danielle was right: it *was* part of his job. He wondered if Grant knew about the discrepancies between what the U.S. sent in food and what the Red Army delivered for distribution.

When Josh looked back at Danielle, he noticed she was wearing a Star of David on a gold chain. He reached out and touched it. "Why are you wearing this?"

"You knew Papa was Jewish. While we were in the re-education camp, Judaism gave us both something to believe in. Every week when I can, I go to a synagogue here in Moscow. The members say that half the people in the sanctuary used to be KGB agents. Now, not so much. I'm sure the KGB still watch who attends and for the moment, they don't bother anyone. You should come with me."

"I will."

"Good. I can introduce you to my fiancée here in Moscow. He's an Israeli."

"Congratulations. Good for you. Who is he?"

"A widower. His wife and children were killed in a terrorist attack in 1986. His name is Avram Gutman."

Josh smiled politely, but his brain had just whited out. *Avram Gutman is Rebekah's cousin!* If Danielle married Avram, she'd be machetunim, a relative by marriage. Did Avram know Josh and Danielle had been serious twenty-plus years ago?

This, Josh realized, is *going to make the discussion with Rebekah even more interesting.*

Chapter 13
The Hits Keep Coming

Wednesday, June 26th, 1991, 0939 Local Time, Moscow

Josh liked living at the Rossiya. If he wanted room service, it was there. Or, he could eat at one of the hotel's many restaurants. If he turned in his laundry in the morning, the cleaned clothes were left neatly folded on his bed or hung in the closet by afternoon. And, he didn't have to do housekeeping. Other than being careful of what he said or left in the room, the Rossiya was growing on him.

He'd become a fixture, and walking through the lobby in an American Navy uniform no longer turned heads. Even so, Josh suspected his arrivals and departures were reported to the KGB and its military intelligence counterpart, the GRU.

On his way to a meeting that Josh *had* to attend to maintain his cover, he told Velasquez, "I like the Rossiya enough to stay there for the rest of the time I'm in Moscow. How do we make that happen?"

"Sir, the ambassador likes his staff to stay in embassy approved apartments. No exceptions unless there is nothing else available."

"Is there anyone else arriving for a long assignment in the near future?"

"I don't know, sir."

"Then use your connections and silver tongue to move me to the bottom of the list."

"Yes, sir, but the ambassador may not approve."

"I like the freedom of action it gives us."

"Understand, sir, but it's against embassy policy."

"Does the ambassador look at the housing list on a daily basis?"

"No, sir, but I'm sure his chief of staff does. The ambassador may be briefed if there's a change."

"Let's worry about that if he asks."

The Same Day, 2016 Local Time, Moscow

The tiny office behind the bar barely had room for two desks and two chairs. A heavy wooden door connected to the hall but it was locked and had two deadbolts. As far as Valentina Kishniev knew, there were only three sets of keys, and she had one of the sets. She carefully opened the deadbolts, then the door.

The owner of the club was standing at the one-way mirror that let him watch what happened in his establishment. "You sent for me, Vadim?" Valentina asked. She didn't know which of her many roles Vadim needed her to fill: manager, host, bartender, or (on very rare occasions) provider of sexual favors.

"Is the booth ready for Comrade Piotr?" Vadim asked.

"Yes. The new girl Galina is already there."

"Good. After she gives Talyzin a blowjob and fucks him, he should be happy. Then Evgeny and I will join him for a chat. Galina is to wait at the bar until we know whether or not Piotr wants her again. Understood?"

"Of course, Vadim. Galina will take good care of the First Deputy."

"Excellent. As always."

Valentina nodded. "Thank you."

"After Evgeny and Piotr have their chat, he and I would like to talk about a business opportunity for you. We think you'll like it."

"I don't know what to say."

"We hope you'll say yes."

* * *

It was almost midnight and Valentina was matching credit card receipts to bills. It was rare for them not to match, but she still sorted through them just to make sure. Afterward, her process was to count the pile of cash and add the amount to the credit card receipts to check to make sure the totals matched what was billed.

Rarely, if ever, was there less cash than there was supposed to be. If one was suspected of stealing cash, you wound up dead. What she had to figure out was how much excess cash there was, because that would be counted as tips. Cash tips were collected at the table and dropped into a locked box. If any of the hostesses were caught pocketing cash from the table, besides being fired, they would be treated roughly until they provided an estimate of how much they stole from their fellow workers. As a result, nothing was stolen. Tip money was given to employees the next time they came to work based on the number of hours they worked at night. Valentina kept a ledger so the club had a record.

Valentina heard Vadim and Evgeny talking as they walked down the hall. Normally, she concentrated on the job at hand and didn't pay attention to their discussions. Tonight, however, she'd just finished the credit card bills and was taking a sip of coffee when the words, "Are you serious?" rang out. There was not much that surprised the club owner; Vadim's tone and words caught her attention.

She looked at the door. It was cracked, not closed. Shutting it all the way would draw attention her.

With her ears tuned, Valentina started counting the bills. Evgeny and Vadim were discussing the price they would ask for assassinating a man named Maksimov. There were two other names Valentina couldn't understand. Their voices turned to whispers, and then someone closed the door.

Valentina finished the night's accounting and put the cash in the safe. There was still clean -up to supervise. She was out the door by 0222 and, as usual, Vadim was waiting to drive her home. As Valentina got into the car, she wondered if she was about to be driven to a dacha outside Moscow, tortured until she told what she heard, and then shot. She smiled, hiding her fear as Vadim held the door open for her.

Thursday, June 27th, 1991, 1033 Local Time, Parsabad, Iran

Two white pickup trucks stopped in a sliding cloud of dust in front of the rusty metal gate of 1045 Firuz Abad, on the northeast side of Iran's northernmost city. The gate was tall and wide, with a sign that read TARANA TRUCKING. A man got out of each vehicle and hurried to the backs of the trucks. They climbed to the truck beds and scanned the area, cradling their AK-47s.

A white Toyota Land Cruiser drove up shortly after and came to a halt in front of the concrete building. Ali Akrami waited for the dust to settle before he got out of the Land Cruiser's passenger seat and walked to the entrance. He squinted in the bright sun as he slipped his sunglasses into the breast pocket of his Pasdaran uniform. The two men with AK-47s followed him inside and down the empty hallway.

Inside a dirty, cluttered office, piles of paper were held down by worn out truck parts. No sign of Tarana Aliyev. Akrami shrugged. If his boyhood friend Tarana wasn't at the desk, he was probably out back, working on a truck.

Before Akrami approached the back door, his guards made sure no assassins were lurking in the shadows of the shop. The dank hallway led past a bathroom reeking of stale urine. Outside, Akrami heard a hammer banging on steel, followed by curse words.

"Tarana, are you here?"

"Who's asking?"

The smart aleck response started one of the bodyguards storming toward the sound of the voice. Akrami waved the man back. "It's Ali Akrami," he called.

With a rustling sound, a man pulled himself out from under a truck. The man was as tall and skinny as Akrami was short and stocky. As for the truck, it was a true classic: a Kahwar 1924, designed, licensed and built in Iran by Mercedes-Benz. Tarana Aliyev wiped his hands with a greasy rag pulled from the pocket of his tan overalls. Aliyev put his hand out to shake, but Akrami held up both his hands as if to say, *I'm not getting my hands dirty.*

He said, "Tarana, we need to talk."

"Here?"

"Yes, here. In private."

"In the office then. My wife won't be here until noon."

Aliyev led the way and made a show of moving piles of paper before he pointed to a chair.

Akrami disregarded the chair and stood in the middle of the room. "I need two BTR-80 armored cars and at least three army trucks. Once you have them, my drivers and crews will take them to an assembly point, probably near Samarkand. I will call you with the delivery location."

Aliyev rubbed the back of his neck. "It will be expensive."

"How expensive?"

"Two million U.S., at least."

"That can be arranged." Akrami wondered how much of the money would wind up in Aliyev's pocket and where the rest would go.

"When do you need to..." Aliyev thought for a few seconds for the right words, "...take possession of the vehicles? And do I get to return them to their owners?"

"They will be left in Uzbekistan by the side of the road. You can let the owners know where to find them after they are unloaded. I need the vehicles for about two weeks after the tenth of August. How soon will you have them?"

"Give me two weeks."

"You know the number to call. I'll be waiting."

Akrami strode out of the building, followed by his bodyguards. Their convoy headed for Parsabad Moghan Airport where an Iranian Air Force Falcon 20 jet was waiting.

The Same Day, 1836 Local Time, Moscow

It was a glorious summer day in the park. Youth teams had set up goals on the field; they were practicing what the Americans called soccer and the rest of the world called football.

Major General Vavilov, grandfather to two young boys, settled his bulky frame onto one of the benches beside of the field. Where the field was grassy, passes stayed on the ground, but where it was bumpy, the ball bounced, making it harder to control. From his own experience as a former player, Vavilov knew that the unpredictable bounces forced players to improve their ball control skills.

"General..."

Vavilov looked up. Standing at attention in his Red Army uniform, Yuri Panichev rendered a salute. The general nodded and touched his cap, but didn't stand. "At ease, Colonel. Have a seat and watch the boys practice."

The Iranian sat and put his briefcase next to him at the end of the bench. "A lovely day, isn't it?"

"Indeed. Four more months before the weather turns to shit."

"It's your home, not mine."

"I'd love to find a place where the temperature never drops below twenty Celsius. Unfortunately, our country has been cursed with a very cold climate. Or perhaps that's a blessing—ask the Germans and the French what they think of Russian winter."

It sounded like small talk, but it was actually a prearranged code. If the general spoke about warm weather, it meant things were going well. If he complained about being cold all the time, there were problems. Since he'd mentioned both, what did that mean?

Vavilov met Panichev's gaze. The general thought Panichev looked like a recruiting poster for a Soviet Army officer, only without the blue eyes and blond hair. "I should have the documents you requested in a week, maybe two," Vavilov said. "Once you do your part, I'll let you know so you can stop by my office to pick them up."

Panichev nodded.

Vavilov put his hands on his thighs and leaned forward. "Did you ever play football?"

Panichev shook his head. "In my village, real balls were very scarce. We were very poor."

"That's a shame. The game is fun... and the ball's bounces prepare you for life." Vavilov stood. "I'll be in touch."

He turned away and walked toward the street.

MOSCOW AIRLIFT

The Same Day, 1939 Local Time, Moscow

The dining room of the largest restaurant in the Rossiya was ornate, historical and ugly. In Josh's opinion, whoever had designed it had combined the worst elements of Soviet architecture. The Rossiya was supposed to be the Soviet Union's proof that it could build and run a world-class hotel. Josh was no expert, but at best, the Rossiya was four, not five star.

As Josh stood in the restaurant's entrance, he saw that Krasnovsky was already there. The KGB general wore a shirt of a color between light tan and army khaki. It might be a faded uniform shirt, but then again, it could have been all that was available at GUM. Most of the time, the department store's queues were long; Russians took whatever was left when they got to the counter.

KGB Major General Krasnovsky arrived at the restaurant early. He'd tried to pass the time by reading a copy of *Isvestia,* but the articles just made him mad. Its reporters were out of touch with reality. Assignments in East Germany and Poland, along with trips to Budapest and Prague, had given Krasnovsky a glimpse into the West. No wonder Russians felt insecure. While he would never say this to anyone, including his wife of forty plus years, Oleg Krasnovsky had become convinced that Communism was a failed system. It didn't come close to meeting the needs of the people. The people the government claimed to be protecting were actually slaves. Healthcare while free, was not very good.

As a KGB general, he enjoyed privileges that ninety-eight percent of his fellow citizens never got. Yet, the government didn't trust Krasnovsky to go abroad, not even for a vacation. Getting an international passport was difficult, and unless your job required frequent travel outside the Soviet Union, the government demanded that you give back the passport as soon as you returned.

As one man, there wasn't much Krasnovsky could do to change the system. What gave him hope was the rising opposition to the Communist Part and its autocratic rule. There was nothing he could do to help the opposition directly—they certainly wouldn't trust a KGB general. Maybe, just maybe, the government might fall in Krasnovsky's lifetime. Maybe it would fall sooner if he gave it a gentle shove.

As long as the government survived, Communist rule was enough to drive a man to drink. Like many of his fellow citizens, Krasnovsky drank a lot. Being drunk make life in the Soviet Union easier to bear.

Josh approached the table. He saw that Krasnovsky had ordered a liter bottle of Stolichnaya and two empty glasses. "Good evening, General," Josh said as he took his seat.

"Please, call me Oleg." Krasnovsky filled the glasses three-quarters full. "Our health."

"Health." Josh took a swallow and winced as the liquid burned its way down to his empty stomach. "General, there's no way I'm going to finish this bottle with you. A glass maybe, but half a bottle, no way!" *Now why did I say that?* Then he knew the answer: he was thinking of his first father-in-law, Artur Vishinski, *may he rest in peace.* He and Josh had shared many a glass of vodka; Josh had always ended under the table.

As if reading his thoughts, Krasnovsky said, "Your first father-in-law was Russian, yes?" He spoke in heavily accented English.

"He didn't consider himself Russian. He was Bessarabian."

"Yes, yes, Bessarabia. It is now part of the Moldavian Soviet Socialist Republic. They were rebels before war and still are. They are hotheads, like Romanians."

"My father-in-law was definitely not a fan of Lenin or Stalin."

"Neither am I."

"What a thing to say, General! Are you a capitalist?"

"I'm learning."

Josh took the comment as an opening. "We're willing to help make your retirement more comfortable."

Krasnovsky's eyes lit up. Before he spoke, he finished his glass and poured a second. With a guilty smile, he raised his glass. "As the proverb says, 'He who drinks to the bottom, lives without mind.'" Krasnovsky waved to a passing waiter. "Let's order. We can eat and drink, so we talk on a full stomach."

Josh ordered pelmni: dumplings filled with a savory mix of minced pork, lamb and beef mixed with onions and garlic. Krasnovsky had soylanka, a thick beef soup with cucumber pickles, tomatoes, onions, olives, capers, allspice,parsley, and dill, all served with a large dollop of sour cream.

Krasnovsky reminded Josh of Artur Vishinski. He gave you the sense he was a cuddly teddy bear... until you remembered he was a KGB general. Josh could see the emotions simmering just below the surface and the pride with which the man spoke of his wartime experiences. Krasnovsky described how they'd attacked a German position at the Battle of Kursk where his company started out with four platoons of five T-34s each. By the time they reached their objective, Krasnovsky's tank was the only one not disabled or burning.

When the story was over, the general said, "Enough about my war. What about yours? You flew special operations helicopters in Vietnam, yes?"

"I did." How accurate was the KGB's file on him? Lying or denying would cost Josh credibility. "I flew mostly combat search and rescue missions."

"Don't be modest. I know you flew your SEALs in and out of North Vietnam many times."

"A few times," Josh admitted.

Krasnovsky laughed. "And I know about Alexei Koniev's defection. At first, we thought he was killed in that messy firefight with all the explosions, but the dental records of the body left behind didn't match Koniev's. It took the KGB and GRU six months to agree he might be in the United States."

Josh forced himself not to respond. If the KGB knew the truth, why hadn't they tried to kill Koniev? They'd killed Arthur Vishinski, a much less important man.

Krasnovsky took no offense at Josh's silence. "You know what I would like to know?" he asked. "How you got into East Germany. But I hazard a guess that stealing a strange helicopter and flying it to Denmark would have been for you, how do you say, a piece of cake?"

"It wasn't," Josh said. "And the weather was really shitty. Very cold and snowy."

"I remember. It snowed almost thirty centimeters, like in Russia." Krasnovsky took a large swallow. "So how are you going to make my retirement more comfortable?"

"We can pay for information, if it's valuable to us. If it isn't, there won't be another chance. The deal will be off and you'll only keep the money we've paid you."

"So this is pay-as-you-go?"

"Yes."

"How much?"

"Each delivery, one hundred thousand dollars in the bank account of your choice."

"A quarter of a million."

Josh made a face and slowly counted to ten, hoping to make the Russian squirm. A quarter million was exactly what Josh was authorized to offer. *Was it worth negotiating? No.* "Agreed."

Krasnovsky smiled. "Under the napkin and the bottle of Stolichnaya, there is a piece of paper with a bank identification number and account number. Why don't you use the napkin to wipe the table and take the paper? Then dessert! Strawberries Romanoff is on the menu."

Josh knew that meant strawberries, whipped cream, cinnamon and brandy. He said, "Strawberries Romanoff it is."

"Excellent. Tonight's conversation will be the first of many for which I am paid. I sound like a capitalist, no?" He lowered his voice. "So what do you want to know?"

Josh didn't speak for a few seconds before he whispered, "What the hell is going on in your government, and who can sell nuclear weapons?"

Krasnovsky eased back in his chair. "Let's eat our delicious strawberries, then take a walk."

Friday, June 28th, 1991, 1845 Local Time, Moscow

Like many Russian buildings designed in the 1890s, the synagogue at 10 Bolshoy Spasoglinishchevskiy was painted a pale yellow brown. A small crowd had gathered outside the entrance. When a black Suburban pulled up, a few people glanced at it, then went back to their conversations.

Josh got out and sized up the people who stood at the top of the steps. He turned back to Velasquez. "I'll be fine, Gunny. Avram Gutman said he'd give me a lift back to the hotel. Even if he doesn't, I can find my way back on the metro. Hell, I can *walk* back to the Rossiya from here."

"Sir, Sergeant Brown and I don't mind waiting."

"It will be a couple of hours."

"No problem, sir. It's our job. Remember, no solo trips."

"I can find my way back!"

"Sir, with all due respect, I'm not worried about you. I'm worried about the knuckleheads in this city who might think you're a rich tourist. I wouldn't want you hurting any of the locals. We'll wait."

"Gunny, I'm not going to order you to go back to the embassy because I know it would put you in a difficult position. You'd have to rationalize your way through the decision as to whether or not you should disobey an order from a superior, and then I'd be faced with the ethical decision as to whether or not I should report your failure to obey an order." Josh took a deep breath. "Soooooo, Gunnery Sergeant Velasquez, I'll give you the option of what you want to do between now and 2130, at which time, if you and Sergeant Brown are still waiting for me, I'll give you an update on my plans for the evening. If you're not here, I'll assume I'm on my own and will see you at 1300 local time tomorrow at the hotel."

A beaming Gunnery Sergeant Velasquez shut the rear door. "Aye aye, sir. I understand the captain's orders and the freedom of action they entail." By phrasing it this way, he avoided saying, *I am glad you came around to my way of thinking,* knowing it crossed an unwritten boundary.

Josh walked past the small group at the entrance and entered the small lobby. It was softly lit with illumination from the sanctuary. Behind the altar, he could see the ark that contained several Torahs written during the reign of Catherine the Great, two hundred and fifty years before.

The Choral Synagogue had survived Stalin's purges and the anti-Semitic policies he'd pursued even though his Foreign Minister, Maxim Litvinov, and many other members of the government were Jews. When Gorbachev took power, he'd rescinded all the government's anti-Semitic rules and regulations. Still, most Jews remained in the closet. They remembered the ploys of Gorbachev's predecessors, who promised freedom of expression, then eliminated those who stood up. The Soviet census showed that greater Moscow contained almost a quarter of a million Jews, or at least Soviet citizens of with Jewish heritage. Only a fraction practiced the religion of their forefathers because they were afraid of prosecution by the state, just as their ancestors had feared the Tsars.

As Josh looked at the walls and ceiling, he wondered how many people had prayed in this building over the years—since the 1880s, when Tsar Nicholas I had allowed it to be built outside what was then the center of the city.

Avram Gutman and Danielle approached. Avram shook Josh's hand. "*Shabbat shalom.* Thank you for coming early."

"My pleasure. I can now add this to the synagogues in which I have prayed."

"And you know my fiancée."

"I do."

A man handed Avram a prayer book, then one to Danielle, and a third to Josh. After the man left, Avram fanned the pages of his book and palmed a sheet of paper.

* * *

It was 2140 when Josh walked out of the synagogue. In the fading light, he spotted the black Suburban sitting out front. A smiling Velasquez opened the door. Josh settled inside, buckled his seat belt and said, "Home, James."

On the folded down seat-rest, Velasquez had left a pad and a pen. As soon as they were under way, Josh started making notes.

1. What info was passed to Gutman?

2. Congregation was about one third foreigners from almost every European country. Why? What business opportunities were they pursuing?

Saturday, June 29th, 1991, 2022 Local Time, Moscow

Arkady put down a well-worn copy of *The Gulag Archipelago*. The banned book had been smuggled into the country five years ago. Many readers had waded through this copy of the book, learning about the people sent to Stalin's network of prison camps. The content was hard to bear; as a police officer, Arkady had seen firsthand how the Soviet justice system abused the rights of citizens. Once convicted, people disappeared into the Gulag and most never returned to their families.

This book was the second smuggled work he'd read by Aleksandr Solzhenitsyn. The first, *A Day in the Life of Ivan Densonovich,* was a depressing story about life in a Soviet labor camp.

Perhaps, Arkady thought, he should have chosen something more cheerful. Summer Saturday nights were always painful. Walking through the city, Arkady ached to see dads playing football with their sons. It was something he wished he could be doing right now. Growing up, Arkady had loved sports; he'd been good enough to play professional football but had decided to join the *militsiya* instead.

On the end table was a picture of his late wife Rachel. She'd contracted sepsis in the delivery room. Both she and the baby had died within hours of each other.

Two medical examiners had told him that pregnancy-related sepsis occurred about seven percent of the time. Unless you were a party bigwig and had access to the special hospitals with the latest in medical technology, sepsis was almost always fatal.

Bureaucrats said that Arkady's son would not be allowed to have his own grave. He wasn't officially a Soviet citizen because he hadn't lived long enough to get an identification number. So the baby they'd planned to name Zvi was buried in the arms of his mother.

Arkady picked up Rachel's picture. After five full years, the tears still came, although they had lessened over time. As often as he could, Arkady visited her grave. Gently, he put the frame down. "Rachel, I miss you so much."

Sunday, June 30th, 1991, 2017 Local Time, Moscow

As Valentina walked up the stairs at her brother's side, the familiar smells of her parents' apartment building reminded Valentina of her childhood and the fun she had. The apartment was small, but she and Arkady had grown up here. She had missed it, but missed her parents even more.

When her father opened the door, both her mother and father welcomed her with tears and hugs. It was as if she had come back from the dead. The get-together ended with promises to visit every week.

On the way home, Valentina looped her arm in her brother's and said, "Arkady, let's take a walk before we get on the metro."

He smiled. It was a good sign when his sister wanted to talk.

They walked in silence for a minute before she said, "I'm glad I came. I can't thank you enough for pushing me."

'I'm glad, too. I like having my kid sister around to tease."

The pair walked in silence again. At last, Valentina said, "I have two things to tell you."

Arkady waited.

"I overhead a conversation between Vadim and Durov."

"Tell me."

"Piotr Talyzin told Durov he wanted the *mafiya* to kill a man called Yakov Maksimov. Who is he?"

Arkady stopped and spun his sister so they were facing. "Maksimov is the *head* of the GRU! If the *mafiya* assassinates its leader, the GRU will rip Moscow apart to find the killers. The killers must realize that. Do they know you overheard them?"

"No. They were in a hallway and I was in the office."

Arkady said nothing. His sister didn't realize how much danger she was in.

Valentina said, "Don't look at me like that. I just thought you could put the information to good use."

"I investigate murders. I'm not in intelligence."

Arkady stopped talking while another couple passed in the opposite direction. "I can't report this. They'll want to know my source, and I can't put you in danger."

"Think of something, Arkady. If Durov's men kill Maksimov, things will be bad for everybody. The idea of a GRU crackdown is terrifying."

"I agree, and I will think about what I can do. What else were you going to tell me?"

"Vadim and Durov are opening a new bar and they want me to run it."

"Oh. Wow!" That was actually reassuring. Vadim would hardly give Valentina a promotion if he knew she'd overheard the conversation. "Congratulations. Where will the bar be?"

"Vadim and I will look at locations this week. Somewhere near where the bigwigs live."

"Good. No more servicing clients."

"I stopped that a long time ago. Katerina still does a little, but only on special occasions. She'll become my head hostess and maître d'. I made it a condition that we'll never have to service another client. It'll be good for both of us."

Good news indeed, Arkady thought. But the other!

Monday, July 1st, 1991, 1105 Local Time, the Pentagon
Admiral Jeff Gainesville sat at his desk and massaged his temples. At 0818, General Feltzer had stopped by Jeff's office to

tell him about a prior meeting with the Chairman of the Joint Chiefs of Staff and the three-star general who headed the Defense Intelligence Agency.

The topic of the meeting had been Josh Haman. Brigadier General Grant had lodged a formal complaint about not being cleared for Josh's mission and not having operational control of his activities. After listening, the Chairman had confirmed there would be no changes to Haman's mission or his chain of command, but pressure was now on Haman to deliver.

Then, at 0900, Jeff had walked into a "stars only" meeting with the CIA and DIA directors responsible for intelligence about Iranian missile and nuclear weapons. Both were openly dismissive of the Mossad assessment. They insisted it was impossible to connect artillery shells to rockets; Mossad, they asserted, was just being paranoid about Iran. Both directors were furious that Jeff was still including the possibility in his assessments.

When Jeff pointed out that Zuni rockets shot by Navy airplanes in Vietnam were not much more than the warheads from five-inch shells mounted on a rocket, he was told he "didn't understand the engineering complexity of the problem." Even the existence of Soviet and East German rocket experts in Iran didn't sway their view. They insisted artillery shells simply couldn't be attached to a long-range rocket.

As the two men walked out, the man from the CIA brought up the name of Jonathan Pollard, who'd been sentenced for spying for Israel in 1987. He warned Jeff not to believe everything the Israelis said. They had their own agenda, and it often conflicted with U.S. interests.

With that kind of attitude, Jeff thought disgustedly, the CIA and DIA were primed to ignore crucial intelligence. Didn't these directors ever study the history of their organizations? The results of ignoring information could prove catastrophic.

Tuesday, July 2nd, 1991, 1155 Local Time, Moscow

In the lobby of the luxurious Hotel Moskva, a line of guests waited to be seated at one of the best Italian restaurants in Moscow, the Yug Restaurant. Hotel Moskva's other claim to fame was that Stolichnaya vodka used a line drawing of the hotel on its label.

Josh went to the head of the line and asked if General Koskov had arrived. The maître d' looked old enough to have survived Stalin's purges; he nodded and said in precise but accented English, "Captain Haman, you are expected. Follow me."

Danielle was already seated at the table in a corner. The men she was with stood up as the maître d' pulled out Josh's chair. Speaking in Russian, Danielle waved her hand, "Captain Joshua Haman, this is Major General Vladimir Koskov and his chief of staff, Colonel Yuri Stoyanovich." Josh shook each man's hand with a distinct pump and sat down.

"Thank you joining us," Josh said.

Stoyanovich answered in English with hardly any accent. "Danielle insisted, and we couldn't resist the invitation of a beautiful woman."

A waiter placed menus on the table. A short handwritten note stapled to the menu listed five specials for the day; it meant they were out of almost everything else.

Josh noticed that Koskov didn't look at the menu. Instead, the man's gray eyes were attempting to bore holes in Josh's body. Was this an attempt at intimidation? Or was Koskov simply bothered by eating a meal with a sworn enemy?

"Captain Haman," said Stoyanovich, "we understand you're here on a special assignment and would like to ask General Koskov some questions. Ms. Debenard didn't tell us anything about you. Would you like to tell us a bit about yourself?"

Josh smiled and looked at the senior Soviet officer. "General Koskov, if you prefer, we can speak in Russian."

"I speak English." Koskov's diction was strongly accented. "If I need clarification, I will ask. Continue."

"Do you want the five or 100 ruble version?" Josh asked. Koskov's expression indicated the attempt at humor was lost.

"You choose."

Josh was sure that both Russians must have read his KGB file. He amused himself by summarizing his career by exactly listing assignments announced in *Navy Times*.

Koskov didn't react to the recitation. When Josh was finished, he simply asked, "Captain, are you married?"

"Yes."

"Children?"

"Two boys and a girl."

Josh was sure he saw Koskov's eyes flicker as he checked off items he already knew. Josh said, "Now, General, it's your turn. Tell me about yourself, please."

"There is not much to tell that you do not know already."

"You'd be surprised. The KGB and GRU have a much easier time getting information on Americans than we have of getting material on Russians. I'm not asking you to give away state secrets. From your medals, I can see you've received awards for bravery in action in Vietnam and Afghanistan. So please, I'm interested in Koskov the man, not the general."

"You have read CIA file on me, no?"

Josh laughed. "Your life is covered in three paragraphs." Josh took a piece of paper from his breast pocket and handed it to Koskov. The document was marked SECRET NOFORN, which meant it was classified as Secret, do not disseminate to foreign nationals. Koskov read it and handed it to Stoyanovich. Josh asked, "Is that accurate?"

"You share secrets so easily?"

"I got permission. It just shows how little we know about you.. So, General, tell me something not on the paper." Josh stared back at Koskov.

"I formed Spetznaz Group Alpha. Andropov gave me order."

Josh cocked his head. After the 1974 Munich Olympics, the KGB formed Spetznaz Group Alpha as an elite counterterrorism unit. It had been frequently deployed to Afghanistan and its members killed the Afghan president as the opening move in the Soviet invasion.

Koskov deliberately refolded the CIA biography and put the palm of his hand on the paper as if to say, *this is now mine.* He had tried to spend his career in the shadows; he was surprised the Americans had gathered anything on him at all.

"What did you do in Laos and Vietnam?"

Out of the corner of his eye, Josh saw Danielle freeze. He waited.

"I was advisor," Koskov said. "The rest is state secret."

Josh shrugged. It had been worth a try.

Koskov gestured for the waiter, who was hovering near the table ready to take their orders. They each picked a "special" and the waiter scurried away.

"Captain," said Koskov, "you have not yet told us why you are in Soviet Union. You are not *nomenklatura.*"

Josh knew Koskov used the word *nomenklatura* in the Soviet sense: bureaucrats and party members who benefit from patronage and favors not granted to the rest of the population. They were the privileged elite. "No, I'm not *nomenklatura,*" Josh said. "I was sent here to make an independent evaluation of the situation in Russia."

"Does your government not trust CIA?"

"Does Gorbachev always trust information from the KGB or GRU?"

Koskov scowled. Josh had expected the verbal fencing, as well as the cold, impersonal tone. After all, the two countries had been enemies and competitors on the world stage since the end of World War II, forty-six years ago. Danielle followed the conversation with a forced smile. She had set up the meeting; her job was over, at least for the time being.

"Answer my question," Koskov said. "Why is highly decorated officer who has experience in special operations here in my country?" Clearly, Koskov was accustomed to receiving answers, not being questioned.

"General, my government thinks the political and military situation here in Russia is... fluid. They want my opinion on the matter. It would help if you told me what's going on."

"You want answer?"

"I do."

"Of course you do. However, I do not like foreigners in my country asking questions when they have no business. Before this century, the Swedes invaded us in the 1700s and Napoleon came in 1812. Then the British and French invaded the Crimea in the 1840s. In each case, we drove them out. Three times this century, foreign soldiers invade sacred Soviet soil. The Germans attacked us in World War I. The French and British along with you Americans along with eight other countries supported the Whites during our revolution and had approximately two hundred thousand troops on sacred Mother Russian soil. You didn't leave until 1921. The Germans attacked us in the Great Patriotic War and it took four years and millions of lives to drive them out. Why? We don't like foreigners in the motherland."

Danielle sensed Josh was about to respond harshly. She kicked him under the table. Her attentive expression never changed, and Josh didn't wince from the pain.

Stoyanovich spoke up. "There's an old Russian saying: *Zhizn' prozhit'—ne pole pereyti.* Life is not like crossing a meadow. In Russia, we know this. We do not expect life to be easy. The Soviet Union and its people are much tougher than America and its allies. We don't need your wealth, your food, or your consumer goods."

Josh mentally counted to five before he spoke. "Colonel, where did you learn to speak English so well?"

"Institute of the U.S.A. here in Moscow. It was preparation for..." Stoyanovich let his voice tail off as if he had been about to say something and had decided, mid-sentence, to stop. It was easy for Josh to draw the obvious conclusion: Stoyanovich had learned English so he could carry out missions in English-speaking countries.

Exactly what kind of missions?

"Colonel," Josh said, "let's stops talking politics for a few minutes. Let's share personal experiences. Are you married? Do you have children?"

Stoyanovich tapped the table with his forefinger as he spoke. "I wish to make one more point, Captain Haman. We are the country who put the first man in space."

And, we're the only country to put a man on the moon. On six different missions. Americans have spent more time in space than any other country by a wide margin. But Josh had not come to play One Up. "How old are your children?"

"Captain Haman, I recognize you do not want to talk about politics any longer, but I thought we are here to discuss the situation in Russia. I am giving you my opinion. Obviously, you do not like what I have to say. Is that not so?"

To make a point, Josh switched to Russian. "It's not that I dislike your views, Colonel Stoyanovich, but I think you're out of touch with reality. The Soviet Union has lost the Cold War because it can't keep up with the West. It can't simultaneously produce food, consumer products, and weapons. You chose weapons, and now your people starving. As other communist countries have learned, it's difficult to control hungry people's minds. Nonetheless, I respect your opinions and appreciate your sharing them with me. Let us say we disagree. In a democracy, that is acceptable. In a dictatorship, it isn't."

Stoyanovich pursed his lips. It was time he changed gears. "Your accent is very good. Where did you learn Russian?" He still spoke English.

"In school. My wife and I have worked with émigré families over the years. I'd speak Russian; they'd speak English." Josh and Artur Vishinski had spoken Russian all the time, but he certainly wasn't going to say that.

Stoyanovich's eyes blinked, but his poker face remained in place. Josh suspected this meant that his émigré work wasn't mentioned in the KGB's dossier.

"Then we continue in Russian," Stoyanovich said. "I have two children. Nicholai is twenty-two and studying to be a doctor; Alexia is twenty and a journalism student at Moscow University. My family and I went on holiday to the Black Sea in June. The year before, I got permission to take a seven-day cruise on a Polish liner sailing from St. Petersburg to Stockholm, Oslo, Copenhagen and Amsterdam, then back to St. Petersburg. We are not completely impoverished in the Soviet Union. Does that answer your question?"

"Colonel," Josh said, "In the West, we don't need government permission to travel outside our country. Nor do we need internal passports and *propiskas*. I might add that we do a pretty good job of feeding our people."

Both Stoyanovich and Koskov stared icily at Josh, while an indifferent waiter plunked their dishes down. Josh's instinct said there was more to the men's animosity than mere national pride. The question was, what?

The meal was eaten in silence. Toward the end, Stoyanovich waved to three officers just entering the dining room with two civilians. "That is General Ulyanov, and the head of our General Staff, General Berenko. I do not recognize the others. Would you like to meet them?"

Perhaps Stoyanovich wanted to prove how well connected he was. "I'd be happy to meet them, thank you," Josh replied.

Danielle pointed in the direction of the party moving toward a table. "If I'm not mistaken, the civilians are Olga Gregorenko, the Deputy Finance Minister, and Seraphim Olshansky from the Ministry of Trade."

Stoyanovich grunted as he got up and went over to the other group. After a few seconds of conversation, Ulyanov headed toward the table. Josh and General Koskov stood up.

Stoyanovich made the introductions. Josh shook Ulyanov's hand. "General," Ulyanov said to Koskov, "after you finish your meal, why don't you and Captain Haman join us? We can talk while we eat." It was clearly an order, and Koskov had no choice but to obey. Josh thought he heard some harshness in the general's tone. Perhaps there was tension between the two men... or it could just be Ulyanov's manner.

"Of course, General," Koskov said. "It will be our pleasure."

Josh paid the bill, noting that neither of the Soviets offered to do so. Stoyanovich, obviously unhappy at not being invited to stay, said he would cancel General Koskov's two afternoon meetings. He turned away sharply and left.

Danielle laid down her napkin on the table. She hadn't been invited to stay either. "I must go." She coolly shook Koskov's hand and left. She headed to the bathroom. In the first open stall, she bent over and used the toilet for support while she retched until her stomach was empty. After flushing the toilet, she pulled herself up and wrapped her arms around her knees as she sat trying to control her shaking body.

MOSCOW AIRLIFT

The Same Day, 1345 Local Time, Moscow

Arkady was surprised when the head of the *militsiya* agreed to see him on short notice. Normally, appointments with Commissioner Sergei Sokolov were hard to get—and then, even if you were lucky, it would take at least a month before he met with you. When Arkady told Sokolov's assistant that the topic was Dolgikh's assassination, she'd promised to find him time as soon as possible.

When the *militsiya* was reorganized 1990, the newly appointed Sokolov's first task had been to clean house. At that time, the organization was known more for corruption and brutality than for effective police work. Sokolov implemented extensive reforms. As part of those reforms, Sokolov created small, elite investigative teams inside the Criminal Investigation Department to solve major crimes. Based on Arkady's reputation for uncovering evidence that led to convictions without resorting to brutality, Sokolov picked him to lead the team concentrating on crimes that were violent, high profile either due to their brutality or the status of their victims and/or difficult to solve.

When Arkady entered Solokov's office, he was mentally reviewing the points he needed to make. He didn't just intend to summarize the case—he wanted to test the political waters and needed Solokov's political support. Without that support, investigating the assassination of a high-level military officer was tantamount to committing suicide.

When Arkady had finished telling Sokolov that he feared other senior officers might be killed in the near future, Sokolov asked what evidence Arkady had. Arkady handed the commissioner a Soviet Navy folder containing sworn statements signed in late May by the four fleet commanders saying they would not take part in any attempt to overthrow the government. The folder also contained an order Dolgikh had planned to send, telling the Navy to stand down if a coup occurred.

Sokolov sat back in his chair and rubbed his chin. Arkady felt his heart rate increase. If Sokolov was aligned with the hardliners, continuing the investigation could put him in an unmarked grave. He was and wasn't surprised that the commissioner told him to keep digging. If another general or major political leader was assassinated, Arkady was instructed to come back and they would discuss what steps to take.

Sokolov went so far as to say he supported what Gorbachev and Yeltsin were doing. They were the ones who'd put him in this job and given him orders to clean house. In the commissioner's opinion, a coup would be counter to the freer, more open society Gorbachev wanted to create. A more peaceful relationship with the West, however, meant the Soviet Union wouldn't need as big an army as it had. Many in the KGB would lose their jobs—a happy prospect for the *militsiya* since the KGB was a rival and often a hindrance to proper police investigations.

At the end of the meeting, Sokolov asked Arkady not to share his views with anyone else and warned him to keep Admiral Dolgikh's documents secure. Arkady promised to do so. Privately, he resolved to keep *all* of the admiral's documents safe—not just the few he'd shared with Sokolov.

The Same Day, 1510 Local Time, Moscow

The black, bullet-resistant Suburban was waiting at the bottom of the steps at the Rossiya's front entrance. Just before Velasquez opened the back door, Josh said, "Gunny, I want to take a detour on the way back to the embassy."

"Sir, where do you want to go?"

Josh rattled off an address near the outermost ring of Moscow. It was one of two given to him by Krasnovsky.

"And what's there, sir?"

"An apartment building." When Velasquez looked quizzical, Josh said, "Gunny, if you don't want to go, I'll take the metro."

Velasquez held the Suburban's door open. "Sir, we have limits where we can drive without the Foreign Ministry's permission. If we take the Suburban anywhere apart from the normal places, someone will tell the KGB and the Foreign Ministry will call the embassy. We try to avoid such conversations whenever possible—the Soviets take a dim view of Americans roaming around their country. So why are we going, sir, and what are you not telling me that I should know?"

In other words, Josh thought, Velasquez wanted to know why Josh was asking him to risk his career and maybe his life.

"It's a long story, Gunny. Sorry to bother you. I'll go out there myself this evening."

"Sir, with all due respect, that's bullshit and we both know it. What's the deal?"

"Let's just go back to the embassy—I have a call to make to D.C. Then we'll go to a SCIF and I'll tell you the story."

"Fair enough, sir." Velasquez made an exaggerated bow and with a sweep of his arm, showed the way to the Suburban. "Our chariot awaits."

Twenty minutes later, Josh sat in one of the mini-SCIF's waiting for Jeff Gainesville to call him back. While he waited, he went over the notes from his mental debrief of his conversations with Gregorenko, Krasnovsky, Koskov, Olshansky, Stoyanovich and Ulyanov.

The phone jangled, and he answered tersely. "Haman."

"Afternoon, Josh. General Feltzer and I are in his conference room. We have several items to pass on to you. Do you want to go first or should we?"

"Sir, I'd prefer you go first, because there are a lot of gaps in what I know. Maybe when I hear what you have, it will fill the holes."

"Then let's start with Iran."

Jeff summarized his conversation of the day before with the DIA and CIA. As much as Jeff wanted to, he did *not* tell Josh about the warning Feltzer had got from senior officers in the CIA and DIA. He hoped it was just bureaucratic turf protection. Whatever they did, it would be played out above Josh's head. Josh needed to keep focused on his mission.

By way of reply, Josh passed on the Mossad's conclusion that a down payment has been made on either nuclear artillery shells or tactical nuclear bombs. He also reported what Krasnovsky had told him: that Ulyanov and others believed a coup was imminent, and that Ulyanov had chosen to sit on the sidelines. Koskov and his chief-of-staff, Colonel Stoyanovich, seemed to be among the plotters.

Gainesville confirmed that the payment for intel received had been made to Krasnovsky. Proof would soon be delivered to Josh in the diplomatic couch. Josh asked if Jeff could get him a covert recording device to make sure he didn't forget anything during future meetings. He was told not to ask the Moscow station head because then the CIA would want copies; if Josh refused, they'd try to make copies anyway.

"Sirs," Josh said, "I need some help here. I need someone as soon as possible trained to look at ground forces and operations and make a determination of what is happening. Marty Cabot would be ideal."

General Feltzer asked, "Where is he?"

"Special Operations Command. Let me note, sir, the Israelis trust him."

Jeff said, "I know you and Marty go way back. We'll try to convince his boss to do without him for a few weeks."

"Thanks."

"This is all good stuff, Josh. Anything else?"

He told the two flag officers he was about to have dinner with several Soviet Naval Aviators he met at the June 22nd embassy reception. "They're helo drivers too," Josh said. "This should be fun."

* * *

When Josh walked into his small office, a pile of clothes lay on the desk. The look of the fabric told him the clothes had been made in the Soviet Union. When he held the jeans at his waist, he figured they would be a bit baggy, but they'd fit.

Velasquez stuck his head in the office. "Ahhhhh sir, you're back."

"What are these for?"

"The trip outside the wire we may be taking. It's best if we look like natives. Before we go, you and I should have that chat. Sergeant Brown volunteered to spend the watch in the comm center where we monitor Moscow police frequencies."

As Josh headed toward the row of small soundproof cubes, he turned to Velasquez. "Expecting trouble, Gunny?"

"No, sir, just being prepared. You're an Eagle Scout, aren't you? *Be prepared* is the Boy Scout motto."

"How'd you know I was an Eagle Scout?"

"I have my sources, sir."

Josh pointed to the first room they came to. They entered and closed the door. Velasquez took one of two chairs and crossed his feet after he sat down. Josh sat on the edge of the other chair and leaned forward.

"Gunny, what I'm about to tell you is known by very few people. It's family history, and knowing it is the only way to understand why I need to go... where I need to go."

Josh told the Marine about the assassination of his first wife Natalie and her parents, starting with Artur Vishinski's six-year career in the Red Army during World War II. By the end of the war, Artur the draftee had been promoted to major and had been twice awarded the Hero of the Soviet Union.

He'd left his unit's bivouac in July 1945 when he learned the unit was returning to the Soviet Union. He'd traveled south on foot, living off the land, intending to head for a port and take a ship to America. Instead, he'd been captured by the Americans and sent to an internment camp. There he fell in love with Rimma Blum, born on the Romanian side of the Moldavian/Romanian border.

Neither Artur nor Rimma had any love for the Russians or Ukrainians: both groups had raided their villages and killed Jews just for the fun of it. By living in the forest and stealing food, Rimma had managed to avoided capture by the Nazis for several years. However, in early 1944, she was caught and sent to the Marienbad concentration camp and forced to have sex with German and Romanian guards. When she resisted, she'd become the subject of medical experiments. The camp was liberated by the Americans before the worst happened.

In the American internment camp, Artur was told he'd be repatriated to the Soviet Union. Knowing he'd be shot as a deserter, Artur escaped. Eventually, he made it to Genoa, where Artur got work on a tramp steamer and through the help of the families that took him in, Rimma was allowed to immigrate in 1947.

Gunny Velasquez listened keenly to every word. Josh clenched his hands as he told the Marine that when his father-in-law saw the Statue of Liberty in New York harbor, he slipped into the water, even though it was December 1948 and the Upper Bay was only fifty degrees. Artur had swum ashore and been taken in by a Jewish family.

"Well, sir," said Velasquez, "his way of getting to the U.S. was tougher than walking across the Rio Grande like my parents did."

Josh took several deep breaths. "Maybe, but your parents had to get to the river first. That couldn't have been easy."

Velasquez nodded and waited for Josh to continue. "Let me make a long story short," Josh said. "The KGB eventually came for Artur, and their agent killed Rimma and my wife with him. Afterward, I stood at the foot of my wife's grave and vowed I would find the KGB son-of-a-bitch who pulled the trigger. Every year, I visit their graves and offer up whatever excuse I had for not finding their killer."

Josh paused to wipe his eyes and gather his emotions.

Velasquez didn't know what to say. Where he grew up in the barrios of El Paso, if someone took out your relative, you were honor bound to return the favor or die trying. Too many of his friends had been killed or were the victims of revenge. The shortest way out of the madness for Velasquez had been to join the Marine Corps.

"So," Josh said, "here's why I want to go to those two addresses. When my diplomatic visa application arrived on General Krasnovsky's desk, he recognized my name from his days in East Germany. Each applicant for a visa has to be researched, so he pulled my file. My file led to another and another and another, until Krasnovsky found the file on Artur Vishinski. A man named Volkov was the one who ordered my father-in-law killed. My wife and her mother were collateral damage."

Velasquez nodded. "If Krasnovsky recognized your name from East Germany, what was that about?"

"I can't tell you the whole story, but suffice it to say, a terrorist organization had a safe house in East Germany. We raided it and put them out of business."

"No shit, sir! I have to hear that story some time."

"I can't tell you."

"Is this the op you were on with Master Chief Jenkins?"

Josh didn't say a word.

Velasquez smiled. "Okay. Back to those two addresses. I assume they're for Volkov and the hit man?"

"Yes."

"Did Krasnovsky give you photos?"

"Not yet. They're coming. Supposedly."

"You just want to walk into these guy's apartments and whack them?"

"I want to validate General Krasnovsky's information. If he's playing me, I want to know."

"How are you going to check it out?"

"First, I want see if the addresses are valid. The hit man lives in a run-of-the-mill flat. Volkov has one of those apartments given to senior KGB officers and other high-ranking officials."

"What if this is a trap?"

"I'm willing to take the risk. But if the addresses aren't valid, I have to put everything Krasnovsky tells me through a different filter."

"And if they're real?"

"Then I have to confront my own demons."

"And you were willing to check these two places by yourself?" Velasquez moved so his face was close to Josh's, as if he were a drill instructor about to distribute wisdom to a recruit. "Pardon me, sir, if I sound like a broken record, but Moscow has gangs who will kill you just for your jeans. Many Soviet policemen would love to beat the shit out of an American just for fun and bragging rights. Then there's the Russian *mafiya*; they make the Italians and Mexican gangs look like choirboys."

"I know about the *mafiya* and the gangs." Josh took a breath. "Gunny, you don't have to go with me. This is my problem."

"Sir, you're either the bravest man I've met or a goddamned fool."

"Probably a fool, but I still have to go. Otherwise, it will haunt me for the rest of my life."

"Are you planning to go armed?"

"Unarmed. If someone stops me and asks for my papers, being armed raises ugly questions."

Velasquez stood to attention and saluted. "Captain, sir, it will be my pleasure and honor to accompany you. Two men together are much less likely to be a target, and neither one of us looks like an easy mark. I'll have the newly promoted Sergeant Brown drive us back to the Rossiya. I'll change in the car and we can work out a plan as we walk to the Metro station."

* * *

It was almost midnight when they got back to the Rossiya where Sergeant Brown waited with the Suburban to take Velasquez back to the embassy and their quarters. The trip into two suburbs of Moscow was covert only in the fact that they were sure no one followed Josh and Gunny Velasquez.

Their rules of engagement were that they would speak only in Russian. If they had to use a second language, it would be Spanish and they would simply say they were reliving their days in Cuba.

The pair went to Rublyovka first because it was the farthest away and both men believed it would be the place they would be noticed if they went there late. The walk from the metro station took them ten minutes and while Josh did not go into the building, the number matched the address given to him by Krasnovsky for General Volkov. They found it interesting that there were pairs of KGB border troops patrolling Volkov's complex that told both men that many senior KGB officials lived in the U-shaped set of buildings.

Bagdonovich's apartment was in a working class neighborhood. By the time they got there after ten, the sun had set and yet the parks and streets were full of people enjoying the warm weather. Other than two drunks who staggered into the pair and whom they helped stagger up the steps to their building, they didn't speak to anyone.

There were no guards patrolling Bagdonovich's. In fact, despite the number of drunks and unruly Soviet citizens yelling and scuffling with each other, there wasn't a policeman in sight. Not seeing the concierge, Josh ventured onto the ground floor and when he heard a door open, he kept walking out the back door forcing him not to turn around. Velasquez met him on the other side of the six-story, rust stained concrete building and they headed back to the Metro.

When he got back to his room, Josh's heart was racing. He took both bottles of scotch from the small cabinet with snacks, soft drinks and dumped them into a glass. After a large sip, he sat in the overstuffed chair in the living room of his suite while his mind raced and his heart slowed down. Halfway through the glass, he decided to take a shower and finish the scotch before he climbed into bed.

Chapter 14
Disintegration

Thursday, July 4th, 1991, 2001 Local Time, Moscow

There were two events Josh had to attend on the Fourth of July. He referred to them as "command performances," and they proved that the Fourth was not a day off to relax.

The first was the embassy's Fourth of July picnic, held for its employees and their families. The menu was traditional: grilled hot dogs, hamburgers, potato chips, and chilled watermelon. The second event was a formal reception where the embassy welcomed members of the local diplomatic community.

While Josh was not a member of the permanent embassy staff, General Grant sent him a note saying he was expected to attend both events. Grant further informed him he was expected to stay until the bitter end.

Each attaché was assigned to host a country for the reception. Josh was given South Africa; he guessed it was because knowing South Africans was not good for a "real" attaché's career. Wearing his Mess Dress, Josh stood by the door until Group Captain Alfred Leuven of South Africa walked in.

Josh introduced himself and welcomed Leuven to the embassy. As someone who'd spent his youth reading books on World War II, Josh asked if Leuven knew any of the South African pilots who'd flown with the Royal Air Force during the war. Leuven did; half an hour of conversation ended with the two of them standing at the bar, waiting for their second beer.

Beer in hand and a plate of hors d'oeuvres in front of him, Leuven asked if Josh would share his experience on helicopter tactics for inserting and extracting reconnaissance teams. Josh tried to play innocent, but the South African wouldn't be fobbed off. Josh asked Leuven to make a formal request; if the Navy approved it, he would be happy to pass on what he learned. Leuven shrugged, smiled, and excused himself to talk with other acquaintances.

While the attachés mingled, a separate event was being held for more senior diplomats. Normally, the Russian foreign minister or one of his senior deputies came to such receptions. This time, however, Boris Yeltsin attended. His appearance was symbolic and significant, sending a message to the Russian people and the world.

Josh milled around for a few minutes, trying to avoid talking to anyone in order to complete a second pass at the buffet table. With one hand holding a glass of beer and a plate with bread, cheese, a pasta salad and fruit, he headed toward an empty table in the corner.

He was enjoying a few minutes of peace when he heard the scraping of a chair and saw Major General Krasnovsky standing there in his KGB uniform. "This is a nice quiet corner," Krasnovsky said.

"So it is," Josh agreed.

"I come to these events because my name is on the visa for every attaché in this room. It's my way of saying the KGB is watching. As the proverb says, if you're afraid of wolves, don't go into the woods." Krasnovsky chuckled.

Josh ate a forkful of pasta salad and nodded to Krasnovsky to keep talking.

"Captain, it looks like you need another napkin. Take this one."

Raising an eyebrow, Josh took it. He felt something inside.

In a low voice, Krasnovsky said, "First, these are the pictures I promised to give you. There are three pictures of the hit man Bagdonovich along with Volkov's latest official photo from his personnel jacket. Bagdonovich is in Moscow waiting for his next assignment. Second, a coup is coming and I'd advise the United States not to interfere. I don't know whom the plotters fear more: Gorbachev or Yeltsin. But the plotters won't arrest either of them until after the coup takes place."

"This is not a good situation."

"You're right. This is going to be an all-Russian affair and could get very bloody. In the next few days, I should have a copy of the movement orders for a no-notice deployment exercise assigned to the divisions in the Moscow military district. Neither Ulyanov nor I think the Army will shoot at its own people. He's more worried about the Spetznaz and the KGB's Group Alpha; you never know what those hotheads will do."

"Do you think a coup might lead to civil war?"

"Possibly."

Josh buttered a chunk of baguette while a waiter cleared his dishes. When the waiter had passed out of earshot, Josh looked down at his plate while he spoke. "General, can you get travel permits for people like me to travel outside Moscow?"

"Where do you want to go?"

"Uzbekistan and Turkmenistan are nice places to visit this time of year."

Krasnovsky laughed. "Why?"

"Hypothetically speaking, if I knew nuclear weapons were being illegally sold to the Iranians, *and* if I knew where the weapons were being taken from... if I knew the transport route, I might try to seize the weapons and give them back to the Soviet Union. As part of the deal, I'd turn over those who sold the weapons illegally—let the KGB treat them as the criminals they are. Unless, of course, there are units in the Red Army I could trust to stop the theft."

Krasnovsky laughed again. "Most units of the Red Army aren't capable of doing much except spending money." He stuffed a chunk of roast beef into his mouth and chewed while considering Josh's statement. "Do you know who the sellers are?"

"No. If I were to look, I'd start with Red Army officers who control access to nuclear artillery shells and portable bombs. Portable enough to be carried by one or two men."

Krasnovsky pursed his lips. He didn't like traitors. "Is this the real reason you're in my country?"

"One of several reasons."

"What do you know about the sale?"

Josh said, "The seller has been paid thirty-six million U.S. dollars. The money is now sitting in a Swiss bank, earmarked for an unknown Finnish citizen. My associates think it's a deposit on the full amount."

"Can you tell me which bank?"

"Bordier et Cie in Geneva. The money can be withdrawn via Nordea in any of its Helsinki branches."

Krasnovsky took a couple more bites. This conversation was becoming more and more interesting by the moment. Capturing the thieves of nuclear weapons would move him another rung up the KGB ladder. That would be good for his retirement. "Captain, I think you know more than you are telling me."

"I've told you everything I've been authorized to say."

"Will you tell me more?"

"It depends on how much you want to help us."

"What kind of help do you want?"

"Not sure yet. Here's the deal. Help us and you get all the credit for finding the bad guys. We want the weapons to stay under Soviet control and destroyed in accordance with the disarmament treaties."

"When will you be able to tell me more?"

"Do we have an agreement?"

"Yes."

"Then I'll share more specifics when we talk next week."

* * *

An hour later, Josh was standing in the hall waiting for the last guests to leave. Velasquez came up behind him. "Sir, are you ready to go?"

"Yes, but I'd like to walk. It will do me good and give me time to think."

"Sir, I advise against it. There are gangs out there who'd see you as an easy mark. We've been lucky the past two times. Neither the KGB nor the GRU nor the MVD nor the gangs noticed. This is the third time and we're pushing our luck."

Josh nodded and he'd already weighed the risks. "I still want to walk. I need time alone." He looked at the gunnery sergeant. "I'm going upstairs to change my clothes. If you want to change too, you can follow me in the Suburban at a respectful distance. If anyone tries anything, you can be the cavalry. Agreed?"

Velasquez swallowed hard. He saw he wasn't going to talk Josh out of walking. "All right. Brown and I will stay two hundred yards behind. Please keep on the sidewalks so we can follow."

"Will do. See you in ten minutes."

* * *

Clad in jeans, a windbreaker, turtleneck and his running shoes, Josh turned right coming out onto Novinskiy. It was sunset and the shadows of the buildings stretched across the street were starting to disappear. The fading sun was on his left, confirming that he was heading south toward Novvy Arbat and toward Red Square. Josh stopped long enough after he crossed Novinskiy to let the black suburban catch up.

He wondered what he'd tell Jeff Gainesville and Avram Gutman about his conversation with Krasnovsky. From his vantage point, the Soviets were the ones who should stop the sale of the weapons. They were capable, but did they have the will? Since the 1980s when they began to replace the U.S. as Iran's primary source of modern arms, they may not want to put that source of hard currency at risk. Beyond that, the sale may have been completed. It might already be too late.

Josh was turning over in his mind what he should say to Gainesville when two men blocked his path. With his mind on the complexities of political intrigue, Josh hadn't noticed that the streetlights just past the Shchusev State Museum of Architecture were out. He guessed by the men's grins and menacing stances that they had him surrounded. A glance over his shoulder confirmed his suspicion.

"You're wearing very nice clothes, comrade," said the leader of the group. "I'm sure your clothes will fit me. I'll take them and the money in your wallet."

"Sorry," Josh said, "but I need the clothes myself. Go buy your own. There are plenty on the black market."

"They cost money. Yours are free. And a rich Westerner like yourself can always buy more."

264

Josh shook his head. He wondered if Velasquez would arrive before this got ugly. He backed up against a wall to protect his six o'clock.

The leader flicked his wrist and a five-inch switchblade knife appeared. He stepped forward, now only one long step from Josh. "If I have to, I will cut them off you. The blood will come out in the wash and I can have them stitched up."

"How many stitches do you think *you'll* need?" Josh asked.

The question took the man aback and made him pause. It gave Josh what he wanted: the initiative. Josh stepped forward and grabbed the man's wrist to control the knife as he bashed his forehead into the man's nose. Then he slammed his knee into the knife-holder's groin, twisting the man's arm down and to the left. The pain from both blows popped the knife out of the attacker's hands. As the man doubled over, Josh shoved him hard; he stumbled back and fell on his butt.

Josh checked on the other three men. Two hesitated, while the third rushed forward in an attempt to grapple. At the last second, Josh jumped aside, stuck his leg out and put his hands on the man's back, sending him headfirst into the wall. Blood streaming from a gash on his forehead, the man fell sprawled to the pavement.

The leader, now deprived of his knife, cursed as he struggled to get to his feet. Before the man could stand, Josh kicked him in the ribcage. He felt the man's lower ribs give way under his foot. The attacker collapsed, screaming in pain to the concrete.

The two remaining men had drawn knives, but they hesitated. The arrival of the Suburban and the sound of sirens made them turn to run, but Velasquez and Brown leapt from the car and quickly disarmed them.

"Captain," Velasquez called, "are you all right?"

Josh had his hands on his hips. He took deep breaths as adrenalin pulsed through his system. "I'm fine. But my sparring partners aren't doing so well." Josh waved in the direction of the first attacker, who was now on all fours. Blood dripped from his shattered nose and split lips, and he groaned in pain. The man who'd gone headfirst into the wall sat dazed on the sidewalk. Blood streamed down both his cheeks from the gash in his forehead.

Not long after, two Volga GAZ 24s screeched to a halt on Vodvizhenka with their lights flashing. Another car with *militsiya* markings blocked the entrance to the nearby Metro station. Uniformed officers came running with their hands on their holsters. A dirty battered car pulled in front of the Suburban, and a *militsiya* officer got out of the passenger seat. He issued orders to handcuff the four men, then walked over to Josh.

"Captain Haman. I'm Lieutenant Colonel Arkady Kishniev of the *militsiya*. On behalf of my country, I apologize for this attack."

"How do you who know I am. Have we met?"

"Not directly. But I saw you at the Choral synagogue, and I asked a friend who you were."

Josh looked at him quizzically, clearly wondering what a lieutenant colonel of the *militsiya* had been doing at the synagogue.

"I assure you, Captain Haman," said Arkady, "I was there to pray, not to spy on those present. My family has been going to the Choral Synagogue for generations."

Josh stuck out his hand. "Well then, Colonel Kishniev, it's nice to meet you."

Arkady took the offered hand and shook it. "Now tell me, what happened here?"

"I was walking from my embassy to the Rossiya Hotel when these four men demanded my money and my clothes." Josh pointed to the man with a bloody nose. "This one attacked me with a knife. It's on the ground over there. I did what I had to do to defend myself. Another tried to tackle me and I shoved him into the wall."

Arkady looked at the blood smear on the wall, then at the gash on the man's head. He tried not to smile. He turned to the uniformed police officers who by now had the four men standing in a row a few steps away. "Arrest them for assault and attempted murder. Send the arrest report to me."

Josh asked, "Will you need a statement from me?"

"Yes, Captain. Here's what I would suggest. Sunday afternoon, my family and I would be honored if you could join us for dinner. Bring a signed statement witnessed by someone at the embassy; that should be sufficient. Oh, and bring statements from your driver and bodyguard as well. For a case this straightforward, it's all we'll need."

"Dinner Sunday?" Josh repeated, bemused. *I doubt this is the usual procedure.*

"Yes, Captain. My parents, my sister, and I dine together every Sunday afternoon. We would be honored to have you as our guest."

Why not? "I accept."

"Excellent." Arkady tore a page from his notebook and scribbled the address on it. "Your bodyguards are welcome as well."

"Thank you."

As Arkady walked away, Josh looked back at Velasquez. The Marine was standing by the open rear door of the Suburban. He had an "I told you so" look on his face. But when Josh approached, all Velasquez said was, "Sorry, sir. We got caught behind a truck and lost sight of you. By the time we caught up, you were ... engaged." His face changed to a big grin. "Your moves weren't half bad for a swabbie aviator."

"I have a wife who has her third degree black belt in karate and is working on a second degree in tae kwon do. Between acting as her practice dummy and taking lessons from the SEALS I worked with in Vietnam... I've learned some tricks." He looked over at the police cars. "How did the *militsiya* get here so fast?"

"We called them on the radio. Then we let the embassy know what was happening. We'll have to fill out a report when we get back. And sorry, sir, but questions will be asked."

In other words, General Grant would be hard pissed.

The Same Day, 1426 Local Time, Quonset, RI

The blue and white thirty-four foot long Luhrs 34 Tournament Sport Fisherman had had a hard life. The prior owner ran it onto rocks at the south end of Conascuit Island in Narragansett Bay. Everyone aboard was drunk at the time, including the man at the wheel. That was enough for the insurance company to refuse to pay for repairs.

After the accident, the boat was towed to a yard in Quonset, Rhode Island. It sat for a year while the owner fought with the insurance company. When he lost the case in court, the owner put the Luhrs up for sale as is to let someone else pay to get it seaworthy again. Anyone who bought the boat would have to patch the hole in the hull, and replace or overhaul the left engine, shaft, propeller and rudder. It was very likely that there'd be further expenses that could not be determined until the engine and gearbox were removed to allow for a more thorough inspection. Although the boat was only two years old, no buyer wanted it in such condition.

However, for Mohammed Safdar, the Luhrs was perfect. He made a low-ball offer and the owner was glad to take it. Safdar had the money wired to the boatyard from a front company and authorized the repairs. As expected, they were about fifteen percent more than the original estimate, but Safdar didn't care. Once the yard finished its work, the Luhrs was certified as seaworthy.

While the boat was being repaired, Safdar completed a course run by members of U.S. Coast Guard Auxiliary at the Port Washington Yacht Club, where club members made their boats available as teaching tools.

Renamed *Swordsman,* the Luhrs was registered in Rhode Island under a fictitious owner's name. Safdar became the proud owner on June 25. Before he set sail, the boatyard's service manager showed him all the systems and coached him for an hour as he maneuvered around the harbor and practiced docking.

Confident he could handle his new toy alone, Safdar eased the boat out into Narragansett Harbor. Once he reached the bay, he opened the throttles for the two 350-horsepower Crusader 454 diesel engines. Looking at the tachometers, Safdar could see he was using just over half of the available rpm. The boat surged through the water nose up and on what he learned was the step—the speed at which the boat is supported by hydrodynamic lift rather than hydrostatic lift. In other words, the drag on hull from the water was less when the boat was on the step than when it was at slower speeds and needed less power to go faster.

Just before sunset, Safdar slowed *Swordsman* to enter the harbor at Port Judith, Rhode Island. His directory of marinas indicated that the one in Galilee Salt Pond Harbor had a well-stocked commissary. He went shopping and gave each of the two teenage dock boys a twenty-dollar tip for bringing his groceries and bags of ice onto the boat. Later that night, Safdar studied the chart of Long Island Sound and his planned 132 nautical mile trip to a marina near Stamford, Connecticut.

Once he reached his destination, Safdar eased the boat into a slip he'd rented for two weeks. Many much larger yachts dwarfed *Swordsman*. Good: it would be that much harder to see his boat. Satisfied that this part of the trip was completed, Safdar cleaned the deck and dropped a bag of garbage in a can at the shore end of the dock. He took a cab to Stamford's railway station before boarding a train into New York City.

Late on the second of July, Safdar returned to Stamford. He'd ordered provisions while in Rhode Island; he found them waiting in coolers near the boat. He stowed away the food and dumped the ice into large coolers designed to keep fish from spoiling.

Safdar left Stamford early on July 3. Two hours and twenty-five nautical miles later, he eased the twin throttles back to let the Luhrs slow to five knots. He didn't want to leave a large wake in Little Neck Bay—he was sure the harbor police were looking for boaters speeding and didn't want the scrutiny a ticket would bring.

Now, on the morning of July 4, Safdar was standing at the end of the pier, waiting for Jim Broughton. The FBI agent had new information they could discuss while spending the night on the boat in New York Harbor and watching the fireworks. Safdar's plan was to leave Little Neck Bay by nine, cruise down the East River, and find a place in one of the designated anchorages in New York Harbor and be one the hundreds of other boats there for the Fourth of July fireworks.

Throughout his trip, Safdar reviewed his plans looking for loose ends. Broughton was definitely on the list: he knew too much. Safdar's bosses in Syria had not answered his request for advice. Was Broughton worth more as a source and a soldier for Allah? Or, did he need to be eliminated?

Monday, July 8th, 1991, 0456 Local Time, Moscow
The jangling of the phone was hard to ignore. So was the sunlight streaming into Josh's sitting room. The brightness

made Josh squint, but he had to admit he enjoyed the reflections from the gold-plated thread on the furniture's upholstery. The phone rang again. *Who the fuck is calling me at this hour in the morning?* He grabbed the phone and said, "Hello?"

"Josh, it's Lev. Sorry to wake you, but I wanted to catch you before the day started."

Josh sat upright and looked around for a pad. Lev Mogen wasn't calling at this hour to exchange pleasantries.

Lev asked, "Do you still stay in touch with Andrew Goode?"

"Yes." Andrew Goode was the head of the FBI's counterintelligence division in D.C. Josh wondered how Lev knew Josh and Goode were friends.

"Do you still trust him?" Lev asked.

"Yes. I had lunch with him just before I left." Josh had to be careful what he said; undoubtedly, the KGB taped all calls to the hotel.

"What time will you be at the embassy today?" Lev asked.

"About seven-thirty. Why?"

"Call me as soon as you get there."

Dial tone.

* * *

Three hours later, Josh took the folding knife that Velasquez handed him and used it to slit open the three-inch thick package sent by Avram Gutman. Carefully, Josh pulled out the contents, putting pictures in one pile and documents in another. Since photos were usually more interesting, he looked at them first. Each had a sheet of typewritten paper taped to the back, then folded over the front. The typist noted the date and location of each picture, as well as who was in it.

Several pictures showed FBI Special Agent James Broughton. Others showed both Broughton and a Middle-Eastern man identified as Mohammed Safdar. The photos were sharp, not grainy, indicating they were taken with a high quality lens not far from the men.

After looking at the pictures, Josh separated them into three stacks: Broughton alone; Safdar alone; and the two together, either walking or sitting on benches along the bicycle path on the Manhattan side of the East River.

The stack of documents included a summary of the surveillance timeline and activities corroborated by the pictures. Josh compared the photos to the summary; often the background of the pictures showed a street sign or address that verified their location.

Another document gave a biography of Mohammed Safdar, starting with his parents and ending with what the Israelis knew about his activities in the United States. The documents had very little on Broughton. Avram's people had found Broughton's photos in high school and college yearbooks, but apart from that, they didn't have much except that he was an FBI Special Agent.

Clipped together were copies of money transfers from an Iranian government agency to a bank in Iran. From the bank, the funds were transferred to another account in Syria, then to a bank in Lichtenstein, then moved to the Canadian Imperial Bank of Commerce in Toronto before being sent to the CIBC's New York office. Finally, the cash was deposited in Chase Manhattan and Citibank accounts in New York. The signee on the Chase account was Mohammed Safdar; on the Citibank account, it was Bashar al Bishi. A separate note said that although the names were different, handwriting analysis indicated that the signer was the same.

Transcripts of three conversations between the two men made up the thickest document. Josh was horrified to read their discussion of potential targets in New York, with

Broughton telling Safdar he would know if any U.S. agency authorized surveillance of the Palestinian.

Josh handed the transcript to Velasquez without saying a word. The Marine read it. "Holy fucking shit."

"We need to call Admiral Gainesville right now."

Five minutes later, Josh was sitting in one of the secure phone booths. He did the calculation: 0904 Moscow time meant 0104 in Washington D.C. Too bad! He flipped the pages in his address book, found Gainesville's home number, and dialed the area code 703 for Northern Virginia.

The phone rang and rang until finally, a groggy voice answered. "Gainesville."

"Good morning, Jeff, its Josh. Pick up your STU-III."

"Give me a few seconds. Do you know what time it is here?"

"Trust me, this will be better than coffee. And besides, Lev Mogen woke me up at 0430 Moscow time."

"Do I need to take notes?"

"Not if you can remember to set up a call or two."

It took thirty seconds for Jeff Gainesville to get to the office he had in his Arlington townhouse. "I'll initiate secure." When the phones finished synchronizing, he simply said, "Go."

It took Josh five minutes to summarize what he'd received.

Jeff said, "Maybe Broughton is undercover."

"Based on the transcripts, I don't think so. Neither do the Israelis."

"So what do you want me to do?"

"I'm on pretty good terms with Andrew Goode, who runs the FBI's counterterrorism operations in D.C. He needs to know. I want to brief him with you on the phone. I'll send the whole file direct to you via diplomatic pouch, then you to hand it to him. Nobody else can touch it."

"Why don't the Israelis give it to FBI directly?"

"The Israelis don't want this go through channels—too much risk of a leak. They want someone who knows good intelligence when he sees it and can take action."

"O.K., but why couldn't this wait until later in the day?"

"The Israelis and I believe one or more of the nukes being bought by the Iranians are headed for the U.S. for use by the Sword of Allah."

"Oh fuck..."

"Yeah. So here's the deal. The pouch will be at State this afternoon, addressed to you. In the meantime, I'll have a friendly chat with Krasnovsky. Let's call Goode now to give him a heads up. Do you want to conference him in now or should I?"

"You do it."

"O.K. here goes. If I disconnect you, I'll call right back."

Josh pushed a button to put Jeff Gainesville on hold and dialed the second number. Another sleepy voice answered the phone. Grumbling, Andrew Goode agreed to pick up the extension in his home office.

"Andrew Goode, meet Rear Admiral Jeffrey Gainesville. He's my boss. Jeff, meet Andrew Goode."

"Andrew," Josh continued, "Since you're not on a secure phone, I'm going to be deliberately vague. Still, I'm sure you'll get the gist of why I called." After Josh summarized what he had, he ended with, "So do you know Jim Broughton?"

"Yes," Andrew said. "He's in the New York office. I can't say more on this phone."

"After you get the material, Jeff and I want a conference call on a secure line with you alone. Admiral Gainesville's aide, Lieutenant Johnson will set it up."

"I'll clear my calendar. Josh, why do you never call with good news?"

"Because people like Admiral Gainesville give me shitty jobs." Josh heard laughter from both phones. "Good night everyone, sweet dreams. We'll talk tomorrow."

Before he hung up, Josh heard the word "asshole" twice.

The Same Day, 0846 Local Time, Moscow

The Zil limousine sped down the middle lane of Leningradsky Avenue toward the center of the Soviet universe, a.k.a. the Kremlin. The car, armored to protect its occupants from rifle bullets, was doing eighty kilometers an hour in the lane reserved for official vehicles.

A second Zil limo followed fifty meters behind the first. Sitting in the back, Seraphim Olshansky heard the shriek of the missile before he saw its smoke plume as it passed over his car and slam into the Zil ahead. Smoke streamed out a hole in its rear door as the car staggered as if it driven by a drunk. Then it erupted in a fireball.

Olshansky's driver floored the accelerator and wove erratically as Olshansky looked over his shoulder. He searched for another missile but saw nothing. As they sped past the burning Zil, Olshansky turned his eyes away. The car had been taking Eduard Schvardze to the same meeting Olshansky was going to at the Hotel Moskva.

They didn't have to call for help. The radio on the console suddenly erupted with police transmissions.

Tuesday, July 9th, 1991, 1423 Local Time, Tehran

In the summer, the Iranian capital was dry and very hot. Everyone sweated and the salt residue left noticeable white rings around the armpits of dark shirts. Colonel Ali Akrami didn't spend much time in the heat—as one of the privileged few, he rode in an air-conditioned Toyota Land Cruiser driven by a chauffeur and protected by a bodyguard.

At a heavily protected building, guards flipped through Akrami's identity documents. While they examined the credentials giving Akrami, his driver, his bodyguard and his aide access to the building, another guard used a mirror on a pole to look under the sport utility vehicle. They even opened the hood to examine the engine compartment for bombs. Satisfied, a guard finally spoke into a microphone. A door with steel grillwork slid to one side, letting the Land Cruiser into an underground parking lot.

His driver was directed to stop in front of doors made of bulletproof glass. Akrami got out of the car and went inside, where both he and his briefcase were searched. When the guard was satisfied Akrami wasn't a threat, he picked up a phone and made a call. Shortly, an elevator arrived and took him to the lobby.

In lobby where the American designed and installed air conditioning and tinted windows kept the interior at a cool and comfortable twenty-two degrees Celsius, Akrami waited for the Pasdaran captain to enter his name in a log and issue him a badge. The six-story structure had been built for an American company whose employees had left after the Islamic Revolution.

The elevator took Akrami to the top floor where he got off the elevator and pressed a button next to a steel door. After a few moments, a buzzer told him that the lock had been released and he could enter the offices of the Pasdaran's special operations group. From this building, orders, money and people were dispatched all over the world.

On other floors, members of the Pasdaran ran the Quds force's administration, recruiting and logistics functions. Veterans of the corps were given preference for administrative duties; it was not unusual to see men in wheelchairs or missing limbs. Staff members were vetted carefully every two years to ensure they were still dedicated to the Islamic Revolution.

People suspected of disloyalty were arrested when they reported for work, never to be seen again. If their relatives had the courage to inquire what happened, they were met by silence or threats if they had not already been arrested.

Workers on the operations floor were in separate "cells" dedicated to supporting specific terrorist organizations sanctioned by the Pasdaran. Akrami often wondered how much money the men and women in this building spent and where the government got it.

No matter how the Ayatollahs spun the news or who they blamed, Akrami could tell the economy was getting worse by the day. Any expression of doubt—even asking if the money spent funding revolutions abroad would be better used at home —could get Akrami arrested. It left him privately wondering where the government got seventy-two million U.S. dollars to pay the Soviets for six nuclear artillery shells.

Soon he was ushered into a well-furnished conference room. Although the leather in the chairs was worn, they were very comfortable. They'd come with the building when it was seized, as had the rosewood conference table.

A voice behind Akrami asked, "All is well with you?"

Ali turned to see the tanned and worn face of Mohaqqeq Damad. Entering the room behind him was the bulky General Qasem Jalali.

Damad looked like an elf: just over one hundred and fifty centimeters tall and at most sixty-five kilograms. Yet, the diminutive Damad had the power to make you disappear. He was the one who'd advocated using young men from families who prospered under the Shah to walk at gunpoint across known Iraqi minefields. Those who'd survived were sent back to their families with a message encouraging them to support the government more enthusiastically.

General Qasem Jalali was almost as broad as Damad was tall. The general was responsible for all the functions in the building. He looked as if he hadn't been in the field for a long time: a strong muscled man gone to fat. As a general, Jalali had no gift for military strategy or tactics, but he was a genius at logistics.

"I am well," Akrami said. "*Inshah Allah.* God has been good to me."

Damad said, "You have been to the Soviet Union several times, I heard."

"Yes, minister."

"Tell me, Akrami, what do you think is happening with the Soviet Union?"

It was not a question he had anticipated. Warily, he said, "There is much uncertainty. The country is split over Gorbachev's reforms."

The wrinkles on Damad's face moved. "We can read newspapers, too. You have met many Red Army soldiers in person, what do you think?"

It was a fair question. Akrami was expected to get to know the people he dealt with and what they thought. It was often a matter of life and death. "Minister Damad," he replied, "they worry about the future. No one knows what will happen under the new Russian Federation. Many generals think a coup is possible, and they fear being forced to choose sides. If they pick the wrong one, they'll be killed."

"What about the Americans? What are they doing?"

"Minister, the food operation will end soon. Then they'll go home."

Damad nodded to himself. "And the weapons we're buying... Is everything ready?"

"Yes, minister. Next week, I go back to Moscow, pick up the transfer paperwork, and send a signal to General Jalali. He'll give the orders to the men who are training to act and look like Soviet soldiers. They'll enter Uzbekistan and pick up the vehicles we've acquired. After that, we'll take delivery of the weapons from the depot. Twenty kilometers before we cross the Turkmenistan border, the weapons will be transferred from the military vehicles to commercial trucks for the trip through Turkmenistan. One by one, they'll be brought to Iran."

"Are you confident your plan will work?"

"With Allah's help, I am. It's a good plan we can easily execute."

Damad asked, "Do you trust your Soviet contact?"

Akrami said, "General Vavilov has seventy-two million reasons to keep quiet. So yes, I trust him."

Damad stared at Akrami evenly. "A lot rides on this mission."

Was that just a statement, a warning, or both? "God willing," Akrami said, "we will be successful."

The Same Day, 1530 Local Time, Washington, D.C.

Andrew Goode was waiting in General Feltzer's conference room when the package arrived from the State Department. Goode's size made him imposing, maybe even threatening. He was big enough to be an offensive lineman in the National Football League and by working out every day, his six foot four, 280-pound body hadn't gone to seed.

An hour after picking up the package, Goode was on the phone with the head of the FBI, getting permission to begin surveillance on Mohammed Safdar and Jim Broughton. The information on Broughton made him sick to his stomach.

It brought back memories from five years ago when Goode headed the agency's liaison office with the Pentagon. He had worked with Josh to catch a spy in the CIA. In the process, they uncovered a sleeper agent for the Soviet Union who'd come into the country as a young boy with the mission of worming his way into the FBI. During the hunt, Josh and Goode had become close friends. What was on the table now would become their second rodeo.

Intellectually, Goode could understand the rationale for becoming a traitor. Emotionally, however, he could never come to grips with it. Only his training overcame his urge to put a bullet into Broughton's head.

Although Goode was in a supervisory role, he spent as much time as he could in the field working with the agents assigned to counterterrorism cases. This assignment, he was sure, would be the pinnacle of his career.

What impressed him about the package he'd received was the level of documentation the Israelis had sent. One of their prosecutors familiar with U.S. evidence requirements must have had a hand in preparing the material. Yet, despite the damning implications of the file, Goode still had two obstacles to overcome.

Even if the Israelis who'd collected the material were in the witness stand, defense attorneys would have a field day challenging their U.S. law enforcement credentials and the legality of the surveillance. Perhaps a judge would throw the evidence out; at the very least, it would create doubt in the jury's minds. While the package was enough to convince the FBI to start its own investigation, it wasn't enough to arrest Broughton immediately, much less take him to trial.

Problem two was the FBI itself. To begin investigating Broughton, the FBI would have to admit it had another traitor in its midst. This was both a bureaucratic and cultural nightmare, and there would be stiff resistance. The dossier ought to have been enough to convince the director to let Goode open an investigation, but he didn't know which way the wind was blowing.

By the time he walked into Feltzer's conference room, Goode had already had a short, tense conversation with the head of the FBI, who was sending a prosecutor to the Pentagon to get a firsthand look at the photos and transcripts. Feltzer was clearly bothered by the delay—every day Safdar remained at large, the odds increased that he'd set off a bomb. If someone didn't stop him, everyone involved would have mud on their faces... not to mention the blood of many dead Americans.

Jeff Gainesville followed the Marine three-star into the conference room. Out of respect, Goode came to an attention. Feltzer dialed the operator, who put the call through to Moscow.

Lieutenant Johnson was sent to wait inside security at the Pentagon's Metro station entrance for the Department of Justice attorney. To allow Admiral Gainesville, General Feltzer and Josh to talk about other topics, Goode was asked to wait outside. Feltzer asked how badly Josh wanted Marty in Russia. He had a choice: go to the Chairman and have the orders rammed down the throat of the commander of the Special Operations Command, or have Josh choose someone else. Josh suggested deferring the request; it wasn't worth pissing off a four-star.

Josh was dog tired by the time he finished this call. As he emerged from the cubicle, he motioned to Velasquez. "I'm going back to the hotel for a nap. After that, I'm changing into my Soviet made clothes. I suggest you do the same."

Velasquez gave him a quizzical look. Josh said, "We'll be going to a place called Vadim's, where you'll ogle the girls and I'll have a chat with General Krasnovsky."

"Vadim's is one of the hottest night clubs in town," Velasquez said, impressed. "It'll be full of foreigners and high government officials."

"That's exactly why I want to go there—we won't be out of place."

* * *

As soon as he entered the Rossiya, Josh stopped at the concierge's desk. The man on duty was old enough to be Josh's father; he watched who came and went in the hotel with a practiced eye. Josh was sure the wizened old man was a veteran of what the Soviets called The Great Patriotic War.

The man smiled as Josh approached. "Do you have the number for Vadim's?"

The concierge nodded. "*Da.* It is very nice nightclub and restaurant. Hard to get reservation."

Dinner with the Kishnievs reminded Josh of dinner with the Vishinskis. No English was spoken, the laughter was genuine and the food hearty. Josh was also able to spend time with Arkady learning the ins and outs of the seeming overlapping and conflicting roles of the KGB, MVD and *militsiya* in Soviet society. The family also gave both he and Velasquez insight into Soviet society and culture that one doesn't read in intelligence reports.

"Good. Please call and ask for Valentina. She's the manager and she knows me. Make a reservation for two in my name. Tell her I need a quiet table."

The man nodded and leaned forward. He whispered in a voice made hoarse from smoking. "Vadim's is good place. No KGB."

Two hours later, Josh and Velasquez emerged from a Metro station and turned right on Kholszunova. Up ahead, about two hundred meters, Josh could see a purple neon sign with the club's name. Three barrel-chested men stood watch over the doorway. Their bearing suggested they had spent more than a few years in the military. The two Americans walked to the head of the line and Josh spoke briefly to the man who was letting in guests. Josh gave him their names and asked him to check with Valentina. It took less than a minute before they were admitted. Like all the other guests, they were patted down before they were allowed to walk up the steps under the frustrated and even hateful stares of those still standing in line.

Inside, the pungent smell of stale tobacco smoke made Josh's eyes water. The smoke hung in a cloud starting a few feet over Josh's head and reached all the way to the ceiling. Large speakers were mounted all around the club; while not deafening, the music was loud; Josh could feel the bass sound pulses through his body. No wonder the concierge had said, "No KGB." There was no way anyone could overhear a conversation in this place. Now Josh knew why it was so popular.

The very noticeable smell of unwashed bodies brought Josh back to his childhood in West Germany in the 1950s. It was a time when deodorants weren't available or popular with the locals, and air-conditioning not widespread. In the spring and summer, body odor was always in the air; walking through stores on a hot summer afternoon was an assault on one's sense of smell. Josh had always liked bakeries and delis—at least there, you could find spots where the pleasant aromas of food won out over the smell of sweat and unwashed bodies.

Valentina was waiting for them near the door. "Good evening, Captain Haman. Welcome to Vadim's. Your friend is already here; he's in back, at a table reserved for special guests."

Josh nodded. "This is my friend, Jesus." Josh used the phonetic pronunciation of 'hay zeus.' "He'll sit at the bar."

"I'll find someone for him to talk too. Does he speak Russian?"

"Just ask him."

Valentina repeated her question in Russian. Velasquez responded with a confident, "Of course," in the same language.

"Excellent," Valentina said. "So do you want to go upstairs, Hay-zoos?"

Velasquez smiled at Valentina's attempt to pronounce his first name. She explained that the upstairs bar was smaller and often used by bodyguards and drivers waiting for their principals. Their bills were added to those of their sponsors. Also, there were girls available and bedrooms.

"No, thank you," Velasquez said. "I'll stay here at the main bar. But it would be nice to have someone to chat with."

"I'll get my girlfriend Katerina," Valentina said. "Pick any chair at the bar. You can have dinner there." She turned back to Josh. "Let me take you to your guest."

Krasnovsky had a glass of vodka in front of him. He set another glass in front of a chair and gestured for Josh to sit. The chair was uncomfortably close to the Sovict KGB general; Josh picked the seat next to it instead. At the waiter's recommendation, both men ordered the steak special and made small talk until the food arrived. Looking over to the bar, Josh saw a striking looking blonde sitting next to Velasquez laughing at something he said.

"To a common purpose." Krasnovsky held up his glass.

Josh did the same and took a swallow. He winced as the liquid burned its way down to his stomach. He thought, *I'll never get used to drinking this stuff neat.* He wondered what Krasnovsky meant by a common purpose. "General, do you want to go first?"

"*Da.* When you leave, Valentina will give you a present. Look surprised. It will contain copies of the movement orders for the 4th Guards Armored and 2nd Guards Motor Rifle Divisions, to be executed any time after August 15. I think the orders are intended to get the army on the street in support of a coup. The coup leaders want to force Gorbachev to resign before parliament gives us our Christmas present on December

25th by dissolving the Soviet Union and creating the Russian Federation. A coup gives them a chance to declare a state of emergency. Then the KGB will be told to restore order. You can figure out what that means."

It took an effort not to react to that announcement. Josh cut off the end of his perfectly cooked steak, took a bite, chewed, swallowed, then said, "If everyone knows this is coming, why doesn't Gorbachev stop them?"

Krasnovsky emptied half his glass of vodka, then topped it off before beginning on his own supper. "Every time a General Secretary dies or is dying, the jockeying for power begins. The losers retire to their dachas or get eliminated. This time, it's more serious. Gorbachev and Yeltsin are hell bent on loosening the controls the government has on its citizens. The hardliners want more control, not less. There's a saying: *The eye can see it, but the tooth can't bite it.* You understand? Who can Gorbachev get to arrest the head of the KGB? Or, the Minister of State Security? Or, the Minister of Internal Affairs? Those men control the police and the entire security apparatus. In your country, perhaps, the president could have such people arrested, but in the Soviet Union..." Krasnovsky let his voice tail off.

Josh worried about how a coup would affect the controls on the Soviet Union's arsenal of nuclear weapons. He wasn't worried about ICBMs—they were locked in their silos and prohibitively difficult to transport. However, nuclear bombs and artillery shells could easily be stolen.

Krasnovsky continued. "One more thing. Volkov is one of the coup leaders, if not the head of the whole operation. If the coup succeeds, General Koskov will head the group punishing the coup opponents and Gorbachev's reformers. Coffin makers and gravediggers will have a lucrative few weeks. I believe Talyzin will replace Gorbachev once he is eliminated. Yeltsin will simply be shot."

"You're KGB. Aren't you in favor of this?"

Krasnovsky drained his glass and waited as a waiter set a new bottle appeared on the table; the Russian poured a glass and took a sip. "I saw the difference between quality of life in East and West Germany. The Stasi knew it could not control the people much longer. It was not a matter of *if* the Warsaw Pact would dissolve, but how soon. We, and I mean all of us, were lucky the East German government fell peacefully. Here in the Soviet Union, I think we may be looking at civil war and I want no part. I had my fill of war long ago, fighting the Germans. I don't want to shoot fellow Russians, particularly if all they want is more freedom. In my quiet way, I am doing what I can to make sure the coup fails."

Josh swallowed hard. For a two-star KGB general, these were astonishing words.

Krasnovsky drained his vodka in one gulp and poured another glass. "Do you know who Anastasia was?"

Josh nodded. "She's the youngest daughter of Tsar Nicholas II. Some people think she escaped the firing squad that killed the rest of her family. If so, she may be still alive today."

"That is the story, yes. My wife's name is Anastasia. Her parents deliberately named her after the Tsar's daughter. Both her parents were members of the bourgeoisie and suffered greatly after the Revolution. Both our fathers ended up in what became the *Gulag*. Then in the early 1930s, the Communists realized they needed engineers like my father and doctors liker hers, and they were released and allowed to work. They were still afraid of the Cheka and its successor the NKVD. When I was selected to join the NKVD, my father was sad and became afraid of me. It was not until after Stalin died that we could again talk as father and son."

Krasnovsky took a deep breath and drank half the glass. "Anastasia is a professor of history. Unofficially, she has spent her life researching what really happened in Yekaterinburg and is an expert on the Romanovs. She is forced to teach the government's story, but that is not the truth. The Tsar's family was murdered in the Ipatiev House. Soon afterwards, the Soviet government demolished the house to destroy whatever evidence remained. My Anastasia believes the Romanovs are in a mass grave near the house. The KGB archives probably contain the exact location and maybe even files on what happened. But of course, the information is a closely guarded state secret."

The general drained his glass and refilled it. "My Anastasia hopes that in a freer Russia, she and other experts can find out what really happened and tell the world. To her, the mystery is symbol of the lies the Soviet government tells its people every day."

Krasnovsky drank half of what was in his newly refilled glass and held it in both hands, studying the liquid as if it would give him strength or wisdom, or both. " So, why am I telling you all this? Neither Anastasia nor I are fans of our government, nor the Communist Party. We want to see change without a bloody civil war. We want to help end the current regime by helping push it over. But, if we do, you can imagine the risk to us and our children."

Josh could imagine their fate all too well if they were discovered. He wondered why Krasnovsky had chosen to speak out; such talk was extremely dangerous.

Krasnovsky held up his hand to keep Josh from asking. "New subject. Fewer than one hundred people control access to our nuclear bombs and shells. Fewer than a dozen officers control the nuclear artillery shells and can authorize a transfer. Every order has to be countersigned by a peer who has authorization, then approved by their superior officer."

"So you're telling me there must be three people involved in the sale."

"At least three. More likely five, maybe six. It would take an awful lot of money for them to take the risk."

"Is seventy-two million U.S. dollars enough?"

Krasnovsky's eyebrows lifted, and he waved his forkful of baked potato in a mock salute. "Definitely. Do you know who wants the shells?"

Josh said, "The money came from Iran. Our intelligence thinks they're trying to mount the shells on a missile."

"Makes sense," Krasnovsky said. "We've exchanged technicians with Iran for years: they work in our nuclear power plants and we help them build theirs. I signed off on the last group who came here about three years ago; I'll look at their visa files. As for the technicians and engineers we send to Iran, I'm afraid that's handled by a different KGB department."

Krasnovsky emptied his glass and plunked it down. After refilling it, he held up the bottle to show it was empty. Josh couldn't help but be impressed by how much liquor the man could put way. He also believed Krasnovsky was too drunk to lie convincingly.

"While I was in East Germany," Krasnovsky said, "I learned we had a nuclear bomb which fit into a large suitcase. I know this because a Spetznaz unit lost one on a training exercise, and it took two weeks to find it. The GRU and the KGB investigated all the participants, believing someone had to be a traitor. However, it turned out the bomb just fell out of a truck. We found it lying in a ditch along a deserted road. The ditch had been flooded and we didn't find the bomb until the water level dropped."

"How big is this thing?" Josh asked.

"About a meter square and a half a meter thick. Close to thirty kilos. Two men can carry it easily. In a war, Spetznaz would parachute behind NATO lines and place them near supply depots or headquarters. Set the timer and run like hell."

"Shit. It is an ideal weapon for a terrorist. Where are these things stored?"

Krasnovsky didn't say anything. He raised his glass, tilted it in Josh's direction and drained it. "When are you going to tell me how you got into East Germany?"

Krasnovsky's just told me that is all he's going to say tonight. Josh asked, "How close to dying is your friend?"

"He has a couple of months to live. Why?"

"Do you know where he lives?"

Krasnovsky shrugged. "South of Berlin in Rütenberg."

"Can you get permission to travel to Germany?"

"Why?"

"I'll pay for the ticket and the two of us can go," Josh said. "I'll tell the story to both of you at the same time. The trip will take three days. Day one, go there; day two, visit him; day three come back. Will the KGB let you go?

Krasnovsky finished his steak and potatoes and put down his knife and fork. He downed the last of his vodka and stood. "Anything is possible in this day and age. Meet me at the Patriarch Ponds on Saturday, one o'clock. I'll be sitting on a bench... provided I'm not in the Lubyanka. Oh, and I trust I've earned a deposit in my retirement account for everything I've just told you! Make sure that happens. And now good night!"

Chapter 15
Transfer Papers

From his flat on the seventh floor, Yakov Maksimov saw the Zil limousine parked at the front door. To get into the guarded compound, the driver and his bodyguard had to show their identity papers and let the car be searched by members of the KGB's Ninth Chief Directorate, the part of the KGB charged with protecting senior government officials.

Maksimov liked to leave the compound around six-thirty and arrive at GRU headquarters before seven. His direct reports would already be in the conference room, ready to update him on what happened since he left the night before, as well as any significant issues needed resolution. However, before that could happen, he had to wait for his car to be passed through the gate. The process of getting into the compound could take anywhere from ten minutes to half an hour, and no entreaties or threats by the drivers could speed things up.

On the ground floor, Maksimov's bodyguard stood by the door. He scanned the courtyard and the surrounding buildings while Maksimov waited inside the bulletproof double glass doors. Satisfied it was safe, the bodyguard walked to the Zil, opened the back door, did another quick scan, and then waved. Maksimov strode to the Zil in his 'head of the GRU' persona.

Maksimov was halfway out to the car when his bodyguard heard the ZZZZZZIPPPPP of a bullet passing close overhead. Instinctively he ducked as he drew his Stechkin APS pistol and searched for the source. A second sang by, followed by the sickening thud of a bullet hitting a human body. Maksimov staggered with a shocked look on his face. He leaned against a wall to stay upright as blood flowed from his chest.

The bodyguard was moving toward his boss when he heard a third bullet zip close by his head. Horrified, he saw blood splatter as it hit Maksimov in the upper chest. By the time he pulled the head of the GRU to safety, the amount of blood on the ground told him that if Maksimov wasn't already dead, he soon would be.

The bodyguard wondered what the GRU was about to do to him.

The Same Day, 1846 Local Time, Moscow

Two smells grew stronger as Josh approached the door. One was the appetizing smell of baking bread. The other was a familiar mix of spices associated with Oriental food.

When Danielle had invited had him to dinner, she'd told him *pad Thai* was on the menu. She'd also said there would a special guest. Since Josh knew that Avram would be present, he wondered who the guest would be.

As he entered the living room, a familiar looking man in his early seventies strode across the floor. Despite not having seen him in twenty-two years, Josh had no doubt that the white-haired man was Jacques Debenard.

The two men hugged, then the Frenchman held Josh at arm's length to look at him more closely. "So Josh, Danielle says you're well."

"I am, Colonel. And I have a wonderful family."

"So I hear. And I understand we will soon be related by marriage."

"Indeed."

He tried to imagine Rebekah meeting Danielle. He hoped they'd liked each other.

* * *

Twenty minutes later, Danielle announced dinner. Josh and Avram went directly to the table, but Jacques made a side-trip to the bathroom. Josh took advantage of Jacques' absence to pull Danielle aside.

Danielle sprinkled peanuts on top of a bowl of noodles topped with grilled chicken. Josh asked quietly, "Does your father know why I'm in Moscow?"

"Not exactly. If he asks, will you tell him?"

"Ask what?" Jacques said, appearing behind Josh.

Danielle said, "Why Josh is here in Moscow."

"I haven't gotten to it yet. I was more interested in his family." Jacques sat at the head of the table. "So, Josh, why are you in Moscow?"

"Gathering information on the food situation." Josh knew how unconvincing that must sound.

"I say bullshit to your answer," Jacques told him. He said it in English out of courtesy to Avram, who didn't speak much French. "The Pentagon wouldn't send a highly decorated officer to count crates of food. That's a job for clerks. So why are you here in Moscow?"

Josh grimaced. His instinct was always to maintain official secrets. If both Avram and Danielle knew the truth, there seemed no point in hiding it from Jacques. He had no choice but to trust him.

Josh sighed. "It's complicated. Mission One is stopping the Iranians from illegally buying small nuclear weapons from the

Soviets. Mission Two is figuring out what's going on inside the Soviet government from a military perspective. I work for a flag officer who wants a second opinion unfiltered by intelligence analysts."

"Father." Danielle held out the bowl of pad Thai. Clearly, she didn't want her father pressing Josh for more confidential information. A chunk of freshly baked baguette on the side of the bowl made it very un-Thai, but both Jacques and Josh appreciated the addition.

The senior Debenard poured them each a glass of forty-year-old Courvoisier. They clinked glasses. *"L'chaim. Good friends and long life."*

Each of them took a sip and repeated the words.

Jacques twirled the noodles expertly on a pair of chopsticks before taking a bite. After swallowing, he looked at Josh. "You know Koskov is here in Moscow?"

"Danielle introduced us. He's one of the hardliners."

Danielle leaned over the coffee table. "The son-of-a-bitch didn't recognize me. That just means I'll have to tell him who I am before I kill him."

Josh thought, *they have Koskov, and I have Volkov. And now I knew why Jacques was in Moscow.*

* * *

It was ten o'clock when Josh had to leave. "Avram, would you like a lift to your place?"

"Yes, thank you."

"My driver should be downstairs. I'll wait for you by the car."

Ten minutes later, Avram got in the back seat. Josh said, "We need to talk about nuclear weapons."

"Now?"

"Can you think of a better place?"

Avram shrugged. "So talk."

Josh took a deep breath. "We have to find a way to stop the weapons from leaving the Soviet Union. That means sharing everything we know. Do you want to go first?"

Avram nodded and spoke for ten minutes while Sergeant Brown circled around the loop known as Novinskiy. There was little or no traffic and Josh was sure the route was giving the KGB trackers fits as they tried to figure out where they were going. Some of what Josh heard was old; most was new. When Avram finished, he looked at Josh and said, "Your turn."

Josh explained why he was convinced the Iranians were going to try to take possession of nuclear artillery shells and a suitcase-size nuke during a soon-to-occur coup. He noted that his source was trying to find out who sold the weapons, where they were stored, and when they were going to be picked up. Josh also promised he could get a limited number of travel documents for Uzbekistan—likely where the weapons would be delivered to the Iranians.

In Josh's mind, the problem boiled down to two questions. First, how to find and retake the weapons without interference from the Red Army, GRU, *militsiya,* or the KGB? Second, in the process, how to make the Soviets look good?

When Josh finished, Avram didn't say anything for full minute. Finally, he said, "If we know where and when, I might be able to get people to help us. There are still many Bukharan Jews living in Uzbekistan and Tajikistan. Many left for the U.S. or Israel in the seventies and our embassy maintains contact with those who are left. We have permission to fly people back and forth to both places. We could arrange for some with military experience to help us."

"Dangerous for their families if they're caught," Josh remarked.

"I thought you said we were letting the Soviets take the glory for recovering the nukes. We can make no reprisals part of the deal."

"Good point," Josh said. "In fact, we could arrange for any Jews in that part of the world to emigrate to Israel or the U.S. if they want. Win-win."

"I like the way you think."

Thursday, July 11th, 1991, 1512 Local Time, Moscow

Grant had a satisfied smile on his face as he opened a file in the computer that was on the back of his desk. He prided himself in believing he had mastered the ins and outs of WordPerfect 5.1 for DOS computers. At the top of the page, he typed UNAUTHORIZED COMMUNICATIONS WITH D.C., then went back and underlined the words. From his notes, he typed the order he had given to Captain Haman: ORDER—All communications to D.C. and the Pentagon are to go through the senior Military attaché in Moscow.

He created three columns. The first contained dates when Josh had disobeyed the order. The second listed methods: phone, message, or pouch. The third column was headed TOPIC OF CONVERSATION. For each entry, Grant typed Unknown, possibly classified.

When he was finished, Grant saved the file as "Disobedience," made sure it was in his directory. To be on the safe side, he saved it to a 3.5" floppy disk and then created another file titled "Failure." The full title was FAILURE TO SUBMIT REQUIRED REPORTS.

At the top of the screen, he typed DAILY STATUS AND ACTIVITIES REPORT. Again, he wrote the order he gave to submit reports by 1700 every day. Under it, he titled the first column with the words DATE DELIVERED. For each date when a report was not delivered, he wrote No. His intent was to list the report serial number for each status report. When he was finished, it was a solid column of No's. Again, it was saved to his hard drive and to the floppy disk.

The third file was titled "Unreported" which was short for UNREPORTED CONTACTS WITH FOREIGN NATIONALS. Again, he created three columns beneath the direction he gave Captain Haman: date, means, and nature of the contact. Under MEANS, he pulled the phone numbers from Josh's bill from the Rossiya, and calls from the embassy to phone numbers not at military installations. The list almost filled a printed page. Like its predecessors, it was saved to both his hard drive and the floppy disk titled "Haman."

Grant planned to update the logs every day based on advice given to him by a friend in the DIA's Judge Advocate's office. The two had served together in the Third Armored Division, based at Edwards Kaserne in Germany. At the time, Grant had been the division's administration officer. His friend said the logs would be the basis for the complaint and charges that would enable Grant to arrest Haman.

Whether or not the charges stuck was immaterial to Grant. What made Grant happy was that once the charges were officially posted, the damage was done. Haman's career would be ruined and, even if the charges were withdrawn, almost everyone in command would assume that where there was smoke, there was fire. As Grant's friend had said, it was legalized character assassination. Haman wouldn't know he'd been skewered until it was much too late.

The Same Day, 0946 Local Time, New York City
Outside the door of Broughton's apartment, the senior FBI special agent put his toolbox down on the terrazzo floor. He nodded to the two other agents who nodded in return and rang

the buzzer. They waited ten seconds. When they didn't hear an answer, they rang again, then knocked loudly on the door.

While they waited, each man pulled on a pair of latex gloves. Not hearing an answer, the second agent took out a small leather folder and inserted the first of two small tools into the lock. It took fifteen seconds to release the dead bolt and another ten to unlock the door.

Inside, they put plastic booties over their shoes so they wouldn't leave footprints or bring in any evidence that could contaminate the scene. The third agent stood by the door as the other two fanned out through the apartment.

The team leader stuck his hand in his pocket to check for the umpteenth time that the warrant was still there. Officially, it was called a Delayed Notice Warrant, but everyone called it a "sneak and peek." Also in his pocket was a normal warrant that they would have used had someone answered the door.

The team spent an hour looking through the apartment: taking photographs and looking for telltales the occupant might have left to warn him that his apartment had been searched. Broughton, after all, was a professional.

The Same Day, 1522 Local Time, Pea Island, Long Island Sound

The boat was out of the wind on the lee side of an uninhabited rock in western Long Island Sound known as Pea Island. On the northeast side, a strip of rocks extended like a bent finger providing a sheltered anchorage. Before deciding to use the small bay, Safdar watched the island from afar without seeing anyone moor there and thought he'd have the sheltered waters to himself during the week.

He heaved a forty-pound Danforth anchor over the side, then waited for the line to pay out as the boat drifted aft in the current. Once the anchor was set, he secured the line on the cleat in the center of the forward deck. From the bridge, Safdar pulled both propeller selectors into reverse to make sure the anchor's twin forks would hold on the rocky bottom. Then he shifted into neutral and shut down both engines.

On the first night he spent in Rhode Island after taking possession of *Sworsdsman,* Safdar measured and re-measured the dimensions of the V-berth to create a rough sketch of the framework that would turn the boat into a bomb powerful enough to cause a bridge abutment to collapse. When he got back to his apartment, he turned sketch into a set of engineering drawings that were distributed to four machine shops. None of which had enough to see the whole design that would create a shaped charge.

Initially, he thought getting the pieces of angle iron and steel plates would be very difficult. It turned out to be less of a challenge than he thought. The plates and frame pieces were hidden in thirty-gallon coolers under layers of ice. The coolers would be heavy, but wouldn't look out of place at a marina.

Getting the welding tanks on board was simple. He repainted the small acetylene tanks to look like scuba diving tanks he carried on board, while also carrying a mask and flippers. The torch and other welding equipment were put in zipped-up duffle bags that looked completely anonymous as he lugged them onto the boat.

It took three days anchored at Pea Island to assemble the jig. Welding inside the cramped V-berth made the summer's 80° temperature even hotter and the fumes made Safdar queasy. Every thirty or forty minutes he went out on deck for fresh air and a drink of water. One afternoon, he tossed a rope ladder over the side and jumped into the 65° water to cool off.

At first Safdar debated taking *Swordsman* to a different marina every night, but he decided that staying at Oyster Bay was the best choice. Its location was convenient and the risk of being compromised was minimal. He was just a wealthy man who took his boat out every couple of days. Buying a hundred gallons of diesel fuel after each trip and giving large tips to the dock boys ingratiated him to the staff.

Friday, July 12th, 1991, 1449 Local Time, Moscow

It had been four days since Krasnovsky lit a fire under the head KGB archivist. The general pushed hard, but not enough to raise suspicions. The archivist was used to strange requests and Krasnovsky's was just one of many. Since Krasnovsky was a frequent 'customer' and polite to the archivist, the general's request went to the top of the stack.

Even so, the process wasn't quick—it would take a few days to pull the records for thirty-six generals. Krasnovsky was keen to know more about the men he suspected were about to sell nuclear weapons, but he had to live with the delay.

Besides, it would give Krasnovsky time to ponder a vital question: once he knew the buyer, whom should he tell?

The head of the KGB's Second Chief Directorate? He was responsible for political control of Soviet citizens and any foreigners residing or visiting the Soviet Union.

The head of the Third Chief Directorate? He was responsible for counterintelligence and surveillance of the armed forces.

It was important to choose the right man. Pick the wrong one, and Krasnovsky would be shot.

The first results he received were records from the KGB Border Guards on Iranians, Iraqis and Syrians who had made at least two visits to the Soviet Union in the past three years. They were rolled into Krasnovsky's office on a cart—thousands of files. Krasnovsky hadn't realized his department authorized so many visas to foreigners. He made a mental note to look into how and why later.

A cursory look at the records told him there was a constant stream of Iranians traveling between Iran and the Soviet Union.

They entered at the crossing points into Armenia, Azerbaijan or Turkmenistan, as well as at all the airports. Each individual had to get separate entry visas into each Russian Socialist Republic and had to specify the destination city.

When Krasnovsky told the colonel heading the immigration records section he was looking for army officers involved in smuggling, he got a cynical laugh. The colonel explained that, under Stalin, they'd arrested and shot twenty percent of the Army officers commanding units along the country's borders. Whether or not they were guilty has been irrelevant. Even if they weren't, Stalin reasoned it was a lesson to others who might contemplate treason.

When Krasnovsky started examining the files in detail, he needed criteria to reduce the possibilities. He decided to play the odds, and look for a man who:

1. Was in his late thirties or forties.
2. Entered the Soviet Union through Moscow or Leningrad by air.
3. May have had his visa renewed several times, and/or
4. Had several identities.

Krasnovsky knew he'd need to get lucky: criterion four drastically reduced his chances of finding his quarry. As he started through the files, Krasnovsky felt energized: hunting for the buyer was more important and interesting than reviewing visa applications. After going through the first twenty or thirty files, Krasnovsky hoped to develop specific instructions that he could pass on to a team of trusted officers who would scour what he anticipated were several thousand files.

Once he got going, he concluded the task was more about gut feelings than pure research. If the KGB had one of those computers the Americans used, the search might only take hours or even minutes. Unfortunately, while the KGB files were indexed, they were stored on a mix of microfilm and paper, so each had to be read by human eyes.

The fifth file caught his eye and he laid it on the side of his desk. Nine files later, his intuition again said, *look at this one more closely*. Before long, he'd gone through fifty and there were five in the 'investigate further' stack.

Krasnovsky selected thirty more files from the cart. By six o'clock, there were fifteen in the 'investigate further' pile and his mind was tired. He decided to go home and sleep, then get back to the job in the morning. In those fifteen files, his gut told him there might be the man he was looking for.

The Same Day, 1859 Local Time, Moscow

The man in the brown uniform with the blue tabs of the KGB looked left and right before he stepped off the curb to cross the street in the Khamovniki district. It was an area where members of the *intelligentsia* and the Soviet political elite lived. Whether he was not paying attention or thinking about something else, witnesses said he probably didn't see the speeding truck.

The truck didn't stop after its bumper sent the sixty-two year old head of the KGB's Fifteenth Chief Directorate flying into a utility pole. The man responsible for the security of government installations was dead when he hit the light post.

The Same Day, 1902 Local Time, Moscow

No one paid attention to the short major general as he emerged from the small bar on Ozerkavskaya in the Zamoskyvarechye area of Moscow. He was neither tall, nor handsome. He looked like anyone wearing the uniform of the Red Army even though he was the head of the military division of the Soviet Union's Supreme Court and its most senior prosecutor. His uniform shirt was unbuttoned at the neck and his tie loosened.

As he headed toward the Paveletskaya Metro station, the general tossed his uniform blouse over his shoulder. He was adjusting his hat when a man hit him on the back of the head with a blackjack. The impact of the small lead balls in the blackjack's leather-covered head sent the general staggering. A second blow knocked him unconscious. A third blow to the side of his head killed him.

The attacker wrapped his arms around the general's chest and pushed him into a waiting panel truck. Inside, the attacker went through the soldier's pockets, found his identity card and wallet, and tossed them between the front seats. Two blocks later, the sliding cargo door of the truck opened and the general's body was dumped onto the street.

The Same Day, 1546 Local Time, Hunters Point, Long Island

Mohammed Safdar backed his Suburban up to the machine shop's loading dock. Three-eighth inch thick plates of case hardened steel were laid on the truck's floor in seven stacks of three. Welded in place, they would direct a blast forward with enough force to weaken and cause a bridge abutment to fail. Safdar smiled, thinking of all the Americans who would die as the bridge trusses collapsed into the East River. As he got into the driver's seat, he stopped to look around. Seeing nothing unusual, he drove off.

As soon as he did, a gray Taurus pulled onto the street. The FBI agent in the passenger seat picked up the microphone. "Unit two is moving and is behind the gray Suburban on 47th Avenue. Unit one, let us know when you're in position."

The Same Day, 2009, Local Time, Moscow

Arkady had finished his bowl of borscht and was washing the dishes when the phone rang. It was Commissioner Sokolov:

two more generals had been murdered. After listening to Sokolov's description of the crime scenes, Arkady decided to go to the site where the KGB general had been hit by a truck.

On the way, he used his radio to talk to the *militsiya* officer on site where the prosecutor was found. The body had been dumped on the street; his skull crushed. No witnesses. Add Schvardze, Dolgikh and Maksimov, and the number of senior officers killed was up to five.

When Arkady got to the 'accident' site, KGB and *militsiya* officers had cordoned off the area. Arkady pushed his way through the crowd but a KGB colonel stopped him; since the dead man was KGB, the colonel claimed jurisdiction. Arkady's pleasant but strong response was that accidents and murders were investigated by the *militsiya*, not the KGB. Unless otherwise ordered, Arkady considered the case his, as dictated by the head of the Moscow *militsiya*. Arkady would happily keep the KGB informed on the progress of the investigation, but the KGB would have no part of it. Soon Commissioner Sokolov arrived in person, and after a discussion with a KGB major general, Arkady and the *militsiya* received sole jurisdiction.

While *militsiya* officers kept onlookers away, Arkady stood where the man had been hit. He was studying the area in search of something that would tell him how the murder was coordinated, when he noticed a different KGB general watching him closely. Arkady headed over, wondering why the man was still there.

The KGB general spoke first. "Good evening, I am General Igor Borodin. Was this an accident?"

"No, sir."

"How do you know?"

"Several reasons. First, if this were an accident, the truck driver would have attempted to stop. There would be skid marks. There are none. Second, the law requires that in cases like this, the driver must stop to help. He didn't. Third, we have statements from witnesses who saw the truck deliberately swerve to hit the victim and drive away."

"May I ask, Colonel, when you were standing in the street, you seemed to be looking for something. Is that so?"

"I was looking for the observation point: someplace an observer could wait with binoculars, identify the target, and signal the truck driver. It would have to be nearby, but with cover so that passersby wouldn't notice."

"Did you see such a point?"

"Yes." Arkady was becoming uneasy. "General Borodin, I'm sorry, but I don't think you told me where you work at the KGB?"

"I'm the senior KGB officer on General Ulyanov's staff. I came from the Third Directorate."

"How did you hear about the accident?"

"General Ulyanov called me—he knows I live nearby. The general thought I might know the victim and asked me to find out what the *militsiya* learned. As you can imagine, General Ulyanov is very concerned. Too many senior officers are being killed."

Before responding, Arkady wondered whether or not Borodin knew that Arkady and Ulyanov had already met about this matter. Ulyanov was convinced that the murders were connected and a coup was in the offing. Arkady agreed with the general's hypothesis. He wondered which side General Borodin might be on.

Borodin simply said, "I will leave you to your job." He walked away, leaving Arkady to wonder if Borodin now considered him an ally or a target.

* * *

When Arkady got back to his office, he pulled four sheets of paper from his safe. Each was a hand-drawn organization chart based on what he knew of Gorbachev's cabinet, Stavka, the GRU, and the KGB.

Making such documents was a crime, but they helped Arkady clarify how the recent murders affected each organization. Boxes with names crossed out indicated the man was dead. To Arkady, the key to solving who was behind the murders was identifying the plotters of the coup.

Saturday, July 13ᵗʰ, 1991, 1122 Local Time, Moscow

Krasnovsky looked at his watch. He was hungry and hadn't had lunch or even much breakfast. Moreover, he needed leave within an hour to meet Josh Haman at Patriarch Ponds by 1300.

He was satisfied with the progress he had made since arriving at 0730. As he looked at the folder in front of him, he saw that he'd gone through almost all of the folders on the cart. His 'investigate further' pile now had twenty-two folders.

He was almost at the last file when a photo jogged his memory. Krasnovsky had seen the face before. He set aside the remaining unexamined folders and went through the 'investigate further' stack. On the fifth from the bottom, the same face stared back at him.

Two names, two current visas. And, if there were two, might there be three? He quickly went back through all the files, both the ones set aside and the ones he'd put back on the cart. He found another match. The man in the photo had a mustache, but Krasnovsky was convinced he was looking at the same man. *Got you, you bastard!* Visas for the same person under different names was ample justification for an arrest warrant.

Satisfied, Krasnovsky sat back... but then a thought hit him. The man had a visa, but how did he travel inside the Soviet Union? Might he masquerade as a Soviet citizen? That meant he would have a *propiska*. In addition, if he traveled abroad under his Soviet identity, he'd need a green *zagranpasport*. He'd also need visas to visit other Soviet Socialist Republics.

All such papers would be reviewed and granted by various KGB offices. Krasnovsky knew everyone who gave such approvals. On Monday, he'd call up those responsible; such checks were common and would arouse no suspicion. He'd start with Russia and Kazakhstan. Krasnovsky was sure that somewhere, this bastard had a *zagranpasport* and a *propiska*.

Since he had multiple photos of the same man, he pulled out the duplicates and stuffed them in an envelope. Maybe Josh Haman and his friends in the CIA could identify the man—in the interests of Glasnost, of course.

The Same Day, 1655 Local Time, Moscow

Despite the air-conditioning, Josh was sweating from the humidity and 90° temperature as he walked into the embassy's secure communications center. His meeting with Krasnovsky at Patriarch Ponds had gone very well indeed, but the area formerly known as the Goat Marsh and it had left Josh clammy and wet from sweat and the humidity.

Besides Velasquez, the only other person present in the comm center was the watch officer on duty. All the other attachés were home with their families, enjoying the Saturday off. Since Josh had his choice of cubicles, he picked the one farthest from the watch officer. He nodded to Velasquez and dialed the number Jeff Gainesville gave him. Time see if the folks in the five-sided puzzle palace were still working.

He was not surprised when Jeff answered right away. Jeff informed him that both General Feltzer and Andrew Goode were in the room. For Josh, it might be near the end of the day, but for them, it was late morning.

Josh asked, "What do you guys have for me?"

Andrew Goode replied, "We did a covert search of Broughton's apartment. He's learning Arabic, but that could be for work. The financial analysis will be back on Monday." Goode summarized of Safdar's activities with the boat. He finished with, "We're convinced that Safdar builds bombs. We're following him closely; we know every place he goes for material. We'll give the DA an airtight case."

Jeff was next. "So, Josh, do you have anything?"

Josh hesitated. "Not for Andrew, no."

"I can tell a hint when I hear one," Andrew said. "I guess it's time to go and let you folks discuss stuff I'm not cleared for."

Once Andrew was out of the room, Josh told Jeff and General Feltzer that Krasnovsky was going to give him the names of the generals who could authorize a nuclear weapon transfer. However, even if they determined who had sold out to Iran, they couldn't just make an accusation. Gorbachev would want real proof, and so far Krasnovsky only had circumstantial evidence. He needed something solid before he could go to the head of the Third Chief Directorate. There was another wrinkle, Josh noted. Before Krasnovsky could blow the whistle, he had to make sure the head of the Third Directorate wasn't involved in the sale or the coup.

At least Krasnovsky had determined who he thought the Iranian buyer was. Josh was sending photos to D.C. and Tel Aviv to let the CIA, FBI, and the Mossad run the pictures through their databases.

Jeff asked, "How soon do you think the Iranians will take delivery?"

"Within weeks," Josh answered. "My gut feeling is they also suspect a coup is coming. They'll try to take possession as soon as they can, so they can use the confusion to their advantage. If we want to catch the bastards, we have to move quickly. How much help can you give me?"

"That's complicated," Jeff said. "The President has decided not to allow any more U.S. assets to enter the Soviet Union. The State Department says the situation is too fluid; they don't want to risk any American lives. The Chairman got his marching orders directly from the President. However, after the Chairman got back to his office, the National Security Advisor called to tell him the president wants the CIA to covertly stop the transfer without leaving U.S. fingerprints behind. CIA doesn't have the info you do, so they want a plan from the Chairman to get this done. You can have whatever resources you need, except people."

Josh said, "So is this like *Mission: Impossible* where the president will disavow any knowledge of our actions?"

He could hear chuckles in the background. General Feltzer said, "Just come up with a workable plan, Josh. We'll see what we can do about people."

"Will do."

Jeff Gainesville's voice was clear through the encryption. "Don't do anything stupid, Josh. I don't want to have to lie to Rebekah."

"Don't worry, she'll be focused on other things. A serious ex-girlfriend of mine is marrying her cousin. I call Rebekah every two or three days, and she brings up the subject every time. *She can't wait to meet Danielle!*"

"Ouch," Jeff said. "You *are* earning your hazard pay."

Tuesday, July 16th, 1991, 1723 Local Time, Moscow

Josh was enjoying a moment of inner peace after spending several minutes on the phone with his children. Even though they presented all the usual problems of teenagers, he missed them.

Sasha had again asked when was he going to get a car. Josh reminded him that it was all about accomplishing a specific set of goals. The more he accomplished, the more his parents would spend on a car. Two days before Josh left, he'd taken Sasha to two car dealers where they looked at cars costing $2500, then $5,000, and so on up to $12,500.

When they'd returned home, Josh had laid out what he referred to as the "car curve." It was an arc starting from the origin going up and to the right. If specific goals were achieved, it added to the amount Josh and Rebekah would spend on a car for Sasha. It was a not-so-subtle way of telling Sasha that getting a car at age sixteen was not a God-given right—it was a privilege he had to earn. To earn the maximum amount, Sasha had to:

1. Become a member of the National Honor Society and get A's in what his parents considered core subjects: AP Math, AP Biology, Chemistry and Physics, AP English, and AP History. An A in an AP class in a foreign language got him bonus points;

2. Show leadership by becoming the captain of either a club, the school soccer team or the varsity baseball team, or else get elected to a class office; and

3. Be in the top five percent of his graduating class.

Those were the main three points. There were others added as reminders for a teenager who needed to understand that with independence came responsibility.

Sasha also had to agree to a set of nine rules about using the car. On the second day he was in Russia, Josh had drawn the curve with the numbers and mailed it to Sasha, along with the typed list of *Rules to Drive By*:

1. No one but family members will drive the car.

2. Any moving violations will lead to immediate loss of driving privileges.

3. If the car is wrecked and Sasha was at fault, the only amount of money Mom and Dad would spend on a new

car—if they decided to buy another at all—would be whatever money they received from the insurance company.

4. Mom and Dad will pay for insurance and routine maintenance. Sasha will pay $50/month for the use of the car and would be responsible for gas and any maintenance caused by neglect, such as prematurely worn tires, brakes worn out before their normal life, etc.

5. Everyone riding in the car must have their seat belt on before the car is put in gear.

6. A drop in grades and/or class standing will result in the loss of driving privileges until grades improve to acceptable levels.

7. No alcohol or drugs will ever be allowed in the car.

8. Occasional errands such as taking Sara and Sean to and from events, trips to the store, etc. will be assigned. Unless otherwise discussed, they take priority over personal trips.

9. Mom and Dad can revoke your driving privileges and take the keys away at any time for disciplinary reasons.

When Josh returned, he expected a signature on both documents before he bought the boy a car. The ball was now in Sasha's court... because at the moment, Sasha was a B student and both Josh and Rebekah were convinced he was loafing.

After a few seconds of musing about the benefits of using peer pressure on teenagers, Josh forced himself to return to the present. Being in Moscow was radically different from being deployed on a ship or away from home on temporary duty at another U.S. military facility. No matter where he went, he didn't feel safe. After all, for years, men and women with the hammer and sickle on their uniforms had been the enemy. Now they were everywhere.

Josh was an aviator, not a special operator. Yes, he'd worked with SEALs and Green Berets, but the danger had always been mission-specific. He was just their taxi driver. Get them in, get them out. Done. Except for one raid in North Vietnam, what they did on the ground was their part of the mission. This was different.

As Josh headed back to his office, Velasquez appeared in the hallway. A thought struck Josh and he said, "Gunny, I have an off-the-wall question for you. Let's go into my office." Once they were inside, Josh closed the door.

"Sir, nothing from you is off-the-wall. Unusual? Possibly. From way out in left field? Very likely. What do you need?"

Josh laughed at Velasquez's response. "Other than rifles and pistols, what kind of weapons do the embassy Marine guards have?"

"Grenades, M-60 machine-guns, squad automatic weapons, light anti-tank rockets, and a few bolt-action sniper rifles. Plus, we have enough ammunition to support a long firefight. Why?"

"Do we have anything that could stop a truck?"

"Other than killing the driver or shooting out its tires, nothing. A NATO 7.62 round will hole the radiator and maybe screw up a fan pulley, but it won't do much to the block."

"So other than an RPG, what could do the trick?"

"From how far away?"

"Four or five hundred yards. Maybe more."

Velasquez thought. "A Barrett M82 would be perfect, sir."

"What's that?"

"A fifty caliber rifle. It can shoot armor-piercing ammo as well as a standard ball round. The armor-piercing round will go right through an inch or so of armor at under five hundred yards."

"So it would go through the armor of one of those BTR's we see all the time."

"Yes, sir. It might not penetrate the front armor, but will certainly go through the top, sides or rear."

"How would you ambush a small convoy consisting of BTRs and three or four trucks?"

Velasquez considered the question. "Ideally, you'd want to be above them and pick a spot where they couldn't get off the road. Take out the lead vehicle and then the last, so the rest are bottled up. Then you can start picking off the others." Velasquez gave Josh a piercing look. "What is this about, sir?"

Josh didn't say anything. His mind was racing.

Velasquez asked, "Sir, what would be in the trucks?"

"Soviet nuclear artillery shells and/or portable nuclear weapons."

"The ones being sold to the Iranians."

"You got it." Josh paused. "Do we have maps showing the roads from Uzbekistan and Tajikistan into Iran?"

"Don't know, sir. I'll find out."

"If we don't have any here, I'll request what we need via the pouch from Admiral Gainesville."

Velasquez paused. "Sir, are you planning to ambush the trucks?"

"I'm setting that aside for now. Our first task is to find out when and where the Iranians are taking possession. Once we do that, we can figure out how to stop them. I want to get a feel for the possible routes so we can look at options."

"Sir, I have a request. I'll put it in writing if I have to."

"Go."

"Both Sergeant Brown and I are Recon Marines. Both of us are scout snipers and very familiar with this type of planning. If you decide to go hunting for Soviet nuclear artillery rounds being carried by a truck someplace in this godforsaken country, Sergeant Brown and I volunteer to go with you."

"Noted," Josh said. "I'll also note your desire to do something incredibly stupid which may leave you dead or headed to the Gulag."

"With all due respect, sir, I'll take my chances with someone who has the balls to sneak into North Vietnam, shut down a helicopter which is, oh by the way, the only way out other than walking, raid a secret missile base, capture a Soviet Colonel, and get out with only one man killed."

"Who told you that story?"

"I have my sources, sir."

"Remind me to wring Master Chief Jenkins' neck the next time I see him."

"It wasn't the Master Chief."

Josh contemplated giving Velasquez a direct order to reveal who told him. No, doing that would be unfair. "Gunny," Josh said, "don't you have some maps to find?"

The Same Day, 1046 Local Time, Long Island City

Mohammed Safdar was not surprised when the manager of the storage facility wanted him to sign a log each time he opened the gate. It made sense. Safdar wasn't worried; he used the driver's license for Bashar al Bishi, which matched the name in which the unit was reserved. Anyone attempting to track "Bashar" down wouldn't get far.

Safdar had picked the place because it was small—only thirty garage-sized units. It had razor wire on top of the fence, which gave some added security. Best of all, the manager gave him a discount after he warned him that the facility's video cameras didn't cover his unit. Safdar made a show of worrying, but was happy to sign the contract.

As he parked his Suburban, Safdar made sure it blocked the door to make seeing inside difficult. At this time of day, he suspected the facility wouldn't have many visitors.

Up until three days ago, the only thing he stored in the facility was his welding equipment and the coolers. On his answering machine, there was a message with a phone number saying his shipment arrived. After writing down the number, he erased the message and then pulled the cassette out of the machine. It went down the trash chute in his building.

From a pay phone, Safdar called the number and the speaker admonished him saying he should have called earlier. Rather than get into an argument, they agreed to meet in the parking lot at Shea Stadium where people park and get on the subway.

Safdar didn't know or want to know the other man's name when he backed his Suburban up to the man's Expedition. The boxes were quickly transferred and Safdar drove right to the storage unit.

With the door open, Safdar could see twenty-five light brown boxes were laid in a neat row. Large letters on twenty-four of the boxes said *Composition C-4*. Underneath, smaller letters listed the U.S. Government part number, contract number, and date of manufacture. Each box contained twenty-four one-pound units of the explosive

From the one box he opened after he took possession of the C4, he pulled out a brick-shaped package. After looking at it through the clear cellophane wrapper, he squeezed the soft claylike material and enjoyed the oily almond smell. Smiling, he went to the twenty-fifth box. It was larger than all the others and contained boxes of detonators. Two coils of det cord leaned against the back wall of the storage unit, along with a spool of copper wire.

Safdar opened the Suburban's hatch and opened the three coolers. He quickly laid the bricks of C4 along the bottom of each cooler. The coiled det cord and wire went into two duffle bags he'd haul aboard the boat. A twenty-dollar bill for helping carry them to his boat would make each dock boys' day.

On his way to the marina, Safdar stopped at a 7-11 and bought enough ice to cover the explosives. He dropped the flattened C-4 boxes into the 7-11's dumpster. It was almost empty and he figured other garbage would quickly cover the boxes.

Chapter 16
Field Work

Clouds and light rain greeted Safdar as he headed toward Oyster Bay. By noon, a new weather front had moved in, clearing the sky and lowering the humidity. The bright sun drove the temperature into the upper eighties.

He sweated profusely as he pressed the bricks of C-4 into place. The frame and plates cut the amount of space in the V-berth in half, leaving only a small area in the bow for him to work in the poorly ventilated space. Access to the hot and stuffy V-berth was only possible through the front hatch.

About halfway through putting the C-4 in place, Safdar needed a break and some water. As he stood up in the front hatch, he noticed a flash of light from a boat anchored just outside the reef and farther to the east. On the fantail, he could see two men and fishing rods. The flash could have been a reflection from almost anything... but paranoia warned him it could be a camera or a pair of binoculars.

As he drank from the plastic bottle of water, Safdar formulated a plan to find out. He walked down the deck and turned on the engine compartment's vent fans. Then he climbed the chrome-steel ladder up to the bridge.

Ignition on, the starters and diesels came to life with a clattering rumble. A gentle nudge of the throttles moved the nose of the heavy Luhrs forward, putting slack in the anchor line. Safdar went out on the forward deck and pulled the line in until the anchor was clear of the water. Next, he got on his knees, grabbed the galvanized steel shank, lifted it out of the water, and put it in the holder mounted on the foredeck. Once it was in position, he secured it with the two fasteners so it wouldn't bounce around.

The Palestinian forced himself not to look at the other boat as he got back on the bridge. Satisfied the gauges were normal, he eased the throttles forward and spun the wheel to the right. Clear of the anchorage, he pushed the throttles up to get the Luhrs on the step.

Rather than go back to Oyster Bay, Safdar headed east in Long Island Sound to Huntington Bay. He pulled into the marina and topped off the tanks before he tied up to buoys reserved for transients for the night. Tomorrow, he planned to cruise to Stamford and dock at a marina. He'd take the train into the city and check into a hotel. With all that activity, if he were under surveillance, he'd surely spot it.

Saturday, July 20th, 1991, 1410 Local Time, Moscow

Velasquez was smiling broadly as he stood in the door of the embassy office. Josh said, "What's up, Gunny? You look like you just won the lottery."

"Sir, if you'll follow me, I have something to show you."

"Lead the way."

They went through hallways Josh had never seen before. At the end of a corridor in the basement, Velasquez entered a five-digit code into a cipher lock next to a steel door.

"Attention on deck." Velasquez's voice carried a tone of authority as he and Josh entered the room. Every Marine inside stopped what he was doing and came to attention.

"As you were." Josh's words sent the Marines back to work. The black rifles on the wall, the sweet smell of gun oil, and the pungent odor of cleaning solvent told him he was in the embassy's armory.

Velasquez pointed to a four-foot long black rifle with a large scope sitting on a workbench. Its barrel was held up by a bipod. Next to it, six box-magazines lay on their flat sides. Two very large bullets stood on the blunt end of the cartridge casing.

"What is this..." The only word coming into his mind was "thing," but Josh knew better than to say it. He'd never seen a rifle this large.

"Sergeant Brown, tell the good captain what the Marine Corps has so kindly sent us."

"Captain, this is a M82A1 fifty caliber recoil-operated semi-automatic rifle." Brown picked up both of the huge rounds. "It fires a six hundred and thirty grain ball and an armor-piercing explosive round known by the name of its Norwegian manufacturer: Raufoss. A Marine Corps sniper can routinely get first round hits on man-sized targets at well over a mile. The official range is eighteen hundred yards, but I assure you, we can hit targets at two thousand."

"How does the Marine Corps use this rifle?"

"To disable trucks and lightly armored vehicles like the BTR-80, or to penetrate walls to get to targets inside a building. If you hit a BMP on the side or in the rear, you can disable it with a single Raufoss round if you're inside eight hundred to a thousand yards."

"And you're trained in this weapon, Sergeant?"

"Yes, sir," Brown said. Josh could hear the man's enthusiasm in his voice. "Both the gunny and I used it in Desert

Storm. I took out a couple of BTRs with it; the gunny dropped an Iraqi colonel looking at us through a pair of binoculars at about fifteen hundred yards. First shot—all we could see was his head and shoulders. Once the man went down, his infantry unit battalion surrendered en masse. The gunny won't tell you this, but he set a record score at sniper school. Despite my best efforts, that record still stands."

"I see." Josh turned to Velasquez. "And why are you showing me this?"

Velasquez smiled. "Clear the room." The Marines who were cleaning weapons put down their rags and left. "Sir, one round into the engine compartment from a Barrett like this stops the truck. A man I trust zeroed this one in before it was shipped, and he sent me the dope on the weapon."

"How many rounds did you get?"

"Plenty. We have 200 ball and 50 Raufoss rounds. Six 10-round magazines."

Josh pondered the Barrett's potential as Velasquez continued. "Sir, General Feltzer doesn't know we got the Barrett. I used your priority codes to get this one from a friend at Quantico. He personally made sure it got on the plane. And no, he doesn't know why I asked for it."

The Same Day, 1206 Local Time, Moscow

Piotr Talyzin often boasted that the conference room near his office was one of the few in the Soviet Union without hidden recording devices. Since the room was used by the head of the KGB, its furnishings were much better than those used by the rank and file. The long teak table and sixteen soft leather chairs came from the Danish design house Dansk.

A buffet table, also from Dansk, stretched in front of the window. It was laden with food not available to the majority of Soviet citizens. The white china had a gold and red band with the KGB logo. The sterling silver utensils had the shield of the KGB molded into the end of their handles. The glassware, also custom made, was the finest lead crystal from Hungary.

Talyzin put his notebook at the head of the table and stood by the window sipping a glass of mineral water. As guests started arriving, some were in uniform while others wore Western-made suits and ties. Each person picked a chair and helped himself to smoked salmon from Norway, sliced salamis from Germany and Italy, and Hungarian ham. Apart from the salad, the only locally made food was the bread. Attendees had a choice of dark pumpernickel or crusty white peasant bread.

When everyone had a plate, Talyzin gently tapped his water glass. "Gentlemen, let me remind you to note in your meeting logs that this is a meeting to discuss additional security efforts needed to protect the food being brought into the Soviet Union. A copy of appropriate notes will be handed out at the end of the meeting."

Heads around the table nodded.

"This will be the last meeting of this group until August 19. We will take power while General Secretary Gorbachev is on vacation in the Crimea. The drunk Yeltsin will be in charge, and the KGB will arrest him. Our purpose is to prevent the Soviet Union from being dissolved and to ensure the Communist Party continues ruling our country."

Again, heads nodded.

"I want to go around the room and make sure we are ready. Let's start with you, Koskov."

"Comrade Talyzin, the Tamanskaya division will deploy around Moscow on the morning of the nineteenth under the cover of a routine deployment exercise. I see no obstacles."

"Excellent. Volkov?"

"By the tenth of August, all targeted opponents will be dead. On the nineteenth, we will arrest Yeltsin, Gorbachev, and the ministers who oppose us. Our committee will then declare martial law. That will give us the freedom to get rid of anyone who gets in our way. The KGB will take care of Yeltsin."

"Yanayev?"

The deputy general secretary of the Communist Party nodded his head. "The party will support our actions." He had been hand picked by Gorbachev, but he was about to betray his boss.

"Pavlov?"

The deputy finance minister had resisted Schvardze's attempts to reform the country's banking system. "We're ready. I don't think the ruble will collapse after we take power. I think the opposite will happen. Stability will help."

"Good, then we're ready." Talyzin held up his glass. "To a strong, unified Soviet Union."

The Same Day, 0849 Local Time, New York City

He'd slept fitfully. Each time Jim Broughton dozed off, he'd wake up only an hour later. Each time, it had taken longer to get back to sleep.

Clutching a mug of coffee and sitting on his couch, Broughton stared at the East River. His emotions cycled from rage to anxiety to feeling violated. He was certain strangers had been in his apartment. The telltale hairs he stuck in the top of the door were gone. The question was, who?

Nothing was out of place, but that just meant whoever had investigated had been careful. If it were the FBI, they would have found the Koran, the prayer rug and his books on Arabic. The bureau would conclude he was learning Arabic and had become a Muslim. No crime in that. Had the bureau put him under surveillance?

If he were arrested, he'd say he was cultivating sources. He'd submitted reports saying so.

What if the intruders were Safdar's cronies? Why would they? Did they mistrust him? Had they or the FBI planted a bug?

Broughton bet it had been the FBI. If the bag team had a warrant, anything they found was admissible in court. So what did they know? When had they started watching? Had they checked his bank and phone records?

Broughton was sure there was nothing in the apartment that could lead to an indictment. Still, if the FBI now mistrusted him, his career was over. The only good news was that he could come out of the closet as a Muslim. Hamas, Hezbollah, or the Iranians would pay handsomely for what he knew about the FBI and its methods.

Broughton's feeling that his home had been violated didn't go away. He went to his desk and pulled on a pair of latex gloves—he didn't want to leave fingerprints on the notes he was going to write. He began to print in block letters tilted to the left so they were distinctly different from his normal scrawl. He also forced himself to apply pressure on the pen in a different manner to further confuse handwriting experts if the FBI ever got their hands on the notes.

7/20/91
Urgent. Need to talk. Usual place.
Nasir

Broughton wrote two notes with the exact same words. They were sent to two P.O. boxes Safdar had instructed him to use. If they weren't picked up, the notes would wind up in the post office's dead letter box because the return address didn't exist.

Satisfied, Broughton walked down 70th Street to the post office, forcing himself not to make it obvious he suspected he was being tailed. Even if the FBI was following him and went to the station's postmaster flashing their badges, even if the postmaster let them look through the mail without a warrant, the chances of finding either of the two letters dropped in the mail slot was slim.

Sunday, July 21ˢᵗ, 1991, 1339 Local Time, Berlin

Josh wasn't surprised that the best connection between Moscow's Sheremetyevo airport and Berlin's Tegel was on PanAm. Under the status of forces agreement, German airlines couldn't fly from Berlin to any European capital. As for Krasnovsky, he insisted on flying with Aeroflot, thinking he would face fewer hassles.

Since Josh got to Berlin first, he met Krasnovsky as the general exited immigration. The Russian was wearing a typically ill-fitting baggy set of dark brown trousers and a white shirt.

"Any problems with immigration?" Josh asked.

"Not really. The immigration officer had seen Soviet passports before, and my speaking German didn't surprise him."

When they got into the rental car, Josh handed Krasnovsky a map with the route highlighted. "I can get us onto the Autobahn south toward Leipzig, but once we get off at Exit Five, you'll have to navigate."

"You're assuming I can read a map."

"General, somehow I think you can. Make believe this VW is a T-34 tank."

"Ah, but in a car, we have to stick to the roads. In a tank, I can go straight ahead through anything, including small buildings."

"True."

Krasnovsky was silent on the drive. He was taking in the changes in East Germany since the wall had come down. It had been fifteen years since he'd moved back to Moscow. There was more car and truck traffic than he remembered to say nothing of a building boom.

Gunter Grünewald lived in a one-bedroom flat with his wife, in one of a string of five-story apartment buildings. He'd moved there when he retired five years ago, before the wall came down. He'd hoped for a peaceful, comfortable retirement. In a united Germany and as a former Stasi general, he'd been interrogated but not charged. As he'd written to his friend Krasnovsky, at least the West Germans had plenty of money to pay his pension.

The former SS officer was slightly stooped and had to carry an oxygen bottle to feed the clear tubes of a cannula. Grünewald and Krasnovsky shared a hearty hug when they met. Josh stood patiently off to the side. When they were finished, Grünewald looked at Josh, his eyes bright with recognition. "Captain Haman! You don't look much older than the pictures I saw of you in 1976."

Grünewald may have been a retired Stasi major general and a lieutenant colonel in the SS, but he seemed delighted as he held out his hand to Josh. When Josh took it, Grünewald put the green oxygen bottle on the floor and held Josh's hand in both of his. "Thank you for coming. It means a lot to me. Old enemies, as Oleg will tell you, can become friends. Please, come in and sit down."

Josh hid his discomfort. Growing up as he had in post-World War II Germany and knowing many survivors of the concentration camps, SS officers and Nazis were the epitome of evil. Revelations from war crimes trials had left an impression on him, even as a kid. He'd seen first hand what Nazis did to people. Long ago, he'd vowed never to allow something like the Holocaust to happen again. As a member of the Stasi and a former SS officer, Grünewald was double dammed. Josh had come as a favor to Krasnovsky. What Josh was going to say, even though it had been approved by Feltzer and Gainesville, increased his anxiety. Josh told himself he was here only because it helped his mission. There was no other acceptable rationale.

Grünewald wheezed noticeably, despite the oxygen. Once he'd sat again, he disconnected the small portable bottle and connected the cannula to a larger one behind his chair. Beate, Grünewald's wife, served a homemade streusel cake and coffee. Once everyone was satisfied, she left the three men alone.

"Does the CIA know you are here?" Grünewald asked in German.

Josh responded in the same language. "I'm not sure, but the admiral I report to does. He approved the meeting."

"*Gut*. I have dealt with enough secrets in my life. The openness of a united Germany is a breath of fresh air." Grünewald paused to inhale deeply and wheezed as he did. Josh could almost feel the rasping as Grünewald's cancer-ravaged lungs struggled to absorb oxygen. "So," Grünewald continued, "I have questions about the time you came into what used to be my country."

Josh nodded.

"How did you get eight men into East Germany?

"Four swam in. Four came by car on the ferry from Sweden."

"Swam in? From how far out? In February, the Baltic is very close to freezing."

"I won't tell you how close we got to the coast, but we knew your radar wouldn't pick up the boat that carried the swimmers."

"Neither we nor the Soviets believed you could swim in water close to freezing."

"I'm surprised," Josh said. "We practice it all the time."

"Really?" Grünewald said. "Both the Stasi and our Soviet counterparts said it wasn't possible. Their theory was your men came in by car through two different checkpoints and spent the night hiding in the woods."

"General, our plan minimized the amount of time we spent in East Germany. The most dangerous part of the mission was the drive our four men made from Zehlendorf to Berlin after the raid."

"Why?"

"Just too many things that might have gone wrong," Josh said. "When they arrived at the Berlin border crossings, they found that your border police had pictures of Marty Cabot and me. We were just lucky that the officer at the Berlin border crossing didn't recognize Cabot. On top of that, we were pretty sure we could steal one helicopter, but two would have been pushing our luck. Aerial photos told us the location of some Mi-4s, but there weren't any Mi-8s nearby. That meant that four of the men *had* to exit by car. With the helicopter out, we could fly the members of Red Hand out with us."

All of this was true... but Josh had no intention of revealing additional details. For example, he didn't mention that he'd been in East Germany weeks before the raid, scouting the terrain, Red Hand's compound, and the route to the helipad.

Grünewald asked, "How did you get the weapons into East Germany? We used dogs to sniff all the cars on the ferry."

"The swimmers brought them in."

"Where did you pick them up?"

"Between Seissnitz and Rostock. I can't tell you the exact location."

"Where did you learn to fly the Mi-4?"

"I studied the manuals. They told me how to start the helicopter and gave me a rough idea on how its systems worked. As helicopters go, it's actually pretty simple."

"You'd never flown one before?" Josh could hear the surprise in Grünewald's raspy voice.

"No. It was a helicopter with a collective and a cyclic stick. Raise the collective and push the cyclic forward, and the helicopter climbs and accelerates. Just like ours."

Grünewald said, "I notice you speak German like a Bavarian."

"I went to a *kinderschule* in Hesse for five years and our *hausfrau* was from Vienna."

"Ahhh, that explains your accent."

Josh nodded. He didn't mention that his mother spoke Yiddish: a German dialect that sounds like a Bavarian accent.

The three continued to chat for about an hour. When they could see Grünewald was tiring, the two visitors made their excuses and left.

Krasnovsky sat silently, staring out the window for most of the trip home. Josh could see the sadness in Krasnovsky's eyes. He'd just seen a very good friend for the last time and seen his own mortality. Josh allowed the World War II veteran to be alone with his thoughts as the car wove through Berlin's traffic to a four-star hotel in what used to be West Berlin.

As they were passing through the central business district, Krasnovsky broke the silence. "You realize you're not going to spoil me with all this capitalist wealth."

"It's part of my secret plan to corrupt you. Since your government won't spring for a decent hotel, you're the guest of the United States."

Josh let the bellman pull both bags from the trunk. Krasnovsky's was battered and looked like a relic from the fifties. Josh's was a blue duffel bag made from rip-stop nylon, a fabric unknown or unavailable for consumer products made in the Soviet Union.

When they checked in, Josh watched with amused surprise when he handed the woman at the desk a Russian and an American passport. After Josh signed the registration form, she gave him two strips of plastic. He handed one to Krasnovsky.

"What's this?" Krasnovsky asked.

"A key. Slide it in the slot above the door handle. You'll see a green light come on, then you'll hear a click telling you the door is open."

"I like old-fashioned keys better."

"Welcome to the rest of the world."

* * *

The steakhouse was a few blocks down the road from the hotel near the Kurfürstendam. According to the hotel's concierge, the restaurant offered the best steaks in Berlin. At Krasnovsky's request, they had gone to a place that served no Russian food.

After their beers and a basket of bread were served, Krasnovsky started reminiscing. "Even though Gunter and I fought on different sides, we shared the same experiences and fears. Both of us lost many friends. The men of the SS were a very close group, so it made their casualties much harder for them to take. We in the Red Army knew we were just cannon fodder. We were told to go forward: it was either be shot at by the Germans or be executed by our officers or a firing squad. The Germans gave us a better chance of survival."

General Feltzer had asked Josh to see if Krasnovsky would leave the Soviet Union. Josh decided it was time to pop the question. "You know if you wanted to," Josh said, "you could walk into the U.S. embassy and defect. We'd welcome you warmly. You'd become a wealthy man for what you could tell us about the inner workings of the KGB."

"I know, but I am a Russian and a soldier. I'm not a Soviet and I'm not a Communist, although I had to join the party to work in the KGB. However, I'm a patriot. My country is going through difficult times, and I don't know if I'll live through it. But how can I desert my country in her time of need?"

"Even if Yeltsin gets his way and the KGB is dissolved?"

"As long as it isn't followed by something worse, dissolving the KGB would help the country. I'd be out of a job, but I can retire. Younger KGB officers can find jobs doing something else. If it gets too bad, I can leave the country, but it would be hard."

"Where would you go?" Josh asked.

"Some place warm all the time! At my age, our winters get to me, but I can't leave now. Who else would help you? Traitors in your CIA and FBI betrayed almost everyone from the KGB and GRU who tried to help your country. I'm one of the few who isn't dead."

"Aren't you afraid the CIA knows about you?"

"Certainly. But as long as you keep the number who knows about me to a very small group you trust, I'm not in any new danger. In my position, I get to see the reports on Soviet citizens who have contact with citizens of other countries. It doesn't take much to put two and two together. I also know what interests the KGB's Second Directorate. As Grünewald used to say to me all the time, you just have to connect the dots. The only problem is that having a few dots doesn't help. You have to know what the connections between them mean."

Josh felt as if he'd been presented with some new dots that were hard to connect with the ones he'd known all his life.

Wednesday, July 24th, 1991, 1106 Local Time, New York City

From the western side of the General Grant Memorial just off Riverside Drive, Jim Broughton looked at cliffs known as the

Palisades. Geologically, they hadn't changed in thousands of years. The twenty-knot wind blowing through them marbled the Hudson River's dark blue water with whitecaps.

Broughton had recommended the park as a meeting place because the open area around the memorial made it easy to spot a tail. If either he or Safdar wasn't in the designated spot, the meeting was off.

Broughton had taken a cab to the memorial and arrived an hour early so he could walk on the park's paths, stop every so often to enjoy the view, and look for tails out of the corner of his eyes. He saw no one. Then again, not seeing a fellow FBI agent didn't mean he or she wasn't there; it just meant they might be good at hiding.

Broughton was admiring two young women as they jogged past when Safdar sat down on the bench and started reading the *New York Daily News*. From behind the paper wall, Safdar spoke softly. "So, Nasir, what is so important?"

"I am almost positive I am under surveillance."

"Why?"

"Someone was in my apartment the other day. Probably the FBI."

"Are you sure?"

"Yes."

"This is troubling," Safdar said. "I think I'm under surveillance too. Nothing concrete, but I thought someone was taking pictures of my boat. Call it paranoia."

"It never hurts to be careful in this business." Broughton turned his head away from Safdar. "How is the boat coming?"

"It's finished. I just have to insert the detonators."

That last part wasn't true. Safdar had already installed the detonators, and a trip switch to set them off if someone tried to dismantle the bomb.

"Excellent," Broughton said. "But I want to take a more active role."

"How so?"

Broughton outlined his plan. Safdar could tell he had thought out all the details.

"Then let us make it so and act quickly," Safdar said. "Allah will be pleased. I'll be in touch."

Broughton said no more. He got up and headed for the street to flag down a taxi.

Chapter 17
True Confessions

Friday, July 26th, 1991, 0832 Local Time, Moscow

As per the instructions of the senior military attaché, only Class A uniforms were to be worn while in the embassy. For Naval officers, from April 15 to October 15, that meant summer whites, which were a pain in the neck to keep clean. When Josh wore them, he made it a point not to brush against anything, lest it show.

When Josh got into the Suburban, Velasquez handed him his schedule for the day. Highlighted was a 0830 meeting with the ambassador. Velasquez added, "And no, Captain, I don't have a clue what the ambassador wants to talk to you about."

Josh was ushered into the ambassador's office, and this time the curtains were open. The ambassador was a wealthy lawyer and power player in the Democratic Party. It helped that he was also a friend of a fellow Texan, the Republican who sat in the Oval Office. The ambassador had a soft soothing voice but was, Josh suspected, not afraid to ask difficult questions. Josh had a feeling the questions *would* be difficult; sitting in one of the side chairs was Brigadier General Grant.

When neither the ambassador nor Grant stood up, the words 'rug dance' ran through Josh's mind. By staying seated, both wanted to signal they were senior to Josh in both position and rank.

Grant spoke first. "Captain Haman, would you please explain your mission to the ambassador and me?"

"I was sent to Moscow to gather information on the activities of the Soviet armed forces."

"I have a staff of competent attachés who do this type of work. I didn't need another. So again, Captain, what is your real mission?"

Shit, this didn't take long. "Sir, I can't tell you."

"Why not?"

Josh was standing at a relaxed position of attention and knew his answer was not going to be popular. "Because neither of you have the necessary clearances."

Grant stood up. "From a military perspective as the attaché and by DIA policy, I am cleared for everything going on in this embassy."

There are people in the Pentagon who'd disagree with you, General.

The ambassador tossed a pen on his desk as a sign of frustration. "Look, Captain, given what is going on in the Soviet Union, we need to coordinate our activities. The last thing we need is an incident. So, please answer General Grant's question."

"With all due respect, sir, I can't. As I suggested to General Grant when I arrived, he should contact his boss in DIA and have him speak to General Feltzer, the J3 on the Joint Staff. If General Feltzer lets me know in writing to give General Grant and you access, I become an open book. Until that happens, I'm sorry but I can't answer your question."

Grant came close thrust his face into Josh's as if he was about to chew out a plebe at the academy. "Captain, I can make it an order. If you don't comply, I can have you arrested and sent home."

"Sir," said Josh, "please let me remind you that my orders clearly stated the embassy and its staff were to provide support: people, facilities, etc. So far, everyone on the embassy staff has been very helpful." Josh took a breath before continuing. "However, the operative word is support, not operational control. No access or knowledge of my activities, nor those of Gunnery Sergeant Velasquez and Sergeant Brown. Again, with all due respect, neither of you is in my chain of command."

The ambassador came around the table and stood in front of Josh. "Don't be a wise ass, Captain. I can send you home in a heartbeat by having your credentials and visa cancelled. All I have to do is call the President of the United States and you're on the next plane out of Moscow. The president is in and at the *top* of your chain of command."

"Mr. Ambassador, if asked, I'd recommend you don't make the call. It could wind up being embarrassing for you. General Feltzer briefs the Chairman almost daily on my mission and the Chairman briefs the President."

The ambassador returned to standing behind his cluttered desk. On the credenza behind him were photos of him with two different presidents. "Captain, my mission in Moscow is to maintain good relations with the Soviet government. Because I don't know what you are doing, I'm afraid you'll stick your nose someplace it shouldn't be and we'll have a preventable mess on our hands. We'll have a hard time getting you out of the Lubyanka, and that's if you don't wind up going home in a body bag. Am I clear?"

"Yes, sir. Absolutely."

"Good. Now get out of here."

With Josh out of the room and the door closed, General Grant didn't wait for the ambassador to speak, he was too angry. "I'm in the process of getting him formally charged. He should be on his way home in in less than thirty days."

"The sooner, the better. Give me enough to tell the President and we'll make sure the asshole is sent home."

The Same Day, 1028 Local Time, Moscow

There were no family photos on the credenza behind Volkov's, only ones of him in the field in Vietnam, Angola and Afghanistan or posing with other KGB officers. Volkov's marriage had lasted only three years. Volkov had married Natalia because he'd thought he needed a wife. As soon as he realized he didn't, he'd intended to shove her out the door. When Natalia figured this out, she'd left on her own initiative and filed for divorce. For years after they separated, the paranoid Volkov had her watched. He was prepared to have her arrested if she made a disparaging comment about the NKVD.

Volkov thought of himself as a priest—celibate and totally dedicated to his church. As a young man, that had been the NKVD. Now it was the KGB. If Volkov needed female companionship, he could buy it for an evening. He considered a wife and children as emotional baggage that could negatively influence a career move or a decision he might make in the field. Koskov, he knew, had been married twice and divorced twice. Once, over two bottles of vodka, Koskov had confided that he'd never marry again. He had tenuous relationships with his four children and non-existent ones with his ex-wives. Divorce in the Soviet Union was relatively simple, and alimony was only paid for six months.

"General Volkov," said his assistant, "General Koskov is here."

"Please send him in."

After the two men shook hands, Volkov pointed to a chair at the table. Once Koskov was seated, Volkov went to his desk and placed some pictures in a folder so he could carry them to the table. " I want to share something special with you," he told Koskov.

Koskov was apprehensive. Although he had fought in Vietnam, Laos and then Afghanistan, he was not yet comfortable in the office of the head of the First Directorate of the KGB, even if the two men had a lot in common and they were both involved in planning the upcoming coup. Fear of the NKVD and its successor, the KGB, was ingrained into every Soviet citizen. Despite Koskov's long and distinguished service to his country, he was not immune to the feeling.

Volkov opened the folder and slid the top photo across the table. It was an enlargement of Josh Haman's face taken through a powerful telephoto lens. The graininess of the black and white picture suggested that the photographer had been several hundred meters away. "Have you ever met this man?"

"I had lunch with him a few weeks back. He is an American Navy Captain named Haman. I filed a report on what was discussed. Why?"

Volkov slid a sheet of paper across the table. It contained a list of names. "Do you know any of these men?"

Koskov looked at the list and his eyebrows went up. "I know two of the officers. They were part of a Spetznaz team deployed to help guard a missile base in Vietnam. They were killed in an American raid."

"One of the leaders of that raid was Captain Haman. He flew them in and out of Vietnam."

Koskov took a deep breath. "He's a skilled pilot. So?"

Volkov moved the pictures to the side and held up the folder. It was six centimeters thick. "This folder is what we know about Haman. It is full of actions against the Soviet

Union. He's a very dangerous man who has killed many of your comrades and mine. Now he's in our midst."

"Are you asking me why I think he's here? Or are you asking me what I want to do about him?"

"Both."

Koskov looked at Volkov. He could see the emotion on the general's face. This was personal—the operations that Haman had stopped must have been Volkov's. Now Volkov wanted revenge: a worrisome emotion. It could cloud one's judgment; it could get you and your men killed. Cautiously, Koskov said, "The official story is that Haman is here to monitor the food deliveries from America."

Koskov waited for Volkov to speak. The general didn't, so Koskov continued. "As for what I would do about him, there are two options. If he's committed a crime against the state, we can arrest him. If he hasn't, the government can still force him to leave. On the other hand, we can kill him. But since we are not at war with the Americans, for anyone in my command to take any action at all, I would need written orders signed by you." *In other words,* Koskov thought, *I don't want any part of this.* "In a few days," Koskov went on, "we start taking back our country. That is far more important than worrying about one American. I don't want us to be distracted by planning to kill one American officer. Unless we have intelligence that Haman will interfere, I would leave him alone until we have a firm grip on power. Then, if you want to eliminate this American captain, we can do it."

So, Koskov had no interest in killing Haman. That put the matter back in my hands. So be it; wet-work is my specialty.

The Same Day, 2138 Local Time, Moscow

For the past several days, Josh had been kept up at night wondering what to do about Volkov and the hit man,

337

Bagdonovich. As much as he wanted to blow their brains out, it was murder and against everything he believed in.

He hadn't told Rebekah or Danielle about Bagdonovich and Volkov, even though it weighed heavily on his mind. Josh kept telling himself that the mission came first. Revenge had to wait until afterward, if at all. He wondered if it was worth ruining his life.

Josh let his mind wander as he stood on the steps of the Choral Synagogue. The Debenards and Avram had just said good night. He was one of the last of the congregants, enjoying the last hour of daylight as he waited for Velasquez and Brown to pick him up.

"Captain Haman?"

Josh turned and saw Arkady Kishniev. Valentina was behind him, walking down the steps with her parents. "Good *Shabbos*," Josh said.

"Good *Shabbos*," Arkady replied. "My parents would like you to come for dinner again Sunday night. It would be again be our honor. And we can talk a little business after."

Josh raised an eyebrow; what little business? All he said was, "My pleasure. What time?"

Arkady thought for a moment. "Between six and six thirty would be fine."

Sunday, July 28th, 1991, 1818 Local Time, Moscow

Josh wasn't sure what to bring as house gifts to repay the Kishnievs for their hospitality. By Soviet standards, they were middle class. He decided to bring what they needed most— food. He and Velasquez spent an hour in the well-stocked embassy commissary; as a consequence, each man had to make two trips to carry the eight paper bags up to the Kishnievs' sixth floor flat. When the bags had been placed in a neat row,

Velasquez came to a relaxed (for a Marine) attention, waiting for orders.

Josh said, "Be back at eight-thirty, all right? Arkady wants to talk with me privately, so we may take a walk. You and Brown can shadow us in the Suburban."

"No problem, sir. See you at eight-thirty."

The Kishnievs protested that the food was unnecessary, but Josh could see they were delighted. As they laid the canned goods out on the counter, Josh described what was in them, speaking in Russian—neither Raisa nor Aron Kishniev spoke English.

The elder Kishnievs were proud to have an American Jew at their dinner table, In a country where one had to report every contact with a foreigner to the KGB or be arrested, Josh wondered if they'd reported the dinner, and if so, what they'd said. He felt it would be embarrassing to ask, so he left it as an interesting but unanswered question.

Dinner was a filling and refreshing chilled *oroshka* made with potatoes, chicken and green onions. After the dishes were washed and put away, Arkady suggested they all go for a walk. The five of them headed down the tree-lined Strovskaya Street between gray and very drab concrete apartment buildings.

The buildings were called K-7s. Chronic housing shortages, particularly in Moscow, forced the Soviet Union to build nine and twelve story K-7s. Soviet rules required buildings with more than five stories to have elevators, but the rule was ignored—elevators were expensive and were rarely delivered on time. The Soviet five-year plans didn't allocate the elevator industry enough economic priority to get the materials needed or the production capacity to meet the demand. The solution was to complete the building and leave the elevator-well empty.

K-7s were made from concrete panels trucked to the building site. Small kitchens and bathrooms, six square meters each, were built as units at a factory and put in place by cranes. The pressure to meet production quotas meant that many of the pipes didn't fit to specifications. Construction workers on the site had to do whatever was necessary to cobble the buildings together.

All K-7s looked the same, except for variations in the rust patterns streaked down the concrete caused by leaking pipes or rusting rebar. Ongoing housing shortages meant that the buildings couldn't be demolished, so the occupants dealt with ever-increasing plumbing and electricity problems.

The Kishnievs were lucky to have been allocated one of the sixty square meters, two bedroom apartments. Other families were crammed into single room flats, either thirty or forty-four square meters. As Aron Kishniev sarcastically remarked, living in a K-7 was one of the joys of being a Soviet citizen. Russians, he added, were good at enduring. "We have endured the Tsars, Stalin, Khrushchev, Brezhnev, Andropov, Chernenko and now Gorbachev. Our "worker's paradise" consists of food and housing shortages, no consumer goods, poor medical care and not one, but two oppressive secret police forces."

"But," Raisa said quietly, as she walked alongside her husband, "it could be much worse. Some of us remember what hell is like," and she fell silent.

Trailed discretely by the Suburban, Josh and the four Kishnievs turned the corner onto Jerusalimskaya, a quiet street lined with large trees. Other families were out walking and keep their distance as if to say, enjoy your privacy. Neither we nor the KGB are listening out here.

A moment later, Josh heard a sound he recognized with a start: a bullet zipping past. His head snapped around. In a corner of a fifth-floor window, he saw the glint from what he was sure was a riflescope.

"Look out!" He shoved Arkady with one arm and Valentina with the other. ZZZZZZZZZZIPPPPPP. The next round smacked the sidewalk just behind them. "Get behind a tree!"

Josh heard another round, this one high over his head as he raced towards the building's entrance. Once under the cover of the doorway, he looked back. Valentina was peering around a large birch tree. Aron's bulk protruded from the other side of the tree; he'd wrapped his arms around Raisa and made sure she was completely concealed.

"What now?"

Arkady had run up and was standing next to him, breathing deeply. Josh asked, "Is there another way out of the building?"

"No, there's only one stairwell...unless he goes out a window."

Josh swallowed hard. He knew neither of them had a weapon; Arkady would have turned in his pistol when he went off duty. "All right," Josh said, "let's go corner the bastard."

"Just a second." Arkady banged on a door and an elderly woman who was supposed to track who comes and when from the building opened it a couple of centimeters. Arkady flashed his badge. He told the woman to call a phone number and give a very specific message. She nodded and closed the door.

* * *

Josh and Arkady had climbed to the fourth landing when Josh heard footsteps coming from below. Velasquez's head popped around the corner. "Sirs, you may need these." He held out two .45s by the barrels so Josh and Arkady could take the handles. "And some of these." He offered each man two loaded magazines. Josh was intensely grateful; *be prepared* indeed!

Arkady slid back the slide on the 1911 pistol. He looked at Josh. "There's only one apartment on the fifth floor where the shooter can be. I'll go knock on the door and say *militsiya*. Anyone inside is required by law to open up."

Josh warned, "If the sniper is in the apartment, you'll get a bullet as an answer."

"Then we have a choice," Arkady said. "We can kick in the door or wait for my comrades to arrive. That could be anywhere from two minutes to half an hour. It depends whether or not the officer who takes the call thinks the old woman is crazy."

"I vote for kicking the door down," Josh said.

"I agree. May I?"

Josh nodded. Arkady walked up the last flight of stairs to the fifth floor landing. He stood off to the left side of the apartment's wooden door.

The police officer rapped sharply three times on the doorframe. "Militsiya! Open the door."

Nothing.

Arkady repeated the knock and the shout.

No answer.

Josh was about to move in front of the door when Arkady held up one finger. Arkady knocked a third time, then jumped aside, just before a single bullet exploded through the door and smacked into the concrete wall behind them. Three smaller bullets punched holes in the wooden door in rapid succession.

"Bolt action rifle," Velasquez said. "Probably a Moisin-Nagant. And a Makarov pistol. Both suppressed."

Josh whispered, "How are these apartments laid out?"

"Everything off a single hall," Arkady whispered back. "Two bedrooms and a bathroom on our left as we go in. The sniper originally fired from the living room. My guess is he's still in the living room—that lets him keep an eye on the street for police, and he can still aim down the hall."

Josh looked at Velasquez. "Suggestions?"

"Yes, sir. Instead of charging in, we kick down the door and stay outside the doorframe. After he fires his rifle, we have one or two seconds to look while he pulls back the bolt to chamber another round. A single shooter will have difficulty working the bolt and firing a pistol at the same time. If there are two people, we're still okay: one of us looks, the other two cover. If the second man pops out, the two of us who are covering can engage him. By alternating looks down the hall, we can confuse him about how many of us there are. Ready, Captain?"

Josh nodded.

"Ready, Colonel?"

Arkady nodded and double-checked to make sure the safety on the unfamiliar Model 1911 was off. He'd read about this well-balanced weapon and now that one was in his hand, he understood why it was a favorite of the American military.

Velasquez took a deep breath. "On three." Velasquez held up three fingers, then two, then one. When he had a balled fist, he slammed his heel against the door just above the knob, then twisted out of the way. The wood splintered and the door banged open against the interior wall. Josh took a quick glance and saw a man dressed in black and wearing a black ski mask at the end of the hallway, pointing a rifle with a scope and a long suppressor tube at the end of the barrel. He fired a poorly aimed snap shot.

A bullet whined by and smacked into the concrete behind them. It left a ten-centimeter circular dent in the wall. The sound of the bullet was followed by the clack of working the action of a bolt-action rifle.

Velasquez took a chunk of wood and tossed it into the hallway. A muffled retort was followed by a zing as the 7.62mm X 39 round flashed by, making another hole in the wall. Josh stuck his head and right hand around the wall, aimed in the general direction of the shooter and squeezed the .45's trigger.

It bucked because he wasn't holding it with two hands. The boom was deafening and was followed by another from Velasquez who dashed into the first room on the left.

"Room one clear."

Josh glanced around the door jam. The shooter was lying prone. The bore of the rifle barrel looked as big as a cannon. "Target is on the floor."

Velasquez waved three fingers at eye height indicating he wanted Josh to move on the count of three. In return, Josh waved back, and when Velasquez got to one, the two American's arms appeared in the hallway with enough of their head to see. The two pistols were enough to make the shooter hesitate. Josh squeezed off a round and heard Velasquez do the same. This time, he came around the door and followed the Marine down the hall.

Josh turned his head long enough to see Velasquez in hand-to-hand combat with another man, also wearing a ski mask. As Josh came into the room, he saw the man with the rifle struggling to shove a five round stripper clip into the magazine. Josh charged forward and yelled, "Stop!" in Russian. The man finished reloading and pulled the bolt back as he raised the rifle.

Josh had no choice and the .45 slammed back in his hand. The rifle jumped as the pistol's .230-grain ball round splintered its stock and sent it spinning out of the sniper's now bloody hand. Josh didn't shoot again—he wanted the man alive, so he lunged and slammed the sniper into the wall. The man grunted as Josh's shoulder broke several of his ribs, then gasped as he tried to breathe. Josh hammered the heel of his hand into the sniper's chin and banged his head into the concrete wall. When the Russian didn't go limp, Josh did it again, harder.

The sniper still didn't go down. He bear-hugged Josh and tried to knee him in the groin. Josh twisted out of the way, ending up too out of position to strike back. The other man clapped his palms against both sides of Josh's head. Fighting disorientation and pain, Josh let rage drive him as he slammed his forehead into the man's nose. The sniper started to lift Josh off the ground in another bear hug. Josh shoved the butt of his hand under the man's chin and pushed up, forcing the man's head back. Thrown off balance, the Russian staggered back against the wall. Josh grabbed the man's head and banged it against the concrete three times, each time harder than the first. The shooter went limp as he slid to the floor, leaving a trail of blood on the concrete. As he went down, Josh yanked off the ski mask.

Josh stared at the inert form. "Bagdonovich!" *Son-of-a-bitch!* He slapped the man on either cheek, trying to wake him up, but the man toppled, his arms limp at his side. Josh picked up the .45 as he glared at the man who'd killed his wife.

Arkady put a hand on Josh's shoulder. "Captain, are you alright?"

Josh nodded. Arkady and Velasquez held a man whose arms were tied around his back by a belt. Velasquez jerked the end of the belt high behind the man's back, doubling him over.

Arkady touched the throat of the man lying on the floor. There was no pulse.

"Captain, how do you know this man's name?" Arkady asked.

Josh could hear the police officer tone in Arkady's voice. "He is a KGB assassin by the name of Alexei Bagdonovich. When he operated in the U.S., he killed my first wife and her parents."

"Are you certain?"

Josh looked at the Russian detective. "Yes.""

Arkady peered into Josh's eyes. "And you know this how?"

"Let us just say we Americans have good intelligence."

"I'd like to believe you." Arkady looked at the Bagdonovich and his assistant attackers. He walked across the room and motioned to Josh to follow him. "I will write this up as an assailant who you killed in self-defense. Nothing more or less, and I will keep the KGB out of it. When we get *this* man back to the station, I will find out who he is. More *militsiya* will be here in a few minutes. I'll stay with them and supervise. Tomorrow, come to my office at ten and I'll take your formal statement that you did not know who the man is. Neither you nor Sergeant Velasquez will be arrested. You helped stop a murder."

"We'll be there. But when you finish here, I suggest you visit Bagdonovich's apartment as soon as possible." Josh recited the address given to him by Krasnovsky. Arkady wrote it down.

"Unofficially, you will tell me the whole story, correct?"

Josh nodded. "I will before I leave Moscow."

Arkady nodded and held out his hand, "I need your weapons. We'll test-fire them tomorrow so we have ballistic samples. They'll be returned to you... unloaded, of course."

Josh popped out the magazine and the chambered round before handing the Model 1911 butt first to policeman. After Velasquez did the same, Arkady turned to Josh.

"Would you please take my parents and Valentina home?"

"It will be our pleasure."

"*Spasibo*. Now get out of here. I have work to do."

* * *

Ninety minutes later, Josh sat sitting in his embassy office. The adrenalin from the fight was wearing off and he could feel the strength oozing from his body. He felt very tired and wasn't sure whether it was simple fatigue from the fight, or astonishment and relief from finally killing the man who killed Natalie and her parents or both. A driving force in his life had suddenly disappeared, and not because of any thing he'd planned or initiated. He'd reacted in self-defense.

Josh sat massaging his forehead. Velasquez arrived with a can of Coke and a glass of ice. "Drink this, sir, you look like you need the caffeine. I'll be down the hall, typing my report and a statement to give to Colonel Kishniev."

Josh waved weakly and kept massaging his temples. He wondered what he'd tell Rebekah. Not the whole story, that was for sure. She'd never got used to the danger he faced, even though she knew it came with his job.

He still didn't know what he'd tell Rebekah, but it was time for their prearranged phone call. Josh took a deep breath and dialed.

Monday, July 29ᵗʰ, 1991, 0950 Local Time, Moscow

Arkady tented his hands under his chin. On his desk were the crime scene photos and the statement made by the shooter who'd survived the attempt on Josh Haman's life. He was now sitting in a cell in the basement. According to his confession, Bagdonovich had promised him one thousand U.S. dollars to help him kill the American, but never said why.

The prisoner's tattoos indicated he was a member of the *mafiya*. So what was the connection between Bagdonovich and the *mafiya*? Was the *mafiya* man just an available gun-for-hire, or did Bagdonovich have more significant *mafiya* ties?

And who'd hired Bagdonovich? The American had said he was a KGB assassin; in a hidden compartment in the floor of Bagdonovich's apartment, Arkady had found four valid passports, plus bundles of U.S. dollars, British pounds, and rubles. Behind a bookcase in another secret compartment, Arkady had found weapons along with cans of ammunition stacked on the floor. All were illegal for private citizens to own, and even for the KGB they seemed extreme. But... there were extreme elements within the KGB. What he'd found was disturbingly similar to what had been in Gabishivili's flat.

This raised an important question: should Arkady show all this evidence to the KGB? No. They had too much incentive to keep buried secrets buried. They'd destroy the evidence, and Arkady himself would disappear.

Should he take what he knew to Commissioner Sokolov? Sokolov had promised to back Arkady's investigations, but the commissioner might still give in to KGB pressure.

Conceivably, Sokolov might take Arkady directly to see Yeltsin. The people around Yeltsin were suspicious of anyone from any of the security forces—even the *militsiya*. The *militsiya* were known to be apolitical but often very corrupt.

Besides, Yeltsin had his own political agenda. He might turn this incident into a political circus in order to embarrass the KGB. That would leave Arkady hanging out to dry. The KGB had a long memory and would know who provided the evidence.

Every one of these options was fraught with political, career and personal risk. Arkady knew there was more to Josh Haman's story.

Since the captain had diplomatic status, he didn't have to cooperate. If that happened, the only advantage Arkady had would be asking the foreign ministry to declare the American *persona non grata*. Josh Haman would have to leave the country within forty-eight hours, which might serve to protect him, but it wouldn't help solve the case.

The phone rang before Arkady could make a decision. It was the front desk sergeant saying his two American guests had arrived. Arkady told the sergeant to take them to a conference room rather than to an interrogation room.

In cases like this, *militsiya* policy was to have another officer present when taking the statement. Arkady brought

Captain Anton Dorotkin. When the two of them arrived, the Americans were already seated. "Good morning," Arkady said to Haman and Velasquez. "Can we get you anything?"

Josh shook his head and set a briefcase on the table. He popped open the brass latches, pulled out a folder and a manila envelope, and set them on the table. Velasquez placed a manila folder of his own on the table, then put his hands in his lap. Velasquez looked uncomfortable to be in the police station—in the neighborhood where Velasquez had grown up, anyone who willingly talked to the police might get labeled as a snitch, which could prove fatal.

"These are written statements," Josh said. "English originals and Russian translations." Josh opened his folder and slid two sets of pages to Arkady. Velasquez did the same. Arkady scanned them for about thirty seconds, then pushed them to Dorotkin who had a pad and a pen ready to take notes. Dorotkin looked at them briefly and made notations on the top of each document.

Arkady said, "The statements look correct. Close enough to my own report that there will be no difficulties. Thank you for being thorough."

"*Spasibo,*" Josh said.

"And I want to thank you for Bagdonovich's address," Arkady continued. "We found enough evidence to confirm your assertion that he was a KGB assassin."

Arkady gestured to Dorotkin, who placed a brown expandable folder on the table and untied the bow before sliding a notebook out of the folder.

"This is Bagdonovich's diary detailing many of his operations. He probably kept it to use to blackmail his superiors if needed. I haven't had time to read it all, but I've read parts. In August 1973, he recorded his orders to kill former Red Army Major Artur Vishinski. In Bagdonovich's three years in the U.S., he killed at least seven other former Soviet citizens and noted he failed to find Soviet Colonel Alexei Koniev. However, we don't know if he was on an official KGB mission or if he was sent by rogue elements within the KGB, or the *mafiya*. I'd bet on rogue KGB."

"Did he write down who issued the orders?"

"No. It states that his orders and information about the target came to a U.S. post office box. No name of his commanding officer."

"So he was controlled by someone else."

"That's what it looks like." Arkady paused. "Of course, that was almost twenty years ago. Who knows if Bagdonovich still works for the same person? It seems he still works for the KGB, and judging from what happened last night, Captain Haman, it appears that his boss wants you dead. Do you know who that might be, and why?"

"Honestly, no," Josh said. "I didn't find out who killed my wife until after I arrived in the Soviet Union. Bagdonovich pulled that trigger because he was *ordered* to do so. Maybe it was the same man who ordered the hit on my first wife's father."

Josh nodded in the direction of the other *militsiya* officer in the room. Arkady took the hint. "Anton, can you give us a few minutes alone?" Dorotkin nodded and left. After the door closed, Arkady turned to Josh. "When operating in the Soviet Union, the KGB can't just kill people. It needs some justification to arrest someone and have a trial of sorts. So who in the KGB is ordering people shot?"

"Can you get access to KGB records?"

Arkady rolled his eyes. "Why are you asking such a stupid question?"

"Because in the KGB's archives, you'll find all the answers. I know the KGB keeps meticulous records."

Arkady thought for a few seconds. "I can't go to the Lubyanka and ask to see the file on Comrade Bagdonovich. After they stop laughing, they'd beat the shit out of me until I told them everything I know. If I didn't end up with a bullet in my head, I'd be sent to the Gulag."

"All right," Josh said. "I'll tell you this: I believe the man who gave Bagdonovich his orders in 1973 was Lieutenant General Nikolai Volkov. He's in the First Directorate. And perhaps he still uses Bagdonovich for killing."

"Why do you think this?"

"I can't tell you."

"Can't or won't?"

"Both."

Arkady scratched the side of his head. Few people in the Soviet Union knew who ran the KGB. Volkov might have the power and authority to order a person killed, but Arkady knew that Volkov would be required to get approval from the Ministry of the Interior and even the Politburo before killing a foreigner who had diplomatic immunity inside the Soviet Union. Of course, that assumed Volkov was following standard procedures. If Volkov wasn't worried about repercussions, he could give the orders without asking anyone first. No one on the Politburo would challenge him over a dead American.

"So, Captain Haman, what do you suggest I do with this information?"

"I don't know," Josh replied.

"Requesting an interview with Volkov would risk my career and even my life. Before I consider it, I need concrete, bulletproof evidence that he ordered someone to kill you without authorization. Without evidence, this investigation will go nowhere."

"I'll see what I can do," Josh said. He thought for a moment. "But Arkady, can you and I have dinner at your parent's house next Friday night before services? I'd like to bring three guests."

The Russian looked at the American warily. He wondered what Josh was up to. He also wondered if a second visit would precipitate another attack—and if his family would be targeted. However, all he said was, "That sounds like an excellent idea. I will assure them that they were not the targets and that your presence will not put them in danger. Let's plan on six o'clock; we can eat and then go to synagogue."

"See you then."

Chapter 18
Arriving

Walking down the hall toward his office, Josh noticed that the office door was cracked open. He lifted a closed fist and turned to Velasquez. Holding his index finger up to his mouth, he pointed back down the hall. In hushed tones fifty feet back in the direction that they had come, Josh told the gunnery sergeant he was sure he'd latched the door when he left the previous night. He asked Velasquez if he had a camera, and the gunny pointed to his desk outside the office.

Neither man spoke while Josh positioned himself in front of the door. Velasquez stood with the camera off to one side so he could take a picture of anyone in the office. Josh mouthed one, two and on three, shoved the door open.

Inside, a surprised General Grant looked up from reading documents Josh had left on the desk. Behind him was the embassy's special security officer who had reset the safe's combination when Josh was assigned the office. The officer was sitting on the floor and twirling the dial, trying to open the safe. The day Josh started using it, Velasquez had changed the combination.

"Surprise!"

General Grant froze and the flash and film recorded his expression for posterity. The special security officer turned just as the flash went off. Josh forced himself to be formal and polite. "General, why are you in my office?"

Neither Grant nor the officer answered. "Okay," Josh said, "let's start with who gave you permission to enter my locked office and attempt to open my safe."

"I don't need your permission," Grant snapped. "These offices are assigned to me and I can enter any one of them at any time. I came here on the assumption you're mishandling classified information."

"That's bullshit. Since you have gone through my desk, you'll have already noticed that there is no classified information anywhere in it or on it. Again, General, why do you want into my safe?"

Grant just stared at him. The security officer got up to leave. Velasquez blocked his way.

"Let's try another question. Who authorized you to come into my office and try to open my safe, when you knew that if you succeeded, you'd have access to information for which you weren't cleared?"

Grant pursed his lips and made a face. Petulance—Josh couldn't help remembering that the man had no combat experience, even though he was old enough to have been sent Vietnam.

"Captain Haman," grated Grant, "you're a menace. All you guys in special operations are hot-heads who don't know how to follow orders." He glared. "I heard what happened last night. The ambassador is fit to be tied. He talked to the Secretary of State, who said he'd talk to the President. The Chairman of the Joint Chiefs of Staff is going to be ordered to recall you. I suggest you go back to the hotel and pack your bags."

Josh spun the STU-III on the corner of his desk around so it was facing him and picked up the handset. Velasquez remained at a loose parade rest blocking the door. The Marine's menacing glare told Grant and the special security officer not to do anything stupid. "First, General, if you look at my uniform, you'll notice I wear the gold wings of a Naval Aviator as opposed to the Trident that SEALs wear so officially, I am not a member of the U.S. Special Forces. For the record, I have flown missions in support of the special forces of several countries. Second, the Chairman already knows—I submitted a report last night. Third, if you remember, I suggested to the ambassador that calling the President would only end in embarrassment." He began to dial.

"Who are you calling?" Grant snapped. Josh thought his voice cracked.

"My boss." When Josh heard Lieutenant Johnson pick up the phone, Josh asked her to put Admiral Gainesville on the line. When she replied that the admiral was in a meeting with General Feltzer and the Chairman of the Joint Chiefs and they didn't want to be disturbed except in a crisis, Josh asked her to interrupt them and let them decide. He gave her a brief description of the events of the past few minutes.

While he waited for Johnson to get the Chairman on the line, Josh turned to General Grant. "In a few seconds, I'm going to tell Rear Admiral Gainesville, Lieutenant General Feltzer, and the Chairman of the Joint Chiefs what Gunny Velasquez and I found at 0711 this morning. I'll also tell them the questions you refused to answer. I expect they'll ask you the same questions, and I suggest you think carefully about your answers. They'll determine whether or not you stay in Moscow. Also whether you retire in the next few days as a Brigadier General, or as something distinctly lower."

When Rear Admiral Gainesville spoke, Josh pushed the speaker button and noted that he had done so before he briefly described what he found. The Lieutenant General Feltzer asked Brigadier General Grant where he got his authorization to open Josh's safe and whether or not he was cleared for the information that it might contain. When he admitted he had none, there was a pregnant silence. After a few more questions, each followed by silence or answers that were challenged by the men in the Pentagon, the chairman said thank you for calling. It was Josh's cue to end the call.

As soon as they heard I dial tone, Grant hissed at Josh. "This is not the end of this. I will see you forced to retire or court-martialed."

Josh smiled at Grant. "Sir, would you please leave my office and do not, repeat, do not re-enter it without either Gunny Velasquez, Sergeant Brown or me present."

The Same Day, 0926 Local Time, Washington, D.C.

The temperature was already in the low eighties with 70% humidity: a Washington D.C. summer day at its worst. Even so, since Special Agent Goode was carrying his pistol he had to leave his coat on. The five-block walk from the Metro Center station left him sweating as he entered the building on 10th Street.

On his desk were photos of Jim Broughton and Mohammed Safdar, along with tracking logs he needed to prepare for his meeting at 1300, when he would brief the Director of the FBI and the Attorney General of the United States. The evidence against Broughton, although circumstantial, was enough to run him out of the FBI. It would not, however, be enough to get Broughton convicted. His defense attorneys could claim he was "just doing his job" and was planning to arrest Safdar when he had an airtight case. Andrew Goode wanted a conviction that would put both men away for the rest of their lives. To get one, he needed much more.

Safdar could be arrested right now. On Monday night, an FBI team had "sniffed" his boat for explosives. The detectors went off the charts. They hadn't tried to board the boat for fear of setting off the bomb. Thanks to the Israelis, they also suspected they knew Safdar's target: one of the bridges in the East River. Warrants to search the storage area in Long Island City and seize any drawings from the machine shops were already issued. The only remaining question was when to make the arrest.

At this point in the investigation, Goode anticipated the director would ask him four questions:

What was the benefit of waiting?

What was the risk in waiting?

Were they sure they could catch Safdar before he acted?

Who was Safdar working with?

The answer to any one of the questions changed the answers to all the others. The permutations and combinations had kept Goode awake all night.

Thursday, August 1ˢᵗ, 1991, 0956 Local Time, Tehran

To the diminutive and wiry Mohaqqeq Damad, the subdued lighting gave the room a somber feeling. There were dark drapes behind the dais on which the members of the National Security Council sat. At each end, the flag of Iran hung on a silver pole. As before, Damad noted there were no nametags in front of the unoccupied high-backed black leather chairs.

Article 176 of the Iranian constitution stated that the National Security Council was made up of the:

- President
- Speaker of Majilis (the Iranian parliament)
- Head of the judiciary
- Chief of the combined general staff of the armed forces
- Ministers of foreign affairs, the interior, and intelligence

- Commander of the Islamic Revolutionary Guard Corps.

In reality, the Supreme Leader and the commander of the Pasdaran made most of the national security decisions, often without consulting the entire Council. Occasionally, the general staff was asked for input. Checks and balances in the style of Western democracies did not exist.

Damad took his place in the front row of chairs, each of which had a small writing desk. He was so short, his feet barely reached the floor. The space was more like a school lecture hall than a conference room. A door opened on the side of the dais. Damad stood while two men in black flowing robes, turbans and long beards walked in. The older man was the Supreme Leader; he took the center seat. Damad was surprised that he didn't recognize the second ayatollah—he thought he knew all the important people in command.

Four men wearing the uniform of the Revolutionary Guards entered behind the ayatollahs. Damad recognized one of the guards as the Pasdaran's commander. The second was head of intelligence for the Pasdaran, and the third was General Jalali. The fourth was a younger man who took a seat at the end of the front row and prepared to take notes.

The Supreme Leader spoke without introduction for preamble. "Damad, thank you for coming on such short notice. We have questions we prefer to ask directly rather than hear your answers through another person."

Damad understood. These men didn't trust their subordinates to tell the truth.

The Supreme Leader spoke again. "Please tell us the status of the nuclear warheads we have purchased for seventy-two million U.S. dollars."

Actually, the figure had risen to seventy-six million, thanks to an extra four million needed to cover bringing the warheads to the Islamic Republic. Jalali knew the correct number and Damad felt no need to correct the mullah.

"Colonel Akrami is in Samarkand right now. He will meet with the soldiers sent by General Jalali. They'll take delivery of the nuclear artillery shells on August 18 or 19 and drive them into Iran. The trip will take about two days. Colonel Akrami has arranged for the trucks to pass through the Turkmenistan border uninspected—the head of the KGB border guards there is a Muslim."

"You're sure of all this?"

Damad forced himself to sound confident, even though he knew that in such operations, you could only be one hundred percent confident after the mission was successfully completed. He didn't want to say everything would work according to the plan because it never did. He simply said, "I'm sure. A Soviet General provided the paperwork authorizing Colonel Akrami and his men to take possession of the weapons."

"Do you think this plan to drive them across Uzbekistan and Turkmenistan will work?"

"I do. Colonel Akrami has prepared well. He believes it's the least risky approach."

Damad went on to describe Akrami's plan as he knew it. When he was finished, the Supreme Leader asked, "Do you think the Soviet's government knows about the sale?"

"Akrami does not think so. Only two Soviet generals know the weapons are being sold. It's a good time for us—Akrami says the Soviet Union is on the verge of a civil war and the theft will go unnoticed."

The Supreme Leader picked up a piece of paper. "Colonel Akrami spent time in the Soviet Army. Do you think he's loyal to Iran?"

"Absolutely. It's true that he was drafted into the Soviet Army and spent time in Afghanistan, but as soon as he came home, he and his family came here to Iran. Akrami joined the Pasdaran and distinguished himself fighting against the Iraqis. He is currently posing as a Soviet artillery officer using a cover General Jalali's staff spent years building."

"So, you're confident Colonel Akrami knows what he's doing?"

"I do. He's one of our best."

"Once we get the nuclear artillery shells into Iran, how soon do you think we can have them installed on the rockets?"

"It will take three days to check out each weapon. Then we'll test them with the rocket's circuitry before we mount them on the missiles. Two or three weeks, maybe a month before we have the first one operational."

The Supreme Leader looked down from the dais. "September 21st is the Prophet's Birthday. We will make it the day the Great Satan and the Jews learn Iran is a nuclear power. Make it so. Allah be praised."

The Same Day, 1008 Local Time, Moscow

Josh waved Velasquez into his office and asked Sergeant Brown to join him. Josh put on a grim expression that Velasquez caught immediately. "What's up, sir?" he asked warily.

"Gunnery Sergeant, you're out of uniform!"

Velasquez gave Josh a puzzled look. "Sir?"

Josh held up a sheet of paper. "This is so bad, the communication officer gave this message to me personally. Chief Grayson demanded I confront you immediately to correct this discrepancy."

Josh paused; he enjoyed seeing Velasquez stiffen with apprehension. "Stand at attention."

Velasquez popped to the position.

Josh stood in front of him, holding up the piece of paper. "This message says you are now a *Senior* Gunnery Sergeant." He reached into his pocket and pulled out the insignia of a Marine Corps E-8. "Put this on and it will solve the problem. Congratulations, and tonight drinks are on you. I will assume the Marine detachment will arrange a proper wetting down that this captain will attend."

A smiling and more relaxed Velasquez took the insignia. "Roger that, sir."

Friday, August 2nd, 1991, 0715 Local Time, Moscow

One of the nightly tasks of the Rossiya's accounting department was manually entering charges to room bills. If charges were made after seven in the morning and a guest wanted to check out, the front desk clerk had to take the room bill back to the accounting department, find the clerk responsible for the room, and have him update the master bill. The hotel asked guests to notify the front desk the day before they checked out. That way, when they arrived at the front desk they could receive an up-to-date bill.

Every morning, but mostly on Fridays, the slow manual system created a line of guests impatiently waiting to pay their bills. Guests accepted the slow pace as one of the costs for staying at the Rossiya, Metropol, but it didn't dampen their frustration.

Every Friday afternoon, two copies of Josh's bill were left on the desk in his room. After reviewing one copy, he initialed each page and signed his name under the total amount before dropping it off at the front desk. The bill was charged to the embassy's American Express card on file with the hotel.

Josh took the second bill to the embassy on Monday morning, filled out an expense form, and made detailed notes where necessary to make it easy for the embassy staffer to approve the bill. After that, Josh stapled the credit card receipt to the bill.

As Josh walked through the lobby, a KGB colonel stepped in front of him. "Captain Haman, a word. It will only take a few minutes." The colonel gestured to three empty chairs. Josh noticed that no other guests were sitting anywhere near them; he assumed the KGB officer had asked the guests to move. Four other KGB men stood nearby to keep the area clear.

Josh saw Velasquez look at the four KGB men; the gunny started to reach for something behind his back. Josh gave a hand signal indicating, "Give me ten minutes," and sat down in one of the chairs. The colonel sat in another, and suddenly Krasnovsky appeared out of nowhere, taking the third.

"Captain Haman," said the colonel, "I am Colonel Iliya Golovkin of Second Chief Directorate of KGB." Golovkin spoke in accented English. "As courtesy, I asked Major General Krasnovsky to join meeting. I believe you two have met on more than one occasion. I understand you speak Russian, no?"

"*Da.*"

Josh wondered if Golovkin knew just how many times he and Krasnovsky met. More importantly, did Golovkin know what they'd talked about?

"Good," said Golovkin. "It's nice to meet an American who speaks more than one language." He opened a soft-sided briefcase and pulled out a folder. In English, he said, "I will get to point of meeting. Subject is death of Alexei Bagdonovich."

Josh crossed his hands in his lap. He said nothing. If the KGB was investigating Bagdonovich's death, it strongly indicated Bagdonovich had still been an active KGB member.

Golovkin held up a stapled set of papers. "This is *militsiya* report filed by Lieutenant Colonel Kishniev. It is very, very thorough. Included is statement given to *militsiya* by you and two American enlisted men. Events in document have been verified by us." he paused, then said, "I am curious how you knew name of the man you killed."

"I'd seen his picture," said Josh.

"Why were you shown picture?"

"He was a known KGB assassin. I was advised to avoid contact with him." Josh had no intention of revealing Krasnovsky gave him the picture. Even if Krasnovsky had turned from friend to foe, Josh didn't want to burn him yet.

"So you hunted Bagdonovich and killed him?" Golovkin asked.

"*Nyet.*" Josh spat the word with more emotion than he intended. The tone clearly surprised the Russian. "As the report states, Bagdonovich *shot* at me while I was walking with Lieutenant Colonel Kishniev and his family. Bagdonovich's associate *confessed* that I was the target. So let me be clear: Bagdonovich was hunting *me*, not the other way around. He fired first."

"Why would he want to kill you?"

"I have no idea. I suggest you take that question to the heads of the First or Second Directorates. They're the only ones with authority to order an assassination inside or outside the Soviet Union. I am sure that one of them must know."

Out of the corner of his eye, Josh saw Krasnovsky wince.

"Did Bagdonovich say anything to you?"

"No. He was trying to kill me, and I was defending myself. I didn't know who he was until the fight was over. That's when I pulled off his ski mask and saw his face."

"Do you know what your government is going to do in response to this incident?"

"No, Colonel, I don't." *And if I did, I wouldn't tell you.* "I do know the United States is very unhappy that the KGB tried to assassinate a senior member of the U.S. embassy who has diplomatic immunity. It is even more puzzling considering that the U.S. and its allies have gone to great trouble and expense to provide food to the Soviet Union. We could have let you and your countrymen starve, but we thought the world didn't need another humanitarian disaster. I find it curious that a KGB assassin tries to kill one of the officers involved in this generous effort. Don't you find it investigating, Colonel Golovkin? If I were investigating this, I'd start there."

Golovkin stared back for a long time. Finally, he stood. "I have no other questions. I would, however, watch behavior, Captain Haman. The Soviet Union does not like foreigners who kill its citizens."

Josh stood so he was eye to eye with Golovkin. "Nor does the United States like when a Soviet citizen attempts to assassinate a member of its embassy staff... especially when that citizen is a member of the KGB."

Krasnovsky quietly handed Josh an envelope. "This is a copy of the police report. Keep it in your records. You'll need it in case there's a trial."

"Trial! Why should there be a trial? I was the *target*, not the shooter."

Golovkin motioned to the KGB soldiers and stood. "Many in the Soviet Union do not see it the same way."

"Bagdonovich was ordered to kill me by someone high up in your organization. Only this time, they missed. I suggest you look inside the KGB not at innocent victims."

"Captain, may I remind you that you went into apartment with illegal weapons, destroyed people's property when you kicked down door and you killed Soviet citizen. If you had waited for *militsiya* to arrive, they could have arrested Bagdonovich who would now being interrogated."

"Colonel, Colonel, that is unmitigated bullshit and you know it. Bagdanovich would have been killed by his handlers because he knew too much and if it got out, leaders within the KGB would be embarrassed. This discussion is over."

Saturday, August 3rd, 1991, 1902 Local Time, Moscow

The embassy was emptier than usual. Many staffers were in the U.S. enjoying their thirty days of vacation, with airfares paid by Uncle Sam. In the communications center where the secure phone booths were located, the watch officer was reading a book.

Making calls on Saturday afternoon were Josh's way of dealing with the eight-hour time difference. Early evening in Moscow was early morning in D.C. Jeff Gainesville and his boss were in their offices in the Pentagon. If they weren't, they could take calls from the STU-III's in their homes. Josh didn't have the same choice.

This Saturday, the normal call time of four o'clock had been pushed to seven because General Feltzer wanted the Chairman of the Joint Chiefs to join the call. Josh waited patiently in the conference room with a secure video conferencing set-up. A big projection screen TV was at one end of the room. It had three cameras: one would be focused on Josh and the others on slides he'd prepared. Finally, all was ready and the conference began.

"Good afternoon, sirs." Josh waited until all of them acknowledged that they could see and hear each other. This was the first time he'd ever been part of a videoconference; looking at screens showing the three flag officers in the Chairman's conference room was distracting. The picture quality was great, but when someone moved, the individual's motions seemed jerky and the video was slightly behind the audio.

"The purpose of this afternoon's call is to discuss our options for preventing the illegal transfer of nuclear weapons to the Iranians." Josh waited for the audio and encryption to catch up. On his left, Velasquez slid the first slide onto the projector.

"In this slide," Josh said, "you can see where the weapons are stored. This information comes straight from Red Light." That was the code name assigned to Krasnovsky.

Velasquez put the next slide into the projector: a map of the area involved. Josh described the road through Uzbekistan and Turkmenistan that led to northeast Iran. He pointed out the best possible route and tapped the map to show the airfields nearest the storage facilities. He explained that the fastest and most efficient way to get the weapons out of the Soviet Union was via truck. Flying wasn't practical—it required the Soviet Air Ministry to allow a non-Soviet registered airplane to fly in and out of Soviet airspace. If the Iranians tried to sneak in a plane, they'd risk having it shot down. Besides, the Iranians would still need trucks to get the weapons out of the depot and to an airfield.

The Chairman spoke while Velasquez changed slides. "Captain, you're willing to bet your life on the information Red Light and the Israelis are providing?"

"Yes, sir. I've worked with the Israelis before. Whatever information they provide is top notch. As for Red Light, I don't think he's playing me. Everything he's given me has been 100% accurate. The way I see it, Red Light has three sets of motives. One is self-interest: we're funding his retirement, so to speak. Two is deeper and more complex. Red Light no longer believes in communism and doesn't like the corruption and inequality of the current system. He wants the Soviet Union of the future to be a better place for his children and grandchildren. Therefore, he wants to do his part to discredit the corrupt elements within the Soviet Union. Third, he doesn't want the Iranians to get nukes. In his mind, Iran is unpredictable, and Moscow is only a short missile flight away from Tehran."

The Joint Chief Chairman said, "I hope you know I'm getting heavy pressure from our friends at Christians in Action to have access to Red Light. They don't like you running a senior Soviet officer when they don't have input or control."

Josh said, "Every time Red Light and I talk, he reminds me he mistrusts the CIA. He knows there are Soviet moles in the agency. If the CIA knows who he is, he's afraid they'll unmask him, and he'll end up dead. Unfortunately, sir, there is precedent for his concern."

"We know. Why does he trust you?"

"Red Light read my KGB file. He also knows that very few people are told what I get from him. I hope you've honored my request and haven't used his name in any documents passed to the CIA."

"He's only known as Red Light," the Chairman said. "Marty Cabot knows who he is, but as far as we know, that's it except for the three of us here, Velasquez, Brown and you."

"Thank you, sir."

"You do know that once this is over, you'll be grilled by the CIA. We gave them the complete list of KGB officers who Red Light says were killed for working with the CIA. The agency is grateful and is actively looking for the moles. They'd still like to talk to him."

"I'll be happy to talk with the CIA, but I won't reveal Red Light's identity. I believe that's why the CIA went along with General Grant's attempt to get into my safe."

"Fair enough. My guess is after this is all over , they may ask you to go back to him."

"I'll cross that bridge when I come to it."

"O.K. What's the plan to stop the Iranians?"

The screen now showed a photo of Colonel Yuri Panichev of the Soviet Rocket Artillery Forces—otherwise known as Ali Akrami. Josh shared what the Mossad had told him: they were convinced Akrami was a member of the Pasdaran or Quds force. He was the buyer and the man tasked with getting the weapons into Iran.

The Chairman held up his hand and leaned forward to speak into the microphone. "Captain, you've been studying this. What do you think Akrami will do?"

Josh t outlined what he believed were Akrami's best options.

The Chairman fired his next question. "Do you see any common weak points in Akrami's potential courses of action?"

"Yes, sir." Josh rattled off the problems faced by the operation: fuel for the trucks, paperwork to get across the Uzbekistan/Turkmenistan border, and only two viable routes by road.

The Chairman asked, "Why wouldn't they go off the road from Tejen directly into Iran?"

"Wear and tear on the trucks, sir. They'd also be pressed for fuel, and they'd travel much slower than on the roads. Not to mention running afoul of KGB Border Guards who aren't in on the arrangement."

The Chairman nodded. "So if they're crossing at Sarakhs, what else is nearby?"

"An airport, sir," Josh said. "As soon as Akrami takes possession of the warheads, I'd start looking for an Iranian Air Force cargo plane sitting on the ramp at that airfield. That is the nearest airport and it has a 13,000-foot runway. So, once we know Akrami has the weapons, I would look for a cargo airplane on that airport."

The Chairman looked at the map for a moment, then said, "What's your plan?"

It took Josh ten minutes to brief what he and Avram had devised. It was simple, but unconventional. The Chairman waited until Josh finished, then said, "Senior Gunny Velasqucz, you have been awfully quiet. You're a Recon Marine; what's your take?" His use of the abbreviated term Gunny instead of Senior Gunnery Sergeant was out of habit and respect. While the Chairman didn't known Velasquez background, Feltzer did. Several times during the work up to Desert Shield and Storm, Velasquez led teams deep into Kuwait to identify Iraqi units and positions. During the Iraqi incursion toward Khafji, his recon team's observation post inside Kuwait was repeatedly attacked by the Iraqi 6th Armored Brigade and repulsed every one.

"It's doable, sir, and not very risky. I like the captain's plan."

"Except that you'll be out in the middle of bum-fuck nowhere without a chance of getting picked up if Mr. Murphy puts in an appearance. But you think the plan will work?"

"Yes, sir."

"You sound like the two-star SEAL I talked with down at Special Operations Command. When I showed him the plan, he asked who put it together. I told him Captain Haman. He said just give the man what he asks for and let him go do it. If the captain needs anyone else to go, there'll be SEALs standing in line. Commander Cabot begged me to send him."

Feltzer asked, "As one tribal member to another, is this your head speaking or your heart?"

"Both, General."

"So you think you can trust the Bukharan Jews?"

"Avram Gutman and I believe they are highly motivated to do what we need, given what we've offered them. We just have to do our part."

"Do you have what you need?" Feltzer asked.

"If we get what we asked for in the briefing document, we're good to go."

The Chairman leaned toward the microphone. "You'll have your answer Monday morning, D.C. time."

Monday, August 5th, 1991, 0701 Local Time, New York

Unable to sleep, Jim Broughton tossed and turned throughout the night. At four o'clock, he gave up and got out of bed, well before the time set on his alarm. Looking east as he sipped coffee, he could see signs of dawn on the horizon. Energized by the caffeine, he headed for the shower where he took extra care to bathe himself from head to toe.

After toweling dry and shaving, Broughton ate his favorite breakfast: dried fruits, walnuts and honey mixed with a dash of vanilla into a bowl of Greek yogurt. This was followed by an English muffin and washed down by a large glass of fresh squeezed orange juice made the night before.

When he'd finished eating and dressing, Broughton turned off all the lights in his apartment and put his keys, FBI badge and ID, electronic access card and pistol in a neat row on the living-room coffee table. Satisfied that everything was in order, he picked up a duffel bag he'd placed by the door and left at 0537.

Broughton took the Lexington Avenue Express to Grand Central Station. From there, he boarded the Number 7 Train to the Willets Point station. No one paid attention to him as he walked the three quarters of a mile across the parking lot, away from the train station and under the Grand Central Parkway. He took the bike path along the edge of Flushing Bay to the World's Fair Marina where *Swordsman* was docked.

Just before seven, Broughton climbed onto the Luhrs. He went through the drill of checking the engine compartments for fumes and letting the vent fans run for at least three minutes before he turned on the ignition and started the engines. A dock boy appeared ready to help him cast off. Broughton returned to the bridge; when he waved, the teenager untied the line holding the bow to the dock. The boy coiled it and tossed it on the deck before doing the same with the one holding the stern.

Broughton shifted the right engine into gear, nudged the right throttle forward, and spun the wheel in the same direction. *Swordsman's* bow moved away from the pier, the ebb tide making it easy. Once it was pointed into Flushing Bay, Broughton pushed both throttles forward until the boat was going about five knots. Even though *Swordsman* was bow heavy, Broughton felt that the boat was eager to go faster.

By the time *Swordsman* entered the East River, the sun was well up in a cloudless sky. It was going to be a hot day in New York City. Broughton could see planes landing at LaGuardia, but he couldn't hear them over the hum of the *Swordsman's* engines. *Swordsman* rounded the north shore of Rikers Island and entered the northern end of the East River. He could see mini-waves from the boat's wake fan out as the boat loafed along at ten knots.

The Same Day, 0705 Local Time, New York City

Less than three miles east of *Swordsman*, Andrew Goode sat in a small conference room where copies of the arrest warrants for Broughton and Safdar lay on a table. Today was the day they were going to arrest Broughton and Safdar. The conference room had been selected because it gave them access to a stairwell that led to the basement. They could remove Broughton from the building in handcuffs without an embarrassing perp-walk through the bureau's office. After arriving at 0700, he reviewed the plan with those in the office and the surveillance teams.

When Broughton arrived, he was going to be asked to attend a meeting and arrested when he entered into the room. This had been triggered by the disappearance of Safdar's boat. On Sunday morning, the boat hadn't been at its usual buoy in Little Neck Bay

The Port Authority Police had begun an intensive, urgent search. After a tense eight hours, two Port Authority policemen found *Swordsman* at a pier at the World's Fair Marina. The New York FBI office was ordered to maintain constant surveillance of the boat; if Broughton, Safdar, or anyone else boarded, they were to be arrested. Goode wanted to capture Safdar alive. Then, as per the plan Goode had given the director on Friday, an explosive ordnance team would board the boat to disarm it.

Glancing at his watch, he noted it was already 0722 and Broughton still hadn't arrived.

Goode headed to the FBI command center. "Where's Broughton?" He received blank looks. "Anyone see him leave his apartment this morning? Broughton was supposed to be tailed."

"By the time we got there at six, he was gone." The speaker was the senior special agent in the command center. Goode thought, *you idiot, why didn't someone call me?* There was no point saying that now. Goode simply regretted that he'd agreed to the Director, who'd wanted to wait until Monday morning. Broughton had once worked for the Director. Because of that, the head of the FBI had trouble accepting that his former co-worker had become a terrorist.

Goode asked, "Where is the team that's supposed to tail Broughton?"

"Still at his apartment."

"Shit! Where's Safdar?"

"We have two teams on him. He tried several tricks to check for a tail. We haven't seen any indication that he's onto us."

"So where *is* he?"

"On the Lexington Avenue Express headed downtown. We have three agents in the same car with him. A fourth got off to report in by phone because our radios don't work in the subway tunnels. As soon as they come above ground, one agent will break off and report in."

"What about eyes on the boat?"

"They're on their way. Should be there in twenty minutes."

"We were supposed to have someone watching the boat 24 by 7! What happened?"

"Somebody dropped the ball, sir. It was in the log as an action item."

Goode felt like cursing. "We'll figure out who screwed up later. Right now, we have to find the boat, and Broughton. What about NYPD or Port Authority cops? How fast can we get them there?"

Another set of blank looks.

Goode struggled to contain his anger. He banged the table with the palm of his hand. Several coffee cups jumped, and one tipped over. No one moved to clean it up. "Goddammit," Goode said. "We have a potential boat bomb designed to bring down a bridge and kill hundreds, maybe thousands of people. C'mon, folks, get your shit together! I want anyone who tries to get on the boat stopped and arrested. Find out how fast the locals can get there! We have a Federal warrant to search and seize the boat, so we can sort out protocol and procedures later."

"Sir, what do we tell the locals?"

"Tell them Broughton is armed and dangerous. If cornered, he may try to bluff his way out using FBI credentials. If anyone has questions, have them call me. Immediately!" The big FBI agent took a deep breath to control his temper. "So we may have lost a boat filled with C4, and Flushing Bay is less than an hour from the closest bridge across the East River. Safdar is headed downtown and Broughton is missing."

"Uh, yes, sir, that sums it up."

Goode looked at his watch. It was almost seven forty *What the fuck happened? These people are supposed to be the cream*

of the crop of the N.Y. office and they're acting like morons.
"Do we still have teams who can go through an apartment?"

"Yes, sir, we have three."

"All right then." Goode again regretted not coming to New York on Friday to take charge personally. "Execute the Delayed Notice Search Warrants on Safdar's two apartments and Broughton's place now. *RIGHT NOW!*"

"Yes, sir."

"Where's the head of the FBI SWAT team?"

"Next door."

"Get the leader and his number two in here now."

The Same Day, 0731 Local Time, New York City

Mohammed Safdar was a man on a mission. His focus on getting to a spot where he could watch what would happen made him predictable and slightly careless. Confident that he'd lost himself in the crowd on the Lexington Avenue Express, he didn't check his six as he hurried up the steps to Chambers Street.

He paused a few seconds to look around, then turned east down Chambers Street toward the East River. In the crowd of New Yorkers hurrying to work, Safdar didn't notice the FBI agent signal his partner.

One agent trailed Safdar while two hurried to get on each side of him. When a fourth Special Agent stepped in front of Safdar, the two grabbed his arms.

The agent in front said, "Mohammed Safdar, I'm Special Agent Giddings from the FBI. I have a warrant for your arrest."

Before Safdar could react, the trailing agent handcuffed him. They moved him to the curb to await the arrival of an FBI car. Giddings recited the Miranda warning as they patted Safdar down and took the camera bag slung over his shoulder.

In it was a Nikon with a telephoto lens, spare rolls of film, a video camera, and a small aluminum box.

The Same Day, 0732 Local Time, East River

Swordsman's twin diesels burbled away, more felt than heard. Broughton was ahead of schedule. He decided to loop around Roosevelt Island before heading back south on the East River. Safdar wanted the bomb to go off at 0800 or shortly after: the height of the rush hour.

The Same Day, 0738 Local Time, New York City

"Sir," someone said to Goode, "NYPD reports that the boat is gone."

"What!"

"It's gone, sir. The NYPD officer on the scene talked to a dock boy who helped the boat cast off about seven o'clock. The boy described Broughton to a T, sir."

Goode scowled. "Get me the head of the Port Authority's aviation unit on the phone ASAP. Same for NYPD. We need helicopters and boats to find Broughton."

"Yes, sir."

"What's the latest on Safdar?"

"No word yet, sir."

Fuck, I wish I were in the field!

The Same Day, 0742 Local Time, East River

With the boat on autopilot and slowed to three knots, Jim Broughton went down the ladder from the bridge to the main deck. In the shelter of the bridge aft of the main cabin, he pulled off his shirt, socks, shoes and trousers. Standing in his underwear, he felt truly free.

He gently pulled white cotton garments from the duffle bag that made up the three pieces of his *kafan,* the Muslim burial shroud. The first to go on were pants that he tied around his waist. Next, he pulled on the top and fumbled with the square unfinished wooden buttons. Last, he pulled on a white *topi* cap worn for prayers instead of the more traditional *taqiyah*. To keep the cap in place, he used a bobby pin to clip it to his hair. For a few seconds, he stood with his arms away from his sides and let the loose white linen flap. Before he went back to the bridge, he faced east and shouted three times: "*Allahu akbar!*"

The Same Day, 0751 Local Time, New York City

Goode paced the command center, trying to calm the churning in his stomach. He reminded himself that no plan survives first contact with the enemy. He fervently hoped that would prove as true for Broughton as it had for him.

"Special Agent Goode," said one of the command center agents. "They're entering the building with Safdar. He should be in Interrogation Room One in less than two minutes."

"I'm on the way. Let me know when you find Broughton or the boat." He heard, "Yes, sir," as he cleared the doorway.

Goode was already in place when an agent lead Safdar into the room and chained him to the chair. "He hasn't said a word since we read him his rights," the agent reported. "He was carrying this when we nabbed him."

The agent held out a small aluminum box with two switches. It had two green lights, two other red ones, and a pullout radio antenna. Goode took it, examined it for a few seconds, then handed it back to the agent.

"All right, Safdar," Goode said, "which bridge is it?"

"Go to your Christian hell, Infidel."

"We know about Broughton. We know about your meetings. So again, which bridge is it?"

"I want a lawyer," Safdar said.

"O.K." Goode turned to the other agent in the room. "Find out which lawyer he wants and make the call. If necessary, call the Federal D.A. to get a public defender. No one, I repeat, *no one*, talks to him. He takes pee breaks escorted by three men and in chains. If he tries anything, deadly force is authorized."

Back in the command center, Goode took it as a good sign that the head of the watch team was smiling. "We have eyes on the boat from a helicopter. The copter is flying a random pattern so it doesn't look like he's circling, but it's keeping the boat in sight at all times. Right now, the boat has just passed under the Triboro Bridge and is north of Roosevelt Island."

"They're sure it's the right one?"

"They can read *Swordsman* on the stern and they've identified Broughton through their binoculars. Here's something odd. He isn't wearing the clothes the dock boy described. He's all in white."

Something niggled in the back of Goode's mind, but it wouldn't advance to be recognized. "Find out if the guys in the helicopter can stop the boat if it's headed for a bridge. I'm going back to the conference room for a few minutes."

In the conference room, Goode grabbed a file and dumped out the pictures. His mind raced as he reviewed the possible targets for the umpteenth time. To drop a bridge using a boat bomb, you needed one with its supports in the water. Which one?

59th Street Bridge? No piers in the water.

The next one south was the Williamsburg Bridge. It had one support out in the middle of the river.

Brooklyn Bridge? All the piers were on land. Same with the Manhattan Bridge.

That made the Williamsburg Bridge the most likely target. Goode was worrying whether his guess was correct when his mind flashed back to what he'd been told a few minutes ago.

Broughton was wearing all white? Oh shit, suicide bombers did that. It was their burial garb! Safdar's detonation box was only a backup in case Broughton got cold feet.

Goode snatched up the intercom. "Find out if the police helicopter is armed, and send the SWAT guys down here, now! On the double is *not* fast enough!"

When two men in black jumpsuits entered the room, Goode demanded, "What weapons do you have that can stop a boat?"

"Disable it or sink it?"

"Disable first, sink if we have to."

"A fifty caliber round in each engine generally does the trick. We can also use our M1A1`s—they fire a 7.62 X 51mm NATO round. It'll chew stuff up, but the fifty is a better option."

"How close do you have to get with the fifty?"

"Under a thousand yards, but closer is better."

"Can you shoot the fifty from a helicopter?"

"We've never tried. If we miss, the bullet goes a long way."

"Will the bullets set off plastic explosive?"

"Not unless we set off one of the detonators by accident."

The Same Day, 0759 Local Time, East River

The 59th Street Bridge loomed overhead. The noise of the traffic on the lowest deck of the bridge—even two hundred feet above him—was loud enough to drown out the hum of *Swordsman's* engines. Broughton checked the clock on the instrument panel, then the watch he'd taken off and placed in one of the cup holders. He was late! Ten minutes late.

The only solution was to shove the throttles forward. As the twin screws bit into the water, the Luhr's bow lifted up. Behind him, Broughton could see the V of the wake rolling toward the river's shores. The wind whipping around his sunglass frames made his eyes water. South of Roosevelt Island, he moved to the center of the river, not giving a damn about the rules of the river.

"James Broughton, this is the New York Police Department. Stop the boat, I repeat stop the boat *now!*"

The loud hailer caught him by surprise. With the noise of the wind and the roar of the diesels, he hadn't heard or seen the police Bell 206 helicopter come up from behind. It was now a hundred feet above him and several hundred feet back. *Two minutes! I just need two minutes. Every second I survive gets me one second closer. Allah help me!*

Broughton spun the wheel to the left as he pushed the throttles as far forward as they would go. The bow rose as the propellers bit into the water and the boat heeled over. One, two three, and he spun the wheel to the right.

There was a flash and the left side of the instrument panel exploded in a shower of splinters and Broughton felt a punch and searing pain in his side. If he didn't know better, he felt as if he was speared. Broughton had to hang on to the instrument panel to keep from falling. He ignored the sharp pain and the blood dripping down his thigh. *Every second counts. Allah keep me alive to finish my mission.*

He spun the wheel left, counted to five and then turned right. The floor behind him erupted. Rounds pinged as they hit the steel ladder. Shards of wood sticking into his legs felt like pinpricks. Broughton looked down and saw see the white fabric of his kafan turning dark red. Blood dripped onto his bare foot.

Looking up and over his shoulder, Broughton saw a man with a rifle and scope lying prone in the cabin of the helicopter. The end of the barrel flashed. Broughton's last conscious thought was, *this is what it looks like when they're shooting at you.*

The first of three rounds from the semi-automatic M1A1 entered Broughton's midsection, just below his sternum. The second copper-jacketed 147-grain 7.62 bullet hit him squarely in the center of mass, exploding his heart before the bullet exited between his shoulder blades. The third went through his mouth, blowing off the back of his head.

The Luhrs kept going in an ever-widening circle; the helicopter maintained position fifty yards alongside. It gave the agent with the Barrett a clear shot at the right side of the boat. Wood and fiberglass flew as the 630-grain bullet hammered through the hull and into the starboard engine. Valves drilled themselves into pistons as the engine seized.

The helicopter repositioned over the other side of the boat. The port engine took two rounds before it belched black smoke and destructed. With no power, the Luhrs slowed to a rocking stop. Broughton's lifeless body slid back and forth across the bloody teak deck like a rag doll.

The Same Day, 1249 Local Time, Governor Island

It was almost noon before the NYPD bomb squad finished towing the Luhrs to the south side of Governor's Island. The location on the hundred and seventy acre island had been selected so if the bomb inside went off, the explosion would do as little damage as possible to the city.

Andrew Goode flew to Governor's Island on a Port Authority helicopter and gave Safdar's transmitter to the head of the bomb squad. In the course of their search, the squad found two detonators besides the one that Broughton was supposed to use. Hidden amongst the explosives was a receiver on the same frequency used by Safdar's transmitter, and another designed to set the bomb off on impact.

With the bomb no longer a threat, an FBI team looked for additional evidence to connect Safdar to the bomb and the boat. With luck, they'd find fingerprints on the steel plates, wiring and detonators. With that, and with what they'd hauled out of

Safdar's apartments, Goode was sure they could make a convincing case to the jury.

By now, Safdar would have to know that his plot had failed. On the helicopter flight back to the Federal building, Goode looked out the window at the city that had so narrowly avoided a deadly terrorist assault. He couldn't question Safdar until the man was represented by a lawyer. None of the public defenders had wanted him as a client. The district attorney was contacting high-profile New York law firms to see if any would take Safdar as a pro bono case for publicity. If one did, the lead Federal prosecutor would have his hands full—unless he could convince Safdar and his lawyer to make a deal that included a data dump on his connections and network. Otherwise, the prosecutor would ask for sequential life sentences to keep Safdar in jail for the rest of his life.

The legal wrangling was out of his control. Goode had done his job. He headed for the observation room, separated from Interrogation Room One by one-way glass.

Safdar was still sitting in the chair. The Palestinian's chin was on his chest. His hands were clasped with his forearms resting on the edge of the table. Despite the manacles and handcuffs, Safdar looked completely relaxed.

"Special Agent Goode," the speaker was Frank Young, the veteran prosecutor from the United States Attorney's office for the Southern District of New York, "the firm of Baker, Brice and Masters has agreed to take Safdar as a pro bono client. Brian Hastings-Mills is downstairs, having his briefcase inspected and being patted down. He's a specialist in ugly, nasty trials where the police believe they have a solid, airtight case. He either gets his clients off or creates enough doubt in the prosecutor's mind to make a deal for a lesser sentence."

"Nice," Good said sarcastically.

"Yeah. So Special Agent Goode, did we do anything which may come back to haunt us in the trial?"

"No."

"Has Safdar been Mirandized?"

"Yes. The other three agents who picked him up witnessed it. As soon as he asked for a lawyer, we stopped talking to him except to offer water. Oh, and he refused our offer of a halal lunch. Twice he was escorted to the bathroom."

"Has he been threatened in any way?"

"No. We've had a videotape recorder running on him since he arrived."

"Excuse me, are you District Attorney Frank Young?"

Goode turned to face a man dressed in what he suspected was a two-thousand-dollar suit. Goode stuck out his hand. "I'm Special Agent Goode. A pleasure to meet you, Mr. Mills."

"Hastings-Mills."

The FBI agent smiled inwardly. *I know, I'm trying to get under your skin.* "My mistake. Do you want to meet your new client?"

Goode gestured to the door. A few seconds later, Hastings-Mills took a chair opposite his new client and Goode double-checked to make sure the video recorder was off. The FBI agent and the DA waited until Hastings-Mills opened the door twenty minutes later to let them in.

The Special Agent and the D.A. brought two more chairs into the room and sat at the table. Two FBI agents took up positions in opposite corners, while a court reporter set up shop at the end of the table.

Hastings-Mills was the first to speak. "I'd like to have Mohammed Safdar unshackled. He will not attempt to harm anyone in the room."

Safdar raised his hands, but District Attorney Young said, "I think not. He's a danger to every American including you, Mr.

Hastings-Mills. The United States will be filing charges against Mr. Safdar for attempting to commit mass murder and unlawful possession of explosives. Those are just the headlines. There's more coming. While you might ask for bail, we're going to ask that it not be granted. He's a flight risk. We've found Lebanese, Saudi, Turkish and Jordanian passports for him—seized in legal searches. Here are copies of the warrants."

Hastings-Mills put the warrants in his briefcase and made a few notes on a yellow pad. "Where do you intend to hold Mr. Safdar?"

Goode said, "You'll be told when he's safely there."

"What happens if I need to meet with my client?"

Young said, "Call me. Either the FBI or the U.S. Marshals will arrange transportation."

"You're making it difficult for me to prepare a defense."

"No one will prevent you from meeting with your client," Goode said. "We're just going to minimize the number of people who know where he's being kept."

"Why?"

"We want to prevent his associates from rescuing or assassinating him."

Hastings-Mills gave a sour look. "When is Mr. Safdar being arraigned?"

"Five o'clock today. In an hour or so, we'll provide you with a preliminary list of the charges and an outline of the evidence we currently have. More will be forthcoming as we gather it. You'll be kept fully informed." Young's tone was pleasant but hard. His task was getting a conviction, and he did not want this one getting away.

Hastings-Mills made a show of writing notes and looked at Young. "Is any of the evidence classified?"

Young let Goode answer this one. Goode looked directly at Safdar as he answered. "We have the boat and its explosives. It didn't go boom as you planned. We also have the boat's driver in custody. We have Safdar's fingerprints on the boat. We've found his stash of C-4 and more. So to answer your question, Mr. Hastings-Mills, the evidence we have isn't classified. We've had Mr. Safdar under surveillance for some time, and we can place Mr. Safdar on the boat and piece together how he built the bomb."

Hastings-Mills took off his reading glasses and put them gently on the table. "I'm sure that somewhere along the line, you made enough mistakes that some, if not all, of the evidence will get tossed."

Young smiled at Hastings-Mills. "We think the evidence will convince any jury of Mr. Safdar's guilt. Any evidence you manage to get removed won't affect the final result." Young put his pen in his pocket. "Oh, before we leave you alone again with your client, I wanted to ask you how good you are extradition hearings. Mr. Safdar is wanted for murder in Israel, and we have an extradition treaty with them. We expect Mr. Safdar will be tried and convicted in the U.S. Then, he'll be extradited to Israel where he may be convicted again. Mr. Safdar, do you have a preference for where you'll be tried? The U.S. or Israel?"

Safdar who swallowed hard several times, and Hastings-Mills put his arm on Safdar's shoulder. "Don't answer. Mr. Young, I wouldn't take extradition to the bank."

"I just thought you'd want to know what you're up against. This could become your life's work. And since it's pro bono, you'll be at it for a long time."

Frank Young and Andrew Goode left Safdar with his attorney. The DA knew that Baker, Brice and Masters were too mercenary to allow Hastings-Mills and a supporting cast of lawyers to spend too much time at pro bono or public defender rates. Soon, they'd start looking for a graceful way out.

MOSCOW AIRLIFT

Monday, August 12th, 1991, 0902 Local Time, Moscow

The main entrance to the Soviet General Staff headquarters was on Znamenka Street in the Arbat district of Moscow. The general staff and the Ministry of Defense occupied several other nearby buildings too, all a short walk from each other. A confident Yuri Panichev, a.k.a. Ali Akrami, entered the building in the uniform of a colonel in the Soviet Strategic Rocket Forces.

After the Islamic Revolution, SAVAMA—the Shah of Iran's feared secret police and intelligence agency—had used its agents and sympathizers within the Soviet military to create the personnel file of Yuri Panichev. Every so often, carefully forged documents were sent to Red Army and KGB headquarters to build the files, on the theory that they would get lost in the blizzard of documents filed and catalogued on a daily basis. By now, Panichev's KGB dossier had background investigations that attested to his education, background and political reliability. His current orders said he was an "artillery and rocket equipment readiness inspector, including nuclear" for the General Staff. In this role, he could go anywhere in the country and inspect any artillery piece, rocket launcher, projectile or missile that the army could fire.

Panichev's documents included a phone number in Stavka anyone could call. The captain who answered was a Muslim from Uzbekistan who wanted independence for his country. He would assure the caller that Yuri Panichev was exactly who he said he was.

Whenever Akrami was in the Soviet Union, he went to his apartment in the Basmanny District of Moscow to become Yuri Panichev. It was an area where many foreigners lived, as well as Soviet military officers. So far, Akrami's comings and goings had gone unnoticed.

After the guard at General Staff headquarters looked at his identity card and waved him through, Akrami walked to the security desk and asked for an envelope addressed to him. The private at the desk shook his head.

Akrami said, "It's probably in the safe."

The private turned to the warrant officer standing a few feet behind him. The officer came forward. Akrami noticed the man wore ribbons indicating combat in Afghanistan. Akrami pretended to survey the lobby while the warrant officer flipped through a logbook. "Comrade Colonel, can you tell me who left the documents?"

"Lieutenant General Vavilov. Do you need to call his office?" Calling Vavilov was the last thing he wanted, but it emphasized the importance of the envelope.

"Ahhh, General Vavilov." From the look on the warrant officer's face, he had no idea who Lieutenant General Vavilov was. "Comrade Colonel, may I please see your identification again before I open the safe?"

Akrami pulled the folder out of his breast pocket. The warrant officer's nametag read Zadornov; he stared at Akrami's laminated ID card for a few seconds. "It is not a very good photo, sir," Zadornov said. "The picture does not do you justice. I suggest when you have time you get a better one."

"Thank you," Akrami said. "Can you check the safe now, *praporshchik* Zadornov?" Akrami let his impatience show.

Zadornov knelt. Akrami assumed he had a small safe under the desk with a combination lock. He could hear the man flipping through papers. After thirty seconds, Zadornov stood, holding a sealed brown envelope a centimeter thick. On it, YURI PANICHEV was neatly printed. The logo of the Strategic Rocket Forces was in the envelope's upper left corner.

Zadornov pointed to a multi-part form taped to the front of the envelope. "Comrade Colonel, please sign for the package."

Akrami scrawled his name, making sure the signature was unreadable. Outside the building, he headed for his flat to review what seventy-two million U.S. dollars had bought.

The Same Day, 1310 Local Time, Moscow

The ride in the Zil limousine from the Lubyanka to the Red Army headquarters took only ten minutes. To give his visit an air of importance, Krasnovsky had the driver drop him off at the underground entrance reserved for VIPs. Normally, the Red Army came to the KGB, but Krasnovsky wanted to make a statement.

The major commanding the guard came to the front of the desk to personally look at Krasnovsky's identity book. Before he called upstairs, he gave a captain a specific order to escort the KGB major general to his destination.

Lieutenant General Vavilov waved Krasnovsky into his office. After offering tea or coffee, which Krasnovsky politely declined, Vavilov sat back behind his desk. "General Krasnovsky, what can I do for the KGB today?"

"Thank you, General Vavilov, for taking time to see me on such short notice." Krasnovsky pulled photos, a visa application, and orders out of an envelope he'd brought with him. He put them face down on the table. "As I told you on the phone, I'm responsible for approving the visas of foreigners coming into our country. I'd like to know if you have ever met this man."

Krasnovsky watched Vavilov's face for a reaction as he placed two photos of Yuri Panichev on the center of the desk. The army officer officer's eyes flickered in recognition; his face flushed.

Trying to cover, Vavilov adjusted his reading glasses as he leaned forward, pretending to be earnest and truthful while he decided what to say. The career artilleryman chose his words carefully. "I believe I have met this man. His name is Yuri Panichev, he is a colonel in the artillery. Why?"

Satisfied with his answer, Vavilov sat back.

Krasnovsky had scripted this conversation in his mind and suspected he already knew Vavilov's answers. This was more than a game, but he was curious as to what Vavilov would say. "How often have you met him?"

"Two or three times. Again, why?" Vavilov couldn't remember the actual number of meetings, but it had to have been at least dozen. He fought down the rising panic in his gut. He was one misstatement from a trip to the Lubyanka. The ZBV2s were not the first weapons he'd sold Panichev.

Krasnovsky said, "This man is not really in the Red Army."

Vavilov paled and felt himself get hot under the color. He decided not to react surprised and said nothing. He wondered how much this KGB officer and the Second Directorate knew. They couldn't know everything, or he'd already been arrested. "Then what is he?"

"Iranian. We think from the Pasdaran—the Islamic Revolutionary Guard Corps. We're not sure of his real name; he entered the country under at least three names that I can find."

"Are you positive?"

"Today, I am only eighty percent sure. If that were a hundred percent, you'd be on your way to the Lubyanka. Rather than bring you in for questioning, I thought I would have a chat with you and hear what you have to say."

Vavilov said nothing. Sweat was soaking his undershirt and dripping down his spin as he tried to figure out how long he had to live.

"Before I pass this information on to the Second Directorate," Krasnovsky said, "what did the two of you discuss?" Krasnovsky quickly held up his hand. "Oh, I know the subject and I know about the money. If you want even a chance of living more than twenty-four hours, I want to know everything about Yuri Panichev, what he wanted, what you sold him, and how you communicate. And, I want it right now."

"Do you want some of the money?" Vavilov asked hopefully.

"Are you trying to bribe a KGB general?'

"No. What I'm offering is financial security. Look at our country. It's falling apart. Even if we live long enough to collect our pensions, the country will be broke. Then what? We get to slowly starve or freeze to death in one of Mother Russia's godforsaken winters."

"We'll talk about money later. Where and when is Panichev going to get the weapons, and who did you pay off?"

"If I tell you, then what?"

"For the moment," Krasnovsky said, "it will be our little secret. I agree the country is going to hell. But at the same time, we can't sell nuclear weapons to a bunch of crazy Arabs."

"The Iranians will tell you they are Persians, not Arabs."

"Be that as it may, they're fanatics and they scare me." Krasnovsky let some time pass to see if Vavilov was going to say anything that he could use to hang him. Hearing nothing, he continued, "I want to catch the corrupt KGB border guards and whoever else is involved here at Stavka. Helping me do that is the only hope you have of staying alive. Once I report this to my counterpart in the Second Directorate, I lose control of the investigation and you, General Vavilov, will find yourself in a basement cell in the Lubyanka. So let's start with where Panichev is now. If you do your part, you may become a hero of the Soviet Union instead of a traitor. Tell me now, or I call the Second Directorate from your office."

Wednesday, August 14th, 1991, 0715 Local Time, Moscow

As Josh walked toward the front door of the Rossiya, the concierge waved at him. The man held out a thick envelope.

When Josh asked who'd delivered it, the concierge shook his head. It had been on his desk when he arrived.

Josh dropped the envelope into his briefcase, wondering if there might be some kind of poison on the paper. Curiosity overcame caution. Once he was inside the Suburban, he used the pocketknife to slit open the top and peer down inside. All he saw was another envelope.

He waited until he was at his office desk before he pulled the smaller envelope out. He slit it open and dumped out three passport-sized folders, each with the logo of the Soviet Union. He opened the top one and was surprised to see his picture on an internal passport allowing him to travel anywhere in Azerbaijan, Turkmenistan and Uzbekistan. It was good for the months of August and September. The other two were similar passports for Velasquez and Brown. They had official looking stamps and the signatures of two men: Major General Krasnovsky and Foreign Minister Viktor Grachkov. He wondered for a second whether if they were real or KGB forgeries. As he fanned through the blank pages where Soviet control points could stamp the document, he found a small folded slip of paper.

> *Pick-up scheduled for 8/19/91 at 117 Strategic Weapons Depot, 39° 24'North, 65° 50' East—approximately 20 kilometers east of Maydayap, Uzbekistan. Your move.*

The Same Day, 1839 Local Time, Tashkent, Uzbekistan

As part of his efforts to ensure the Communist Party maintained control, and to homogenize the country's population, Stalin had forced resettlements. Siberians were sent to live in the western part of the Soviet Union; Uzbeks were sent to Belorussia; Ukrainians were forcibly moved to Siberia. Those who objected wound up in either the Gulag or a grave.

As a result, Uzbekistan's capital Tashkent had a Russian flavor. It had new buildings built in the same manner as the rest of the Soviet Union, blocky and unless it was for a government agency, little attention to style. Pressure to meet the current Five Year Plan drove design and construction techniques and rather than on quality. Tashkent also had a expanded airport that had more military than airline flights and supported what many locals thought was an occupying force: the Red Army.

The Soviet "stans"—Kazakhstan, Uzbekistan, Turkmenistan, and Tajikistan—bordered Iran and the two other non-Soviet "stans": Pakistan and Afghanistan. Their strategic value was that they pushed U.S. bases farther from Moscow.

The countryside of the Soviet-controlled "stans" was dotted with intercontinental ballistic missiles silos and weapon storage sites. Low population density, remoteness and as distant as one could get from the United States made the 'stans' ideal places to store nuclear weapons. If they leaked, no problem: no population centers would be endangered. If a few locals died, the world would never find out.

Ali Akrami could have bought a plane ticket to Tashkent, but he decided on a two-day train ride in a first class cabin because he didn't want anyone looking into his briefcase. If they did, they'd find the transfer papers and two hundred thousand new rubles in cash. He had a similar amount of money in his suitcase, held in a sealed package with the logo of the Red Army.

The menu was simple and the portions small. It seemed that the only thing plentiful on the train was vodka. As a first class passenger, a bottle of vodka was put on the table along with one of mineral water. While everything worked in his compartment, it was clear that Soviet Railways was not spending its budget on upkeep. His bathroom needed a good cleaning and the fabric on the bench that folded into a bead was threadbare and needed replacing.

The train passed through land with few trees and almost no visible water. The region resembled northeastern Iran, where Akrami had grown up.

Akrami emerged from the train carrying his bag and briefcase. Tarana Aliyev found him and saluted. The tall, slender mechanic was dressed in utilities and wearing the insignia of a captain.

"Colonel Panichev, welcome to Tashkent. I am Captain Moshen Zangeneh."

Panichev returned the salute and let "Zangeneh" pick up his suitcase. As they started down the platform, Akrami waited until there was no one nearby. He quietly asked, "Is everything ready?"

"Yes, sir. We have a camp outside the city. No one bothers us. We have papers to get fuel and supplies from any army depot."

"Excellent."

"Ali, do you have the documents?"

"In my briefcase. Now take me to my hotel. I'm not supposed to report until tomorrow morning. Since this is a surprise visit, I'll ask for a briefing on the storage locations. We can confirm the locations, the number of weapons at each, and their security plans. I won't tell them the site I plan to inspect near Samarkand because it's supposed to be unexpected. If we aren't closely watched during the inspection, we'll try to take a few extra warheads. I don't think anyone will notice."

Aliyev nodded as they walked through he crowd."

Akrami continued with his update. "Tomorrow, you head there. We knew we wouldn't find out the exact location of the weapons until I got the papers. I will follow by train after the briefing and meet you in Samarkand."

"Are you afraid we'll be discovered?"

Akrami opened the passenger door to the small GAZ truck and looked across the roof. "In this business, it's always a possibility. However, we have a good plan, and with Allah's help, we will succeed."

"I hope we don't need Allah's help."

Akrami laughed. "Tonight, my friend, let us have a nice dinner."

Thursday, August 15th, 1991, 0856 Local Time, Tashkent

The military district headquarters was the easiest building to identify on the base: the gray concrete building, essentially a six-story rectangular box, was the only one with the national flags of the Soviet Union and Uzbekistan on either side of the steps. It was also the tallest building in Tashkent, and perhaps most distinctively, it had a grass lawn: a rarity in dry Uzbekistan.

On the first floor just off the entrance, Major Svi Yaniv reviewed the rotation of the soldiers stationed at the security desk. He had been in the Soviet Army for almost fifteen years and had spent three tours in Afghanistan with the 5th Guards Motor Rifle division. Yaniv had been awarded the Hero of the Soviet Union, the highest award for courage and bravery under fire. He'd also received the Order of Alexander Nevsky for leadership. His assignment as the head of security was a reward for his distinguished service and his time fighting the Mujahidin. As a bonus, this assignment was close to Samarkand, the city where he'd been born and raised.

Looking at Yaniv who preferred to wear his utilities to work rather than the more formal brown uniform of the Red Army, he looked like one of the natives. Only on those days he was required to wear his dress uniform, would one see his ribbons and know that he was a highly decorated officer. Yaniv was informal, yet professional with his staff that issued badges to anyone allowed access to any military facility in the district. He didn't yell or scream and followed the adage when dealing with his men that leaders "praise in public, chastise in private."

Regulations stated that every visitor and every worker assigned to the headquarters needed a badge showing their picture. Different departments had badges with different colored stripes. Visitor badges had three red diagonal stripes across the badge; the top center would display the man's picture, under which was his name and rank.

Like any bureaucracy, regulations required a form to be filled out for every visitor. Yaniv kept a copy in his office; another went to the military district's administrative office; a third went to the paymaster; and a fourth went to the department that the individual was visiting. Each copy included the photo taken in Yaniv's office. At least two extra prints and the negative were kept in the security office's files, cross-referenced by badge number, date, and last name.

Photos were stapled in place on the completed form. Only when Yaniv was satisfied that everything was completed properly, did he sign the final form. A copy of the form was then clipped to a copy of the soldier's orders. Once this process was completed, the photo was laminated to the badge and issued. Completed rolls of film were processed at night; when the prints were dried, they were stapled to the forms.

When Major Yaniv was given this assignment, he'd been told his office would issue only a few badges a week. He was always surprised at the end of the week when he totaled the number and usually found it was more than a hundred. As was his custom, when Yaniv went through the pile, he singled out the ones he thought they deserved special attention. For some, policy required sending a copy to the KGB or GRU.

One man's orders caught his attention. They specifically authorized Colonel Panichev and a small team to inspect nuclear artillery shells. For the Central Asian Military District, inspecting nuclear weapons was not unusual. The district was dotted with missile silos and storage sites containing much of the Soviet Union's nuclear arsenal. Along with notifying the KGB, Yaniv made a copy of the orders and the badge form. He clipped one of the spare pictures to the forms before carefully folding and slipping them into the breast pocket of his fatigues.

Friday, August 16th, 1991, 1428 Local Time, Moscow

By two in the morning, a slow moving warm front and its thunderstorms had pushed in from the west. While they banged and lit up the sky, the storms dumped four centimeters of rain on the city. It was going to be a hot, humid day in Moscow.

Panichev's file reached Krasnovsky desk shortly after he got to the office. He was just starting to read when the phone on his desk jangled. As a major general, Krasnovsky had two lines: one official and one private. The light flashing was his private line. Only a few people had the number, although anyone at Krasnovsky's level in the KGB could look it up. He answered the phone. "Krasnovsky."

"This is Lieutenant General Volkov, Second Directorate."

"Good morning, General Volkov. What can I do for you?"

"I am looking at the dossier of an American captain named Joshua Haman. I see that you approved his visa."

"I did. The request was in order and approved by the foreign ministry." Krasnovsky was wary—he knew Volkov was ruthless, and his enemies went to early graves.

"In the dossier," Volkov said, "I came across a report you wrote while working with the Stasi."

"I was a KGB liaison officer to the Stasi and provided information when asked. My job was to keep the KGB fully informed about Red Hand. My analysis is in both my file and Haman's."

"That's part of what prompted my call. On at two occasions, this Captain Haman prevented KGB and Cuban officers from repatriating a senior CIA officer who had been serving the Motherland for almost twenty years. Did you see that?"

Krasnovsky was familiar with the events. The woman in question hadn't wanted to live in either Cuba or the Soviet Union. Twice, Haman stopped KGB teams from kidnapping her. Undoubtedly Volkov was angry because the CIA had ended up debriefing the woman on KGB activities, and it had affected other operations. Krasnovsky held his silence.

"Then there was Vietnam," Volkov said. "Haman captured a Soviet Colonel named Koniev. Koniev then betrayed his country by giving away surface-to-air missile secrets. In light of this pattern of interference, I find it astonishing that you approved his visa."

Volkov, you and I both know that Koniev defected. You also know he had every reason in the world to be unhappy with the Soviet Union: its doctors were incompetent and he lost both his wife and daughter to pneumonia. "General Volkov, Haman's diplomatic visa was approved by the Foreign Ministry. I simply signed it."

Volkov ignored Krasnovsky's statement. "I see notes in Haman's file stating you met him several times. Is this true?"

"Yes, it is. We met at an Embassy event. I wanted to size up the man who, as you so correctly pointed out, has caused trouble in the past." He did not want to pretend he was ignorant of Haman's accomplishments.

"Tell me what you think of this man."

"I think the KGB's assessment is accurate. If we were at war, he would be a very dangerous opponent. As it is, he is here under the banner of peace. We discussed the historical significance of American famine relief efforts around the world, particularly those of the 1920's." That was a subtle jab. It was more than likely that members of Volkov's own family had been saved from starvation by President Hoover's foreign policy. "Unlike most Americans, he knows history."

"What do you think about sending him home in a box?" Volkov demanded abruptly.

"I don't make those decisions, sir," Krasnovsky said. "Haman has diplomatic immunity. Killing him would cause an international incident."

"The Americans would certainly protest. In a few days, they'd forget about it. They are easily distracted. And they are cowards, afraid to make a public stink."

"General, their protest might be stronger than you think."

"Are you aware that someone tried to kill Captain Haman a few days ago?"

"No, I hadn't heard that," Krasnovsky lied.

"You may be interested to know the Americans have said *nothing*, officially, about the attempted assassination. That doesn't sound like a strong protest, does it?"

"They may be waiting until the *militsiya* gives them their final report."

Volkov could hear the discomfort in Krasnovsky's voice. He liked making people uncomfortable. Many times in his career, Volkov had had the power of life and death over targets and his own men. He enjoyed it; particularly knowing he could pick and chose who lived and who died. Making a fellow KGB general squirm was a bonus. "General Krasnovsky, accidents happen. That's something you may want to remember." Then there was a click.

Krasnovsky's hand was shaking when he hung up the phone.

Friday, August 16ᵗʰ, 1991, 2149 Local Time, Moscow

The trip from the U.S. embassy in the Arbat District of Moscow to the Choral Synagogue a few blocks east of Red Square would normally take about twenty-five minutes. The two Marines dropped Josh off a little before seven, then returned to the embassy for dinner. To be on the safe side, Velasquez and Brown had left the embassy at 2100 to pick up Josh at 2130, knowing he often would stand on the steps and chat with his newfound friends before he was ready to go back to the Rossiya.

Normally, it was a straight shot down Mokhovaya Street, but an accident was holding up traffic. Exasperated by the delay, Brown made a U-turn and went back to Zanamenka Street to go past the Kremlin. Navigating the black Suburban, with all its armor and run-flat tires, was easier on the wider streets than the labyrinth of smaller ones that made up much of Moscow's street map. Brown had been a driver since arriving in Moscow, and knew the streets of central Moscow well. To make up time, he stayed on the road by the Moscow River until he made a left turn on Yauzsky Boulevard and another on Solyanka to bring him to the front door of the synagogue.

Brown was just about to shift his right foot from the gas pedal to the brakes when he saw the distinctive muzzle brake and flash compensator of an AK-47 poke out of the rear window of a four-door GAZ Volga sedan just ahead. The staccato bark of the rifle was barely audible through the one-inch thick bulletproof windows, but repeated flashes meant the gun was firing on automatic. "Hang on!" Brown yelled, and he slammed the accelerator to the floor, aiming the Suburban at the GAZ. As the Suburban bore down on its target, both Velasquez and Brown saw a man come out of the front passenger door, lean on the hood and spray the steps of the Choral Synagogue with bullets.

The Suburban weighed almost nine thousand pounds. When it slammed into the rear bumper of the three thousand pound GAZ, the lighter car folded like an accordion. Before the two vehicles ground to a screeching halt, the GAZ's trunk was shoved into the back seat, pinning the driver against the steering wheel.

Velasquez grabbed the .45 from the door holster and jumped out. The man who'd been leaning on the hood was sprawled on the ground; his gun had been knocked from his hands. Velasquez held his .45 at a low ready position. When the shooter began to reach for the AK-47, Velasquez yelled, "*Stoi, stoi!*" He didn't have to add "Or I'll shoot." The .45 leveled at the man's chest said that for him.

The man shook his head to get his blond hair out of his eyes and maybe to clear his head. Velasquez could see colored tattoos on the man's neck and forearms. "*Ne delayte etogo.*" Don't do it.

The Russian sneered and grabbed the AK as he dove for cover. It was a mistake. Velasquez's .45 barked twice. The first round caught the Russian in the lower chest, the second in his abdomen. He screamed in pain and the AK clattered to the pavement.

Velasquez kicked the AK well away from the Russian, keeping the pistol pointed at the man's chest. Blood leaked between the man's fingers as he lay on his back, groaning.

In the background, Velasquez could hear sirens. Time was short. "Who are you? Who sent you?"

"I am *mafiya*. That is all you need to know."

"Who was your target?"

"The American. Haman."

"Who hired you?"

"I don't know."

The man tried to lift his head, but his eyes rolled up and his head dropped back as he died. Velasquez turned to see Josh and Brown yanking on the driver's door of the GAZ Volga. Inside, the driver's forehead was resting on the flattened steering wheel, now just a few inches from his chest. Velasquez put his fingers on the man's neck and shook his head. "Sir, don't waste your time," he said to Josh, "He's gone."

Velasquez saw a bloody mess through the back window of the car. Satisfied there was no immediate threat, Velasquez turned to Josh. "Sir, are you O.K.?"

"I'm fine. We got everyone behind the columns and then into the synagogue. No one got hurt. Arkady is here someplace, so I am not sure who the target was."

"Sir, you were. Look at their tattoos. They were *mafiya* and someone put a contract out on you."

Clearly, Josh thought, *we must be stepping on someone's toes. Is it the KGB looking for payback for Bagdonovich's death? Or, the generals selling nuclear arms? General Grant and the ambassador are going to be so pissed—and not, unfortunately and unfairly, with the Soviets.*

He was sure they would want him to stay on the embassy grounds, but he couldn't do that and do what he came to Moscow to do. *So what do I tell Grant?*

Josh sighed. Briefly, he talked to Arkady and agreed to give his statement the next day at the embassy. Josh got into the Suburban. Brown had looked over the vehicle and declared it fit to drive. The only damage was that the grill, the bumper cover and left headlight needed replacing. The motor pool could deal with that when they got back to the embassy.

Saturday, August 17th, 1991, 1526 Local Time, Moscow

When the Ambassador and General Grant knocked on his office door, Josh stood up and welcomed them. There weren't enough chairs for all three of them.

"What happened last night?" Grant demanded.

Josh said, "You'll be pleased that no one was hurt, thanks to the actions of Velasquez and Brown—"

The ambassador interrupted. " Do you know who wanted to kill you?"

"No." *The less said the better. Arkady is convinced someone in the KGB is tasking them, but doesn't know who.*

General Grant said, "We think you need to lay low and avoid going out in public. Until the police find who put out the contract, we—the Ambassador and I—think you should stay here in the embassy."

"Is that an order?" Josh asked.

Grant made a face. "If I made it one, I suspect you would ignore it."

For once, Grant and I agree. After a moment, the ambassador surprised him with what sounded like genuine concern. "Please be careful. I don't want to have you killed on my watch."

The Same Day, 1937 Local Time, Moscow

The line to get into Vadim's was at least fifty people long. Many were unhappy that some guests were allowed to go straight in without waiting. Sons and daughters of high-ranking party members yelled threats describing what would happen if they weren't let in immediately.

The burly bouncer ignored all protests. His employer's connections with the KGB and *militsiya* would prevent party hacks from shutting Vadim's down. If a complainer persisted, one of two things might happen. He or she could get an informal visit from a messenger who'd negotiate some sort of payout to soothe hard feelings. If the *mafiya* felt truly threatened, the unpleasant second option resulted in a long hospital stay, or a trip to the morgue.

Krasnovsky arrived at 1937. He was early: he'd received a message around three in the afternoon saying that a table at Vadim's was reserved for him at eight o'clock. It could mean only one thing—Josh Haman wanted to meet. With such a head start, Krasnovsky was already a glass and a half into a bottle of Stolyichnaya when Valentina ushered Josh to the table. By that time, the bar was packed. On the dance floor, the dancers barely had room to turn around without stepping on someone's toes.

As Josh sat down, Krasnovsky poured him a glass of the vodka. Both knew that nothing of interest would be discussed until Josh had finished that glass. It took three swallows, but Josh got it down and instantly regretted drinking so quickly. "So, General," he said, "who wants me dead?

Krasnovsky gave Josh a quizzical look. Josh recounted the Friday night attack telling him that the *militsiya* identified the shooters as *mafiya*. So who in the KGB has contacts in the *mafiya* high enough to put a contract out on an American who isn't a threat to the *mafiya* at all?"

Krasnovsky shook his head. "It could be anyone. Let me quietly dig around."

In truth, Krasnovsky suspected it was someone in the Second Directorate. Volkov or perhaps Talyzin have the power. Conceivably, it could have been someone from the First Directorate—tasked with espionage overseas—or the Third Directorate—responsible for military counterintelligence—or even the Seventh Directorate which tracked foreigners on Russian soil.

"Thanks." Josh broke off a chunk from the crusty dark pumpernickel bread and popped it in his mouth before he took a sip from a new glass of vodka. Neither settled his stomach. The *mafiya* was an unseen, dangerous enemy whose motives were unknown. If they were working for the KGB to help move the weapons to Iran, his job had got a lot harder and more dangerous.

"Have you arrested the people selling the warheads?" he asked.

"*Nyet.*" Krasnovsky's tone was emphatic. "Arresting them would raise too many question about how and why I knew. I would wind up being the subject of an investigation and it would not end well."

"As of yesterday, Panichev is in Tashkent." Josh slid a piece of paper across the table. It was the badge application form Panichev had filled out in Tashkent, along with a copy of Panichev's orders.

Krasnovsky snatched up the piece of paper and studied it for at least a minute. "Shit."

"So, general, what are you going to do?"

"Have another chat with the bastard who issued the movement orders." Krasnovsky put the sheet of paper down on the table. "What about you?"

"I can recapture the weapons, but I need your help." Josh spent two minutes outlining what he wanted. Krasnovsky made a face, finished his vodka, and refilled the glass. "O.K., even if there's a coup, I'll make sure the KGB or the *militsiya* does its part and arrests the thieves. None of us want bombs in the hands of madmen. You gather them up, call me, and I'll take care of the rest."

Sunday, August 18th, 1991, 0846 Local Time, Tashkent
Yuri Panichev strode up to the guard's desk at the military district headquarters. He flashed his badge. The guard, good soldier that he was, came to attention and saluted. "Colonel Panichev, sir, I have a message for you."

"Excellent. May I see it?"

"Yes, Colonel." The private went to the safe and withdrew a sealed envelope. He handed it to Panichev.

"Thank you, Private." He smiled and walked out. Alone, he opened the envelope and extracted the hand-written sheet. His smile faded as he read the words.

1602 17 August 1991

Colonel Panichev,
There will be a short delay in giving you access to the weapons you are assigned to inspect. In two days, I will provide information on their exact location.

Major General Vavilov

Angrily, he crumpled the paper.

Chapter 19
Not For The People Nor By The People

Monday, August 19th, 1991, 0446 Local Time, Moscow

The rumbling and clanking beneath Josh's window sounded like a bulldozer in the street. Curious, he slid the curtains back a few inches. For a moment, the sun, already high in the sky, blinded him. Eight tanks that he recognized as T-72s were parked with their 125mm main guns leveled at the other side of Red Square.

The first move of the coup? Josh yanked the curtains wide open to give him a full view of the square. Four eight-wheeled BTR-80 armored cars flanked each street entrance. Soldiers had set up barriers to stop and inspect all vehicles. In the middle of the square, eight more T-72s were backed into a circle with their guns facing outward. Inside the circle, four trucks bristling with antennas were parked back to back in two rows. A canvas tent covered the area between the trucks.

In front of the main entrance of the Kremlin, more BTRs and T-72s were arranged as a barricade. Soldiers were inspecting every vehicle and individual wanting to enter. Josh grabbed the small pad by the phone and quickly drew up the deployment, noting the numbers and positions of the tanks and armored cars.

Josh pulled a pair of jeans from the closet, put on a golf shirt and his running shoes. He quickly folded a complete uniform and packed all the garments into a gray duffel bag.

Next, he grabbed the small satellite phone he'd been given: the one with an encryption option. It could call anywhere in the world. He pushed the first number on the speed dial. It took almost three seconds for the signal to go from his room in the Rossiya to the satellite in a geostationary orbit twenty-three thousand miles above the earth. The satellite relayed his call to another satellite before sending it to a ground station in the United States. A computerized switch recognized that Josh was calling a phone number issued to Gunnery Sergeant Jesus Velasquez assigned to the embassy in Moscow. In accordance with its programming, the switch validated both sending and receiving numbers, then accepted the call. It then resent the signal to a satellite over the east coast of the U.S., where it was forwarded back to the communication satellite that covered Moscow. Six seconds after Josh sent the coded message, it arrived at Velasquez's phone sitting on the dresser next to his bed.

He was wide-awake and answered the phone. "Velasquez."

"Captain Haman here. I think the coup has started. There are Soviet troops all over Red Square. There will probably be roadblocks between the embassy and the hotel. Both you and Brown had better wear civilian clothes. We can all change into uniform when we get to the embassy. How soon can you get here?"

"Less than twenty minutes, unless we get held up by a roadblock."

"Good. We're going to do a little recon on foot."

"Aye, aye, sir."

Josh had a quick breakfast and looked at his watch before he stepped outside. It was 0548, and Velasquez was bounding up the hotel steps two at a time. His muscular chest and arms were barely hidden by his golf shirt.

Two convoys, each with eight BMP-3 armored personnel carriers, clanked into the square from different directions. They parked in a separate group with their armored fronts facing outward as seven-man squads exited from the back hatches. Unlike the T-72s which had their main guns leveled, the BMPs thirty-millimeter cannons were pointed toward the sky. The squads quickly formed up in front of their officers, and then took positions around the BMPs with their AK-47s slung over their chests.

Josh walked to a BTR parked where Ilyinka Street headed away from the square. A soldier sat on the flat section of the hull in front of the driver's compartment. The barrel of the vehicle's 14.5mm machine-gun was fully depressed and pointed off to the side.

"Where are you from?" Josh asked the soldier in Russian.

"Sverdlovsk. You English or American?"

"American. How did you know?"

"By your clothes. No one in Russia can afford clothes like those unless they are *nomenklatura*." The private spat out *nomenklatura* as if it was a dirty word. His relaxed posture showed he was comfortable talking to Westerners.

"What unit are you with?" Josh asked.

"2nd Guards Tamanskaya Motor Rifle Division. We're based just outside the city."

"When were you drafted?" Josh guessed he didn't have much time with this young man, but it was too good an opportunity to pass up.

"Two years ago. Next month, I get out." Looking around to make sure no one was within hearing distance, the soldier leaned toward Josh and lowered his voice. "I was a fool to report when drafted—many of my friends ignored the order. I didn't have a job, and the Army was better than starving. Where do you live in America?"

"San Diego, California. Are you getting enough to eat?"

"We get two meals a day: more than my mother and father get. In their last letter, they were eating only once a day. It is not enough." The soldier stopped talking when he saw his platoon commander running toward him.

As Josh hurried away, the officer screamed at the young man for talking to a foreigner. Before the officer could catch them, Josh and Velasquez disappeared into the growing crowd. They walked to another roadblock, but at this one the soldiers refused to talk.

As Josh passed one of the tanks in front of the hotel, he spotted a tank commander leaning out of his turret. "Why are you here?" Josh asked.

"It is an exercise."

"Have you been issued ammunition?"

"A full load for the machine-gun. Only half for the cannon."

"Do you know why?"

"Our orders are to prevent an attack on the Kremlin by a mob trying to take control of the government. That's bullshit. I'll leave my tank before I fire on fellow Russians."

The Same Day, 0826 Local Time, Moscow

The documents General Grant wanted from D.C. arrived in the diplomatic pouch. After the envelope was logged in, it was delivered to his office where he made three copies: one for himself, one for the FBI officer on the embassy staff, and one for the personnel files on each of the attachés.

He called the senior FBI Special Agent to his office and gave him the papers authorizing the arrest and detention of Captain Joshua Haman, United States Navy. Grant asked him to go to the Rossiya and arrest the naval officer. If they found Velasquez, he was to be arrested as well.

After the FBI officer left, Grant called the embassy's security officer and told him that when Velasquez or Haman showed up, they were to be detained until formally arrested. If Brown showed up, he was to be brought to Grant's office for questioning. Grant figured he could intimidate the young Marine into divulging useful information.

The potential coup happening outside didn't interest Grant. He was about to ruin Haman's career, and that would make his day.

The Same Day, 1141 Local Time, New York State

The convoy moving Safdar to a facility closer to New York City consisted of three polished vehicles. A first generation black Ford Taurus was followed by a black Chevrolet Suburban. The third car, several hundred yards behind, was another Taurus. At 0530, the convoy pulled out of the Federal Prison near Saranac Lake, New York, built on what used to be the Olympic Village for the 1980 Winter Olympics.

For security purposes, the convoy commander decided to take a detour to make it harder for them to be ambushed. Peekamoose Road, also known as State Route 42, wound and twisted roughly northeast, then southeast. The convoy headed toward the intersection with Route 55 where the commander would decide whether the vehicles would take State Route 55 or 42 to State Highway 17 and then down to New York City. Once they got into traffic, the red lights and sirens would come on.

The trip was necessary because Hastings-Mills wanted to meet with his client the day before Safdar appeared in Federal Court. Hastings-Mills intended make two motions. The first was a request for the government to reconsider bail, even though he was certain it would be turned down. The second was a request to move Safdar to a more convenient prison in Otisville, New York, or to the Sing Sing State Prison just south of Ossing. Ossing was on the east side of the Hudson River; getting there would be an easy drive along the Taconic State Parkway. Hastings-Mills was looking forward to driving to Ossing or Otisville in his recently restored 1966 Series 1 Jaguar E-Type painted a metallic British Racing Green.

Two days after the announcement that Safdar had been captured, an unknown individual called Hastings-Mills to say that an envelope containing two hundred and fifty thousand in cash would be left at the firm's front desk to cover Safdar's legal expenses. The caller, who had an accent Hastings-Mills couldn't place, said more money was available if the lawyer could talk the judge into setting bail. The envelope had a note with a phone number to call if the law firm needed more cash. Without going into details, Hastings-Mills informed his partners this was no longer a pro bono case.

At the last second, the driver of the first Taurus saw the small spikes scattered across the road. He wrenched the wheel left to miss them, but didn't. The tires blew out. As the car slewed to a stop, six canisters of a white sweet-smelling gas enveloped the vehicle.

Seeing what happened to the car in front, the driver of the following Suburban slammed on the brakes and turned the wheel to stay out of the white smoke. The armor-plated version of the sport utility vehicle weighed close to nine thousand pounds and hard braking caused its nose to pitch down, unloading the rear wheels. The rear brakes locked and a cloud of tire smoke rose around the Suburban as it slewed drunkenly to a stop. More white smoke enveloped the car and the driver became unconscious before he could finish the 180-degree turn.

The driver of the third car, seeing the first two in trouble, also tried to execute an emergency turn. He was too late. The smoke obscured several rows of spikes that ripped open its tires. By the time the Taurus came to a stop, grenades landed on each side. It too was engulfed in a cloud of white gas.

A dozen men dressed in black came out of the woods wearing masks and carrying strange looking pistols. They tested the doors of the Suburban. One door was unlocked because the FBI agent sitting in the passenger seat had started to open the door before he fell unconscious. For the other cars, the men fired darts with a powerful narcotic to knock out the occupants.

The open door on the Suburban made things easy. Safdar, like everyone else in the car, was unconscious. Bolt cutters were used to cut the chains that held him in the car. He was lifted out and carried to a waiting hearse with the coffin slid almost all the way out of the vehicle. Before the lid was closed, one of the masked men emptied a syringe into Safdar's arm.

Satisfied, the man closed the coffin's lid. With the help of two others, he slid the coffin back into the hearse. The man with the syringe handed his mask to one of the others before he climbed into the passenger seat of the long black Cadillac funeral car. The other men clambered into a fifteen-passenger Chevrolet van. It and the hearse headed south toward Westchester County Airport.

It took thirty minutes to reach the general aviation ramp. The hearse stopped next to the passenger door of a Gulfstream III with its auxiliary power unit running. A uniformed member of the U.S. Customs and Immigration walked to the hearse. The hearse's driver asked if the inspector wanted to look inside the coffin. He shook his head no.

Inside the plane, two of the fore and aft facing seats had been removed so the coffin could be strapped down. The driver of the hearse and other men in black suits from the Gulfstream carried the coffin into the cabin. Satisfied, the customs agent stamped everyone's passports and headed back to the general aviation terminal.

The Same Day, 1737 Local Time, Washington, D.C.

It had been a long afternoon. District Attorney Frank Young's folder containing his notes on Safdar's activities had grown to almost four inches thick. Some of the heft was due to the black and white pictures. The balance came from documents, surveillance reports, and pads full of notes.

Three hours ago, he'd gotten a call from Hastings-Mills asking where Safdar was. District Attorney Young called Goode, who said Safdar was on his way to the courthouse for his hearing.

Meanwhile, a captain from the New York State Police had come upon the two Tauruses and the Suburban. He was responding to a call from a motorist; the spikes in the road had blown out the motorist's tire, so the man had put on the spare and driven back to a gas station to make the call.

A New York State Police helicopter was first on the scene. It circled until road was closed in both directions. Canisters of knockout gas and spikes littered the highway. By the time FBI agents arrived via helicopter to take control of the crime scene, helicopters from all the major news networks were circling overhead.

Back in the city, District Attorney Frank Young stepped in front of the podium in the press briefing room. "Earlier this morning, a group of people conducted a precision military-style operation to abduct Mohammed Safdar from FBI custody. They used spikes to stop the cars and knockout gas to put the escorts to sleep. No Americans were injured. Mr. Safdar is the only person missing. There is no indication that guns were used or if Mr. Safdar was shot. I refuse to speculate on who conducted this operation. No terrorist group has claimed responsibility and as many of you know, Mr. Safdar is wanted in several countries."

Young stopped and shouted questions followed. The D.A. hadn't finished with his statement, but he decided it would be better to answer a few questions first.

"What kind of gas was used?"

"It's called ZF. It contains a quick-acting narcotic. Anyone who breathes the gas goes to sleep in seconds. I'm told that only side effect is a headache when one wakes up. ZF is not available on the commercial market so we're checking into possible thefts of the gas. The attackers used twenty-four canisters."

"How did they stop the vehicles?"

Young described the spikes on the road. "We're interviewing the agents now and will have more information later."

"Do you have any idea of who might have carried out the kidnapping?"

"As I said, I'm not going to speculate. Thank you all for coming."

Tuesday, August 20th, 1991, 0716 Local Time, Moscow

Avram had just walked into his office when the phone rang. He picked it up, expecting Josh Haman. Instead, Lev Mogen told him that the man Avram had identified back in 1987 was now in Israeli hands.

Gutman nodded slightly. In 1986, Safdar had designed a bomb that killed Gutman's wife and two young children. If the Israelis had him in custody, justice would be served

The Same Day, 0730 Local Time, Haifa, Israel

Mohammed Safdar sat alone in a cell. He was awake and manacled. In front of him was a bowl of fruit and yogurt, along with a spoon. Both were untouched.

A balding man stood patiently while the heavy metal door was opened. The man used a cane as he entered—a leg wound during a commando operation in the 1956 Arab-Israel War had left him with a limp. As he got older, the effect of the wound got worse.

"Good morning," Lev Mogen told Safdar. "Welcome back to Israel. I hope you had a restful trip." Mogen spoke in Arabic. He tilted his head with his ironic attempt at humor.

"Where am I?" Safdar demanded. Whatever drug they'd used to knock him out had left him with a pounding headache.

"You're in a prison cell outside Haifa. It is used to hold war criminals." Mogen pursed his lips. "Adolph Eichmann spent a lot of time in that very chair."

"How did you get me here?"

"We drugged you, put you in a coffin, and flew you to Tel Aviv. It was a nice coffin with a foam mattress and holes to let oxygen in. Much nicer than the one you will have."

"Are you going to put me on trial?"

"No."

"The Americans will be angry when they figure out you kidnapped me."

"Who'll tell them? We see this as solving a problem for them and saving them millions of dollars. In America, you'd be found guilty after a very expensive, drawn out trial and spend the rest of your life in jail. Here, the end is different. '

The Same Day, 1332 Local Time, Samarkand, Uzbekistan

The air-conditioned air inside the Air Force C-141 dissipated as soon as the passenger door was opened. It was replaced by dry hot air blowing in off the arid land west of Uzbekistan's second largest city.

The aircraft commander, who had flown many missions carrying food into the Soviet Union, told his three passengers that a KGB officer would board the aircraft, check the identities of the crew against a list, and sign the manifest before they could begin unloading the pallets of food. The manifest was had been set on a cardboard box containing food and left just inside the passenger door. It was one of a dozen on board that would be given to the men who refueled the plane. In the Soviet Union, a box of food ensured better service than a pile of rubles.

Only when the C-141 was empty would the ground crew be allowed to refuel the plane for the four-hour flight back to Sheremetyevo airport. The KGB officer would again inspect the interior of the airplane just before the flight crew closed the doors.

The pallets of food went to a small hangar where a team of civilians from the European Union watched as they were loaded on Soviet Army trucks for the trip to local food stores. From there, the food was supposedly made available to Soviet citizens.

A dour-faced KGB lieutenant colonel quickly compared the passports of the six-man Air Force crew to the list. He stopped when he got to the passports of the three passengers in civilian clothes. He studied each of the diplomatic passports and the Soviet documents allowing them to stay in Samarkand. Each passport had two thousand-ruble notes folded inside.

"Why are you here in Samarkand?" the KGB man who did not wear a nametag asked Josh.

"We have business with the government of Uzbekistan."

"All three?"

"Yes."

"What kind of business?"

"Food distribution."

If he'd inspected their luggage, the KGB officer would have found their desert-colored utilities. If he'd asked them to open the three boxes they'd brought with them, it would have given him apoplexy.

"How long you stay?" he asked.

"Three to five days."

The man grunted. He reeked of cigarette smoke and his pockmarked face gave him a sinister look. He reached into his pocket and pulled out a stamp and inkpad. Using his knee as a table, he stamped each passport, and then scribbled his initials and the date.

"Welcome to Uzbekistan." He picked up his box of food and drove off in the small truck that he had parked in front of the C-141.

After the KGB officer left, a Soviet made Zil-130 truck pulled up in front of the three Americans. It had been frequently repaired, then painted in different uncoordinated shades of gray. Avram Gutman got out of the truck and walked up to the three Americans standing on the ramp, "Welcome to Samarkand."

Wednesday, August 21st, 1991, 0916 Local Time, Maydayap, Uzbekistan

Masud Khayayev came on duty at 0730 this morning at the 117th Strategic Weapons Depot of the Soviet Rocket Artillery Forces. He was told to expect a convoy sometime in the morning by the camp's commander, Captain Kupka. He was the second person who told him to expect one today. The first was the mysterious man by the name of Faheem who contacted Masud. He asked Masud to make sure the trucks got in and out without a problem. If he did, Masud's children, Ahmed and Hassan, would receive the best medical help whenever they needed it.

In the past, when Masud's children were sick, he and the other Muslim guards could count on Faheem to find doctors who brought medicine and treatments not available even at the Army hospital in Samarkand. At first, Masud wondered why he was never told the doctor's last names. Faheem would only say they were trained in the best medical schools in the world. To Masud, that meant they weren't trained in Russia.

They Khayayev's lived in a small hut about half a kilometer from the base along with the other families of the enlisted men. At first, he was proud of the little with the corrugated steel roof in which his family lived. Food was always a problem. It wasn't about money; there just wasn't much food to buy, and what was available was very expensive. Even the Army was down to two meals a day. With the fifty thousand rubles Faheem paid for each load, Masud's wife could buy food and clothing for years to come. Each time she went to town, Masud cautioned her to be careful with the money. If she spent it too easily, people would start asking questions. When Masud's enlistment was up in two months, he wanted to go to either Samarkand or Tashkent to find work and eventually bring his family. If that didn't work out, they still had enough money buried under the floor of their hut to live comfortably for years.

The whines of transmissions and the clash of gears warned Masud Khayayev that trucks were coming up the winding road that led to the depot. The guarded facility was in south central Uzbekistan, tucked into a saddle between two small hills, one hundred kilometers west-southwest of Samarkand. The first vehicle to appear was a little GAZ-69, then a BTR-80 armored car followed by three GAZ-66 trucks and another BTR. The GAZ-69 light truck was dwarfed by the 2.5-meter height of the BTR-80s.

Despite the early morning summer sun, Masud felt cold. As the trucks approached, he slung his AK-47 over his shoulder and stepped out of his red painted sentry hut. He stood next to the striped pole that blocked the road. When the driver of the GAZ-69 handed him his papers, the driver whispered, "God is great."

Masud responded with, "God is in paradise." He made a show of examining the truck driver's documents in case the pig of a Russian who commanded the garrison was watching.

The driver said, "Faheem is grateful for your help."

Masud grunted in reply, not wanting to appear to engage in a friendly conversation. Another guard who was an infidel walked around the trucks and armored cars to inspect them. Their markings were correct. The papers had all the right stamps and signatures to allow the convoy to enter. That was all that mattered to Masud.

Doubt and the fear of being blamed made Masud hold up a hand. "I'll be right back. Everything appears to be in order but I still need the guard commander's approval to let you enter." He didn't want to put his neck in the hangman's noose if something bad happened.

Inside the administration building, Masud knocked loudly on the frame of the office door. "Captain Kupka, sir, the convoy is here. They've come to pick up artillery shells for the garrison near Bukhara and to take some old weapons to a destruction facility. Their papers appear to be in order. Shall I let them in, sir?"

Masud's Russian was better than the average soldier from Uzbekistan because he'd assumed he might need to use the language someday. It was one of the reasons Masud had been promoted to sergeant. He dreamed of a day when knowledge of Russian wouldn't be needed.

The captain glared at him. "I'll decide whether they enter. Understand, Sergeant Khayayev?"

"Yes, sir." Masud let himself appear humble, happy that the infidel Kupka would shoulder any blame.

"Have you inspected each soldier's papers?" Kupka asked.

"Yes, sir. The driver of the lead truck gave me all their identity books. I then walked to each vehicle and compared the pictures in the identity books to those of the drivers and the work party."

Masud guessed Kupka wouldn't take the time to go out and inspect each man and his papers personally. The captain was much too interested in playing ten chess games at once by mail and telephone. Ten boards were arranged on the big table in his office.

Masud often wondered how the Russian Army picked officers for this kind of duty. Were they screw-ups, not good for service anywhere else, or was it random? Kupka wasn't a bad man for an infidel. He was just bored with being here and no different than the other Russian officers in the unit.

"Bring the officer-in-charge of the convoy in here. On the double."

"Yes, sir. At once." Masud was breaking out in a sweat as he walked back out. *Faheem will not be happy if there is a problem.*

The leader of the convoy, a lieutenant whose papers identified him as Moshen Zangeneh, reluctantly followed him to the office. Masud assured him that meeting the captain on duty was routine.

Zangeneh timidly tapped on the frame of the cramped office. "Captain Zangeneh reporting as ordered, sir."

"Papers." Kupka didn't even look up from the array of chess sets he was studying. Only after Zangeneh's papers sat on the table for a few moments did Kupka shift his attention from the chessboards to the disheveled Zangeneh.

"You look like a bandit, Captain. Your uniform is a disgrace. What unit are you with?

"Supply Regiment, 51st Guards Armored Division. We've been on the road for almost two days. We stopped last night about sixty kilometers from here to get some sleep. We're short of everything, sir."

Kupka picked up the pile of documents and flipped through the pages before stopping to examine one. He looked up at Zangeneh, then flipped through the rest angrily. He hadn't joined the army to guard an ammo dump in some godforsaken place! He'd become an officer after the Russian Army left Afghanistan. He'd wanted action and volunteered to go to Chechnya. Instead, he'd been sent Maydayap. He was convinced he could lead men in battle, if given the chance. Chess was the only thing that kept his mind alive in this dump out in the middle of nowhere.

Kupka stood as he handed Zangeneh his papers and checked a chart on the wall. "Khayayev, show them to bunker six. See that Captain Zangeneh and his men get all the help they need."

Zangeneh replied, "I brought a detail to do the loading. Your men can go about their duties."

"Suit yourself."

Masud thought it strange that the two armored cars also entered the compound with the trucks. Normally, troops escorting ammunition shipments were more interested in taking a nap or finding something to eat and letting Masud and his comrades load the trucks.

* * *

Ali Akrami rode with Zangeneh in the GAZ-69 light truck. Instead of being Colonel Panichev, Akrami was dressed as a warrant officer. His cover as Panichev would be blown after this mission, but it would have served its ultimate purpose. Posing as a warrant officer created some distance from his cover as Panichev. Akrami was confident his papers as a warrant officer would pass cursory examination, but they'd quickly fall apart if he were interrogated. His back-up plan was that as a warrant officer, he was less conspicuous than as a colonel and could say he was observing the depot's security and storage procedures. The key, he kept reminding himself, was not to be captured.

In the bunker, Akrami walked between the rows of crates, stopping to read the markings on each stack. In one corner of the room, eight olive drab boxes caught his attention because they looked like large suitcases. He brushed off the dust covering the label and forced himself not to cry out in excitement as he popped open the latches. For second, he stood there not believing in his good luck and thought, Allah was looking out for him. In front of him was a man-portable 2-3 kiloton RA-115 nuclear weapon. According to the markings, each one weighted thirty kilos. His bosses in Iran would be very pleased because they could be turned over to Hezbollah or other Islamic organizations..

Akrami decided to put four RA-115s on each truck right behind the truck's cabs so there would still be room for two artillery shell crates tied down end to end. His men could sit on the benches that ran the length of the truck beds.

Loading took over an hour and a half because Zangeneh and his crew had to match the serial numbers on the papers with the numbers on the 250-kilogram crates holding the ZBV2 nuclear artillery shells. Keeping each truck under its maximum load was critical: the first fifty kilometers of the journey would be on unimproved dirt roads where too much weight would risk breaking an axle. However, after that, all the roads were paved. As long as there weren't too many potholes and traffic permitted, Akrami planned to travel as close as they could to the truck's maximum speed of eighty kilometers per hour.

From his office, Captain Kupka watched the convoy depart the facility. When they were out of sight, he went back to his desk and dialed a number. "They just left." he said into the phone. There was no reply nor did he expect one so he hung up. His role was over and maybe it would lead to a unit someplace outside of Uzbekistan.

After hanging up the phone, Major Svi Yaniv checked the time, dialed the number to a local hotel, and was put through to a room.

The call was answered. "You're on," Yaniv said. "Departure time 1128."

* * *

Avram Gutman rapped sharply on three room doors in the hotel. Five minutes later, he and the three Americans were back in the canvas-topped Zil-130 truck. Josh had the passenger seat; Velasquez and Brown rode the back. At a small repair shop on the western edge of Samarkand, Avram stopped at the single pump and started refueling. When they pulled out, another dusty light blue truck Zil-130 followed. Its canvas back covered a cargo bed.

On the road, Josh consulted the map several times. Frustrated, he eventually tossed it onto the dash. Road signs were almost nonexistent and landmarks were few and far between. There were distance markers every kilometer, but most were bent or unreadable from the dust.

Josh turned to Avram. "Do you know where we're going?"

"Akrami can pick from three routes from the storage facility. The fastest and best goes straight south to Kasan once they get off the storage area's access road. The BTRs won't have any problem with the dirt road, but the loaded trucks will have to go slow. If they average twenty kilometers an hour on the dirt road, they'll be doing well. Once they get on the main road, between traffic and rough sections of pavement, they'll be lucky to average sixty kilometers an hour. Akrami's second choice goes seventy kilometers west before it heads south. The locals say the road is much worse until it intersects the main road to Turkmenistan, but it's shorter in terms of distance. The third option goes northwest and we don't think Akrami will take it—it adds a whole day to his trip. So we've got teams watching choices one and two."

Josh knew not to ask how they got a Sayarat Maktal team and their equipment into Uzbekistan. One of Sayarat Maktal's specialties was desert reconnaissance; while this wasn't a desert like ones in the Middle East, it was close enough. Josh said, "What if they ditch the BTRs and switch trucks right away?"

"Soviet nuclear weapons leak small amounts of radiation," Avram said. "Not enough to be a danger, but enough to be detected. If Akrami tries some sort of deception, our surveillance teams have Geiger counters—we can identify any vehicle carrying the weapons. He could, of course, have brought lead lined boxes, but those would be large, heavy and difficult to transport, assuming he could even get some."

"How many men do you have in the other truck?"

"Ten. That gives us a total of nineteen. We have four in two-man teams watching the roads. We also have an American SEAL named Richard Carlson. He's an expert on nuclear weapons and knows how to disarm them. I was told the two of you worked together back in 1976. He volunteered for this mission."

Josh nodded. "Carlson is a good man." Marty Cabot probably set that up. "So nineteen men. We were told that Panichev has thirty, plus two armored cars and heavy machine-guns."

"Numbers won't matter if we act smart and catch them by surprise," Avram said. "If there's a battle, it'll be a short one."

"Have your men picked an ambush site?"

"We've scouted two on each route."

Josh was silent for a moment. "You know, smuggling is an art form in this part of the world. Illegal as hell, but many people do it. We need to think like smugglers."

"I agree."

Once he had the weapons, Akrami would want to get to Iran as soon as possible. Nonetheless, It was still possible that the Iranians could do something they didn't anticipate or that Mr. Murphy would show up. What other possibilities were there? Transfer the weapons to fully fueled commercial trucks this side of the Turkmenistan border? That was conceivable, but where could Akrami make it happen? The only thing that Avram and Josh assumed was that Akrami had papers to allow him to go from the Central Asian to the Turkestan Military District either in a military convoy or as commercial vehicles.

What if he had a fuel truck in his convoy? They'd been told there wasn't one, but he might pick one up along the way. Otherwise, he simply had to stop to refuel. His trucks had a range of between 200 and 250 miles, much too short to reach the Iranian border.

He could just buy fuel from a local gas station, but to do that, Akrami would need the necessary forms. The Soviet Army never paid cash; if Akrami did, it would make the station operator suspicious. He might have hidden a cache of diesel fuel somewhere, protected by trustworthy guards but that was an impractical plan. Besides, hiding enough fuel for four or five trucks would be difficult, and his whole operation would be at risk if the fuel were stolen. Final possibility: he could stop at an Army post. Josh rejected that idea; the risk of exposure was too great.

Josh stared out the window. The land was only green where there was water. The rest of the country was flat, featureless, and sandy brown. Water in the irrigation ditches stretched off into the distance and explained the green colors in the fields. Every few kilometers, the cab filled with the putrid smell of human and animal waste.

Josh tried to imagine what it had been like for traders and their caravans of pack animals traversing this barren land without a compass. Journeys from "Cathay" to Europe had taken years. Finding enough food and water to keep man and beast alive along the Silk Road was only one problem. Disease and bad weather took their toll, made worse by roving bandits who preyed on the caravans and demanded payment in return for safe passage. It had to have been a nightmare. Only the sense of adventure combine the lure of huge profits would have made it worthwhile.

Avram broke the silence to ask about the other looming crisis. "What of the coup?"

"The big question," Josh said, "is whether the Red Army will fire on its own people. When I left Moscow, there were tanks and roadblocks all over the place. Gorbachev is in the Crimea. The new State Committee on the State Emergency put out a communiqué saying they rejected the new treaty creating the Russian Federation government. They promised to 'maintain law and order' during the emergency."

Avram downshifted as he braked and followed the other truck off onto a dirt road. Five hundred meters farther, the two trucks stopped side by side. "Communication and bathroom break," Avram explained.

Josh had just finished relieving himself when he heard his satellite phone ring. He pushed the ACCEPT button. "Captain Haman," said a voice, "this is Master Chief Grayson from the embassy. I need to speak to Gunny Velasquez. It's important."

Josh handed the phone to Velasquez, who walked off to get some privacy. He listened for thirty seconds and said, "That's bullshit," loud enough for Josh to hear. Velasquez walked a few more meters and rattled off numbers and names. After Grayson acknowledged that he'd copied everything down, Velasquez ended the call and walked back to the group.

"What's bullshit?" Josh asked.

Velasquez grimaced, wondering how much of the conversation to tell his boss. "Sir, General Grant reported us as AWOL to his DIA boss in D.C. The Master Chief is going to get it straightened out."

Josh started to say what he thought of general Grant's maneuver and then stopped. Being reported AWOL meant a warrant was out for their arrest! Well, he'd deal with that when he got back. The mission had to come first. He simply said, "Understood."

Just after Velasquez gave Josh his phone back, Avram pulled out a similar device. When Josh gave him a puzzled look, Avram smiled, "Americans don't have a monopoly on new technology. But this call is private." He shooed Josh away. "Go introduce yourself to the rest of our tribal members. The Israelis all know about you, the Russians not so much. Take the two goyim with you."

Avram stepped off to the side and dialed a number. He spoke for a minute in Hebrew before ending the call.

The Same Day, 1354 Local Time, Moscow

Volkov walked toward his office past rows of desks arranged in what the west would call cubicles. It was not until he reached the door that he realized how quiet the floor was. Most of the work areas were empty. He wondered where the men assigned to those desks were. The younger generation of KGB officers were not as dedicated as Volkov had been at that age. The young were soft... but eventually, experience would harden them.

Volkov put all that out of his mind as he slumped into his chair. Day two of the coup: some actions had gone as planned, but most hadn't. Gorbachev was under house arrest and his dacha was cut off from communication. Yet somehow he had managed to tell the media he rejected the committee's authority.

Some traitor had allowed Gorbachev to talk. The guilty ones must be found and eliminated.

The newly created State Committee on the State of Emergency had shut down all the newspapers and radio stations except those controlled by the party. From what Volkov saw and read in the reports, it wasn't having the desired effect. The show of force hadn't intimidated Moscow's residents.

426

Barricades manned by unarmed citizens were preventing anyone from entering the nation's parliament building. Other citizens openly ignored the committee's curfew and were out demonstrating in the streets.

The commander of the Moscow military district had been ordered to convince the protesters to peacefully disperse. If they didn't, the general was authorized to use the KGB's Alpha Force commandos to force them out. If that happened, Volkov worried that Alpha Group would leave a pile of corpses that would be perceived as an untidy mess. Volkov saw it as reducing the number of opponents to the coup. Despite the unit commander's reassurances that his men would minimize the shooting, once bullets started flying, the amount of blood was unpredictable and that is what worried Volkov.

Volkov decided that finding Boris Yeltsin was the most important task. Yeltsin was supposed to have been arrested as soon as his plane from Kazakhstan landed; somehow, though, he'd slipped through the net. Volkov thought wryly, *whoever searched for Yeltsin didn't check the right bars.*

He didn't know that one of the unread folders on his desk contained a report about Haman, Velasquez and Brown. It gave their arrival time in Samarkand and the hotel where they stayed. It also stated that Haman had left hurriedly in a truck with three other men. A note in the folder asked for instructions.

On the other corner of Volkov's desk was an order he'd signed personally: to detain, interrogate harshly, and hold Captain Joshua Haman of the United States Navy until he could be deported.

The Same Day, 1529 Local Time,
On the Road Between Quarshi and Bukhara, Uzbekistan
The two trucks were parked in a small grove of trees whose shade lowered the temperature by ten degrees. Josh noticed the

welcome coolness as he went from bright sun to into the trees' shadows. His sweat evaporated quickly in the dry humid air.

In the Soviet Union, road maps were classified documents. Soviet cartographers were encouraged to draw cities many kilometers away from their actual location. Being caught with a map based on U.S. satellite imagery would land them all in a KGB interrogation center, so Josh was careful to open it only when those he could trust were around.

Frustrated, Josh wonderd for the umpteenth time if they had missed the Iranians. When he heard the ring of Avram's satellite phone, he hurried toward the sound. He saw Avram twirling his hand over his head in the universal signal to mount up. By the time Avram was ready, Josh was sitting in the driver's seat of the lead truck, revving its engine.

"I'll drive," Josh said, "you play commander."

Avram smiled, "Ever driven a Zil before?"

"Nope, but I watched you. It has five gears, a clutch, a brake and a gas pedal. I think I can manage. What's the news?" The truck didn't buck too badly as Josh coordinated the clutch and gas pedal to get it moving.

"Our targets are taking a break on the main road about twenty kilometers from here. No tanker. We have a surveillance team half a kilometer in front of them. The other will join us when we stop. We'll figure out then how make our move."

The Same Day, 1606 Local Time, On the Road to Bukhara

Rather than stand looking over the shoulder of the mechanic from the contingent of Quds soldiers, Ali Akrami stood on the shady side of the GAZ and waited for his report. He looked at his watch and noted they were two hours behind schedule. They could make it up either by driving longer tonight or by leaving earlier tomorrow. Before he could make a decision, however, he needed to know what was wrong with the truck.

"Colonel Akrami."

He turned around to see Zangeneh approaching, accompanied by a man wiping oil off his hands.

Zangeneh said, "The transmission on the third truck is failing. I can get it into first or second gear, but not third or fourth. If we keep driving, the transmission will fail. It needs to be replaced."

Akrami picked up the map and pointed to a place where they could pull well off the road. "Can we make ten kilometers?"

"Probably. The driver will be limited to second gear and a speed of ten kilometers an hour."

Akrami nodded. "Get everybody back on board right now. We'll stop where I showed you and spend the night. We'll transfer the crates to the other two trucks in the morning and leave the truck behind."

On the road, Akrami picked up his satellite phone and dialed a number. He said, "A truck broke and we're running late. We should still be able to rendezvous tomorrow. Will call you when we know when."

"We'll be ready." Dial tone.

Both men knew that satellite phone calls from this part of the world would be noted by almost all the intelligence agencies. The longer they were on the phone, the greater the chance that the KGB or GRU would record the call and maybe take an interest.

The Same Day, 1742 Local Time, Moscow

The hot summer afternoon was made more stifling by the lack of wind. The exhaust plumes from the idling diesel engines of the armored vehicles created a light blue cloud in the open area in front of the two wings of the parliament building.

Lieutenant Colonel Lev Zubinsky, the commander of the motorized infantry battalion, placed a platoon of tanks and two platoons of infantry at each of the intersections and set up his command center just in front of the gate. He ordered his men not to drive their vehicles onto any of the grassy areas around the building or to knock down any trees. Once this was all over, he wanted Moscow to look as though absolutely nothing had happened, no reminders. He was sitting in the back of his command truck when the radioman handed him the handset. "It's Major General Konarev, sir."

Konarev was the Tamanskaya division commander. Zubinsky put on the headset. "Zubinsky here, sir."

"Colonel, your battalion is ordered to support the storming of the parliament building. Alpha Group teams are moving into place. Have a BMP crash through the barricades in front of the main door at the time they specify. You will provide Alpha Group with whatever fire support they require. Do I make myself clear?"

Zubinsky scowled. "Sir, we've been watching the building all day. The citizens in the building are not armed and they've done nothing wrong other than occupy the building. They aren't ransacking it or damaging it in any way. They may be protesting, but they aren't violent."

"Colonel Zubinsky, you have your orders."

"Sir, we'd be killing innocent Russians. Who are the crazy people who issued these orders? It could turn the public against the Red Army."

"The State Committee on the State of Emergency has given us our orders. We are soldiers. It's our duty to obey them."

"Are you sending me written copies of these orders?" Zubinsky asked.

"Colonel, are you are refusing to carry out your orders?"

"No, sir," Zubinsky said. "I just want them in writing, so I can present them at my court martial when I'm accused of killing innocent Russian citizens."

"I'll send you what you need," Konarev said. "Just accept that this is necessary for the good of the Motherland."

The fuck it is, Zubinsky thought. *There's no way I'll order my men to shoot my fellow Russian citizens peacefully protesting against what they think is an illegal coup.* He pondered the situation for a moment and realized that was only one way to put an end to it.

Zubinsky switched his radio to the short-range tactical circuit that connected him to all the vehicles in his command. "This is Zubinsky. All units turn your guns away from the parliament building and shut down your vehicles. We're wasting fuel. Unload your weapons. Do not fire, repeat, do not fire on the protesters." His radioman had overheard his conversation with General Konarev; the man looked at him quizzically. "Everyone do it, and do it now," Zubinsky said. "That's an order! Acknowledge!"

Zubinsky grabbed the two megaphones his battalion had been issued and left the command vehicle after logging the acknowledgements to his radio operator. Jogging forward, he climbed onto the first T-72 tank and stood on top of its turret. Zubinsky was over two meters tall; when he'd been younger, he'd had to fold himself into the tight confines of first the T-55, then the T-62. Now it was the T-72. He put one foot on either side of the tank commander's hatch and flipped the switches of both megaphones to the ON position. A tone came out of each, telling him they were active. He held both a few inches from his mouth and faced the crowd behind the barricades. He thought, *I'm about to commit suicide: either by getting shot here and now, or by a firing squad after my court martial. Someone has to stand up to these crazy people who want the Soviet Union to return to what it was under Stalin.*

Zubinsky ran his hands through his blond hair and watched as one by one, turrets whined as they turned. The square, which had been filled with the noise of idling diesels for the past eight hours, was now eerily quiet.

He turned to face the parliament building. "I am Lieutenant Colonel Lev Zubinsky, commander of the second battalion of the 117th Motorized Infantry Regiment of the Tamanskaya Guards Motorized Rifle Division. I stand for Russia and support the elected president Boris Yeltsin and General Secretary Gorbachev I do not support the State Committee on the State of Emergency. The army has ordered me to fire on you. I will disobey this order and will not, I repeat, *will not* order my battalion to fire."

From the open windows of the parliament building, Zubinsky could hear cheering. A few minutes later, a stocky man with a shock of white hair emerged surrounded by a group of wary citizens. The older man was helped onto the tank, then onto the turret of the tank on which Zubinsky was standing. Boris Yeltsin held up tank officer's hand.

From where there were standing less than a hundred meters away, Danielle and her father saw the two solitary figures on top of the olive green tank. They watched as crewmembers climbed out of their vehicles and infantrymen unloaded their AK-47s, putting the weapons away in the racks of their BMPs. Tension evaporated, at least for a few minutes, and cheers rang out for Zubinsky and Yeltsin. Cameramen from Western networks recorded the scene while excited reporters spoke into their microphones.

* * *

When Konarev heard what had happened, he ordered the battalion's executive officer to arrest Zubinsky. The request went unanswered. He then called the leader of the Alpha Group team and ordered him to shoot Zubinsky, then arrest Boris Yeltsin. The man said he didn't have a good shot at either one.

Frustrated, Konarev called Talyzin. When Talyzin didn't answer, Konarev called Vladimir Koskov, who said he was on his way to Red Square where he'd take charge. The State Committee on the State of Emergency was going to institute martial law and a strict curfew by any means necessary.

The Same Day, 1806 Local Time, East of Bukhara, Uzbekistan

The Zil-130 rolled along at a comfortable eighty kilometers an hour. Despite the heavy steering and the ineffective vacuum assist for the brakes, Josh found the lightly loaded truck easy to drive. Occasionally, he slowed to wait for a small herd of goats or sheep to cross the road, but for the most part, the traffic was light. He'd double-clutched a downshift to climb a hill, and as they came over the top, there was Panichev's convoy. There was a huddle around one of the aft wheels of the middle GAZ-66 four-wheel drive truck. At the front end of the convoy, a man was talking on as a satellite phone.

Ten kilometers later, Avram told Josh to turn off onto a dirt road. The other truck followed. Once they were stopped, Avram huddled with the two members of the Sayarat Maktal, Eli and Isaak. Josh waited as the nearby truck engines made loud crackling noises as they cooled.

Avram issued orders to Eli and Isaak. "You two take up a watch position. We'll move off a bit farther and wait to see if they spend the night or continue on. The smugglers aren't taking off a tire, so my guess is they have a transmission or rear axle problem."

When Avram looked his way, Josh said, "All right, we've found our targets. I say we strike as soon as we can."

Chapter 20
Joint Foreign Combined Take Down

Thursday, August 22nd, 1991, 0011 Local Time, Uzbekistan

Thursday, August 22nd, 1991, 0011 Local Time, Uzbekistan

With the half moon, clear skies, and no human-made light for miles around, the stars stood out like distant flashlights. To Josh, driving the truck was like flying over the ocean at night, but instead of water underneath a helicopter, he was crossing sandy rocky soil in which Uzbekis struggled to make things grow.

They stopped at a wadi to make their final plans. On the dirt between the trucks, one of the Israelis drew a map of how Panichev's six vehicles were parked in a clear area off the road about a kilometer from where they stopped. Arrows pointed to how the assault team would approach the convoy from two different directions. The idea was to force the Iranians away from the trucks and into an open field with no cover.

Since they'd arrived at the wadi, Josh and Avram had received two reports on the convoy. The first report said the smugglers were towing the disabled GAZ-66 to a turnoff where they could park well off the highway in a wide-open area. The second noted that one of the GAZ-66s was backing up to the one being towed.

"They're going to be crowded with thirty people and six weapons in just two trucks and two BTRs. Have they started moving the weapons from one truck to the other?"

"No. My guess is they'll start at first light. Right now, they have four sentries out and the rest are sleeping."

"Any signs they're using the infrared sights on the BTR's main gun?"

"No," Avram said. "The engines aren't running and the turrets aren't moving."

Josh made sure the magazine in his AK-47 was seated and the safety was on. He looked up at the sky. When he flew on nights like this, there was almost enough moonlight to read a chart. Tonight, however, the moonlight was his enemy. It might let the enemy see the assault team as they worked their way over open ground. Their goal was an irrigation ditch about a hundred and fifty meters from Akrami's trucks. Even at this distance, the smell from the mix of mud, rotting vegetation and animal waste wafted over the assembled group.

Velasquez sat fifty meters to Josh's left with his forearms resting on his knees. The M82A1 Barrett lay between the two Marines, along with an ammo can with six extra ten-round magazines. Their other weapons were .45s that they'd brought from the embassy.

For most of the flight to Samarkand, Josh had listened to the good-natured joshing between Brown and Velasquez about who was better with the Barrett. Velasquez had finally allowed that Brown could be the shooter—at the range they were firing, he said even Brown couldn't miss and wouldn't need him as a spotter.

The team moved out in three groups. Josh and Avram acted as the command group. Velasquez went with Brown off to their flank. Ten Bukharans and two Sayaret Maktal made up the second group and main attacking team. The surveillance team of three, including Richard Carlson, had the task of taking out the sentries; they'd be the short side of the L-shaped attack.

Josh sprawled on the ground in the shadow made by a small scrubby bush, trusting it would make him harder to see. The cold steel of the .45 Model 1911 in the small of Josh's back was comforting, but it was only a short-range weapon. His AK-47 lay in the dirt next to him with a spare magazine taped to the one inserted in the well. He'd given his other two spare magazines to one of the Bukharan Jews; he hoped he wouldn't regret it. Weapons were easy to get on the thriving Uzbek black market, but ammunition wasn't.

They were a long way from any farmhouse, but the noise of a firefight would travel far over this desolate land. It might draw curious onlookers who could compromise their mission. Telephones were rare in this rural area, but there only had to be one. Even though the nearest Red Army garrison was fifty miles away, they could arrive in time to interfere with the last stage of Josh's plan.

He was studying the easily recognizable silhouettes of the BTRs when he heard Avram's satellite phone buzz softly. There was short whispered exchange in Hebrew, then Avram held up two fingers.

Josh had crawled to within a hundred meters of the trucks. Brown was off to the side behind a rock outcrop; if a firefight broke out, he was to fire Raufoss rounds into the BTR turrets. If needed, he'd destroy the truck's engines.

A hundred meters away from the western end of Panichev's convoy, Richard Carlson sighted the two sentries he was assigned to take out. He hadn't practiced with the rifle he was about to use and hoped it was close to being zeroed. This was the first time he'd fired a SVD-63 (a.k.a. a Dragunov sniper rifle) since the Soviet weapons familiarization course he'd taken in 1975. At a hundred meters, if the scope was anywhere close to being aligned, he was confident he'd hit the target.

Carlson felt the pressure on the small of his back from the spotter's fingers. He would tap three times and on the third, both Carlson and the other team member would squeeze their triggers. Take out one sentry each, then shift their aim and shoot the remaining two. Hopefully, all four sentries would be down in seconds. After that, the others would attack.

One press from the spotter. Two, a pause and Carlson let out his breath. Three, and the Dragunov barked. Through the scope, he saw his target stagger, drop his AK-47 and go down. The other man spun in the direction of the noise, giving Carlson a full frontal view. The Iranian sentry let loose a long burst from his AK-47. The rounds sung harmlessly over Carlson's head. Carlson jerked the trigger and the shot missed. Cursing softly, he now had a tougher shot because the man had crouched down, looking for a shooter. Squeeze. A nearly simultaneous flash and bang and the man toppled over.

"Let's go," Carlson said.

The three men leaped out of their hide toward the first BTR. They could hear its starter cranking over, then the vehicle's engine fired. The turret began turning and the three men weaved as they ran toward the parked vehicles.

The Iranians, now awake, came tumbling out of the trucks and tried to mount a defense. At least six attempted to rush toward the attackers, but the Bukharans fired short bursts from the hip and cut down all six. The remainder hid behind the truck tires, darted quickly out to fire, then ducking back.

As soon as he heard the first shots, Moshen Zangeneh knew what to do. He was shouting instructions as he leapt from the rearmost GAZ truck. After getting his men in position to return fire, he dashed to the next truck in line. Dirt flew up around his feet as he covered ground. Satisfied that his men were well positioned and returning fire, he headed toward the rearmost BTR. He'd already figured where the attackers must be. In the BTR, he could use the heavy machine-gun to break the ambush.

Sergeant Brown spotted Zangeneh when he made his first dash between trucks. Zangeneh's actions convinced Brown he was either a senior NCO or an officer. On the second move, Zangeneh got under cover before Brown could get a shot off. As soon as the Iranian emerged from cover, Brown squeezed the trigger on the Barrett. The recoil shoved him back in the dirt, but he didn't miss. The fifty-caliber Raufoss bullet hit Zangeneh's left biceps muscle and severed his arm before it went into his chest and exploded, splattering body parts on everything within ten meters. The man's head flew five meters through the air before it banged against a truck and hit the ground, leaving a bloody trail as it rolled to a stop. The rest of Zangeneh's torso, from the hips down, crumpled in a heap.

Seeing the turret of the front BTR start to move, Brown aimed and squeezed the trigger. In the scope, he saw the flash of the hit and heard the dull clang of an armor-piercing round going through steel.

As Carlson approached the BTR, he heard a loud bang and the 14.5mm heavy machine barrel went skyward. At the front of the vehicle, Carlson peered around the large tire. The side-hatch flew open and two Iranians clambered on board. Carlson knew he couldn't let them get the heavy machine-gun into operation. Cautiously, he moved along the side of the armored car until he got to the open hatch. Red light from the interior shone on the desert floor, and voices spoke in a language he didn't understand. Without a grenade, he had no choice but to do the one thing he dreaded: a close-quarters battle inside the unfamiliar confines of a Soviet armored car.

The lack of gunfire told Josh there was a lull in the fighting. The Bukharans only fired when they had a target. In the starlight, Josh could see bodies lying around the trucks, as well as three more down by the second BTR.

"We need to force the issue," he whispered to Avram. "The longer this goes on, the worse it gets for us. I'll take Velasquez and work around to the other side so we can come at them from a direction they don't expect. Do you still have comms with the other team?"

"I can reach them."

"O.K.," Josh said. "I'll pull back to the drainage ditch, then follow it around."

"How will I know when you're in position?"

"I'll flash my white flashlight twice, then pause and do it again. At the end of the second flash, Velasquez and I will start with the westernmost BTR and work our way forward. You guys keep them pinned down."

Avram signaled he understood then got busy with the satellite phone.

* * *

The two Israeli snipers kept the Iranians pinned down under the two trucks that were parked back to back. Every time they got a target, they fired and an Iranian went down.

Alone, Carlson listened for a few seconds. Judging by the sounds inside, someone was struggling to move a heavy object. Since there was no time like the present, Carlson held the Makarov pistol out in front of him as he stuck his head in the door wishing he had a .45.

Under the turret, he could see a man with his back toward the door. The man seemed to be pulling on what looked like a body, but in the dim red light of the interior, it was hard for Carlson to be sure. He fired twice from five feet. He felt the concussion from the pistol's muzzle blast, and despite earplugs, the noise battered his ears as it reverberated inside the steel hull. The man he'd just shot fell forward, bleeding from two holes in his upper back. A second man sitting in the driver's seat tried to bring his AK to bear, but Carlson shot him in the face. Carlson pulled the corpse back only to find another body, its face shredded by spall from the Raufoss armor piercing round. The blackened, jagged hole was just below the gun sight.

Exiting the BTR, Carlson emerged to find one of his teammates crouched by the rear wheel. The man was talking into the satellite phone while his partner lay prone, watching the trucks.

Two men emerged from behind a GAZ-66 truck and ran towards what was now Carlson's BTR. He listened to their footsteps and let them get within ten meters before he stepped around the front of the armored car and shot each with the Dragunov.

One of the Bukharans yelled in Uzbek, then in Russian. "We have you surrounded. Give up. You have no place to go, and it's not necessary for more of you to die."

"Allah Akbar!" a man yelled in reply. "We may die here, Infidel, but many of you will die too." The man punctuated his comments with a long burst from an AK-47.

* * *

When Josh emerged from the ditch, he crouched as he ran as fast as he could toward the BTR. Halfway there, he tripped and went face first into the dirt. His AK landed with a soft thud ten feet away. Velasquez grabbed Josh under the arm and helped him up. Both were surprised they weren't shot at.

Spitting foul-tasting dirt, Josh peeked around the rear corner of the second BTR. In the moonlight, he saw men looking in all directions, but mostly toward the Bukharans and the other BTR. Near one of the trucks, a man was talking into a satellite phone who looked like Akrami and he was only twenty yards away.

Josh had to spit out a clump of mud. "Man with a radio or phone," he said softly. "I'll pop out and shoot him. When I do, all hell is going to break loose, so cover me. Plenty of targets to our right."

Velasquez nodded. Josh held up three fingers and took a deep breath. He showed his index and middle fingers and exhaled. After Velasquez acknowledged the index finger, Josh put both hands on the .45 and popped out. The man with the phone spotted him, but before he could move, two .230-grain slugs slammed him back into the truck tire.

Josh shifted targets and fired single shots at silhouettes until the weapon clicked empty. Jumping back behind the BTR, he did a combat load and released the slide. Velasquez lay next to the wheel, pumping out shots until Josh heard a noticeable click, signaling that the Marine's weapon was empty. That was Josh's clue to come out of hiding. When he did, a bullet ricocheted off the vehicle's armor while two more kicked up dirt by his feet. Spotting the muzzle flash, he pumped off two rounds and heard a scream.

"Stoi, stoi!" Stop, stop! The words were yelled out first in Russian. Something else was yelled in Farsi, but Josh didn't understand that language. He assumed it also meant, "Stop!"

As Josh peeked around the front of the BTR, men were standing up with their hands in the air. Iranians emerged from their hiding places and tossed their AKs on the ground. Richard Carlson and the two Israelis joined Josh as he motioned to the Iranians, directing them to move to a clear area away from the vehicles, near the Bukharans who had yet to break cover.

Carlson stayed with Josh and Velasquez as they herded their captives into a circle well away from the trucks. The Israelis made sure no one was left in the vehicles and as they found their weapons, they were tossed into a pile.

Josh was starting to relax when he heard two noticeable pings followed by a third. Carlson yelled "Grenade!" just as three dark hissing objects rolled toward them on the ground. A short distance away, someone yelled, "Allah Akbar!"

Josh dived. He was still in the air and heading toward the ground when the first grenade went off. He felt a stinging sensation on his left thigh and another in his butt. Between the bangs of the grenades, he heard the staccato of AK-47s being fired. When he got up, he saw Velasquez had a bloody shirt.

Rolling on his back, he saw three Iranian's pulling the pins on three more grenades. He pumped two rounds from his .45 into one and the other two were shredded with bullets. None of them got the pins fully out before they were killed.

"Are you alright, sir?" the Marine asked, coughing. "The fucking bastards did this to us during Desert Storm. We should have known better."

He collapsed into Josh's arms. Josh lowered him gently to the ground. The back of Velasquez' BDUs was oozing blood.

"Brown! Take care of Gunny."

"Yes, sir, but you're wounded too."

"I'll live. Anyone else hurt?"

"I'll check."

"Good. Find out, take care of the injured, and then come find me."

By now, the Bukharans were standing around a group of men sitting on the ground. Some of the wounded Iranians groaned in pain. Brown soon found Josh and told him that Velasquez would be fine, but needed surgery to remove about two dozen grenade fragments.

Relieved, Josh limped back to the truck. He found the man who'd had the radio struggling to breathe. The man's uniform was soaked in blood. "Akrami?"

The other man nodded weakly.

Josh pried the bloody phone out of the man's hands. He spoke in Russian. "To whom were you talking?"

"Headquarters in Tehran." Akrami wheezed and blood foamed from his mouth.

"Who are all these men?"

"Quds." Akrami coughed and his face contorted in pain. "Who are you? KGB or GRU?"

"Neither. I'm an American. The rest are Israelis and Bukharan Jews."

"Figures."

Akrami's head slumped. Josh felt for a pulse. There was none.

The Same Day, 0140 Local Time, Moscow

The citizens occupying the parliament building reinforced the barricades at the entrances, under the direction of a people's deputy who was a Red Army general. Earlier in the day, Zubinsky's battalion had been ordered to pull back after it refused to fire on the protestors. In the square where Lieutenant Colonel Lev Zubinsky once had his command post set up, the KGB Alpha Group had set up its own.

By comparison, it was much smaller: centered around two trucks with large boxes mounted on their frames. One was a communications center. It had cables hooked to the other box, which held a large conference room, several work stations, and a small communications room.

In the conference room, Koskov ordered everyone out of the truck before dialing a number.

"Talyzin."

"Koskov here. I want to confirm an attack by the Alpha Group is a go for 0200."

"Yes, attack at 0200. Tell them to clear the building and try not to make too many martyrs."

"I will."

"We're counting on you," Talyzin said. "We need to put down this rebellion quickly. Capture Yeltsin alive."

"My men will do their duty," Koskov said.

He rang off and picked up a handset to a secure radio. The people had to bend to the will of the State Committee on the State of Emergency. A message needed to be sent, and he knew he was the man to send it. "This is Koskov," he said. "Attack is a go at 0200. Shoot anyone who resists. Find Yeltsin and kill him."

"What about prisoners?"

"Take prisoners only if it doesn't endanger the lives of your men."

"Understood."

Koskov came back into the conference room to refill his coffee cup. He was surprised to see a woman standing next to a fit-looking elderly man. "How did you get in here?" he demanded.

"There are no guards outside, General. They are all either following your orders to suppress resistance, or refusing to start a civil war." Danielle heard how cold and controlled her voice was, almost as if someone else were speaking.

Casually, Koskov poured coffee and stirred in two lumps of sugar. "You, I know," Koskov said to her. "Who's he?"

"I am Colonel Jacques Debenard, French Foreign Legion, retired." Jacques looked straight into Koskov's eyes and spoke in English knowing Koskov didn't speak his native language "Remember when you were an advisor at Laos Re-Education Camp Number 3?"

"You bring up ancient history? I am a busy man. Get out!"

"Danielle and I were what you might call guests at the camp."

"Ahhhhh. But what does that have to do with me?"

Jacques's voice was cold. "For months, you and your men raped my daughter. When she found out she was pregnant, she committed suicide by walking into a minefield."

"We were at war. Ugly things happen." Koskov settled himself in the largest, most comfortable chair and used peripheral vision to scan the room. His sidearm, he remembered with a silent curse, was on a desk in the back of the trailer. "I fucked a lot of women in that camp. I liked the younger ones. If I remember correctly, your daughter squealed like a pig when I took her virginity. There are no living witnesses, apart from you two; it will be your word against a respected and decorated Red Army general. No one will believe you, and no one will care if they do. So, what can you do to me, old man?"

"I don't need a court to get justice," Jacques said.

Koskov tilted the large chair back and looked the former legionnaire in the eyes. "Don't threaten me, old man. Leave. Now! Or, I will have you killed. Not arrested, killed. Both you and your... damaged daughter here. Did we fuck her too? I don't remember... Danielle did you enjoy it too much to kill your self?" He sneered at Danielle, who stood stone-faced and still.

"General, think of me as your judge and jury." In a smooth practiced motion, Jacques pulled out a Makarov pistol with a long suppressor and fired one shot. It hit Koskov squarely between the eyes. The general collapsed back into his chair, blood flowing from the hole in his forehead. While Danielle turned the chair so it was facing the back wall, Jacques laid the pistol on the table and pulled off the deerskin gloves he was wearing and stuffed them into his pocket.

The Same Day, 0613 Local Time, Uzbekistan

By the time the soft light of early morning was casting shadows, Richard Carlson had inspected all six nuclear artillery shells. At the same time, Avram had some of his men examine the trucks to determine which ones were still usable.

Carlson's loud exclamation, "Holy shit!" brought Josh at a limping, painful run. He arrived simultaneously with Avram. Inside the truck, Carlson had pulled back a tarpaulin and was staring at four olive drab containers. "These are RA-115s! I've heard about them, but I've never seen one."

The batteries of Carlson's flashlight were fading, but he still had enough light to check the seams of the bomb cases for potential problems. Satisfied that the closest container wasn't going to explode or arm the weapons, Carlson popped open the latches. Sitting on top was a small instruction book with a series of pictures. Carlson studied them for a few seconds before handing the book to Josh. "The first set of pictures tells how to arm the bombs. The battery indicators suggest they still have juice, so I think the best thing to do is take them out of each weapon. That should disarm them."

"And if you're wrong and you actually arm them?"

"Then none of us are going to be around to worry about it."

Josh turned to Avram, who shrugged. "How can we help?"

"Pray these puppies don't go off!"

Neither Josh nor Avram moved as Carlson took off the battery-pack's access panel. He studied it for a few seconds before he unscrewed the connector holding the wires to the dry-cell batteries. Nothing clicked or started to whir. The battery indicator went to zero and all three men exhaled loudly.

"There may be more of these on the trucks," Carlson said. "If so, it's one down, God knows how many to go." He looked at the others. "Can you get Sergeant Brown up here so he can log these weapons?"

Josh looked at Carlson and then at Avram. We don't know if Akrami has a back-up force on the way or the Army was notified. We need to get on the road. How long will this take?"

"Ten minutes." By the time Carlson finished disarming the RA-115s, the Israelis had searched the bodies for documents and had photographed each of them. The dead were stretched out in a row. Their blood blackened the sand.

Avram told Josh, "I had one of my people check the trucks to see which are still roadworthy. We have our two Zil-130s, one of the GAZ-66s, and the little GAZ-69. The other two GAZ's are shot up and we don't have the parts or the time to fix them. We're siphoning fuel out of them into our vehicles and into gas cans. We should have enough to get back to Samarkand without refueling."

"What about the BTRs?"

"I thought we'd just leave them here. They're no use to us. Sergeant Brown did a good job of putting holes in the turrets with the armor-piercing rounds."

"It's a shame we can't take them," Josh said. "How's their fuel?"

"The gauges say they're just over half full. That would be enough to make it back to the airport."

"Do we have anyone who can drive one?"

Avram said, "I don't know, but it can't be too hard."

"Get them started," Josh said, "and let's take them. Put all the bodies on one of the trucks, then fill it with as many prisoners as will fit. Lash them to the benches. They're not going anywhere without papers. Our people will ride either in the BTRs or trucks."

Just before they left, Josh pulled out a sweat-stained piece of paper and dialed the number scrawled on it. A gruff voice answered. Josh asked to speak with General Krasnovsky. After thirty seconds, the general came to the phone.

"Mission accomplished. We're seventy kilometers from the airport."

"Good. And Akrami?"

"Dead."

"I'll take care of the next part. All hell has broken loose here in Moscow."

Krasnovsky hung up. There was some degree of worry that a satellite call would catch the attention of the KGB and trigger an investigation. However, given what was happening in Red Square, the people who listened in phone calls were probably distracted.

The Same Day, 0733 Local Time, Moscow

When Arkady showed up for work, two members of the *militsiya* examined his identification before letting him in the building. Once inside, he understood why. Black-clad members of OMON, the *militsiya's* special operations and tactics unit, had taken over the first floor. Six were loading magazines for their AK-74 assault rifles. The holding room normally used for criminals was now a crowded makeshift command center. Radio sets had been propped up on stacks of empty ammo boxes.

Arkady walked to the armory to obtain his Makarov pistol and holster. There he was offered a second pouch with three extra magazines. That was a first. The man in charge said, "You aren't required to take the extras, but with everything that's happening around the parliament building, headquarters recommends it."

"What has happened?" Arkady asked. "Yesterday, the protestors were just occupying the building. When I went to sleep, the army had pulled back."

"Yes, sir, the Tamanskaya Division was sent back to its barracks because several of its commanders declared their loyalty to the country, not the special committee. Last night around two, Alpha Group attacked the building. No one knows who's winning or how many have been killed."

"What about our OMON?"

"Commissioner Sokolov says he only takes orders from Yeltsin or Gorbachev. There is one OMON team here and another closer to Red Square. Most people I know support the protesters, not the committee."

Arkady nodded. He knew what he had to do. He yelled at Dorotkin to get a car and meet him out front in five minutes. He opened his safe and pulled out a folder holding everything from his investigation into the murders of senior officials. All of it went into a battered leather briefcase that smelled of dill pickles. The smell always embarrassed him; one time, a package of pickles had leaked and he'd never been able to get the odor out of the leather.

Arkady's badge got him past the guard in front of the communications center. The watch officer saw him come in. "How can I help you, sir?"

"What's the latest at the parliament building?"

"The OMON commander at the scene refused to attack without written orders from the commissioner and a signed arrest warrant for each Member of Parliament."

"Do we have any men nearby?"

"Just a few blocks away. But army paratroopers pointed the cannons from their tanks at our men's trucks."

"That's not good."

"I agree," the watch officer said.

"How many protestors dead?" Arkady asked.

"We don't know. There's been a lot of shooting. The protestors were unarmed, and you know those hotheaded Alpha Group guys. See a citizen, shoot a citizen."

"Do we know if President Yeltsin is safe?"

"We're not sure. Some reports say he's still in the building, but others say he was smuggled out. We just don't know."

"What are your orders?" Arkady asked.

"Stand by ready to respond. Our trucks are in the back, loaded and ready to go." The watch officer looked at him. "Do *you* have any orders for us?

Arkady shook his head. "There's no need for the *militsiya* to get mixed up in this mess. We'll wait to do the police work once this is over. Then we may need your men to make the arrests."

The watch officer sighed. "This is not a good day for our country."

"You're right," Arkady agreed. "I'll be back." He didn't add *to do my part to save the country from bastards like Talyzin.*

The Same Day, 0825 Local Time, Uzbekistan

The sun was well above the horizon and beating down from a cloudless sky. The steel of the BTR was already hot to the touch. Josh liked standing on the commander's seat with his head and shoulders in the wind as the vehicles ran at a steady eighty kilometers per hour. He'd never ridden in an armored vehicle before except for a few minutes on his first NROTC summer cruise, learning about the Marines.

Driving at that speed, every ripple in the road sent pain through Josh's body as the shrapnel in his thigh and butt touched nerves. Both wounds had stopped bleeding, but it would take a surgeon to get the pieces out.

The Same Day, 1350 Local Time, Tehran

Mohaqqeq Damad had been in the Expediency Council chamber before. It was dark and somber, almost like a funeral parlor. Damad looked around to see if members of the SAVAMA were present to arrest him. No one in sight. Damad relaxed, but still feared the worst. His bodyguard waited impatiently for him to enter the chamber so he could sit down in one of the comfortable chairs outside the room.

When the three robed men entered the chamber, Damad stood up. Because he was so short, the table on the dais was almost two meters above where he sat and the men's heads, even higher.

"So, Damad," said the leader, "there is bad news from Uzbekistan."

"Yes, your Eminence. It seems our shipment of nuclear artillery shells was intercepted. The convoy was attacked after a vehicle broke down."

"What happened to our men?"

"We do not know yet."

"Have you talked to Colonel Akrami?"

Damad looked grim. "He called me on his satellite phone while they were under attack. I have not heard from him since."

"You assume the Russians captured him?"

"I do. Someone must have turned him in. Or he is dead." Thankfully, Akrami knew little about Iran's network inside the Soviet Union. When the KGB dug into his personnel file, they would only find what amounted to a well-written novel.

"So," said the Supreme Leader, "we do not have the nuclear artillery shells to mount on the missiles." He pursed his lips and leaned back in his chair. After a few seconds of staring at the ceiling, he looked at Damad. "It is God's will. We will find another way to get nuclear weapons, even if we have to build them. Decide what you want to do with the foreign technicians. If they ask to leave, let them do so, then silence them with an accident. In the meantime, General Damad, your job is to find another way to buy nuclear weapons. The Pasdaran will help as needed. Money is not an object."

Damad bowed his head in acknowledgement. The Supreme Leader turned to the general sitting next to him. "We can continue to have Hezbollah strike the Israelis. When we have weapons, Iran will attack both Israel and America."

The general, who was wearing the uniform of the Iranian Revolutionary Guards Corps, nodded.

The Same Day, 1715 Local Time, Moscow

The table was the work of a skilled artisan. Its alternating strips of black and white Birchwood had perfectly fitted seams, but the mars and scratches on the table's surface showed that it had seen better days. What dominated the room was the credenza matching the table. It held a well-stocked bar and glass shelves full of Hungarian lead crystal glasses.

The room was not in the parliament building. Rather, it was in a small suite of offices near the Kremlin that Boris Yeltsin maintained so that he could meet quickly and privately with his rival for power, Gorbachev. As the General Secretary of the Communist Party, Gorbachev ran the party and Yeltsin supposedly ran the country, but in a country where the party was the government, conflicts naturally arose. They would end when the Soviet Union was dissolved on December 25th, 1991 and Yeltsin would be the country's sole leader.

Still, both men were reformers. Yeltsin was the first president chosen in a relatively free election, and he wanted reform faster than Gorbachev. The activities of the past few days reinforced his desire to shut down the KGB.

Commissioner Sokolov sent Arkady to Yeltsin when the murders of senior leaders began to happen. Yeltsin had ordered Arkady to keep digging and gathering evidence; the time was coming when evidence would be needed.

All Arkady could think about on his way to Yeltsin's office was, *the time has come.* The door opened and Yeltsin's secretary, a matronly woman in her fifties, stuck her head into the conference room. "The President will be here in five minutes. Make it quick, he's moving locations to stay away from the KGB."

Arkady nodded. He rearranged his information into three piles and wrote the four points he wanted to make on a pad. Each point was supported by evidence in the stacks in front of him.

"Good afternoon, Colonel," Yeltsin said, hurrying into the room. "What do you have for me on the bastards from the Lubyanka?"

Arkady looked at the man. He looked liked he hadn't slept for days. He smelled as if he was staying awake by a mix of coffee, tobacco and booze. "Mr. President," he said, "I have a great deal. I hope you can put it to good use."

The Same Day, 1832 Local Time, Samarkand

Twenty kilometers from Samarkand, Avram called a halt. Ostensibly, this was to refuel the trucks and the thirsty BTRs, but it really was a chance to talk with Josh about the plan's next step. What worried Josh most was that Mr. Murphy hadn't yet managed to screw anything up for them. Maybe, Josh thought, Mr. Murphy couldn't find Uzbekistan on a map or didn't have a visa.

Josh's fatigues showed large sweat rings under his armpits and bloodstains on his pants. He ran his hand through his hair and felt his scalp rough with grit. He was sure that mud and dirt on his face around his Ray Bans gave him the ski goggle look.

One of the Bukharans said there was an entrance to the airport used only by police and emergency vehicles. The guards were local police officers; they were often drunk and would be intimidated by a convoy guarded by two BTRs. The Bukharan drew a map in the sand and Brown copied it into his notebook.

As the convoy approached the airport, three well-used commercial Zil-130s joined the procession. Through the fence surrounding the field, Josh could see an Air Force C-141 parked on the same ramp where he'd disembarked a few days before.

Its silver paint gleamed in the sun. Nearby stood three GAZ-66 trucks and another BTR.

When the guard at the airport gate saw the BTRs, he held up his palm of his hand to stop them. He jogged out to lift the pin on the entrance gate. Once he had the gate unlocked, he walked it open, and then gave Brown an exaggerated bow. The Marine gunned the engine of the BTR and led the convoy into Samarkand International Airport.

Brown followed Avram's instructions to park nose to tail behind the BTR that was already beside the C-141. The two trucks with the weapons parked opposite the armored cars, followed by the truck that held the prisoners and the bodies.

The extra Zil-130s made a tight turn, then backed up and stopped so their tailgates were ten meters from the C-141's ramp. As Avram headed toward the C-141, Major Zvi Yaniv walked up and handed him a package of small red folders.

With the three Zil-130s in position, two Bukharans dropped the tailgates and started helping a group of women and children get out. They formed a line in front of Avram; he handed them each an exit visa and checked their names off on a list. This gave the C-141's loadmaster ample time to guide each family to seats in the cargo compartment and help them buckle their seatbelts.

Josh leaned against a BTR for support while he sipped from a large bottle of water. The expressions on the Bukharan Jews going to a new life in Israel alternated between fear, confusion, bewilderment and excitement as they boarded the airplane. He could only imagine what they were thinking as they left the "comfort" of their homeland with only the clothes on their back and headed to a strange new land. This airlift—Josh's airlift— brought to life the true meaning of the Passover Seder service prayer that ended with "Next year in Jerusalem." For these fifty families, the dream would become a reality in less than twenty-four hours when they walked off El Al's flight in Israel.

Behind Josh, Captain Kupka and two Soviet Artillery officers approached the truck where Dick Carlson waited to help them examine the ZBV2s and R-115s. The men had brought a test set to make sure the weapons hadn't been tampered with.

Josh's interest in the future immigrants was interrupted by the sound of tires skidding to a stop. Out of the lead GAZ-66, a KGB captain emerged in battle dress followed by a dozen armed soldiers wearing the uniform of the KGB Border Guards. Each carried an AK-47 in the ready position. They gathered in a semi-circle with their weapons leveled at Josh.

Their leader looked at a photograph then said, "Captain Haman, I am Captain Bogdan Fedin of the KGB. I have orders to arrest you and bring you to Moscow."

Josh was too tired and achy to argue. He made a wry smile. "For what reason?"

"Murder. I am to arrest you and wait for a plane to take you to Moscow."

Josh pointed at the C-141. "I have a plane right there."

"A Soviet Air Force plane will be sent once I report you are in my custody."

"You know I have diplomatic immunity, right? Even in the Soviet Union, the KGB doesn't arrest diplomats."

"We do if a crime has been committed. My orders say you murdered a Soviet citizen. Therefore I can arrest you."

"The man was ordered by a KGB general to assassinate me and I killed him in self-defense. This was confirmed by the *militsiya*. I guess in the Soviet Union, the truth doesn't matter."

"*Militsiya* is not KGB. It will be for a KGB court to decide, not me. My job is to take you into custody until you can be transported to Moscow."

"Well, Captain Fedin, I'm about to get on this plane and it will land in Moscow about four hours after it takes off."

"I cannot allow you to leave."

"Sure, you can. Come with me. There's plenty of room. Bring some of your men along."

Fedin wasn't used to being challenged. He also didn't like what he saw: a group of men who looked like soldiers. Then suddenly, two squads of Red Army soldiers appeared seemingly out of nowhere.

"Captain Haman," said Fedin, "my orders authorize me to shoot you if you resist."

"I'm not resisting, Captain Fedin. In the United States, this is called a discussion."

The Russian took a step toward Josh. "I see your clothes are bloody. If you're injured, we can give you medical attention."

"No thanks."

"If you were in some type of fight, you may have committed another crime."

"I was preventing a crime," Josh said.

"What kind of crime?"

"Theft of Soviet nuclear weapons."

"So you, an American, here in Uzbekistan, prevented criminals from stealing some of our nuclear weapons. You are making a joke, no?"

"No joke. My prisoners are members of the Iranian Revolutionary Guard Corps. We killed twelve and captured eighteen. All are on the truck, waiting for you to take them prisoner. We have all their forged as well as their real papers."

"Impossible!"

One of the Israelis pulled back the canvas of the truck. Fedin strode to the Iranians who were wearing Soviet Army uniforms.

"These are Soviet soldiers. You killed members of the Soviet Army. That is a crime punishable by death."

Josh held out the documents and identity tags that had been taken from the captives. "If you check these out, you'll find they're phony. Most of these men don't speak Russian. One of the dead men is Ali Akrami, who has been posing as a Red Army artillery officer name Yuri Panichev."

"I don't believe you."

Josh held up his satellite phone.

"Captain Fedin, if you give me the name of the general who signed your orders, I'll be happy to call him. I warn you, you're making two mistakes. One, you are holding up this flight which is waiting for me to board. And two, you're standing between me, medical attention and a bath."

Fedin stepped toward Josh and unbuckled the flap on his holster.

A voice behind Josh called, "I wouldn't draw my pistol, Captain."

Fedin's hand stopped with the pistol only partially out of the holster. "And you are?"

"Major Zvi Yaniv, security officer for the Central Asian Military District. If you pull your pistol, my men have orders to shoot all of you KGB. For a change, it would be citizens killing the KGB, not the other way around."

Yaniv's head and shoulders had risen out of the hatch in the turret of the BTR. He continued, "We have just taken possession of the weapons Captain Haman recaptured, along with the survivors of the Iranian commando unit. The Red Army will be happy to allow the KGB to participate in the interrogation."

Fedin scowled at the soldiers surrounding him. "This is nonsense. The Army doesn't tell the KGB what to do. I have orders to arrest Captain Haman, so get out of my way or I'll report you to my commanding officer."

"Captain Fedin," Josh said, "I'm getting on this airplane. If you want to die, try to stop me." Josh nodded to Major Yaniv.

Yaniv pulled back the bolt to charge the RPD light machine-gun he carried. The clanging sound could be heard over the whine of the C-141's auxiliary power unit. Yaniv leveled the weapon at Fedin. "As an Army officer senior to you, I order you to put down your weapons or we'll shoot you."

"I am KGB. We do not report to the Army."

Yaniv shook his head. "Captain Fedin, you can order your men to lower their weapons, or you can die right here and now. You have three seconds to make your decision. Three...."

Fedin looked around. Yaniv's detachment stood on their flanks with AK-47s pointed at the KGB Border Guards. When Fedin shoved his pistol into his holster, his men lowered their rifles.

"Captain," Yaniv said, "tell your men to put their rifles on the ground. My men will remain here until Captain Haman and the American Air Force plane leaves."

"Then what? I have my orders. What do I report to Moscow?"

"Say you saw Captain Haman depart for Moscow. But I don't think anyone will pay attention—if you've been seeing the same mess of contradicting orders that I have, our comrades in Moscow have other things on their mind. However, if you want to call someone in the KGB, I suggest you call Major General Oleg Krasnovsky. He's the one who authorized Captain Haman's mission and mine. Or, we can use Captain Haman's satellite phone to call General Krasnovsky right now. I'm sure he'd be happy to talk to you."

Fedin glared at him. "You will pay for this day, Major. The KGB does not forget when its authority is challenged."

"If Yeltsin has his way, the KGB will have its teeth pulled." Yaniv yelled for Captain Kupta. When Kupta's round face appeared from the back of the truck, Yaniv handed him the machine-gun and saluted. "You're in charge now."

Kupta saluted back. Yaniv pointed to the aircraft. "Captain Haman, please board the plane. Everyone, including my family, is waiting for us."

Josh nodded and walked stiffly up the ramp as the number one engine began to whine. Yaniv saluted Fedin and Kupta before he hopped onto the ramp. By the time the C-141's ramp was closed, three of its engines were running and the airplane was taxiing toward the runway.

Saturday, August 24th, 1991, 0928 Local Time, Moscow

The lines at the international airline ticket counters at Sheremetyevo weren't really lines. They were mobs of people shouting for the attention of a ticket agent so they could get one of the few seats on a Western airline flight out of the Soviet Union.

Danielle showed her diplomatic passport to an Air France employee who was trying to create order out of chaos. The Air France woman held up her finger and disappeared into an office behind the counter. Out came the station manager.

"Colonel Debenard... Miss Debenard... please come with me."

It took less than two minutes to issue Debenard his ticket to Paris and to walk him through customs and immigration, where a bored KGB officer took a quick glance at his documents and stamped his exit form and passport. The Air France employee waited while Danielle kissed her father good-bye, then ushered him to the first-class lounge.

Chapter 21
Revenge is Sweet, But Not All It's Cracked Up to Be

Monday, August 26th, 1991, 0711 Local Time, Moscow

At first, Josh thought he was dreaming. Sun streamed into his hotel room through a crack in the curtains. The phone rang, and then stopped. Then it started again. He had showered at the Israeli embassy's infirmary after they stitched the gashes made by grenade fragments. He'd waited until the doctors finished pulling the shrapnel out of Velasquez before he had Brown drive him back to the Rossiya. They'd gone to the Israeli embassy because they knew as soon as they set foot inside its walls, Grant was going to have them arrested.

Exhausted as he was, he hadn't been able to get to sleep. His mind wouldn't stop running through the past few days; mentally, he kept writing the report that Gainesville would require. Eventually, he'd taken one of the sleeping pills he'd received from the Israeli doctor.

That had been at 2311. What time was it now?

The ringing of the phone was replaced by pounding on the door. Reluctantly, Josh got out of bed and pulled on a pair of jogging shorts. "Who is it?"

"Arkady Kishniev."

Josh fumbled with the lock and cracked it open. He half expected KGB or *militsiya* officers ready to slam open the door and handcuff him.

Arkady nodded to the hotel manager, who disappeared down the hall. As Arkady entered, he told Josh, "You look like shit!"

"I'm glad I look the way I feel." Josh was still struggling with the fog of exhaustion. "What brings you here?"

The *militsiya* colonel pulled a sheaf of folded papers from his briefcase. He plopped them on the table. "These are arrest warrants I'm serving today. At the top of the list is General Nikolai Volkov. Do you want to witness the arrest?"

"Absolutely."

"Then meet me in the lobby in civilian clothes as soon as you can. I have some apple juice, bread and cheese you can eat in my car. Oh, and if you like, you can call General Krasnovsky and see if he wants to join us."

* * *

The back seat of Arkady's Volga was cramped and smelled of body odor. Josh wondered how many criminals had sat in the seat before him. Behind Arkady's car were two more each with four *militsiya* officers, and a van with a twelve man OMON team.

When they reached their destination, Josh winced in pain as he unfolded himself from the back seat. When he'd first arrived in Moscow, he had asked Brown to stop in front of the Lubyanka so he could take a good look; however, this was the first time he would see the interior. Climbing the steps, Josh had to admit that the building was even more imposing than it was from the street.

A smiling Oleg Krasnovsky was waiting for them in the entrance area. He watched with amusement as the officer in charge of the guard detail protested the arrival of the *militsiya* without permission from the head of the KGB. Arkady placed the first arrest warrant in front of the very young-looking officer. "Lieutenant, this is my permission slip. President Yeltsin personally signed it. We have already arrested the head of the KGB, as well as several others for treason and attempting to overthrow the government. If you insist I need permission to enter the Lubyanka, then I'll arrest you for obstructing justice. I have an OMON platoon waiting outside."

"But Colonel," the lieutenant said, looking down at his logbook, "how do I record your entry?"

General Krasnovsky leaned over the counter. "Just write that the colonel and his men are here on official business. Add my name to the log as their sponsor, if you wish."

As they rode up in the elevator, Josh looked at Arkady. His shoulder tabs now had the three stars of a full colonel rather than two of a lieutenant colonel. "So when did you get promoted?" Josh asked.

"President Yeltsin promoted me at the same time he signed the warrants. Commissioner Sokolov has already approved it so I should have the paperwork in a few days. And they look much better."

"Congratulations."

Arkady nodded, not to be rude, but he was on a mission. Their group consisted of a *militsiya* colonel followed by eight armed *militsiya* officers walking two by two, then a KGB general and a casually dressed man who was walking gingerly and who was obviously a foreigner. They got stares, but no questions or interference as they strode down the hall to Volkov's office.

The eight *militsiya* officers remained in the corridor, while Arkady, Krasnovsky and Josh walked right past Volkov's surprised administrative assistant and into the general's office.

Volkov stood in the middle of the room, holding a stack of files he had just taken from the safe of his spacious office.

"Who are you?" Volkov demanded.

"Colonel of *Militsiya* Arkady Kishniev."

Volkov pointed at Josh. "Why do I know you?"

"Who he is will be clear in a moment." Arkady spoke with an air of authority. For his entire professional life, he had longed for the day he could arrest a senior KGB general.

Volkov bristled with anger. "I don't have time for games, Colonel. The *militsiya* doesn't have jurisdiction in the Lubyanka. Get out before I have you thrown out."

"General Nikolai Volkov, you are under arrest for treason, for plotting to overthrow the government, and for conspiracy to commit murder overseas and here in the Soviet Union. We know some of those murders overseas weren't sanctioned by the Politburo. Other crimes may be added after we finish our investigation."

"By whose orders am I being arrested?"

"President Boris Yeltsin."

"Bullshit. He doesn't have the authority to have me arrested. I am KGB."

Arkady laid a piece of paper on Volkov's desk. "You *were* KGB. These papers, signed by President Yeltsin, strip you of your rank and position."

"Fuck you. He has no authority to do such a thing. Get out before I call the guards and have you shot."

"No you won't." As if on cue, the eight *militsiya* officers appeared with their guns drawn. Volkov's administrative assistant, a lieutenant colonel, cowered in the corner of the office.

Volkov glared, then turned to Krasnovsky. "What's your role in this?"

"I am witnessing your arrest." Krasnovsky didn't bother adding, *and your demise.*

"Bullshit. You're involved up to your neck. Traitor!"

"A more accurate description would be loyal law-abiding citizen and servant of the people."

Volkov turned to Josh, who was standing quietly off to one side. "And who the hell are you?"

"I am Captain Joshua Haman, United States Navy. I thought you might want to meet the man you tried to kill more than once. At your trial, I'll testify to your involvement in a triple murder in the United States and your recent attempts to kill me."

Volkov reached downward.

"I wouldn't do anything rash." Arkady had his Makarov pointed at Volkov's chest. "At this range, I can wound you and add resisting arrest to the list of charges, as well as attempting to kill a *militsiya* officer. So, General, come around to this side of the table. We can look through these files you were holding and see if they contain evidence. I can assure you that any files related to national security won't be taken."

The rattle of gunfire outside in the hallway made everyone freeze for a second. Josh recognized the softer prattle of suppressed weapons. He saw Volkov reaching for a pistol and launched himself into a chest-high tackle. The impact slammed Volkov against the wall. The Makarov Volkov was drawing from his holster skittered off to the side. Josh landed a right cross on Volkov's jaw, stunning the man. Josh snatched up the weapon and slid the slide back a few millimeters to make sure it was loaded.

"There are seven rounds in this gun," he told Volkov. "The first goes into your head. The remaining six are for whomever comes through the door."

Volkov sneered. "You won't leave this room alive. What you hear is the sound of the Alpha Group fast reaction team coming to my rescue. I pushed the alarm and soon, you will be either dead or in the custody of the KGB. Then you'll *wish* you were dead."

The sharp barks of Makarovs were followed by short bursts of suppressed automatic weapons and shouting. Volkov's assistant had his knees drawn to his chest as he sat in the corner at the end of the couch, trying to make himself as small as possible.

As they he watched and listened, Josh could Volkov's face was swelling as he kept the Makarov aimed at the man's chest. Arkady and the eight other *militsiya* officers crouched behind the administrative assistant's desk with their weapons drawn. The Alpha Team remained out in the hall, content to maintain a standoff. They knew that rushing in would mean Volkov's death, so they waited.

Krasnovsky, the old warrior, sat relaxed on Volkov's couch with his hands in his lap. Josh reflected that the old man was probably thinking, *if I am going to get shot, I might as well be comfortable when I die.*

Sporadic gunfire sounded from the hall. Then it stopped and was followed by a series of shouted commands that were muffled by the office walls. A moment later, Arkady stood and let out a deep breath of relief. The rest of his men relaxed and came out from their cover.

Militsiya clad in black fatigues with OMON patches on their sleeves entered the outer office. In front of them, they shoved six men of the Alpha Team, all of them wearing camouflaged fatigues. The leader of the OMON team unbuckled his helmet and pulled off his black knit baklava.

"Colonel Kishniev, sorry we were late." He pushed one Alpha Team man to his knees. The others followed.

"How many were killed?" Arkady asked.

"Two of them dead, two wounded. They weren't expecting us to come at them from behind. My men are holding four more at gunpoint, but I don't think they have the stomach to start a shooting war with us."

Arkady nodded. "Let the Alpha Group men collect their dead under your supervision. Get the wounded to a hospital. In your report, please note they were doing their job. They didn't know they were following the orders of a general who had been relieved of his duties and who will be treated as a common criminal."

The captain saluted and left a four-man team for protection in case any other Alpha Group squads responded to Volkov's alarm. When they were gone, Josh yanked Volkov to his feet and waited while the ex-general was handcuffed. Then Josh shoved Volkov hard enough to bang his head off the wall. When the KGB general regained his balance, Volkov stood sullenly in a corner glaring at whomever looked at him. His aide stood meekly off to the side while he was handcuffed. Arkady wanted him more for information on where to look in Volkov's files than as a witness. He was not the target of his investigation.

Arkady pulled more files from the open safe, including what looked like a diary. He flipped through the pages, and then tossed it to Josh.

"You'll be interested in this."

Seeing the dates, Josh worked back through the handwritten pages until he found an entry for August 15, 1973. *"Bagdonovich reports he killed the traitor Major Artur Vishinski and two women, probably Vishinski's wife and daughter, at their home in San Diego on August 11, 1973. Usual calling card left."*

Josh's eyes blurred. He turned over other pages and found similar entries before he put the diary gently down on the edge of the desk. Bagdonovich had not been the only killer on the loose in the U.S.

"You fucking son-of-a-bitch!" Before anyone in the room could react, Josh took two strides toward Volkov and hit him with all his strength in the stomach. Volkov's face went red as he doubled over in pain. When he lifted his head gasping, Josh hit him on the temple with a downward blow. Volkov collapsed to the floor. Blood gushed from his nose and from a cut on his cheekbone.

"Who ordered these killings?" Josh demanded.

It took Volkov a long time to answer. When he finally recovered enough to speak, he glared at Josh defiantly. "*I* ordered them. *I* had approval of the head of the KGB to kill them as traitors to the Motherland."

Josh said, "You're lucky I don't kill you right now."

"We were at war with America," Volkov replied. "We still are."

"You killed innocent men and women who weren't on the battlefield. That's not war, it's murder."

"Your father-in-law was a deserter. He left his unit."

Josh had to take a deep breath before he could reply. "Artur Vishinski left *after* the Great Patriotic War ended. He didn't want to live under Stalin anymore. He was tired of the pogroms and the Cossacks raiding his villages. He wanted his *freedom!*"

"You are military," Volkov said. "You must understand deserters should be shot."

"Only after a trial, and only if they leave in the face of the enemy. Artur Vishinski served his country with honor and was awarded the Hero of the Soviet Union twice. His desire for *freedom* to live where he wanted, do what he wanted, and pray in a synagogue was far more important than his loyalty to Mother Russia. He did his duty for the Soviet Union and all he wanted was to live in peace."

Volkov struggled for breath as blood streamed down his face. "We hunted down a deserter to let the world know the Soviet Union does not allow its citizens to abandon the Motherland in its time of need. Besides, the world wouldn't miss one more worthless Jew."

Josh's eyes widened. He grabbed a handful of Volkov's tunic hard enough that buttons popped off and fell to the floor. "Look at me, you worthless piece of shit. I am A JEW. Jews found you and will make your crimes public. You don't deserve to walk on this earth."

"So are you going to pull the trigger?" Volkov made a face showing his contempt. "You Americans don't have the courage to pull the trigger. Besides, it will never get to trial. I am KGB and I was doing my duty. This coup will pass. The Soviet Union will live on, and the KGB will maintain order."

"Don't count on it."

The Same Day, 1030 Local Time, Moscow

The room stank of disinfectant. Its rough gray concrete walls needed a good cleaning. A table's rusty legs were bolted to the floor of the basement room. The only other furniture in the room were four chairs, two on either side of the table.

Arkady put the folders he'd removed from Volkov's office on the table. He put one chair in the corner and waited until the recording officer sat and said she was ready before turning to the Captain Dorotkin who was standing in the doorway. "Bring prisoner Volkov in."

Volkov shuffled in restrained by manacles on his legs. A chain connected the manacles to his handcuffs. Volkov clanked as he walked and his face was still puffy from Haman's blows. His cheek was covered with a bloody bandage. Volkov's uniform was wrinkled, dirty and bloodstained.

Arkady helped Volkov settle into his seat before a guard used two large padlocks to secure Volkov's chains to rings in the floor. The guard stepped back and stood by the door.

Volkov stared while Arkady made a show of looking at the folders and reading their contents. He let five minutes go by before he slid two sheets of paper across the table. "Citizen Volkov," Arkady said, "this is the warrant for your arrest and the sheet listing the current charges. The charges now include treason. The coup has failed and you were one of its leaders. I am sure the state prosecutor will add more to the list later. Please read the current list of charges."

Volkov glanced them over, and then slid the paper back across the table. "These won't stand in court. I am KGB. We are the Committee for State Security. We decide who has committed crimes against the state, not the *militsiya*."

Arkady presented Volkov with several papers clipped together. They listed fifteen names, ten of which were crossed off. Accompanying the list were forms with the names of individuals and the assassins assigned to kill them. Gabashivili was on three; Bagdonovich was on two, including the one filled out in pen to kill Gabashivili.

"I don't think you understand," Arkady said. "These papers show you recently ordered the assassination of Soviet citizens: members of the Red Army and Navy and the government. Stalin and Beria are long gone. Murder in the Soviet Union by anyone for any purpose is illegal. Finding the murderers is the job of the *militsiya*."

"Are you going to torture me to get a confession?"

"I don't have to. Much of the evidence is in your own handwriting. I also have the blank authorization documents you got signed in advance by your superiors, so that you could add the names and reasons after you had someone killed."

"I was following orders."

"That's what Hitler's generals said. For you also, it is bullshit. You were *giving* the orders. And, you were involved in the coup up to the top of your KGB head. So, Citizen Volkov, I'm not going to torture you. Others might, but not me. I like to let the evidence speak for itself... and I have enough to send you to the Gulag for the rest of your life, or to have you stood up against a wall and shot. I suggest you answer my questions."

Volkov glared at him. "Are you Jewish like the American captain?"

"Why do you want to know?"

"If you are, your religion is more important than your loyalty to your country." Volkov spat on the floor. "The Jewish bastard Olshansky sold his country down the river. We didn't need the West's food. Soviet citizens would have suffered, but they would have survived because true Russians understand the need for sacrifice."

"I'm not going to discuss politics with you," Arkady said. "But it's hard to sacrifice when you are starving, your children are sick and dying, and you have no hope of a better future, while KGB officers feast on caviar and imported steaks."

"You didn't answer my question," Volkov said. "Are you Jewish?"

"Yes, I am."

"Jews can't be trusted. Any Jew who wants to leave, we should let him go, and good riddance."

Arkady simply stared back without expression. "Do you want to tell me about your role in the coup?"

"No."

"How about your involvement in the assassinations of senior officers of the Soviet military?"

"Go screw yourself."

"Are you going to answer any of my questions?"

"No. Go fuck yourself, you goddamn worthless Jew."

"Then we're done." Arkady motioned for the recording officer to leave. When Arkady got to the door, he told the guard, "Hold him in solitary confinement. Bread and water only."

The Same Day, 1356 Local Time, Moscow

Josh kept a set of his summer white uniform hanging on the door of his office in case he came in wearing civilian clothes and needed to change. His wounds hurt; he was glad he could make the pain go away with two aspirin every four hours. He was just buckling his belt when there was a knock on the door. He was about to answer when General Grant opened the door resplendent in his green shirt and olive drab pants.

Grant was holding a folder and smiling. His plan was to arrest Haman and then, to further embarrass him, have him walk down the row of cubicles and offices in hand cuffs on his way to a cell. It was to be his victory walk to show that no one challenges his authority. "Where have you been for the past four days? The ambassador wanted all the attachés in the embassy to provide information and analysis on the coup. Your absence was noted."

"General, sir, I was doing my job."

"And what job was that?"

"I suggest you ask General Feltzer, sir," Josh replied. "I'm sure he'll answer your questions. I can't and I'm tired of you asking." He regretted those last words as soon as he spoke them —a symptom of his exhaustion.

"I notified the Pentagon that the three of you were absent without official leave. The DIA's Judge Advocate General has also filed charges against Senior Gunnery Sergeant Velasquez and Sergeant Brown."

"With all due respect, General, I can tell you that both Gunnery Sergeant Velasquez and Sergeant Brown were with me on an authorized mission. They distinguished themselves in the conduct of their duties. I suggest you contact General Feltzer or Rear Admiral Gainesville and ask them to read you in so we can tell you what we were doing."

Grant made a face. "What I want is your ass out of this embassy as soon as possible. There are enough crises around here and we don't need you creating another one. The Marine guards are on their way up to arrest you on a variety of charges, including improper handing of classified material, deliberately disobeying orders given to you by a senior officer, conduct unbecoming of an officer, being AWOL...the list goes on. When word gets around the Pentagon that you've been arrested, many flag officers will cheer. Your career in the Navy, Captain Haman is over. You'll be lucky not to spend time at Fort Leavenworth."

There was a gentle tap on the doorframe. It was Sergeant Brown, along with two Marines, each carrying a holstered .45 and wearing an MP armband on their left sleeve.

Brown marched to a position three feet in front of General Grant. He did not salute. "General Grant, I'm here to deliver orders relieving you of your duties as the senior military attaché here in Moscow. These orders were issued by the Chairman of the Joint Chief of Staff, and endorsed by the Chief of Staff of the Army. They directed the head of the Defense Intelligence Agency to have you relieved, effective immediately."

Brown held out a manila folder so that Grant could take it and look at the papers inside "My orders are to escort you out of the building and to your quarters where you will pack your bags. From there, you will be escorted to Domededovo Airport where you are to board the first U.S. Air Force airplane headed to Rhein Main Air Base. You will remain on the base until you are flown back to the U.S. to face disciplinary action."

"This is bullshit," Grant spluttered. "These orders are forgeries to protect Captain Haman."

"General Grant, sir, the originals arrived by the diplomatic pouch and were authenticated by Master Chief Grayson. He also received a second set of orders assigning Navy Captain Williams, the senior Naval Attaché, as your temporary relief. He is presently in your office inventorying your classified material. Your personal items will be shipped back to you in the U.S."

Grant turned to Josh. "This isn't over, not by a long shot. I'll have your ass if it's the last thing I do."

Josh shook his head. "General, you fucked up. You're lucky you didn't get anyone killed unnecessarily. My report will detail your attempts to get unauthorized access to a mission for which you had no authorization." He stepped back. "Sergeant Brown, please get your prisoner out of my office."

Brown was grinning ear to ear as he saluted. "Aye, aye, sir."

Josh watched the Marines escort Grant down the hallway. Feeling much less tired than before, Josh sat down at his desk. He'd just started editing his notes when the phone rang.

"Josh, Admiral Gainesville here. I'm on a speakerphone in the tank at the JCS command center. With me are all the joint chiefs and General Feltzer. No one else. They have a few questions for you."

"Yes, sir."

"This is the Chairman. What does your source in the KGB say about the coup?"

"It's over and it failed. The *militsiya* have arrested most, if not all, the plotters. I don't know all the names except Volkov, Talyzin and the Minister of the Interior, Boris Pugo. Pugo has committed suicide. "

"How have you confirmed this information?"

Josh said, "I know the *militsiya* colonel who arrested Volkov and the others. The arrest warrants were signed by Yeltsin and given to the colonel to execute." Josh paused, wondering if his next statement could make the shit hit the fan. "I was there when Volkov was arrested."

"Where did that happen?"

"In his sixth floor office in the Lubyanka."

"You were in the Lubyanka?"

"Yes, sir."

Josh was expecting *a what were you thinking? Or, were you out of your fucking mind to go voluntarily into the Lubyanka?* Instead, a calm voice said, "Tell us about the arrest."

Josh described what he'd seen, and what Arkady had told him about his meeting with Yeltsin. Josh didn't mention Krasnovsky. When Josh was finished, the Chairman said, "You realize that neither the CIA or the DIA, nor the attachés in Moscow have reported any of this."

"Sir, they need to get out more," Josh said. He regretted his words the second they left his lips.

"What do you mean?" the Chairman demanded.

"The attachés were told by the ambassador and General Grant to remain in the embassy during the coup. They should have been walking the streets and talking to Soviet soldiers. Several soldiers from the Tamanskaya Guards division told Gunny Velasquez and me they weren't going to fire on their own people."

There was a long silence. Finally, the Chairman said, "Great work on getting the weapons back. What will the Russians do to the officers who sold them?"

"I don't know, sir."

There was a long silence, then the Chairman spoke again. "Captain, I'm thinking about replacing General Grant with you."

"Sir, I respectfully would like to decline and come home. It's been an intense few weeks, and I don't think I'm the type of party animal needed to be a successful attaché."

The Chairman laughed heartily. "Noted. Captain, you've developed more intelligence and contacts in two months than these guys have done in years. You still may wind up being ordered to stay in Moscow."

"I understand, sir. But, I would respectfully ask the general not to order me to do so."

Tuesday, August 27th, 1991, 0001 Local Time,
Zurich, Switzerland

Fund transfers between banks began seconds after the clock passed 0000. For Lombard Odier, the computer began sending funds electronically to banks based on the sequencing number for the transfer. Buried in the long list was a transfer of $71,892,000 to a bank in the Seychelles. Once the money was received, another SWIFT transfer order was waiting to send the money to a bank in Lichtenstein, from where it was transferred to the First Caribbean National bank in the Cayman Islands. Each transfer had the appropriate authorization codes, so they could not be disputed. Because the transfers were properly authorized, General Vavilov would not know they'd been made until he saw his next bank statement. By then, the funds would be long gone and there'd be no way to recover the cash.

Since the banks in Lichtenstein and the Seychelles didn't have money transfer agreements with Lombard Odier, each took twenty-five basis points or one quarter of one percent as a transfer fee. If by some chance the funds had to be repatriated, the banks would resist because it meant the fees would have to be refunded.

Once the money was credited to the account in the Caymans, an electronic note was sent to a bank officer telling him call a number in Zurich. The person who received the notification smiled and called his boss at Mossad headquarters in Tel Aviv.

$71,892,000...that left $108,000 in Vavilov's account plus any accrued interest. The amount had been carefully chosen to ensure that it was above Lombard Odier's minimum account balance of $100,000. $108,000 was also picked because 108 was six times eighteen; multiples of eighteen are traditional amounts that Jews give for gifts. The money from Vavilov's account went into a special Israeli government fund to help Jews emigrate from the Soviet Union. By leaving Vavilov with $108,000 plus any accrued interest, they were leaving him a gift.

The Same Day, 1837 Local Time, Moscow

The dinner table was loaded with food. All six diners were smiling. The elder Kishnievs were happy to have both their children present, plus the two foreigners. Josh was honored with the seat at the foot of the table, opposite Arkady's father. A beaming Raisa put a steaming plate of stuffed cabbage emitting its pleasant sweat pungent odor at each end of the table.

"So, Arkady, my son," said Aron, "what's the latest news?"

"The coup is ended and the plotters have been arrested. Soon everything will be back to normal for everyone except mama and you."

"I don't understand. Why won't things be normal for us?"

"Father..." Arkady used the formal term rather than *nána* or papa, "You know that at the end of the Seder service, we always end with the statement *next year in Jerusalem.*"

"What does a prayer have to do with the coup?"

"Nothing... but by the end of the week, you, mama and Valentina will be in Tel Aviv."

"No, not possible!"

"It is. Avram has arranged it. Avram will help Valentina find a job and the Israeli government will support you and mama."

"What about you?"

"I have work to do here, but I'll follow in a few weeks when it's finished. Avram will help me get a job as police officer, once I learn Hebrew. And I promise I will find another wife... maybe sire some grandchildren!"

"Good." Raisa Kishniev's stoic face reinforced the finality in her voice when she said, "No one in this family will ever return to the Soviet Union."

Wednesday, August 28th, 1991, 0639 Local Time, Moscow

It took Josh an hour to pack his bags as he gingerly moved around the suite. The few souvenirs he'd bought were already in the mail; they'd arrive in San Diego within a few weeks as Parcel Post packages.

The side pouches in his B-4 bag were stuffed and he was putting hanging clothes into the center section. Another duffel bag was packed with shoes and clothes. His carry-on contained toiletries and two sets of casual clothes. All he had left on the bed was what he would wear on the flight home.

Tomorrow, Velasquez and Brown were going to pick him up at eight to take him to the embassy for a formal checkout. From there, he would be driven to the airport for the early afternoon Pan Am flight to London, where he would catch a non-stop to D.C. Rebekah had already announced she and the kids would meet him at the Marriott in Crystal City.

Josh had just finished shaving when he heard a knock at the door. Not expecting room service, he pulled the .45 out of its hiding place, slid back the slide to make sure a round was chambered, and flicked off the safety. "Who is it?"

"Arkady."

Josh unlatched the deadbolt and popped open the door, staying on the side covered by the door. When he saw Arkady was alone, he put away his pistol.

"Good morning. To what do I owe the pleasure of this visit?"

"Are you going to the embassy today?"

"Velasquez is picking me up around nine. Why?"

"Call him and tell him to pick you up at 1000 instead. Then get dressed and come with me. A suit would be appropriate."

"Are you going to tell me why?"

"Not here."

Ten minutes later, Josh was ushered into a conference room in the parliament building across from the hotel. Workers were still clearing debris and cleaning up from the attacks. Standing in the room were two Soviet officers: Major General Krasnovsky and the General of the Red Army, Dimitri Ulyanov. All the Russians came to attention when the door was opened. A stocky, white-haired man entered the room. He walked over to Josh who also stood at attention.

"You must be the American, Josh Haman." Yeltsin spoke in Russian.

Josh could smell the alcohol on his breath as the President gave him a traditional Russian hug and kissed him on both cheeks. As many times as Josh had experienced the ritual, he still didn't like it. Nevertheless, he was sincere when he said, "I'm pleased to meet you, Mr. President."

Yeltsin turned to an aide who handed him a small dark blue box. "These generals have told me what you have done on behalf of the Union of Soviet Socialist Republics. Besides saying thank you, I have the honor to present you with the Order of the Red Star. Normally, it is only given to our citizens for exceptional service in the defense of the Soviet Union, in war or peace. We have had a little of the former. Now, under my leadership we hope to have a lot of the latter. Foreign Minister

Grachkov told me he will get approval from your government to allow you to wear this medal. More importantly, however, on behalf of the highest levels of our government, our country wants to thank you for what you have done."

"Thank you, sir. I am honored by your gratitude." Josh knew it sounded stilted, but it was true.

A tray appeared with five glasses, already filled with vodka. Yeltsin handed a glass to each man before taking the last for himself. "To a job well done. May both nations live in peace."

All of them emptied their glasses. Josh never drank alcohol before breakfast, but there was always a first time. On an empty stomach, the vodka made his head spin.

"Now," said Yeltsin, "I would like to stay and talk, but there is much to do." He shook Josh's hand and left the room.

Arkady handed Josh the medal box and a folder containing a written citation in Russian. "On to our next stop."

"There's more?" Josh asked.

"Indeed," Arkady said. "As you Americans say, it is a chance to finish some unfinished business."

Fifteen minutes later, Arkady stopped in front of a drab-looking pale yellow building. As they waited for the guard to examine their papers and inspect the car, Arkady said, "This is Butyrka Prison. Unlike Lefortovo and the Lubyanka, this prison is run by the Minister of the Interior. It was originally built in 1879 as a prison from which there was no possibility of escape. Today, the *militsiya* use it to keep citizens either awaiting trial or those who have been sentenced and are awaiting transportation elsewhere. Hitler's nephew Heinz was brought here when he was captured and tortured to death in 1942."

Arkady grimaced at the thought of Hitler. "This is a pretty grim place. I decided it would be appropriate for Volkov. In the past, many Jewish dissidents were kept here, so we put Volkov in the cell once occupied by Yevgenia Ginzburg. You know her?"

Arkady didn't wait for an answer. "She wrote *Journey into the Whirlwind* and *Within the Whirlwind*. They were books about the purges in the 1930s. They did not make Stalin happy. Ginzburg survived eighteen years in the *Gulag* before she was released."

"Oh." It was all Josh could say. Prisons made him very uncomfortable.

Arkady laughed. "You are not being arrested." He signed the logbook, and then clipped a badge on Josh's suit pocket. The hall smelled of disinfectant desperately trying to cover up smells that Josh didn't recognize. He suspected the disinfectant was covering up vomit, rotten or burned flesh, blood, feces, urine and other ugly, smelly things. Distant sounds echoed and bounced off the stone walls.

They walked in silence for some time, until Arkady stopped at a door and opened it. Inside were a wooden table and four metal chairs, two of which were bolted to the floor. "We'll wait here," Arkady said. "Someone will bring us something to drink. And this is for you." Arkady opened his briefcase and pulled out the diary he took from Volkov's office. "You can have this. We don't need it anymore—we copied everything from it, and we have the KGB archives to verify the information."

Josh removed the two wide rubber bands that kept the well-worn book together. There was a paperclip on the August entry about his in-laws.

Arkady said, "It may help your police close some cases. Our people are copying pages from KGB dossiers of assassinations in America. I'll deliver them to the legal attaché in a few days. I'm sure your FBI could use them."

"Thank you." Josh looked at the diary, afraid to touch it. It was a key to unlock memories hidden for years. "So why are we here in the prison?"

"I'm waiting to be called to witness the administration of Volkov's sentence."

"So soon?"

Arkady nodded. "Volkov is being given a taste of his own KGB medicine: quick trial with a predetermined guilty verdict and execution of his sentence. The only difference is that here we have real evidence, not lies."

"What's his sentence?" Josh asked, knowing the answer.

"Death by firing squad." Arkady paused. "He still considers himself a servant of the people. He wants his fellow citizens to look him in the eye when they pull the trigger." Arkady looked at his watch. "It's scheduled for 0830. If you wish, you can witness it too."

Josh swallowed hard and took off the jacket of his charcoal gray suit. "I have a better idea."

* * *

Five minutes later, Josh was standing with a Mosin-Nagant bolt-action rifle holding a single 7.62 x54mm cartridge. Josh recognized it as the shorter carbine version of the long rifle originally designed in 1891. It was the Russian Army's rifle of choice in World War I and World War II.

Before Josh entered the courtyard, the commander in charge of the execution went through the drill making sure Josh knew the commands and what to do. He was told he would be about ten meters from the prisoner; he was to aim at a circle pinned on the man's chest. This prisoner would be standing at attention. Not blindfolded. After Josh fired, the commander would check to see if the prisoner was still alive. If he was, the commander would shoot a bullet into the man's head as a coup d'grace.

Josh followed the *militsiya* captain into the courtyard. It was raining, not heavily, but enough to make the cobblestones glisten. Josh was given a rubberized nylon poncho and a hat to keep dry.

Volkov stood in front of a pockmarked concrete wall that had clearly taken its share of bullets and been patched many times. Josh wondered if he'd be so calm in the same situation. But when Volkov saw the lone shooter, he screamed, "Not you! Not a Goddamn American Jew!"

With the rifle in the ready position, Josh said, "Ironic, isn't it? I hope you go straight to hell!"

"Load," the captain called.

Josh rested the rifle on his right hip as he slipped the single 7.62 X 54mm rimmed cartridge into the breech. He pushed the bolt forward and down, locking it in the firing chamber.

"Safety off." Josh used his thumb to ensuring the weapon was ready to fire.

"Aim."

Josh pulled the rifle hard against his shoulder and looked down the 514mm long barrel, aligning the front and rear sights on the red circle on the man's chest. Looking at the circle made it look like he was shooting a target, not a man. *Fuck it!* Josh made a slight adjustment of his sight picture.

"Fire."

Josh squeezed the trigger. A spray of blood and brain matter hit the wall behind Volkov as his body buckled and toppled over.

The Same Day, 1313 Local Time, Moscow

The air-conditioning in the Red Army's General Staff building couldn't keep up with the heat and humidity. Krasnovsky wasn't surprised he was sweating—it was almost 37° Celsius outside and the humidity was nearly a hundred percent. Later in the day, it was supposed to start raining.

The KGB officer knew where he was going. He wasn't carrying a briefcase—he didn't need one. He was only there to deliver a message as he walked past the major sitting outside the Vavilov's office.

Inside the office, Vavilov looked up, surprised. "General Krasnovsky! What can I do for you? You should have called and I would have had something sent up from the mess for you. Tea?"

Krasnovsky closed the door. "No, General Vavilov. This will only take a minute."

The artillery officer said nothing.

Krasnovsky stood with his fingertips touching Vavilov's desk. "By noon, tomorrow, you will submit your request for immediate retirement. Use any excuse you want, but your career is over."

"But Oleg, I'm not ready to retire." Vavilov kept his voice soft.

"Yes, you are. Your request will be on Comrade General Ulyanov's desk by noon tomorrow. If not, I'll be duty-bound to report your attempt to sell nuclear weapons to the Iranians for seventy-two million U.S. dollars. This will lead to a trial, after which you'll be given the choice of being hung or shot."

"And if I retire?" Vavilov asked.

"Nothing will be said. Consider it a favor for helping me."

"How do I know I can trust you?"

"You don't," Krasnovsky told him. "Right now, I am the only one in the KGB or Red Army who knows the full extent of your treason. Much of the paperwork has been destroyed. However, there are men outside this country who have copies of all the evidence. They know as much as I do so if I have a fatal accident, they will turn the information over to the KGB and the *militsiya* and let them fight over what do to with you. As part of this deal, you will give me a list of all the others involved in this matter. They too will be given a choice. Leave the army, or be court-martialed, then hung or shot. Double-cross me, and you will face a firing squad within twenty-four hours."

Vavilov squeezed the ample flesh under his chin. "I need time to think about this."

Krasnovsky thought he saw a wisp of a smile. "If you try to leave Moscow, you'll be arrested. You're on a watch list. Oh, and don't bother checking on your money. Almost all of it is gone. When you've resigned, you can live wherever you want, but I don't think a Soviet General's pension will go very far in another country. Come to think of it, it won't go very far in our socialist paradise."

For the first time since he met the man, Krasnovsky saw fear in Vavilov's eyes. "Remember, retirement papers on Ulyanov's desk by noon tomorrow. He'll be in his office. I suggest you bring them personally, so they aren't lost or mishandled. If they aren't there on time, you'll be arrested shortly thereafter."

Tuesday, September 3rd, 1991, 0802 Local Time, Washington D.C.

The effectiveness of the Pentagon's air-conditioning system was evident as Josh came up the escalator from the Metro station into the waiting area. He set down his briefcase and a heavily taped box wrapped in brown paper so that he could pull his badge from the pocket of his shirt.

The guard at the turnstiles said, "Captain, sir, what's in the box?"

"A notebook containing a classified report."

"Do you mind if we inspect it?"

"You can X-ray it."

The guard said, "We need to open it and look inside."

"You can't pull it out," Josh said. "You don't have proper clearance."

"We understand, sir. You can watch while I open the box and look."

Josh was still jet-lagged and emotionally worn out despite the day he'd spent with his family. He wasn't in the mood for fighting. "Sure," he told the guard, "go ahead."

Lieutenant Johnson was waiting for Josh when he finished with security. Always the cheerful soul, she held out her hand. "Captain Haman, welcome back!"

"Thanks," he said, shaking her hand. "It is soooo good to be back in the states."

"How's your wife? I talked to her several times and she's so nice."

"She has to be—she's put up with me for all these years."

Johnson smiled. "Rear Admiral Gainesville and General Feltzer are expecting you. I'll escort you—it'll give me a break from sorting through all the message traffic. The admiral has me divide each pile into RELEVANT and DUMB. You wouldn't believe what some commanders put in their messages!"

"Oh yes I would, Lieutenant. And they get even dumber and stupider when you're at war."

"I can believe it. Trust me, I've seen my share of them."

A few minutes later, Josh was sitting at a conference table with Jeff and Feltzer. Josh slid the thick notebook out of the box.

"What do you have?" Jeff asked.

"My report. The first section is a copy of the report I've already sent you via courier. The second section is my diary. It was typed day by day, so there are some inconsistencies: over time, I learned things that contradicted previous entries. The diary also contains a number of photographs taken while I was there. The third section lists the names and ranks of the Soviet officers I met and a summary of their backgrounds. In

485

Krasnovsky's case, there's only the code name, Red Light, because I don't know where this document might land in future."

"Understood."

Josh pulled a sterling silver Parker fountain pen from his shirt. "I used this pen to write my initials in blue ink on each page of each copy. Gunny Velasquez and Sergeant Brown did the same in red ink—they helped me pull the file together. Dick Carlson initialed the pages detailing his notes on the Soviet nuclear weapons and how we captured them in green ink."

Feltzer looked at the notebook's cover. "It says this is one of three copies. Where are the other two?"

"Avram Gutman from the Mossad has one. The third is in a very secure place for safekeeping outside this government."

Feltzer's expression hardened. "Some would say that hiding a copy is a violation of your clearance."

"With all due respect, sir, I don't know who'll see this document, how it will be used, or even where it will be stored. If anyone tries to distort what happened or alter this report, I want an honest copy for ground truth."

"Who else knows where the extra copy is kept?"

"Nobody. You'll have to trust me, general; it won't be given to anyone unless someone here in D.C., Moscow, or Tel Aviv does something stupid."

Feltzer made a face but didn't pursue the subject. "Do you know Krasnovsky's plans?"

"No. Yeltsin wants to dismantle the KGB. Krasnovsky doesn't think that will happen, but if it does, he doesn't know where he'll go next. I think he'll be offered a job in whatever organization replaces the KGB. Either that, or he'll retire. Leaving the Soviet Union will be difficult for him—he knows too much for them to let him go."

"Do you have a way of communicating with him, openly or covertly?"

"Yes, sir, both."

The general started flipping pages in the report, stopping occasionally to read. When he got to the section on the capture of the weapons, he studied the diagrams drawn by Sergeant Brown. "This document is very, very thorough. I look forward to reading it later." He slid it to Rear Admiral Gainesville. "Jeff, you read it first and then I will."

"Yes, sir."

"Good. So, Josh, how did it feel to play Moses?" The tone and smile on the Marine general's face changed the tenor of the meeting.

"It felt great! I helped get fifty extended families out of the Soviet Union and into in Israel. All of them had been oppressed, harassed and even killed for generations. It's truly a blessing that for them *next year in Jerusalem* actually happened. I'm glad I helped."

"Do you know how many more are left?"

"Avram told me the Soviets have agreed to give permits to any Bukharan Jews who want to leave. All they have to do is apply. He estimates there may be twenty thousand left. Those in the military have to finish their obligations, but then they can leave."

"Would you be willing to tell my congregation this story?"

"Of course," Josh said, "I can give them an unclassified version of the story. The report has an attachment on Bukharan Jews and their history. They've been living in the area for more than two thousand years. They trace their ancestry to two of the Lost Tribes of Israel: Naphtali and Issachar. Their ancestors migrated to that area when the Assyrians occupied Israel."

"I'll have to read up about it." Feltzer looked up when the door cracked open. "Yes, tell the Chairman I'm on my way." As the general stood, the other two men did likewise. "Captain, a job well done," Feltzer said. "I'll tell the Chairman you're back safe and sound. I'll have a précis of your report on his desk tomorrow. When are you going back to San Diego?"

"As soon as Rear Admiral Gainesville releases me." Josh looked at Jeff. "I was hoping to be there by the weekend."

"Stick around until I talk to the Chairman," Feltzer said. "He may want to talk to you personally."

"Yes, sir."

"Do you know what your next assignment is?"

"No, sir. It was put on hold until I finished in Moscow. I was going to stop by the detailer to see what's available—I'm due to rotate out sometime in November. If possible, I'd like get command of a ship as my next sea-duty assignment."

"Noted," Feltzer said. "But don't see the detailer. He'll try to stick you with some useless procurement job here in the Pentagon. Look into this, Jeff, and let me know what you can find."

Sunday, September 8th, 1991, 0826 Local Time, Beirut

It had been eleven days since the news of Safdar's abduction broke. Everyone who Rami Dagher knew at Hezbollah's offices suspected the Israelis had kidnapped Safdar. On everyone's lips was the obvious question: What does Safdar know about our current operations? Several people had turned to Dagher for an answer; after all, Dagher was the man who'd initially recruited Safdar and recommended him to the Iranians, and as of May 5th, 1991, Dagher had become Hezbollah's operations director. His organization's mission was to recruit, train, deploy and equip bomb designers and suicide bombers, as well other units that could conduct attacks in Israel, Europe and the Middle East. It was the job he'd wanted for years. Now, Dagher was on his way to a meeting in Damascus. One item on the agenda was his assessment of Safdar and how much his capture would affect Hezbollah's operations. His conclusion was: Not much.

When Dagher stepped out of his apartment building, he heard a distant boom. He looked at the gray sky to determine if he was hearing thunder or artillery fire and saw a bolt of lightning. Even though the Lebanese Civil War had ended almost a year before, Dagher's first thought was that it must be a bomb or artillery shell exploding.

Dagher's apartment was six blocks west of Damascus Street, the old demarcation between the warring factions of Maronite Christians and Muslims. With the civil war over, life in Lebanon was returning to some semblance of normalcy. By the end of the war, more than 100,000 people had been maimed, 150,000 killed, and 900,000 displaced from their homes. Hezbollah had emerged from the chaos as both a military and political force; it now controlled all the areas where Lebanon's Shi'a population lived.

For Dagher, life was good. Even though he was allocated a driver and bodyguard, he preferred to get behind the wheel of his 1987 Mercedes 300. He was buckling his seatbelt as his bodyguard/driver scanned the area. Besides inspecting the car every time before either one of them drove it, the bodyguard was always worried about snipers. Satisfied there were none, he got in beside Dagher.

Dagher eased the car into first gear and looked in side mirror to see if traffic was clear for pulling out onto Abdul Wahab el Inglizi. He noticed a motorbike coming and waited until it passed.

What he didn't hear over the noise of the traffic was the clunk from a magnet attaching a shaped charge to the driver-side door. Neither he nor his bodyguard paid attention to the rider when the motorbike parked two hundred meters down the street. Dagher turned the wheel and gunned the engine to get out into traffic. The Mercedes had moved less than a hundred meters when a boom rattled windows all along the street.

The steel backing around the hollow shaped cone directed the explosion toward the interior of the Mercedes. The copper cone became a molten 1700° Celsius jet melting a three-centimeter hole in the door. The fireball incinerated everything in its path and the pressure wave crushed what was not burned.

Neither Dagher nor his bodyguard was alive when the Mercedes careened into a parked car. Smoke poured out of the smashed driver's door and the shattered front window. Satisfied that Rami Dagher was dead, the motorbike driver put the radio transmitter back into his pocket and drove off. Twenty minutes later, pieces from the dismantled transmitter box were in three widely separated trashcans in West Beirut.

The Same Day, 0930 Local Time, San Diego

The sun was still low enough on the eastern horizon that the trees in the Jewish section of the Mount Hope cemetery cast shadows on the three headstones. Each had a row of small pebbles on the top, signifying that someone had visited the site.

A solitary figure stood at the foot of the headstone on the far right. He had just placed another pebble on the top of the tablet-shaped piece of gray granite. Below the Star of David were chiseled the words, *Natalie Vishinski Haman, December 3, 1950—August 11, 1974 Loving Wife, Wonderful Daughter.*

At a respectful distance behind the man, a woman and three children stood holding hands. None spoke. All were watching the man at the grave.

Josh Haman bowed his head and spoke softly. "Natalie, it took me seventeen years and fourteen days to avenge your death. While I was in Moscow, I learned the name of the man who ordered the killing of Artur. He was an anti-Semitic KGB general by the name of Nikolai Volkov. He sent assassins around the world to kill Soviet émigrés whom the KGB thought were threats. Your father was on the KGB's hit list because of his efforts on behalf of his brothers and other Soviet Jews who wanted to emigrate, and because the KGB considered him a deserter. The murder was Volkov's way of reminding Soviet émigrés that the KGB could kill them anytime, anywhere. Artur was the target; you, my first love, and your mother were in the wrong place at the wrong time. I killed your killer, Boris Bagdonovich, after he tried to kill me."

Josh took a deep breath. He was amazed how calm he was. He had rehearsed this speech several times on the way, but the words coming out weren't the ones he planned to say. "A few days ago, after a trial for crimes he committed inside the Soviet Union, Volkov was sentenced to death. A man I met in Moscow —a man who became a friend—was the arresting officer. He invited me to witness the man's execution. For reasons I still don't understand, I volunteered to be the one-man firing squad. It could have been rage or anger. It could have been a chance to get revenge on the man who ordered Artur's killing."

The words were flowing in an uncontrolled, unrehearsed stream, finally undammed after seventeen-plus years. "My bullet hit Volkov right between the eyes and blew his brains out. It was cold-blooded, legalized murder. Afterwards, even though I had the satisfaction of knowing that despicable man would no longer walk the face of the earth, I felt guilty. All these years I've thought about what I would do if I ever found the man who killed you. In some respects, my desire for revenge drove me in ways I don't understand. Now I've killed both the man who murdered you and the man who ordered the killing. Yet, I feel empty and uncomfortable with what I did. Even though I avenged your death, the rage and anger in my mind hasn't gone away. These bastards took you from me for no reason. I hope they rot in hell."

Josh found himself nodding as he spoke softly and gently. "My actions can't bring you back, but they do end a search I began the moment that I learned the KGB killed you. As I've told you before, I have a great life with the lovely Rebekah and our three wonderful children. Looking down from the heavens, I hope you're proud of what I've accomplished. I hope you're proud of *me*. So good-bye for now. I'll come back and report all the mitzvahs my family and I enjoy. Natalie, now you can rest in peace."

Wednesday, September 11th, 1991, 0729 Local Time, Damascus, Syria

Dagher was the second person that Safdar had identified. The first name he gave to Lev Mogen was the man he'd met in Damascus in 1988 just before he left for the U.S. The man was probably in his mid-to-late sixties, and even though he spoke Arabic without an accent, Safdar was sure he wasn't a native Syrian.

For some reason, Safdar could see the man's face today as clearly as it had been then. The man had dark hair graying on the side, black eyes, and oval-shaped head. If you squared off that head, it would look like a trapezoid.

In the next session, Mogen brought a sketch artist with him. Safdar described the man's face in detail, down to a birthmark next to his right eye. After a few minor corrections, he told the sketch artist that the drawing was accurate, at least as he remembered the man's face.

Two days later, Mogen came in with a stack of photographs and a pile of files. Quickly, Safdar helped Mogen reduce the number of possibilities from twenty to four. Safdar decided he wasn't ready to meet Allah in heaven. He knew the more he helped the Israelis, the longer he would live. After saying thank you, Mogen left.

Three days passed and Mogen again showed up with the four folders, plus a new set of pictures. Some were close-ups; others had been taken at a distance. Safdar put his thumb and forefinger under his chin and rested his elbow on the table as he studied the photographs. After thirty seconds, he tapped one of the photographs. "This is the man."

"Excellent."

"Who is he?" Safdar asked.

"SS-Brigatenführer Hans Graebner. He's wanted for murdering thousands of Jews near the Pripet Marshes in Belorussia. At the time, he was a Standartenführer in the SS Cavalry Regiment—roughly equivalent to a colonel. Later, he committed many more war crimes.

"How did he get to Damascus?"

"His father, Gerd Graebner, was in the German Foreign Service and based in Cairo before the war. The father's mission was to try to get the local Arabs to revolt against the British. In Palestine, he allied himself with Kamil al-Husayni, who'd been appointed the Grand Mufti of Jerusalem by the British but was forced into exile after he led an Arab revolt in 1939. During the war, al-Husayni worked with the Germans and the Italians. He even met with Hitler, and got his support in opposing the creation of a Jewish state. Graebner's father was in that meeting. He died in 1950."

Lev paused and looked at Safdar. "Isn't this all familiar? I would have thought you would have known about al-Husayni and his alliance with Hitler."

"No, not really."

Lev shrugged. "Well, after the war, al-Husayni got himself reinstated as the Grand Mufti of Jerusalem. He and Gerd Graebner started recruiting former German soldiers to help them, because they knew war would come once the State of Israel was created. The Odessa network helped the son, Hans, sneak out of Europe right after the war. He got to Jerusalem and started to work with his father for al-Husayni. Hans speaks Arabic along with French, German and we think, English. After the war for independence, Hans Graebner disappeared but turned up a few years later as a military advisor to the Syrian army. Then he disappeared from our radar again. About three years ago, we learned he was working for the Iranians and Hezbollah."

Once Safdar confirmed that his contact was Graebner, Mossad agents began watching him. The German followed the same routine every day. After a brisk thirty-minute walk starting at 0600, he returned to his flat, showered and had breakfast. At 0728, he unlocked his car and drove to a compound outside Damascus that the Mossad knew was a Hezbollah training camp. He left the camp at 1730 and drove home. After dinner, he took another brisk walk before returning to his apartment.

The Israelis had four choices. One, they could press the Germans or the Russians to request Graebner's extradition from Syria based on outstanding war-crimes warrants. The extradition process and a trial would take years, assuming they could even get him out of Syria. Graebner might well escape before he was extradited, or he might die before he was tried.

Two, they could kidnap Graebner and bring him to trial in Israel as they had with Eichmann. This option had its own set of operational and political risks.

Three, they could just assassinate him. Given his strict routine, it would be easy.

Four, they could leave him alone.

A group gathered in the prime minister's office to discuss the issue: the prime minister, the minister of justice, the head of the Mossad, and Lev. They immediately rejected options one and four. Two was eliminated because of the potential political and legal circus. After that, the discussion about killing Graebner was simply about how to do it. Consensus took twenty minutes; Mogen walked out of the meeting with clear directions.

Assembling and testing the weapon took two days. Getting men to carry out the mission took another. They were sitting in another car in Graebner's garage when he got into his Citroen DS19 and could clearly see the Nazi. They waited until he picked up the envelope sitting in front of the instrument cluster. When he opened the envelope and started reading the note inside, an Israeli pushed a button on the transmitter, locking the doors and windows. He then flipped a switch to release Zyklon B inside the car.

Zyklon B gas was used in the gas chambers in the concentration camps. It was made by Degesch, a German chemical company that marketed the gas as Cyanosil. After the war, Degesch resumed production of the hydrogen cyanide gas for use in pesticides.

Graebner frantically tried to get out of the car but couldn't. The Israeli's pushed the remote they brought with them to open the garage and drove away. The police arrived later in the day after someone noticed him slumped over the seat. They found a note written in German:

Brigatenführer Hans Graebner,
We thought you might like a taste of your own medicine.

Saturday, September 15th, 1991, 2156 Local Time, San Diego
The sun was starting to morph into an orange ball on the horizon as it began to slip out of sight. Already, damp air from the Pacific made the evening feel cooler than it was.

Rebekah wore a light sweater as she sat on the couch facing west. She'd stretched her legs out onto a small ottoman. The deck on the back of the house was large enough to allow the couch and chairs to face either east or west. When the sat on the back deck, they faced west to watch the ocean and the sky.

Josh filled Rebekah's glass with chardonnay and handed it to her. He set the almost empty bottle onto the coffee table and sat down so he could pull her close and rest his head on her shoulder.

"The stuffed shells were fabulous. Thank you. It's so nice to eat a home-cooked meal."

"After living the life of Reilly in a luxury hotel in the heart of Moscow, you wanted something *I* cooked?"

"Always. Mind you, I think prison inmates here in the U.S. get better food than what you get in most restaurants in Moscow."

Rebekah put down her wine glass. "You look drained and worn out. No, let me rephrase that. You look like hell."

"I feel like someone stuck a tube inside me and sucked out all the energy."

"How ugly was it?" she asked quietly.

"What part?"

"Killing Volkov."

"It made me sick. Arkady took me to a bathroom afterwards and I retched. I didn't just throw up. I convulsed. Then he took me back to my hotel. It took me ages to clean away the stink of vomit."

Rebekah looked at him. "Why did you volunteer?"

"It seemed like the right thing to do. I hated Volkov and everything he stood for. I thought killing him would purge my mind."

"Did it?"

Josh shrugged. "Time will tell. Volkov's death clearly ended a chapter... but I don't feel closure. I feel guilty and I don't understand that." Josh took a deep breath. "Revenge isn't all it's cracked up to be."

"You and I were brought up believing murder is wrong."

"But he was a cold-blooded killer," Josh said. "I think he enjoyed it."

"You need some time off."

"I have it: three weeks leave."

"And you're going to take every minute of it," Rebekah said. "But that's not what I mean. You need time away from trying to save the world. You've done your part. Let someone else do it for awhile."

Josh shook his head. "I'm not ready to retire."

"I'm not asking you to leave the Navy. Just take a desk job or something less stressful. Give yourself and your body time to heal. You're not twenty-five anymore."

"I'm aware of that." Josh could feel the humidity raising aches and pains where he'd been injured.

Rebekah was silent as the sun lowered into the sea. "So what's next?" she asked softly.

"The Chairman of the Joint Chiefs hinted that he wanted to make me senior attaché in Moscow. My answer was a polite *not no but hell no*." Josh sipped his wine, and then emptied the rest of the bottle into his glass. "I hope they'll give me a ship. I want to be captain of a ship before I retire. Command at sea is what it's all about. I've had tours as squadron CO and XO; I did well. Command of a ship is the next rung up the ladder."

Rebekah rolled her eyes. "So have you asked the Navy to give you a fast ship so you can go in harm's way?"

Josh chuckled at her use of John Paul Jones' famous request to the Continental Congress. "I don't know if it'll be a fast ship, or if I'll have to take it in harm's way... but Jeff

Gainesville knows what I want. They won't give me a destroyer or an aircraft carrier; at best, it'll be one of the major amphibious ships."

"So you'll be back on sea duty?"

"Yes. But CO tours are typically no more than eighteen months. Even shorter if you run aground or into another ship."

Rebekah made a face. Sea duty meant she'd be both mother and father to their three children for a large portion of the assignment. During the entire time, she'd be the "captain's wife." That came with a set of traditional duties. To avoid thinking about that, she said, "So tell me about Danielle."

"There's not much to tell..."

Rebekah gave him a little push. "Oh, yes there is!"

"It's in the past. Danielle and Avram are engaged, so really, there's not much to tell."

"Bullshit. Out with it, Haman!"

"I gave you a précis while I was in Moscow. Where do you want me to start?"

"The beginning would be a good place."

Josh gave his wife a sanitized history of his relationship with Danielle. He left out the juicy parts, focusing on Danielle and her father escaping from Laos.

"Is she pretty?" Rebekah asked.

Josh knew there was no right answer. "Are you asking if I think she is better-looking than you?"

Rebekah smiled. "Of course."

"Then the answer is no."

"Liar, liar, pants on fire." Rebekah took a sip of wine. "I'm going to assume you slept with her."

"Not since my first tour in Vietnam. Long before I met you."

Rebekah leaned over and kissed him. "Good answer."

Josh returned the favor with a deep, long, French kiss, happy the inquisition was over. For the time being, they could do what consenting adults do at home.

The ringing phone stopped their kissing. Since the phone was on her side of the couch, Rebekah picked it up. "Hello." She listened for a few seconds, then spoke in rapid-fire Hebrew. She and her mother used it when they didn't want anyone around them to understand what they were saying. The only words Josh understood were *mazel tov*. She said it several times.

Josh finished what was left in his wine glass and waited until his wife put the phone down. "So?" he asked.

Rebekah was grinning like a Cheshire cat. "It *is* official." She took a long drink of her wine. "Avram's mother called my mom to let us know Avram and your ex-girlfriend are getting married on the first Sunday in December in Haifa. I'll get to meet the beautiful Danielle and a former member of the French Foreign Legion after all. There are some Russians coming as well. How exciting!"

Josh couldn't tell if she was being sarcastic or teasing him or both. He let her continue.

"We'll get the formal invitation in the mail within a week. You need to plan on taking at least fourteen days leave because you, me, and the kids are all going. We'll spend a week there having fun, and it will help them understand their heritage."

Josh smiled. "I'm in!"

The End

Historical Backdrop for *Moscow Airlift*

Long after most of us are in the ground, 1991 will be viewed by historians as one of the most eventful and significant years in world history. Seven events relating to the Soviet Union that either culminated in or happened during 1991 had a significant long-term effect on the history of the world. All were woven into *Moscow Airlift's* plot.

When the year began, the Soviet Union was financially, economically, culturally and politically in trouble. Its citizens, emboldened by Gorbachev's policies of *perestroika* and *glasnost* and the declarations of independence by its own republics and the defections from the Warsaw Pact, were becoming more vocal in their opposition to Communist Party rule. They clamored for better quality Soviet made and Western consumer goods along with an improved standard of living. Shortages of everything from food to medicine were part of the daily fabric of life.

The problems the Soviet Union faced in 1991 were the culmination of years of attempting to compete with the West while dedicating twenty to twenty-five percent of its economic output to defense. By contrast, the U.S. spends less than four and Nato nations are required by treaty to spend two.

The core of President Reagan's strategy to end the Cold War was to bankrupt the Soviet Union by forcing it into an arms race it couldn't afford. The Soviet Union didn't have the resources—money or technology—to keep up with the West. The deployment of stealthy aircraft made its entire air defense network obsolete. Add a viable missile defense known at the time as Star Wars and suddenly, the Soviet Union's fleet of ICBMs was obsolete. New equipment deployed by modernized NATO and U.S. armed forces made them technologically and qualitatively superior to what the Red Army and its allies could field.

Gorbachev was trying to convert the Soviet economy to one that could compete in the world and needed a currency that could be used as the basis of financial transactions. His problem was simple to explain, but difficult to fix. Valuing transactions with the Soviet Union was extremely complex and potentially risky because the ruble was not traded on Western currency exchanges so its value was impossible to establish. Western governments and businesses had little faith in the stability or the long-term value of the Soviet currency.

Compounding the currency exchange problem the Soviet Union faced was its historically low foreign currency reserves at the beginning of 1991. It had been selling natural resources, primarily gas and oil to the west to earn U.S. dollars and British pounds to pump up its reserves. Gorbachev was depleting those reserves on foreign goods faster than they were earned. In short, the Soviet Union was running out of cash and the financial and economic problems are the basis of event #1.

Inflation was high and on the verge of going out of control. During the year, the Soviet 50 and 100 ruble notes issued in 1961 were withdrawn from circulation, effectively devaluating the ruble. Soviet citizens could only convert old rubles for new ones at a rate of 500 rubles per month. At the time, the Soviet Union didn't have a banking system similar to what we have in the West. Many if not most citizens hoarded cash in their homes because they didn't trust Soviet banks to protect their cash. The reissue of new rubles made their life savings almost worthless.

When 1991 began, the Soviet Union was in deep trouble financially and Gorbachev and many in the West knew it. What we didn't know was how bad it was.

Another historic problem is that the Soviet Union and now Russia can't feed itself. This problem continues to plague Russia to this day. 1990 figures show the Soviet Union's farm production had been dropping an average of five percent per year while the population grew at three percent over the past three years. To make up for the shortfall, the Soviets bought grain and meat from the West, primarily the U.S. and Canada. To this end, they agreed to a historic grain deal in March 1990 to buy up to 14 million metric tons of grain a year from the U.S. The only problem was that the Soviet Union was broke. It simply didn't have the cash to pay for the grain when it was delivered. To that end, the U.S. gave the country credits so U.S. farmers could be paid and the Soviets could eat.

In June 1991, the United States faced pressure to cut off grain sales to punish the Soviet Union for its repressive actions in the Baltic States of Latvia, Lithuania and Estonia. Nevertheless, the U.S. offered $1.4 billion in loan guarantees to pay for the grain. If these guarantees hadn't been made, the Soviet government wouldn't have enough to feed the country. This is the second significant event that influenced the development of *Moscow Airlift's* plot. A potential food shortfall and emergency shipments is the genesis of *Operation Deny Famine*.

Event #3: is the combination of Desert Shield and Desert Storm. Together, these constituted the largest military operation since World War II. After a month-long bombing campaign, the Allied Coalition ejected the Iraqi Army from Kuwait in 100 hours. Josh Haman's role in Desert Storm was similar to the role I played during what is now known as the First Gulf War.

In March 17th, Soviet citizens voted on a referendum that would lead to the dissolution of the Soviet Union. Seventy-seven percent voted in favor of dissolution and only twenty-two said no, don't do it. This is event #4 set in motion two events. One was the parliament setting the date, December 26th when the Soviet Union would no longer exist. It also put in place the conditions that lead to the August 19th coup.

MOSCOW AIRLIFT

Officially, the Warsaw Pact died on July 1st, 1991 and is event #5. Its demise began when in a December 1989 speech at the U.N., Gorbachev announced he was unilaterally reducing the number of troops in Easter Europe and his country was going to assume more of a "defensive posture." The reality was it had been dead for almost a year because its member states had voted for independence from the Soviet Union in 1990 and most of the Red Army had come home. Three countries—Poland, Czechoslovakia and Hungary—were members of the Desert Storm/Shield coalition and sent troops to Saudi Arabia.

Event #6 was the coup in the Soviet Union. Several members of the Politburo tried to take power in August 1991 to prevent Gorbachev from dissolving the Soviet Union at the end of the year. Even though its citizens overwhelming voted to dissolve the Soviet Union and the newly and relatively freely elected Russian Parliament sets the date, change, hardliners within the KGB and Communist Party saw it as a threat to their power. The events depicted in *Moscow Airlift* follow the timeline of the attempted removal of Gorbachev. What's fiction are the actions of the books' characters during the coup.

When the Russian Federation was officially created on December 26th, 1991, it was a nation in financial, social and political trouble. Many of the former Soviet republics had already declared their independence from the Soviet Union and used the creation of the Russian Federation as an excuse to move farther from Moscow's influence. On December 26th, event #7 takes place when Yeltsin became the federation's president and Gorbachev was out of office.

One of he more interesting rumors about the end of the Soviet Union is an assertion made by Sergei Treyakov, a senior KGB officer who defected in 2000. He claimed the last official head of the KGB—Vladimir Kryuchkov—supposedly sent US$50 billion worth of Communist Party funds to an unknown location in the last days of the Soviet Union. The funds still haven't been found. One can only wonder if Gorbachev could have used those funds to help solve his country's financial problems in the late 1980s.

Iran and its quest for nuclear weapons also plays a major role in the plot. When the Ayatollah Khomenei took power after the shah was overthrown in 1979, he was not interested in nuclear weapons because Iran didn't have the expertise to develop them. He was afraid of outside influence affecting the Islamic revolution and opposed bringing in foreigners from any country to help.

After Khomenei's death in 1989, his successors thought differently even though Islamic Republic of Iran signed the Nuclear Non-Proliferation Treaty affirming it did not aspire to acquire or develop nuclear weapons. President Hashemi Rafsanjani wanted nuclear weapons to threaten Israel, European countries, the United States and even the Moslem countries on the south side of the Persian Gulf.

Shortly after Rafsanjani took office, he turned to the Russians, the Chinese and the North Koreans for help. By 1990, it was obvious the program had moved from just producing electrical power to creating material for use in nuclear weapons. Over the years, Iran tried all sorts of subterfuges to hide its nuclear weapons program and/or acquire deliverable nuclear weapons. With Obama's Iranian deal in place, experts say it's now a matter of just a few years before the Iranians have a deliverable nuclear weapon.

Marc Liebman
April 2018

MARC LIEBMAN

About The Author

Marc Liebman
Citizen Sailor, Businessman and Author

Marc retired as a Captain after twenty-four years in the Navy and is a combat veteran of Vietnam, the Tanker Wars of the 1980s, and Desert Shield/Storm. He is a Naval Aviator with just under 6,000 hours of flight time in helicopters and fixed wing aircraft. Captain Liebman has worked with the armed forces of Australia, Canada, Japan, Thailand, Republic of Korea, the Philippines and the U.K.

He has been a partner in two different consulting firms advising clients on business and operational strategy; the CEO of an aerospace and defense manufacturing company; an associate editor of a national magazine, and a copywriter for an advertising agency.

Marc's latest career is as a novelist, and six of his books including, *Moscow Airlift,* are listed below.

MOSCOW AIRLIFT

Cherubs 2
Big Mother 40
Render Harmless
Forgotten
Inner Look
Moscow Airlift

A seventh, *The Simushir Island Incident* will be released in November 2018.

Big Mother 40 was ranked by the readers who buy books on Amazon as one of the top 100 war novels.

Forgotten was a 2017 Finalist in Historical Fiction in the Next Generation Indie Book Awards, a Finalist in Fiction in the 2017 Literary Excellence Awards and rated as Five Star by Book Favorites.

Inner Look was also rated Five Star.

The Liebmans live near Aubrey, Texas. Marc is married to Betty, his lovely wife of 48+ years. They spend a lot of time in their RV and visiting their four grandchildren.

If You Enjoyed This Book
Please write a review.
This is important to the author and helps to get the word
out to others
Visit

PENMORE PRESS
www.penmorepress.com

All Penmore Press books are available directly through our
website, amazon.com, Barnes and Noble and Nook, Sony
Reader, Apple iTunes, Kobo books and via leading bookshops
across the United States, Canada, the UK, Australia and
Europe.

Big Mother 40

By

Marc Liebman

Big Mother 40 is a story well told and one in which aviation and special warfare veterans of the Vietnam conflict will identify, and about which they will tell their friends. Younger readers will enjoy the book simply as a great adventure.

— Michael Field, Captain USN (retired) Wings of Gold, Winter 2012 issue

Liebman skips macho combat images to plunk us into the deeper connections of war, from fear and courage to the truer realms of human relationships. His detail is authentic, and he lends even greater validity to the operations he describes with valuable author notes at the back of the book including a historic analysis of the time, military glossary and roster of characters. Despite the book's intensity and detail, the story is fast-paced. For a book you won't forget, you have to read BIG MOTHER 40.

PENMORE PRESS
www.penmorepress.com

RENDER
HARMLESS
BY
MARC LIEBMAN

Car bombs set by a group called Red Hand are going off all over West Germany, killing American, British and German citizens. Red Hand's manifesto reads as if it was copied from Nazi propaganda. Now, just four years after the 1972 Olympics massacre of Israeli athletes and three decades after the Holocaust, the West German government is facing its worst political nightmare: Germans are once again killing Jews – and former Nazis who want to create the Fourth Reich may somehow be involved.

The West German police can't find the shadowy members of Red Hand, so the American and British governments decide to act covertly. Josh Haman, part way through an exchange tour with the Royal Navy's Fleet Air Arm, joins the team led by his friend and SEAL Team Six member Marty Cabot. The hunt takes their team into East Germany to execute their written orders, which tell them "to find, neutralize and render harmless to the United States and her allies the members of Red Hand."

PENMORE PRESS
www.penmorepress.com

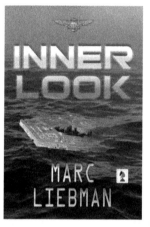

INNER LOOK
BY
MARC LIEBMAN

International Espionage, NKV Russian
Intelligence , US Intelligence, CIA,
Argentina spy story, Peril at Sea ,
Helicopter stories , Sea stories,
After John Walker and Jerry
Whitworth are arrested for passing top-
secret information to the Soviet Union,
the project Inner Look is initiated to
determine if there are any other spies operating within the government
intelligence agencies. Navy SEAL Marty Cabot and naval aviator Josh
Haman are assigned to the project in the hopes that their
unconventional approach and out-of-the-box thinking will yield more
answers.

Cabot and Haman discover that the security leaks go higher up than
anyone imagined. Furthermore, the leaks have compromised many of
their missions. For Josh and Marty, it's not just about national
security, it's personal.

Their pursuit turns international, taking them into dangerous waters.
Nothing but their skills will keep them alive when the KBG sends
assassins to silence the traitor and neutralize the threat they pose.

PENMORE PRESS
www.penmorepress.com

CHERUBS 2

BY

MARC LIEBMAN

In combat, there is a fine line between being overly cautious and cowardice. It's Josh Haman's first tour in Vietnam and he's fresh out of the training command - a "nugget" in Naval Aviator parlance. Josh Haman has to figure out on which side of the line the combat search and rescue detachment's officer-in-charge stands. Untested and without a lot of experience, he has to make a career and life and death decision and live with the consequences.

Josh gets his first taste of the unpredictability of Naval operations when he is picked to be a pioneer in flying helicopters in Navy special operations. He, and Marty Cabot, a Navy SEAL, become pawns in inter-service politics. The two of them are ordered to fly missions that could, if not carried out successfully, have international consequences

PENMORE PRESS
www.penmorepress.com

Penmore Press
Challenging, Intriguing, Adventurous, Historical and Imaginative

www.penmorepress.com

CPSIA information can be obtained
at www.ICGtesting.com
Printed in the USA
FSHW010418150419
57251FS